Dedicated to Clint Fletcher

<u>Wednesday, August 20th, 2014</u>

8:11 AM

St. Charles, Missouri

Today is Sara's first day at a new school. St. Charles High School, home of the Fighting Pirates, is her sixth high school in six years. While this would be unusual for most, it is routine for the one issued her most recent alias only last night. Relocation is required for every new mission assigned.

Sara is a spy.

Despite being the age of a sophomore in college, Sara blends among high school students. This is due to an extremely low-calorie diet and daily pill regimen, standard protocol for all Natashas.

The new girl, whom most mistake for frail, moves about the flowing torrent of students. The mid-August air is thick with humidity and unique brand of energy exclusive to the first day of school. A blend of excitement and anxiety. Everyone is affected to a degree—everyone save the Natasha insinuating her way through the congested hallway.

Sara camouflages herself with a demure manner. Chin down, eyes forward, she passes as though walking between raindrops.

A fan of neither posturing nor affectation, the Russian is surrounded by both; the environment is charged with teen spirit. Immune to the emoting and rambunctiousness, the operative goes about her progressions. The 712th product of the Natasha Program does not allow commotion to distract her.

Wending through squealing girls and chest-bumping boys, the five-foot-six operative passes by as though invisible. En route to her first hour class, Sara approaches a mass of football players gregariously conversing in the middle of the hall. Oblivious to their inconvenience to those coming and going, they take no notice of the willowy girl along the trail of those flowing around them.

The noise and commotion are pushed away by the spy with crystal clear focus.

Natasha 712 has spent nearly six years in the field—the standard length of time for a Natasha's deployment. She understands this to be her last mission. Upon completion, she is to return to Moscow. The girl with sandy-blonde hair falling just below her shoulders does not concern herself with what is to follow. Her only purpose is to serve the Russian state.

Her kind are conditioned to neither worry nor wonder.

This time her name is Sara. Last time it was Ruth. The time previous was Esther. A common Jewish name could always be used, if beneficial, to Jewish heritage on her mother's side. But the last name, always Smith, never bound her, should Jewish heritage prove disadvantageous. Furthermore, Smith is a common surname, making Natashas more difficult to track.

Antiquated ideas from the Cold War era affected protocols until the end. Natasha 712's class of 2008 was the last.

Addressed simply as 'Twelve' throughout training, the agent with a brand-new cover has never had a first or last name of her own. She is a Natasha and nothing more. The hazel-eyed operative is on a need-to-know basis. Unless something pertains to the completion of a state-sanctioned objective, she does not need to know. Sara does not care about what she does not need to know.

The curve-less girl passing a noisy cluster of squealing girls and a teacher with a comb-over is incapable of thinking back on her childhood. If she could, her earliest memory would be of a facility much like an orphanage. Her fate decided previous to conception, conditioning began shortly after birth.

Natashas are less miracle of nature, more product of design.

After familiarizing herself with the building, the spy has committed the exits, restrooms, blind-spots, reflective surfaces, and general layout to memory. The girl wearing secondhand clothes nears her locker. Eyes seemingly fixed on her empty locker, the one with full lips but sunken cheeks uses her peripheral vision to scan side to side.

Having begun in 1962, the Natashas are Russia's oldest female spy program – though not the only. In 1974, the Cold War went on to produce the Shannons, a sister program for the more delicate realm of corporate espionage. Since the beginning of the program, all Shannons were raised alongside Natashas in Leningrad (now St. Petersburg) until age ten. Then protocol mandated a divergence of program participants. Separated for the first time since birth, the Natashas and the Shannons were transported to their respective schools for very different forms of training.

Unlike the Natasha Program, the Shannon Program remains operational.

The Natasha, noting a vamping girl to her left and a primping boy to her right, has not seen a Shannon since 2004.

Maintaining her meek countenance, the agent closes her locker door and heads to First Hour.

From birth to age ten, the strictly controlled facility served as the perfect setting to prepare their young minds for what lay ahead. Though the environment of St. Petersburg was intense, it was mild in comparison to that of The Institute.

Once distanced from the clustered mass of those socializing in motion, Twelve takes a mental note of the few whom notice her. Looked up and down by boys and girls alike, the looks are typically short-lived.

The spy is glad to be discounted so summarily. It is her objective to be hardly remembered at all.

The orphanage-like setting in St. Petersburg was a cross between a state-sanctioned elementary and a Catholic school run by the most stringent of overseers. This was where the spies-in-training were taught reading, writing, arithmetic, apathy, obedience, and the ideals the most ardent Soviet at the height of the Cold War. Indoctrination began shortly after the cradle.

The Natasha is keenly aware of her surroundings, like a finely calibrated seismograph that can sense earthquakes hundreds of miles away. Sara keeps track of those who look her way. The opposite sex hardly pays her any mind at all.

The Natasha passes the band room.

When Natashas 701 through 716 left St. Petersburg at age ten, they were like all Natashas before them: hardened, obedient, inured to pain, and ready to begin the Spartan education of the near-mythological program.

Eyes down and shoulders rolled forward, the 106-pound Natasha appears harmless. Her stomach, ever knotted from her diet, makes a shy posture all the easier to maintain. After a glance up and down, a boy makes no effort to mask his disapproval. Sara is satisfied with the boy's superficial judgment.

Contrary to how Hollywood portrays spies, the ideal spy is neither attractive nor charming. In reality, the optimal spy gains no attention at all. Spies need to blend.

With a deadness in her eyes and no makeup covering her blemishes, the Russian glides past dark blue lockers and open classrooms in route to class.

The Institute, AKA "The Natasha School", is silent now. Finally put to rest after having been officially shut down long before. The crumbling facility is no longer a spy factory, no longer the place where cruelty conditions and repetition refines. Tales of The Institute readily dismissed as the love child of rumor and exaggeration. Beyond consideration of a 'rational' person, the truth remains entangled within the vines of the facility since relinquished to the forest.

Twelve, a member of the final class to graduate from The Institute, is not totally invisible to everyone. Her fashion-mag-skinny figure does not escape the attention of those who believe a form as sparse as hers the ideal. The Natasha catches an envious glare in the reflection of a tinted window as she passes.

8:15 AM
The spy, who is yet to answer to her new alias, arrives at Mr. Colliet's Advanced Biology classroom just as the first bell of the day sounds. Every student now has four minutes to get from wherever they are to where they need to be.

One by one, students arrive. None suspect the scrawny fawn sitting nearest the pencil sharpener of being an assassin.

After an initial rush, the remaining students straggle in.

Serving dual functions allowed The Institute to survive financial famines. The facility provided not only an optimal setting, but also ideal candidates for those with an interest in clinical research impossible for any government to sanction publicly.

The 'First Gen' Natashas – those created by way of selective breeding until 1968 – were given names. Those since, created by way of in vitro, numbers. Any embryos failing to survive gestation or delivery were relegated to dictation in The Institute's impeccably maintained records. For all intents and purposes, Natasha 001 is considered the 'first Natasha'.

Maintaining her flat gaze on the tall, skinny teacher, the Natasha carries out the standard threat assessments as attendance is taken. Every student, male and female, are evaluated for weakness. The agent scanning from the back of the class goes about her progressions.

"Sara Smith?" says the teacher with a mustache.

"Present," answers the Natasha. A few heads turn, but only for a moment. Most are far too deeply invested in their own reality TV show of life to pay the new girl (sporting a couple spots of acne) any mind.

The research and development portion of the program was run by a father-son team, the former having recruited the latter in 1965. Subsequent leaps forward were almost exclusively due to the son's innovation and complete lack of scruples.

The Natashas made excellent guinea pigs for two reasons: the environment of The Institute minimized variables, offered optimal conditions for controlled experimentation; and the total lack of oversight that enabled the duo to pursue their studies without the stifling burden of human rights considerations. The father had not experienced such freedom in a clinical setting since his days as a young man in Berlin. Present since the initiation of the program, the former Nazi remained until his retirement in 1990.

Modern Natashas are unaware of having been modified, as all manipulation and experimentation since 1998 was done in the embryonic stage or under the guise of medical care. Long past are the days of invasive, often painful procedures.

While the methods of the father-son tandem would be wholly condemned, the results spoke for themselves. Natashas created after 1988 gained significant genetic improvements: greater speed, endurance, caloric efficiency, mental plasticity, strength, bone density, pain suppression, and markedly quicker recovery from injury.

Though not all Natashas are equal, even the weakest possesses the physical prowess of an Olympic athlete.

While genetic advantages and training make Natasha 712 what she is, her daily pill regimen keeps her how she is.

The wallflower in the back row has no idea how long it will be before her next mission, but she is not thinking about that.

Having analyzed the movement, physique and demeanor of the males in the room, she deems Mr. Colliet the most capable of inflicting harm. Despite his age, the forty-three-year-old assistant wrestling coach is the most fit and physically capable person in the room – thus, primary threat. Though his demeanor indicates a statistically low likelihood of attack, the Natasha has no intention of dropping her guard.

Should a situation arise, the metal pen in her right hand will aid in her defense.

From 1968 onward, The Institute was structured like a high school; four classes in progressive stages of training, graduating one class per year. The final batch of Natashas, numbered 701-716, arrived in 2004. Sara's first year, her class shared the facility with three other classes; by 2008, her class was the only on otherwise empty grounds.

During their four years at The Institute, the Natashas had to master the arts of espionage and assassination. With so much material to cover, measures were taken to hasten the learning process. Such measures included sleep deprivation, borderline starvation, and corporal punishment.

Twelve of the original sixteen members of the 2008 class survived to graduation. Two fatalities occurring in St. Petersburg, two at The Institute.

Wearing thrift store blue jeans, the agent with a Nordic face sits still as a stone.

From the back of a classroom plastered with biology-themed décor, the Natasha sees what the teacher pretends not to notice: light whispering, a note being passed, a girl two rows over reading a text. The 712th Natasha does not care. Aside from mild agitation, a properly functioning Natasha experiences hardly any emotion at all. The blue pills see to this.

The student with three kills under her belt notices what others do not: the basketball player whose stride has been shortened by an old knee injury. The construction worker whose punch would be compromised due to wear and tear on his shoulder and elbow from repetitive hammering. A brawny custodian with posture betraying chronic lower back pain. Experts at spotting tells, Natashas sniff out weakness.

Sara observes Mr. Colliet. He twists his body more to his right than his left when turning to the class, indicating a long-healed neck injury — but no physical limitations of consequence otherwise.

The spy who has only been Sara Smith since 9:38 last night comes off as aloof. Some assume her to be moody, shy, or perhaps even sleepy. A blank canvas, she reflects whatever disposition people believe they see. Sitting in the back row, Sara is like a cat, bored yet hyper vigilant — living only in the moment. Poised, she is ready to act in an instant.

The Natasha is issued a textbook she recognizes from a school attended two years ago.

Sara Smith, the Natasha who was Ruth Smith until this time yesterday, was delivered by her previous handler to her current handler last evening. Both her last two handlers were named John Smith. She could immediately tell her new handler is ill

A woman Sara understands to be his subordinate escorted her into her private quarters. A bedroom she found most unsettling. The arrangement, the colors, the smell. Unlike any room she has entered before. The Natasha silently waited for the heavyset woman with copper-colored hair and thick Sottish brogue to leave the room. Once alone, she put her few belongings away and remained in the room until morning. Uneasy for her surroundings, and leery of the woman's intermittent peering in, the new arrival sat on the edge of the bed in the dark.

At 4:21 AM she fell asleep on the carpeted floor near the bed. Fortunately, Natashas require little sleep.

Upon being summoned to the kitchen by the subordinate, the Natasha was informed her superior was still asleep. Then the second-in-command encouraged her to violate diet protocols. The woman named Joanna Smith attempted to issue two days' worth of calories in a single meal.

Sara is unwilling to take a directive from anyone besides her handler, especially a female.

Because the blue pills dampen the portions of the prefrontal cortex most responsible for personality and introspection, Natashas possess little desire (and a diminished ability) for thinking of the past. Rendered all but incapable of inner

monologue, their entire focus is fixed within the moment. Natashas sense, detect, acknowledge, perceive, and calculate. Though flesh and blood, they are virtually machines. A series of progressions, routines, and if-then protocols.

Sara Smith would be taking notes if the majority of her classmates were – but they are not. For this reason, she sits still, one hand atop the other, not taking notes.

Natasha 712's class was introduced to killing in 2006. After morning conditioning, the Natashas were led into the dingy shower area where a wooden chair awaited. Once all were ushered inside, a bound and hooded man was dragged in. Whimpering and begging in a language the twelve-year-old Natashas did not recognize, he was forced into the chair.

> *Natasha 712 was the second in line. The second to be handed the small caliber pistol. But the first in her class to kill.*

The pangs of having refused breakfast cause the spy wearing a faded blue t-shirt and old tennis shoes to shift in her seat. No matter how hungry, Sara will not eat until her handler says it is okay.

> Natasha 712 has not taken her pills since 4:00 PM yesterday.

> Sara listens to Mr. Colliet go through the motions of the first day of a new school year. Her stomach growls.

Natasha 708 was first in line. Given a .22 caliber pistol, she was ordered to execute the hooded man in the chair – his weeping echoing about of the five-by-five-meter shower. Clustered in the space lined with dingy brown tiles, the pack of adolescent Natashas awaited their turn. To the left of their ex-Spetzna instructor, a single shower ran to wash away the blood soon to flow.

Waif-like compared to her more robust female classmates, Sara's chair-desk combination is wide enough for herself, plus a half.

The purpose of the hood over the men's heads was to make the exercise easier, less personal. Natasha 708, the girl with eyes like no Natasha before her, did not refuse to execute the man whose head was being forcibly held in place by a meaty palm; she only hesitated. Hesitation equals failure. Her punishment was swift as it was brutal.

In the showers thick with mildew, the one who had failed to carry out the directive in a manner deemed satisfactory, was made an example of before those awaiting their turn.

The instructor, unmoved by the bloodcurdling screams of the seventy-eight-pound Natasha curled in the corner, issued punishment by way of a rubber hose.

The grading scale at The Institute was 'satisfactory' or 'unsatisfactory'. Natasha 712 did not hesitate upon receiving the command. Nor did any of the others. Condemned men were dragged in one by one. Most of them sobbing; each were shot and dragged away. The 708th Natasha, or Eight, went last.

Some men flopped and flailed more than others after being shot. Some did not flop at all. Their blood went down the drain just the same.

Skilled at hiding in plain sight, Mr. Colliet has already forgotten Sara is a new student. Having only seen her name on an amended attendance sheet yesterday; he believes her a local he simply doesn't recognize.

Intense as The Institute was, it was not without times of slower pace. Nighttime was for 'Americanization' courses. On all nights, except those with scheduled nocturnal exercise, the Natashas would watch American television shows and movies, and listen to American music. The Institute had not updated its study materials for some time.

Despite the deadening effects of the blue pills, the program participants did experience a measure of what can only be identified as pleasure. For Natasha 712 it was the music of Britney Spears, and any scene in Friends with the character Monica.

Now and then a classmate turns back to look at the new girl with perfectly symmetrical features. The furtive looks, disguised as a glance at the clock above Sara, are held longer by those of her own gender. The spy feigns obliviousness.

The operative with oily skin and pimples (caused by the white pills) does not need to look at the clock. The wristwatch of the boy two desks forward in the next row over is plainly visible when he props his head up on his hands.

The white pills maintain strength despite her diet.

While the male instructors focused on espionage, killing, and 'Americanization', the females — caretakers, overseers, and teachers — saw to the nurturing of ideals: Russia good; America bad; all American males seek to violate and injure Russian women. No element of The Institute was without purpose.

The Natashas are wary of males due to the realistic understanding that their hand-to-hand expertise is of little use in a head-on fight with a much larger, far stronger, aggressive male.

Though American males have yet proven the aggressive creatures so thoroughly demonized in her training, Sara keeps an eye on all eleven males in the room. In addition to the awareness of all escape routes, the spy who identifies as Twelve is never without a defensive object in hand.

After graduation in 2008, the class dispersed. Natasha 712's first handler was a stoic man named Bill Smith who lived within five miles of Wichita, Kansas. The Natasha, newly arrived on US soil, posed as his niece. A semi-retired spy himself—same as all Natasha handlers—Bill Smith's cover was that of a mechanic.

Blind in one eye, missing the tip of his right index finger, and marred with burn scars on his face, Bill Smith strictly saw to his duty. Despite his gruff disposition, he was consistent and never abusive toward the second Natasha placed under his watch. Her first handler provided what was required of him – no more, no less – while she awaited her first mission from Moscow.

As required, Bill took blood samples after six months and sent them by courier to the lab that regulated the medication regiments of all Natashas in the field. Under Bill Smith, the daily dosage for Natasha 712 did not change.

Having already taken Advanced Biology two times, Sara could easily ace the course along with every other course, but she does not. Academic excellence draws attention. Somewhere between a B- and a C+ is her target range.

Sara senses restlessness in the room as the first hour nears its end.

Her first assignment. Carl Beckerdeit, father of a male classmate, was an engineer for Boeing. Her mission was to bypass his home security system and gain access to his personal computer. Sara, then Mary, mirrored the hard drive and installed undetectable spyware before slipping out the backdoor. She completed the assignment within nine days.

Ordered to finish out the semester to avoid gaining unnecessary attention with a mid-semester move, Natasha 712 remained Mary Smith until her next identity was issued. During the interim, the operative was 'decommissioned' by her handler until further orders arrived. Her blue pill regimen was tripled, reducing the Natasha to a near zombie-like state. Kept in a dense fog for almost seven weeks, the groggy spy realized both a new handler and identity when the fog lifted. Second alias, Deborah Smith.

While her female classmates accentuate their features and assets, the Russian – who has developed little since her arrival in America six years ago – makes it a point to dampen what little she does have. No makeup, drab clothing, and a tight sports bra keeps the operative gray a world of color. The pink pills – estrogen suppressors – ensure Sara's chest will stay much like her back.

Two-and-a-half pink pills per day and a low-calorie diet are why she has yet to have her first menstrual cycle.

9:09 AM

The bell sounding the end of first hour rings.

Those most anxious to leave rush for the door. In the methodical way she goes about everything, the operative

- 16 -

collects her green notebook, new textbook and stabbing pen, then trails the stragglers into the maelstrom.

Like a moth, silent and barely there, Sara Smith navigates her schedule. After Advanced Biology is American History, then Trigonometry, followed by English 4. Three more classes after that and the Natasha who skipped lunch is picked up by the woman who dropped her off. Copper hair perfectly spun into a bun, the gal with brogue thick as Guinness waits along the street nearest the North entrance.

The ride back to the rock home on the edge of town is silent; the Natasha eyes the driver with her periphery. Watching without looking, the spy rides with her eyes straight ahead.

Her pale green eyes on the road and both hands on the wheel, Joanna Smith knows she is being watched. A spy's wife for almost thirty-five years, she is familiar with many of their methods.

After fifteen minutes of heavy silence, the late model Buick pulls onto the lane leading to the small home alone on a hill. Lady carefully pulls into the carport extending from the white, barn-like shed setting just the other side of the drive.

Stepping lightly as a cat, Sara follows Joanna through the chain-link gate, along the patio, past the bench swing and up the three steps leading to the front porch.

Her stomach groaning, Sara trails through the front door. Once into the narrow utility room leading to the kitchen, the cinnamon rolls Joanna removed from the oven right before leaving causes the spy's mouth to burst with water.

"I've been baking today," says the rosy-cheeked lass, gesturing for the guest to follow. Sara trails Lady to the right as she walks into the dining area between the kitchen and living room.

At the head of a walnut table large enough to seat eight, sits Sara's handler John Smith, his thick, white hair freshly combed. Now under the brightness of a sixty-watt bulb, the Natasha can see he is sicker than initially believed.

The man with fresh sleep lines sports a welcoming smile.

"Welcome," John says warmly, nodding toward the chair Joanna has pulled out for her.

Though suspicious of the woman – certainly not wishing to turn her back to her – Sara sits down.

Joanna leaves the room; silence is the sound as John Smith takes in the sight of his new charge.

Joanna soon returns with a package. During the continued silence, she gently places one item after another – a syringe, four ampules, cotton balls, rubbing alcohol, and a few forms – on the table between Sara and John.

Sara can tell her new handler has smoked cigarettes for a long time, spent a lot of time in the sun, and would be an inch or two taller were he not slouched.

John can hardly believe the skinny girl sitting before him is a Natasha. After all he has heard of her kind, he assumed she would have fangs and claws and glowing red eyes.

The man appearing ten years older than his sixty-three years, smiles despite his pain. He wants his guest to feel welcome. Patiently, he waits for his lady to leave.

"Welcome," he repeats softly. "I am sorry I could not speak to you last night. I was a bit under the weather."

He does his best to let his guest know he means no harm. Voice a bit shaky, the man retaining traces of the handsomeness from his youth tries to appear less sick than he really is.

Sara remains silent. No question was asked, and no directive issued. Therefore, there is no need to speak.

"My name is John and you've met my wife, Joanna. You may call her Lady if you like." John says with a measured calm.

Her mouth watering from the cinnamon waft, the Natasha sits statuesque.

"First things first," John Smith draws a ragged breath. "We must pull some blood. You've done this before?" The question is rhetorical.

Sara nods to the man demonstrating respectful caution.

"Now, I would draw your blood myself, but..." John pats the air and laughs. "...but my hands are not as steady as they used to be." He huffs a few raspy breaths. "You'd probably prefer my Lady to do it. She used to be a nurse."

Sara says nothing.

"She is very gentle and would do nothing to hurt you. You wouldn't do anything to hurt her, would you?"

"No, I will not." Sara speaks for the first time. Expressionless and distant, the young spy seems vacant, even soulless, to the couple given only six days' notice of her arrival. John has told his wife little of the Natasha legend.

Though made uneasy by the Natasha's vibe, Lady rounds the table and takes the seat to Sara's left. The Natasha turns her chair. With the man she calls Babe looking on, Lady carefully draws one vial after the other. Her arm laid out on the table; Sara sits unfazed.

"There you go," Lady says in her songbird voice, pressing a cotton ball to the crook of Sara's arm. "Wasn't so bad, was it?"

The Natasha looks to John, uncertain whether she would answer Lady.

As though dismissed, Lady disappears around the corner, into the utility room. Two spies sit alone.

"Now that *that's* done," John pats the tabletop. "I understand my Lady has been trying to get you to eat, but you haven't. Are you hungry now?"

"I eat as directed," Sara answers without inflection.

John's lips tighten into a smile. "While you are with us, you are directed to eat whenever you are hungry." These words cause Sara's brows to knit quizzically. It's the first expression John has seen on her gaunt face. "Any time you are hungry, all you have to do is let my Lady know and she will make you something to eat." John's smile broadens. "Probably more than you can eat. Just do the best you can."

"You just let me know what you want, dearie!" Lady's voice flutters around the corner.

"She really likes cooking for people," John whispers as though telling a secret.

Sara does not know what to make of this.

What in the world are we going to do with this girl? wonders the man fending fatigue. John Smith clears his throat before continuing. "I am sure you noticed I am sick." Sara does not respond. "I will not always be available... so anything my Lady says is the same as if it came from me. Do you understand?"

Though unsure what to make of the words she hears, the Russian does understand. Sara nods. Stomach twisting, her toes curl inside badly worn tennis shoes.

"I don't know how other handlers have done things," he continues, although having a pretty good idea, "but we will probably be different from what you are used to. Do you have any questions?"

"It is past time for my pills."

"My Lady will make sure you get all the pills you need." He nods with a grin. "If you need anything, just let her know."

The Natasha nods her understanding.

"I can tell you my Lady has been looking forward to feeding you. She says you need some meat on your bones!" Smiling deepens the wrinkles along his cheeks and corners of his eyes. A sudden coughing fit wracks his frail body.

Sara remains still, watching her handler hack and cough as the matronly Scotswoman announces, "There's plenty of food in here if you want to eat!"

"Do you want to eat?" Seconds the man regaining his composure.

Sara nods her head.

Good, this is progress, John thinks to himself.

The flurry of activity in the kitchen causes John – almost always called Babe – to smile once again. The refrigerator door wide open, Lady places item after item upon the counter by the stove.

A debilitating wave of fatigue strikes Babe. Sara watches John's energy drain away.

"I would very much like to continue talking and getting acquainted", his voice fading, "but I am going to have to lie down and rest my eyes."

Lady, realizing what is happening, swoops in to see to him.

"Why don't you go to your bedroom and see what's waiting in there for you?" the stout Lady ushers Sara out of the room. She doesn't want the young woman to see Babe in such a state.

Sara returns to the living quarters she finds so disconcerting. Puzzling is the sight of a television resting atop a stand at the foot of the bed. The TV wasn't there last night. She assumes Lady is using her quarters for storage.

Sara gazes about the ten-by-twelve-foot room.

She would not feel any more out of place were she standing on the surface of the moon.

Lavender curtains match the comforter and pillowcases. To one side of the bed, an off-white dresser with antique brass handles; the other side, a desk with a vanity mirror and sliding drawer for a laptop. Full-length mirrors on sliding closet doors reflect the North-facing window above the twin size bed. A ceiling fan lazily circulates air tinged with the scent of jasmine emanating from the air freshener plugged below a nightlight.

Too much comfort. The Natasha would feel far more comfortable with a cot in a basement or tool shed.

Still as a statue, Sara awaits the directive to return.

After a couple of minutes, the heavy gal who moves swiftly returns to the kitchen (just other side of the bedroom wall). Now that her Babe has been tended to, food preparation can commence. "No rules against eating in this house!" Lady sings over the sound of a *Tupperware* lid coming off and microwave turning.

New aromas soon join the already glorious scent of cinnamon rolls. Sara's stomach growls again.

Awaiting the directive to return, Sara runs her fingers along the waist-high dresser. She has never had a dresser before.

"Have you ever had Swiss steak, dearie?" Lady calls from the kitchen.

This is unusual. Generally, the Natasha is summoned when a superior wants to speak to her. And is not further addressed until standing before him. Now she has been asked a question without having been given permission to leave her quarters.

After a delay, Sara responds, "No."

"Then you're in for a treat!" Lady's enthusiasm enriches her voice even more. A moment later, "You a-comin'?"

Understanding this to be a directive, Sara exits her quarters. A few steps to the right bring Sara to the small, round table where Lady and Babe take their morning coffee and meals.

Sara stands idly as Lady finishes situating the impromptu feast.

An intoxicating blend of scents, the salivating girl has never smelled anything so divine.

"My pills," Sara obediently reminds.

"Oh, yes." Lady sighs, turning to the cupboard above the four-piece toaster oven. On her toppy-toes, she reaches into the dark-stained cabinet. Her back to Sara, she gets the pills Sara will be taking for the evening.

"Here you go," Lady chirps, palm speckled with pills.

After a glance, Sara flatly states, "These are not my pills."

"These are better," Lady whispers with a wink.

Sara looks down at what should be two-and-a-half blues, two-and-a-half pinks, and one-and-a-half whites. Instead, she sees one big peach-covered pill, a burgundy pill, and two clear gel tabs. Vitamins

"Go on," Lady insists again.

Sporting the expression of one fearing poison, the Natasha extends her hand.

"And to wash them down," Lady hands her guest a tall glass of cold grape juice.

As instructed, Sara reluctantly puts the pills in her mouth, washing them down with a gulp of grape juice. The chilled sweetness causes green-gold eyes to widen and nostrils to flare. Lady glows at the small victory.

"Now," Lady whispers, smiling widely. "Let's get some food in you!"

Lady hands her guest a bone-white plate with a midnight-blue border. The famished Natasha stares down at the plate growing heavier with each scoop. Swiss steak, mashed potatoes, macaroni and cheese, and green beans. Hardly any of the dark blue border remains visible.

"Do you want to eat here in the kitchen, or in your room?" Garlic toast pops from the toaster.

"My... room?" Sara is confused.

"Yes," Lady answers, placing toasted bread atop the heaping plate. "Your bedroom."

"The table," she eventually answers, baffled at the idea of being given the choice of where to eat.

Sara sits in the spot where Babe reads the newspaper every morning. Hesitantly, she takes a small bite of mashed potatoes.

Glad at finally seeing the skinny girl eat, Lady anxiously inquires, "Do you like it, dearie?"

Her brain awash with sensation, Sara does not hear the question.

Lady watches her guest scoop another bite. Then another.

Sara chews and swallows faster... and faster. The event turning ravenous, a feeding frenzy is soon under way.

The Natasha lords over the plate like an animal, tearing off chunks of Swiss steak with her teeth and shoveling spoonfuls of potatoes and green beans. She chews just enough to get food down so she might shovel more. The sounds of snorting, chomping, lips smacking, and a fork scraping plate fills the kitchen. For a time, Lady sees only the top of her guest's head.

The flurry of consumption is short-lived. Once roughly half the food is eaten, Sara abruptly stops. Eyes wide and breathing labored, the Natasha is taken aback at what has just transpired.

Lady, stunned at having seen her guest eat like someone rescued at sea, feels a curious concern for the girl slumping forward. Sara breathes shallowly. Shifting and squirming, the flurry of gluttony is proving painful.

"Are you okay?" Lady asks.

Feeling on the verge of rupture, Sara manages an uncomfortable "Yes."

"Well let's get you into your room," Lady says, wondering if the girl has ever been full before.

4:21 PM

Sara's bedroom

From the fetal position on her bed, Sara watches Lady hook up the very old DVD/VHS player to the only slightly newer television. Shifted in search of relief, she only now realizes the television is for her. Neither grateful nor displeased, the uncomfortable operative simply observes.

Lady turns to the suddenly sleepy Sara. "Have you seen *Grease*?"

"*Grease*?" Sara asks between panting breaths.

"*Grease*, the movie?" Lady cocks her head to one side. "You've never seen the movie *Grease* before?"

"No," Sara answers, wishing Lady would go away. The operative with an enhanced tolerance to pain is unaccustomed to the hurt of being stuffed. Her eyelids grow heavy.

Lady disappears, only to return waving a VHS tape in the air. "Now, I haven't seen the remote for this thing in ages," she informs as the tape disappears into the machine, "but I *do* have the remote for the television."

Sara can hear the tiny motors inside the dual-purpose machine.

Lady presses Play, and the classic begins. After a bit of fast-forwarding, the debilitated assassin is watching the animated intro. Music fills the room.

Unable to move, the Natasha blankly stares at the screen.

"Here you go," Lady softly whispers, laying the TV remote next Sara on the bed. Pulling the door nearly closed, she goes to check on her husband. Periodically returning to check on the one she calls "that poor girl", the dessert-pusher later brings a bowl of hot apple crisp in melting vanilla ice cream, just in case Sara decides she might want some.

6:02 PM

After peeking in with a gentle knock, Lady enters the room as credits begin to roll. She smiles at the sight of an empty bowl on the stand.

Sara's eyes pop open at the muffled sound of floorboards under carpeting.

Lady smiles. "Did you enjoy your show?"

"Yes," Sara answers, despite having fallen in and out of sleep throughout the movie.

Nodding happily, Lady understands her visitor is one of few words. "Would you like to watch another movie? We have an entire box of movies in the living room."

Sara shrugs, not knowing what to say. She has no preference. The Natasha's tongue glides in search of bits of apple crisp hidden in the recesses of her mouth. Her stomach hurts.

"I'll see if I can find another movie you might like," says Lady, turning for the door. "And maybe a cinnamon roll."

From her side, the Natasha laid low watches the graceful gal sashay from the room.

6:12 PM

Lady returns with a cinnamon roll, a glass of milk and a VHS of *Dirty Dancing.*

7:41 PM

Lady quietly places another cinnamon roll and more milk on the stand next to the bed in case Sara wants another.

9:22 PM

Lady turns off the television, drapes a sheet over the sleeping spy, and turns off the lamp on the small desk. The nightlight glows.

Pausing at the door with a sorrowful look, Lady sees not an operative, but a young girl. A thin, unfortunate, vulnerable young girl she wishes she could do more to help.

"Sweet dreams, dearie."

Just before turning to leave, Lady's pale greens fall on the old tennis shoes with frayed laces and worn soles. This gives her an idea.

Thursday, August 21ˢᵗ, 2014

8:07 AM

Hallways of St. Charles High School

The Natasha with five pieces of French toast, bacon, buttered toasts, and orange juice in her belly, makes her way down the hall. Walking with the same slouched posture as the day before, today it is due to being too full to stand up straight.

Breakfast was inhaled much the way of dinner last night – in a frenzy.

Eight minutes until the initial bell. The Natasha slips through the crowded hall, scanning for possible threats, and eavesdropping on bits of conversation swirling around. Roving patrols for intel, Natashas have the auxiliary purpose of data collection. Ears like radar, they scan the air for information of possible consequence.

After dodging traffic — dipping to avoid the arm of a girl flailing excitedly, and nearly getting stepped on by a football player walking backwards without looking — Sara nears her locker. Of the six snippets of conversation overheard, two were about the football game next week, one was regarding a musician she has never heard of, one dealt with a possible schedule change, and the remaining two were the hushed conversations of female students talking about other female students.

Sara stopped to listen to the females speaking low, using a different ploy each time to disguise her eavesdropping. Once pretending to tie her shoe, the other searching her pockets for a small item such as a key or note.

During both of what seemed intimate conversations, the one listening for state secrets heard the word *bitches*. Dismissing the chatter as hearsay gossip, the Natasha continued toward her locker.

But that's not all she notices.

The curve-less girl with more energy than normal also detects the emotional fatigue following the first day of school, a hostile glare from a petite brunette passing by, and – most consequent in the moment – the anxious stare, peeking through a cluster of people.

Stifling a burp, Sara spins the combination knob. 4, 12, 36.

The suspicious girl with brown hair and wire-rimmed glasses remains at her locker, eight doors down. She has no idea that Sara, appearing to be looking inside her own locker, is in fact keeping tabs on her closely.

Conclusions drawn in a snap, Natashas think not in a stream of words, but bursts of calculation.

Threat detected. Shifting eyes, nervousness, diminutive comportment. Could be another operative feigning timidity and meekness the same way I do. If indeed an agent, either poorly trained or new to the field. Which would explain the hesitation and failure to conceal surveillance. Possibly a diversion for a second agent. Could be a tandem. Sara turns. Full sweep. In search of a possible secondary. *No viable candidates detected.*

The potential threat continues to stare. The Natasha does another sweep for an accomplice. None detected.

A solution is formulated in the blink of an eye.

8:11 AM now. Four minutes until the bell. Lead threat to less crowded area and eliminate. Bathroom nearest band room is most remote. If she follows me, I will kill her there. Strangulation.

Sara decides to stay in place. Observe the threat, scan for weapons. Then lead to the restroom as previously decided upon.

Sara pulls her Advanced Biology book from the top shelf of her locker; the perspiring Megan Herlbrecht searches for courage enough to approach.

Megan is a junior with a good heart an unparalleled desire to be liked. She has been waiting to approach, welcome, and befriend the new girl ever since noticing her about the same time yesterday. Megan, who is considered neither attractive nor particularly unattractive, keeps her thumb firmly on the pulse of the social world she so desperately wishes to be a part of.

Despite knowing everything about every social group and clique, she is not *actually* part of any of them.

Awkward in most ways one can be, Megan is as excitable as a bunny. Unfortunately, her spastic manner and runaway anxiety – her defining characteristics – undermine her ambitions of acceptance. Megan fears rejection more than death itself.

Megan considers approaching, then decides not to. Standing by her locker – located where the juniors end and the seniors begin – she wavers. And then, with her heart pounding like that of a soldier crossing open space under sniper fire, she goes for it.

Taking short steps, chin down, Megan heads Sara's way.

Sara readies for an attack from the subject clutching a black spiral notebook (possibly obscuring a weapon) as she approaches. Primed to strike, the Natasha clenches her metallic pen in her right hand. *Stab the neck, stab the face,* thinks Sara, preparing to strike.

"Hi," Megan manages, stopping just shy of mutilation.

Still gripping her improvised weapon, Sara gives a flat "Hello." She waits, wary of any quick movement.

"Um, well, yeah... I'm Megan," begins the girl crimping behind her notebook. "I, um, I saw that you are new because... well... I have gone to this school forever and I have never seen you – well, not *forever* forever, but the whole time I have gone to high school, you know, has been this one..."

Eyes darting side to side, the Natasha does not know what to make of the prattling stranger with the sweating upper lip.

"...and like I said, I saw you are new and I know what it's like to be new to places, well, not new to *school* but, you know, new to *places,* and I know what it's like not to know anybody and since I am from here and, you know, like, know people, you can ask me any question if you have any questions. My name is Megan by the way—" Megan stops to breathe. "What's your name?"

"Sara Smith."

"Ohmygosh!" Megan gushes. "That's such a pretty name!"

Sara stands frozen. She has no training for this.

"I know, like, a hundred Saras—well, not a *hundred* Saras, but a bunch, like maybe four or seven, but anyway, like I was saying, I can help you find your way if you need help knowing how to find somewhere because I know where everything is, and I pretty well know what's going on because, well, you know, I hear stuff, but I'm not nosy..." the talking continues.

The longer Megan jabbers on, the more noticeable the glossy sheen on her forehead becomes.

With no protocols for one such as Megan, the Natasha experiences a sort of short-circuiting. Like a boxer pinned against the ropes, Sara finds herself cornered by the by the girl yammering on and on and on.

Saved by the 8:15 bell. The frenetic chatter stops with an abrupt departure and promise to talk again later. The operative has no idea what just happened.

Somewhat disoriented, Sara heads for her first class.

8:32 AM, 1st Hour
Mr. Colliet's Advanced Biology class
A lioness posing as a house cat, the Russian sits at her desk in the back row. The discomfort of having overindulged having passed, the Natasha finds herself with an inexplicable desire to get up, leave the room, and run around the building as fast as she can.

She has never had a compulsion like this before.

On the second day of school, Sara draws a few more looks from students, but not many. Having fully committed the facility's layout to memory and completed a cursory threat assessment, the spy finds herself in the next phase of relocation—gaining a general understanding of the social construct of her new environment.

Natasha 712's first assignment, as Mary Smith, under the handler Bill Smith, involved the father of a female classmate. Stealing the cellphone of Emma Beckerdeit assisted with her mission.

Though unlikely, Sara Smith's assignment could be to eliminate the father of a fellow student. Or mother, sibling, or grandparent. She knows this. With no feelings either way, the operative sits calmly composed, ready for whatever may arise.

9:00 AM

It has been forty-one hours since her last round of pills. Most importantly, it has been forty-one hours since her last round of blue pills. She has never gone this long without a blue.

9:06 AM

Something unprecedented occurs.

Bits and pieces of Megan's jabbering cuts in like an overlapping frequency. "...the tall blonde girl, Julie, is one of the 'The Bitches' but she totally isn't a bitch..." and "...Lexi is a sophomore..."

And just like that, focus returns like a channel changing back.

The spy shrugs off the incidents and goes on with her morning.

9:15 AM, 2nd Hour
Mr. Schibi's American History class

Two minutes into class, Sara has noticed Julie Woodard's absence. The same Julie whom Megan pointed out in the hall. The leggy girl with platinum hair and hourglass figure made a point of going to the counselor's office to change her schedule. Few students drop Mr. Schibi's class. He is a popular teacher most students find entertaining.

The spy soon experienced the overlapping signal once more. "...she drives a Range Rover..." and "...The Bitches are the clique of popular girls that everyone talks about. A couple of them are nice, but most of them are – well, bitches...". The Natasha's focus snaps back.

Annoyed at the intrusion, Sara shakes her head. Unwanted recall is disruptive. The Natasha redoubles her focus.

9:22 AM

Experiencing agitation, the Russian funnels her focus on the laissez-faire teacher seldom without a coffee mug in hand. Mr. Schibi, a pear-shaped man with a broad face and teeth yellowed from smoking, is talking about George Washington when it happens again. Agitation graduates to anger. Attempting to regain control, the Natasha goes through her progressions. And then goes through her progressions again. And again.

The effect of the two-and-a-half blues she took forty-one hours and twenty-two minutes ago lessens with every passing hour.

9:47 AM

The Natasha's mind slips away again.

Flashes from the past burst into Sara's mind. A beautiful home at night. Pillars. A pristinely kept lawn. American flag proudly on display. The zoned-out assassin sees the picture she passed along the hallway after slipping through a second story window. She sees her latex-covered hands. Her left holding a bottle of Scotch while her right empties the lethal contents of a glass vial.

Sara's consciousness snaps back into the moment—jarring is the return. Skipping anger, straight to rage. The Natasha would slap herself if not for the attention it would draw.

Laughter rises at something the dryly sarcastic teacher just said. Sara is clueless as to whatever that might have been.

Natasha 712's second assignment, as Deborah Smith, near Fort Riley, Kansas, was the elimination of Brigadier General Raymond Hayes. After six days of stalking, she slipped into his home through a second-story bedroom window. While the general was sound asleep, she poisoned the bottle he poured from every night.

That was her shortest stay with any handler.

The spy grows restless. Edgy. The malfunctioning Natasha desperately wants to get up and walk around. Her eyes – otherwise flat – are opened wider than usual and fully dilated. The change is slight, but progressive as portions of the Natasha's prefrontal cortex comes back online.

Parts long rendered dark fire once again.

The chemical straitjacket loosens.

10:03AM
The bell ends second hour.

Usually one to wait for the room to clear, Sara is up and out the door like a rocket. Students soon fill the corridor around her. Chin down and jaws clenched, a deeply agitated Sara threads her way past as though everyone else were standing still.

It helps to be up and moving.

The Natasha finds a measure of relief in the noise and commotion. Searching for her center, the operative using the alias 'Sara' tries to rally her focus. Chatter all around, slamming locker doors, an announcement over the PA.

A dull pain begins behind squinting eyes.

Some students move quickly. Some possess no urgency at all. Minus her usual awareness, Sara clips the shoulder of a girl stepping back without paying attention. The grazed girl is saved from the ground by a friend nearby. Sara is six steps away before the words "That was rude!" or "What's her problem?!" enter the air.

The Natasha continues on.

Only upon arriving at her locker does Sara realize she forgot her history book. The one who has known little worse than frustration or agitation experiences a surge of raw anger.

Temper rising, Sara pivots back to the classroom for her book. After a few steps, she realizes it is logistically better to get her Trigonometry book *then* go by Mr. Schibi's room on her way to math class.

Sara does not realize she is thinking in words, rather than cognitive shorthand like any properly functioning Natasha. *What the hell is wrong with me?*

Despite her malfunction, the Natasha notices the glowering sneer out of the corner of her eye. Shelly, one of "The Bitches" Megan talked about, stands with her arms crossed and hip cocked. The tiny brunette with a defiant chin, blazing green eyes, and shiny locks swept behind her right ear, holds an unfriendly pose. Mouth tight, she chews the inside of her cheek, making no effort to hide her dislike.

For a moment the line-of-sight is broken by the mountain-sized football player who was so disruptive in her sixth hour Home Economics class yesterday. By the time he moves out of the way, the one known as 'Napoléon' is gone.

That's the second time she has looked at me like that, Sara thinks in words.

10:07 AM

The bell signals the beginning of third hour.

Sara sits in the last row of Mr. Godfrey's Trigonometry class. The cracks in her concentration worsening, an electrical storm rages behind aching eyes. The loud clap of Mr. Godfrey's hands cause everyone but Sara to jump.

"All right class!" He charges into the room, flashing a toothy smile. "Let's get started!"

Head Football Coach Ray Godfrey (like his older brother, Assistant Football Coach Mike Godfrey) is a powerfully built man capable of putting on pads and playing the game same as twenty years ago.

Focus temporarily regained, the spy maintains her concentration on the 220-pound teacher for a while – then another lapse. It just happens.

A memory flashes.

From a third-party perspective, Sara watches herself get struck with an open hand. She sees the face of her previous handler, John Smith. She sees the squalid basement he provided her. The water heater. The cot she slept on. So vivid is the recall, she can smell the mildew.

Like being bumped at a stop sign, her mind snaps back.

Pulled deeper each time, her affliction is worsening.

10:11 AM, 3rd Hour

Mrs. Harding's Junior English class

Chewing on her pen, Megan assesses her encounter with the new girl. Eyes forward, sitting still, she projects the very image of a student paying full attention, when in fact, the mind behind her brown eyes races at a speed her lips could never achieve.

Ohmygosh! I just know that Shelly, who has to make sure everybody knows she's the boss, is going to be mean to Sara, and that's so sad because I can just tell that Sara is a nice person and I would like to be friends with her... I hope she likes me... What if she thinks I'm a dork? She didn't seem too freaked out earlier. We didn't talk for very long so she can't think I'm too weird, right? It's okay if she thinks I'm a little weird because, if she does, I can make up for it later...

Reliving the conversation, Megan's inner monologue streams in looping swirls. At a thousand frames per second, the brief exchange is replayed and dissected time and time again. Megan worries for her new friend. Her new friend who is a senior.

Giddy at the prospect of having a senior as a friend, Megan can't wait for lunch.

10:45 AM, 3rd Hour

Mr. Godfrey's Trigonometry class

Sara has gone over forty minutes without a lapse in focus or unsummoned memory. Forty minutes without a malfunction. Honing her focus, the top button on Godfrey's shirt is the center of the universe.

Sparkling eyes track he fiery educator. His teaching style, much like his coaching style – up-tempo and enthusiastic – gives Sara's attention a moving target.

Focus narrowed, the Natasha clings to the present. *Stare at the button. Stare at the button. Stare at the button.*

11:24 AM

Lunch

Sara Smith enters the packed cafeteria two minutes after Mrs. White dismisses fourth hour English. Angry, deeply concerned, and starving, the Natasha veers toward the 'a la carte' line at the far side of the cafeteria.

The social pecking order is on unmistakable display. The round tables on the far end serve as an unofficial VIP, while the long white tables with bench seating are for everyone else.

The few noticing the new girl manage to forget her just as quickly – but the Natasha does not care. Fresh off another episode, Sara's focus is on the pressure building behind her eyes. A pain working its way from the front of her head to the back.

Headache worsening, Sara gets only fries and a sports drink.

Eyes punished by florescent lighting; she pays with the twenty-dollar bill Lady gave her and turns in search of a seat. A flash strikes again.

Sara is approaching a store front. A jewelry store. She feels the heat of the day, asphalt under her feet.

Lost in a reverie, Sara shuffles past rows of long white tables in search of an open space.

Consciousness divided between the present and the past, she sees her reflection in the tinted glass of the store's front door.

"Sara!" a voice excitedly cuts through the hum of a hundred conversations. "Over here!"

Sara snaps back into the moment. She turns toward the source of the noise.

Remembering none of the steps taken from the register to where she is currently standing, Sara sees a wide-eyed Megan spastically waving for her to come join her and her three friends. Knowing it would draw more attention to refuse the flailing Megan, the Natasha with a worsening case of vertigo heads over.

Somewhat off-balance, Sara carefully takes a seat near the end of one of the long tables. The introductions begin even before she is fully seated.

"Lexi, Karen, Angela, *this* is Sara, and Sara, *this* is Lexi, Karen, and Angela!" Megan enthusiastically gestures, overly enunciating each word. "This is the Sara I was telling you about this morning. She just moved here and..." the one talking with her hands goes on to make much of what was no more than a brief encounter. After a bit, Sara goes deaf Megan's rambling. The background noise seems louder than it is. Those all around seem closer than they are. Sara's head throbs.

As though on autopilot, she puts a French fry in her mouth. Then another. She feels wobbly, despite being perfectly still. After a bit, the pain behind her eyes begins to subside. Sara somewhat returns to the moment.

As Megan continues on as though she and Sara are better acquainted than they really are, Lexi – the petite sophomore with curly brown hair and big brown eyes – can tell something is wrong with Sara. While Karen simply assumes Sara to be shy, Angela also realizes something is wrong. For the sake of being polite, Lexi and Angela pretend not to notice.

Feeling better, but dizzy, Sara remains in the moment. Anchoring her attention to Megan's blistering stream of words, she soon realizes that the junior who is her new friend (whether Sara wants her to be or not) has steered the conversation around to her own favorite topic, The Bitches.

"...and next to her, the one who is sickeningly pretty, that's Tiffany Springfield." Megan doesn't have to point her out, as Tiffany looks like a *Sports Illustrated* swimsuit model posing among normal teenagers. "She's dating Jet Ryan whose real name is Jed Ryan, but we call him Jet because he's really *really* fast and anyway, Tiffany – everybody says her boobs are fake, but they aren't because she got them in eight grade – everybody hates her because of how pretty she is, which might be kind of why she is such a total b-word, but I didn't say that."

Megan blathers on. But as she does, the strangest occurrence begins. Rather than struggling to maintain focus, Sara is drawn into them. Pulled more and more, as though by a magnet growing in strength. Her headache fades.

"Okay, you see the little one?" Megan asks, pointing with her head. Sara instantly recognizes the brunette who has been of shooting daggers her direction. "That's Shelly Thompson. She's a senior and *everybody* hates her, but she is somehow super popular, and like, queen bee of the group because she is super tough and moved from Jefferson City last year, and dates Jensen Hallowell. He's the super gorgeous quarterback who will probably definitely go professional..."

Sara eats fries while she listens.

Point by random point, Megan bounces from one member of the group to the next. She relishes the opportunity to display her archive of knowledge. Alleged fact after alleged fact, the girl with a theatre major's manner blisters along. Tone and inflection express her opinions as she goes.

"...and the girl with wavy dark hair is Devon!" Megan gushes. "Devon is the nicest one of them and she used to be, like, captain of everything and *"leader"* of The Bitches," says Megan, making air quotes, "only they weren't called 'The Bitches' back before Shelly came along."

The pressure behind her eyes all but gone, Sara comes to understand that; Shelly usurped the group, uses bully tactics, and dominates the preeminent group with her tiny iron fist.

Megan has yet to take a single bite of her food.

"Devon is still the captain of the dance team, but only because Shelly isn't on the team." Megan informs in an intense, but hushed, tone. "The reason Shelly isn't on the dance team is because Mrs. Halpern's daughter, she graduated last year, was the senior that Shelly got into a fight with when she first got here. Her name's Emma Halpern. Anyway, Shelly got into a fight with her and, like, knocked two of her back teeth out..." Megan informs, nodding toward Lexi, Karen, and Angela for confirmation.

Sipping her blue sports drink, Sara does not notice Shelly Thompson giving her the evil eye yet again. The girl with hair pulled into a scrunchy lets it be known that she does not care for the new girl.

In a high whisper, Megan goes on with what is essentially the narrative of a reality TV show entitled *The Bitches*. Their boyfriends are the supporting cast. The rest of the school, extras.

11:49 AM, 4th Hour
Mrs. White's English class

After a lunch break that seemed to pass in an instant, the Natasha is back in her seat. Headache fully returned; it roams from one part of her head to another. The alternating of sharp and dull pain returned less than a minute after Sara got up from the lunch table. After throwing her untouched lunch in the trash, the speed talker followed Sara almost to the door of Mrs. White's classroom. The spy rubs her temples.

11:52 AM

The grandmotherly teacher wearing floral perfume and the same horn-rimmed frames her own English teacher might have worn, resumes her one-woman war on the prepositional phrase. Heart beating faster than normal, Sara strains through her headache to pay attention.

Sara's condition mutates as it worsens. No longer sharp and shallow, the intrusions are softly insidious, pulling the Natasha's consciousness under and away like some tentacled sea creature, silent and stealthy. The more gently she drifts away, the deeper she goes.

Eleven minutes later, it happens again.

Feeling much the way one does upon discovering themself the victim of a pickpocket, the Natasha looks around the room, then up at the clock. Minutes have been stolen.

"Grrr..." Anger meets helplessness.

More than forty-four hours since her last pills.

Hands resting atop one another, Sara doubles down on her focus. Mouth dry, eyes wide and head pounding, she zeros in on Mrs. White. The bridge of Mrs. White's glasses.

While the Natasha struggles to get back on track, Megan thinks of ways to further the relationship that has become her life's focus. Though Sara doesn't know it, she has a new best friend.

12:27 PM, 5th Hour
Mr. Stuart's Government class
The wiry teacher with a Tom Selleck mustache and frenetic energy, all but skipped the usual first day formalities. Sense of urgency ever engaged, the man who coaches wide receivers, defensive backs and special teams was lecturing within ten minutes of calling attendance. Sitting in her assigned seat, the agent breathing sharply through her nose steels in for battle against the mystery plaguing her. Sara concentrates on the man who talks nearly as fast as Megan.

Mr. Stuart's excitable disposition and darting movements serve to aid Sara's effort. She maintains for a time. Then slips. Megan's voice barges in, like a radio switching on its own. The Natasha goes deaf to Mr. Stuart's regarding all three branches of government.

The audio track of Megan plays.

"...Michelle, she's the short blonde with big boobs who just left, she's like only kinda-sorta one of The Bitches, but *kinda*-sorta not, because the only reason she is part of them is because of Devon, who is *super* nice, is trying to help her because, I think, she feels sorry for her because she has low self-esteem and she will... well... I guess, pretty well let any guy who tells her she's pretty sleep with her, which is

- 43 -

sad because – wait! Did I tell you her parents are divorced? Not that it matters, because my parents are divorced, and I don't go sleeping around – because I am not like that – because I believe that..."

Megan's chatter replays even *faster* in the spy's mind. The dialogue skips ahead.

"...Tiffany's dad invented the laser—or, you know, something to do with lasers or something—so he is like super rich, and well, he isn't her *dad* dad because her real dad is in France or China or something and her mom left him for a doctor. Yeah, so Tiffany's mom was like a supermodel by the way, but anyway, Tiffany's stepdad is like super crazy rich and every year she gets a new Mercedes, or some other sporty rich-girl car. And, so, people hate her for it and, you know, I think it's more the fact that she is so super pretty because she got a modeling contract when she was fourteen, but I guess all the pictures are in Europe because she goes there all the time, like, every summer..."

1:12 PM
The bell ends fifth hour.

Realizing her condition has mutated once more, Sara hurries as if to outrun whatever torments her.

Rubbing the wall as she speed-walks past, Sara experiences yet another attack. She sees the glass door of the strip mall jewelry store once again. This is not a flash like before, but a streaming recall.

The Natasha sees her reflection around the OPEN sign in the tinted glass. Her image grows larger as she nears. Wearing a blonde wig, big sunglasses, and tissue-stuffed bra, the assassin looks nothing like herself.

She hears the *'ding'* when her palms push the door open. Feels the gust of air conditioning on her skin. Sees the sparkle of diamonds, sapphires, rubies, silver, gold and platinum. It was the fourth jewelry store she stopped at that day.

With a welcoming smile, the portly owner greeted his unassuming customer with a hearty "Good morning!"

Henry, Sara recalls. *His name was Henry.*

This event led up to the Natasha's third and most recent, kill.

Her mind skips ahead. Passing through a velvet curtain leading to the back of the store, Sara sees the cluttered office area in route to the restroom she requested to use. A quick scan of the disorganized area reveals the purpose of her ruse.

On the counter, across from the restroom not meant for public use, sat the venom used for cleaning stones. Cyanide. Every Natasha who graduated from The Institute knows that small, privately owned jewelry stores offer the best chance of procuring the amber-colored death.

The girl straddling the past and present arrives at her locker. Going through the motions, she places her Government textbook on the top shelf before closing the dark blue door. Home Economics is next, no textbook is necessary. Carrying nothing more than her green notebook and pen in her sweating palm, the dazed Sara turns for her next class.

The memory plays on.

The past feeling as real as the present—if not more—Sara sees the syringe in her hand, discreetly, siphoning three milliliters of poison through a one-inch, eighteen-gauge needle. Less than enough to be missed, more than enough to kill dozens.

The faltering mind skips ahead.

Standing in front of the sink, the bar of soap next to the faucet is bright yellow. A framed picture of a firetruck hangs above the toilet. The tiny restroom smells like peppermint.

The assassin gives a flush for effect. As the water swirls, she slides the loaded syringe into a toothbrush holder. She unlocks the door and walks out.

Down the front of her faded jeans and under her shirt, she has what she came for.

1:15 PM

Hands trembling, the Natasha enters Mrs. Espinoa's classroom. She takes her seat.

As other students file in, the Natasha relives purchasing forty-one-dollar earrings, pushing the heavy door open and stuffing the wig, sunglasses, earrings, and receipt deeply into a stinky trashcan around the corner.

Sara awakens fully to the present.

Out of sorts, as though waking from surgery, Sara realizes where she is – but with only the faintest recall of having traveled from one class to another.

"What did I do with my Government book?" Sara wonders, headache returning. Terribly out of step with herself, the Natasha is yet to notice she can hear her own thoughts in the form of words.

Long, deep breaths. Sara dwells on the shiny wooden apple on Mrs. Espinosa's desk. Vibrant red, it catches a shimmer.

Oblivious to the boys goofing off beside her, and two girls speaking in hushed tones, Sara's entire universe begins – and ends – upon the apple's glossy shine.

Her temples throbbing, palms sweating, and stomach twisting – hazels gaze into the glare.

1:22 PM

Mrs. Espinosa (whose classroom includes six workstations with stoves, sinks and microwaves) gets the day's project underway.

Sara continues staring at the apple; Russell Martin does the same thing he did yesterday.

Russell Martin – the six-foot-four, 250-pound senior linebacker with fiery red hair, a face covered with freckles, and grades the Division One football scouts wish were better – is persistently disruptive. Prone to antics one might expect from a sixth grader, he often competes with teachers for attention. Fortunately, the seasoned educator knows *exactly* how to deal with the students she calls "rascals".

"Now, for just a moment, I would like for the entire class to turn their attention to Mr. Martin because *he* would like us to notice him."

Russell's pasty skin reddens as his yellow smile melts away. The man-child slumps in his seat. The spotlight turns out to be too warm for his liking.

The crafty teacher patiently holds her gaze. Russell's ears turn beet-red when he gets embarrassed. "Well?" insists the unshakable gal in her thirty-second year of wrangling teens. "Nothing? Okay, so long as Mr. Martin has nothing more to add, I'd like for everyone to get into groups of four or five so we can make some 'no-bake' cookies!"

Mrs. Espinosa enjoys her job so much; she claims to have never worked a day.

Present, but not in the moment, Sara is invited to join a group of four by a friendly girl. Since the other girls are already well-acquainted, it is easy for the malfunctioning Natasha to stay off to the side.

"Turn your heat on *low* and put a *half* stick of butter..." Mrs. Espinosa says loudly enough for the whole class to hear.

But Sara does not hear. Though her body is in Sixth Hour Home Economics, her mind is back in yesterday. Mrs. Callahan's Seventh Hour Physical Education class.

From her vantage on the pull-out wooden bleachers, the Natasha sees the other twenty-eight girls in the class. Few actively listen as the thick-limbed coach runs down the semester's syllabus. Her droning voice echoes in Sara's head same as it did in the otherwise silent gymnasium.

"Two weeks of volleyball. Two weeks of archery. Two weeks of basketball." In her low, coarse voice, the rather masculine woman goes on to explain how the boys' and girls' class will alternate between indoor and outdoor activities, weather permitting.

Sara can feel the hard surface of the bleachers and smell the industrial strength cleaners used by the custodian. Lost to Seventh Hour yesterday, she doesn't notice her headache is all but gone. Submitting makes the pain go away.

As though stuck in a trance, Sara stands off to the side while the others in her group melt butter, measure cocoa, pour oatmeal and socialize. Staring into yesterday she sees Tiffany's face. So crisp is the vision of the teenage Aphrodite.

Memory transfixed on the one who sat the farthest from the rest of the class, Sara's recollection is set to the backdrop of Mrs. Callahan explaining how a partition will come down in the middle of the basketball court on days of inclement weather so that both the boys' and girls' classes can use the gym. This information was of no consequence to the flawless one.

Sara watches the one with lustrous brown hair halfway down her back send a text without looking down. Deigning herself to even be in such a class, the girl who looks like she should be wearing a tiara and sash will not be participating in any of the activities. She will not be sweating, messing up her makeup, or running the risk of a broken nail. While the others are "doing whatever", Tiffany will be talking to someone—should she choose to do so—while walking laps, periodically ducking off to check her phone.

Immediately dismissed as a non-threat by the Natasha yesterday, the one wearing designer clothes and unamused expression is at the center of Sara's focus today.

The sound of Russell's obnoxious cackle jerks Sara back into the present. He sprayed someone with water.

The pain in her head and eyes surges. *What is wrong with me?!*

2:06 PM
The bell ends sixth hour.

Fatigued, but glad to be in motion, the Natasha shuffles out of the room.

2:10 PM

The bell sounds the start of seventh hour. The class has a five-minute allowance to change into the navy-blue shorts and white t-shirt issued yesterday, and report to the benches for roll call. The fact that Sara cannot be seen undressed by her peers complicates matters on a day that has been bad enough already.

Like all Natashas, Sara has scars.

While many females find changing clothes in front of others uncomfortable, Tiffany is an exception. Spared no expense by nature, the one granted an exquisite figure and cinnamon tan takes no measure to assuage any pangs of self-consciousness her innate perfection might inspire.

While the rest of the class scrambles to change as quickly and discreetly as possible, Tiffany takes her time. Once down to her lacey undergarments, she stops to fiddle with an earring as though she has all the time in the world. The blue and white locker room all but empties.

Right about the time Tiffany is fully dressed, the locker room door bursts open. In charges Shelly.

"You made it!" Tiffany emotes while shutting her locker. Shelly turns the dial on her padlock.

"Yeah," Shelly snipes acidly. "That retarded secretary bitch in the counselor's office just fucking sat on her fat ass and stared at me while she was on the phone." The pint-sized brunette tells while quickly changing. "My transfer slip was *right* there where I was pointing! Did she reach over and get it?" Shelly vents. "*Noooo!* She closed her window and turned the fuck around." The quick-eyed spitfire yanks up her shorts, then pulls her hair into the scrunchy always on her wrist.

Tiffany goes along. "That explains why she's forty and working as a secretary in this shitty school."

Within thirty seconds of opening her locker, Shelly is changed and headed toward the door. Though in a hurry, she isn't in too much of a hurry to shoot the new girl an unfriendly look on her way out.

Finally alone, the student who is two pounds heavier than yesterday slides out of her thrift store jeans and peach t-shirt and into her physical education attire.

Natasha 712 has reason to remain unseen while in a state of undress. Were any of her classmates to see her lithe body uncovered, they would notice a horizontal laceration across her abdomen. The textured discoloration of an abrasion along her ribs. Traces of a scrape on her right hip. Whispers of countless scratches, nicks, cuts, and other marks collected during her years at The Institute.

Though her scars are hardly offensive to look upon, they would be impossible to miss.

The most difficult to explain would be the vertical marks along her upper back. Whip marks. Punishment for failure; they were received while held over a desk.

Out the door as roll call begins, the Natasha arrives at the last moment. The faded scars on her thighs and knees are veiled by baggy dark blue cotton/polyester shorts with white trim. Only the crystalline marks on her shins are visible.

Anticipating another episode, Sara waits for her name to be called.

Tiffany and three others are soon walking the perimeter of the gymnasium while the rest of the class is playing volleyball. In order to make class—and life—simpler, Mrs. Callahan pre-selected the teams during her lunch hour.

2:50 PM

So far, Sara has made it the entire class without a single lapse or loss of focus. The activity and busy environment seem to help. No images flash in her mind, nor do any scenes from the past replay. Even better, Sara doesn't hear a peep from the yammering voice that has plagued her brain since lunch.

2:55 PM

Mrs. Callahan, with a whistle and her husky voice, releases class to change out.

Anticipating dismissal, Sara left for the locker room two minutes early and has already changed into her thrift store clothes and worn-out shoes. Passing by students only now entering the locker room, the Natasha makes her way down the empty hall lined with athletic trophies and plaques. Walking past the water fountain (and stand stuffed with pamphlets for the armed services), she heads for the heavy glass and metal doors below the snarling pirate mascot painted above.

Blinding sunlight, heat and stifling humidity greet the spy who has had a bad day. Unable to get away from the school fast enough, Sara cuts across the grass to the Buick waiting along the street.

Lady notices the less-than-happy expression on Sara's face.

The Natasha lowers herself into the car – air-conditioner running full blast – and shuts her door. Eyes forward, she says nothing as the pleasant chill cools her skin. Goosebumps raise along skinny arms.

"Sooo..." Lady says with her songbird voice, "how was your day?"

"Good afternoon," is all the Natasha says, her troubled eyes forward. Even if she could articulate her malfunction, she would never report it to a female.

Dismissing the awkwardness, the rosy-cheeked Lady cautiously pulls onto the congested street. Soon, after a few stops and a right-hand turn, the two are headed the direction of home.

Natashas are supposed to be incapable of having any kind of mood. Sara is in a bad one.

The floodgate opens wider. For the first time since the pills began, Sara hears her inner voice. *Don't let it happen again!* Squinted eyes locked on the yellow lines passing underneath, Sara clings to the present. *It's happening again!* The Natasha slips. And then slips some more.

Lady can tell something is wrong.

Sara falls back into the immediate past.

While Tiffany walks laps with the other girls, Shelly continues letting her teammates know she wants nothing more than for them to get out of her way. For the last few minutes, Sara has felt a way she never has before. No headache, not hungry, bounding with energy.

Four teams – two games going at once – volleyballs bouncing everywhere.

"Either play right or take your fat fucking ass for a lap!" Shelly shouts at her teammate.

"Miss Thompson!" Coach Callahan barks at the basketball team's top scorer. This isn't the first time the coach has been forced to reprimand the fiercely competitive Shelly. The one with lemur-like athleticism led her team to three wins – shooting Sara dirty looks all the while.

Though she should have no feelings at all, the new girl has been alternating between being intimidated by the tiny tyrant and wanting to kill her. Kill her. Intimidated. Kill her. Intimidated. Neither emotion lasts long enough for action.

Sara looks straight ahead through the windshield. Cold air blowing in her face, she sees not the back of the Jeep Grand Cherokee ahead, but Shelly's face; her ponytail loose, makeup sweated off, her quick eyes. Sara sees the lock of raven hair, plastered to her sweaty cheek.

Watching the little bully run roughshod over the other teams has stirred something within. Sara's curious awe of the one so mighty is accompanied by a yearning to see her put in her place. The compulsion intensifies as time goes on. Still yet to play Shelly's team, Sara watches from across the way.

Driving two miles under the speed limit, Lady would very much like to converse with her new charge, but waits. Made uneasy by Sara's vibe, the pleasantly padded woman feels much the way she might were she transporting a wild animal. Though Babe has told her little of the Natashas, her intuition tells her 'Beware.'

During the lightning storm in her brain, Sara feels the gym floor beneath her feet. She feels the extra spring in her step. She feels the urge to unleash the prowess she hides all day, every day. The Natasha gets another mean look from Shelly.

"Did you make any friends at school today?" Lady asks. Sara does not hear. What the passenger with a thousand-yard stare does hear is Mrs. Callahan's whistle.

The game begins. Shelly is a one-woman team all her own. The score is close. The ball is popped up by a sliding Shelly. After a high arch, it hangs above the net, begging to be spiked. Shelly rises.

After three swift strides, Sara leaps over her teammate.

Smack!

Shelly eats the spike.

Sara snaps out of her daydream to realize they are home.

Climbing the gradual incline of the straight lane entering from the South, the new Buick rolls past the thirty-year-old house surrounded by chain-link and under the carport.

Disoriented and exhausted, Sara gets out of the sedan. She is careful not to bump the door on one of the posts supporting the aluminum roof. A bit woozy, she follows the swift-footed gal toward the house.

What in the world is wrong with you, child? wonders Lady.

Walking through the narrow utility room, the spy stops. *Cinnamon rolls!*

8:02 PM

Suffering the effects from her third feeding frenzy of the evening, the Natasha is curled atop her comforter once again. Curtains drawn. The ceiling fan swirling lazily above feels nice. Fatigued in a way she has never known, the operative feels broken. Laying in the dimness, Sara finds a macabre peace at what must be rock bottom.

Twenty-one minutes pass. Sara, eyes vacantly adrift, hears a gentle knock. Her door opens.

"Are you still awake, young one?" asks Lady, voice as soft as rose petals.

"Yes."

"Babe is awake and would like a moment with you."

The operative nods before rolling onto her side. *I am soooo fuuull,* feels Sara, shuffling out of her bedroom.

After a turn out of her bedroom and a few steps through the kitchen, Sara passes through the utility room and out the door. It is dusk. Though still hot and muggy, it is far more pleasant outside than a few hours ago.

Around the corner, chains squeak lightly. Once down the porch, Sara finds Babe swaying slowly. He is enjoying the sunset.

"Hello there," he greets, wrinkles deepening with his widening smile. "Did my Lady feed you enough?"

Sara stifles a burp as she nods.

"Come, sit." Babe scooches over.

Lagging behind herself, the Natasha takes a seat beside her superior.

"So," John begins, shifting his body. "What do you think of the place?" Waving his hand like a wand.

"The residence is good." The Russian does not know why her superior is asking her opinion.

Lady looks down from the window above the kitchen sink. His smile warms her heart. Her Babe hasn't smiled often since his diagnosis.

"How are the children at your school?" John asks in Russian. "Are they nice to you?"

Sara sucks in a sharp breath. Her body tenses. Spies are not to speak in Russian. Ever.

"They are nice." Sara answers in English.

"They are nice, are they?" John continues in Russian, one brow raised. He knows how teenage girls can be.

"They are Americans," Sara does not know what else to say. This makes the man with a 1950's style chuckle. Her presence lifts his spirits.

Smiling, he turns to the lowering sun. Even though it is eighty-five degrees, the semi-retired spy wearing jeans, a yellowed t-shirt, and slippers rubs his hands as if he were cold.

"I haven't been taking my pills," Sara volunteers in a flat tone. John waves dismissively while reaching for the pack of smokes in his shirt pocket. He draws a cigarette with his lips the way he has done countless times before. Sara sits by as he lights up with a scratched Zippo.

During a long drag, the handler deep in thought sets the refillable lighter on the ledge near his left elbow. He blows a cloud of smoke into the air. "I know... I know about the pills." John veers to another topic. "I'd much rather hear of your school friends. Are they really nice?"

"I have only spoken to one person. She is nice." Sara answers, shifting in search of relief. She has eaten so much tonight.

"What's her name?" asks John, smoke crawling out of his mouth. Looking upon Sara, the weathered man steals a glance toward a sunset too beautiful to ignore.

"Her name is Megan. She is a junior." Sara sees her wire-rimmed glasses and boxy face. "She is a source of information regarding other students."

"It's okay if you would like to speak Russian. No one is around." John tries to calm the uneasy spy.

"But the rules—"

"Rules, rules, rules... so many rules." John interrupts in English. "Too many rules." He pulls again from his cigarette.

At a loss for words, Sara sits silent.

What seems an eternity passes before the man with paunch shifts her way. "While you are here with my Lady and me, the rules will not be the same as you are used to." A grinning John leans in. "As long as you don't drink up all my good vodka!"

"I would never steal any of your belongings." Sara rushes to assure.

John chuckles. "I know," he calms the one who takes everything literally. "I know."

Without warning, John's energy drains much the way it did last night. He puts his hands on his knees. *Ahh, shit,* he thinks, fatigue and dizziness setting in. The guy letting out a long breath knows he will need to find his bed soon. John clears his throat. "For the time you are with us, you will not be taking any more of the pills." John can tell a difference in Sara already. "Do you know the purpose of the pills?"

"No," Sara answers, having only a general idea.

John's gray eyes turn toward the city. Cars pass along the bottom of the hill. The spy who has aged several years over the last few months considers explaining the purpose of each pill, but decides against doing so. "I believe you will be better without them." With this, John's energy fades. He lowers his chin to his chest.

Lady is soon out the door, down the steps, and at her husband's side.

Having been issued no directive, the Natasha stands by, watching the stout lass help her wilted husband to his feet. Supporting himself between the railing and Lady's sturdy figure, John makes his way up the steps and into the house.

The door closes, leaving Sara alone on the swing. A slow push of air travels up the slope of the hill like a hot breath. Her mind depleted, the one feeling as though in a vacuum just sits, shoulders slumped. Zoned out, she stares at a spot along the edge of the patio. The swing creaks as she sways. Everything feels so far away...

Hazel eyes fix upon a random spot on the concrete. A tiny chip along the edge of the patio beckons her gaze. Sara sort of zones out. Peacefulness.

The sun continues to retreat. Cars zoom in the distance. Lady asks if Sara would like some pie.

8:47 PM

It has happened again. Crumb speckled plate on her nightstand, the Natasha has laid herself low once more. *I was full* before *I even took a bite,* thinks Sara. An episode of *Friends* casts a glow. *I like Joey and Monica best,* she thinks. No thought lasts long in the mind coming apart.

Short, choppy breaths. *I'm never eating like this again,* she swears.

9:15 PM

Lady turns off the television and drapes a sheet over the girl fast asleep. "Sweet dreams, child."

Resting so deep as to near a coma, Sara appears to be at peace. But behind closed eyes is a mind ablaze. Millions more synapses coming online by the minute.

Polar opposites. Irreconcilable. Unable to occupy the same psychological space—the Natasha and girl whom nature intended continue to rise. Continue to diverge.

The mind underneath struggles to accommodate.

Friday, August 22nd, 2014

8:31 AM, 1st Hour
Mr. Colliet's Advanced Biology class
Megan sits beside Sara. Not being able to talk is painful for the friend who seized the initiative by changing her schedule to be in First Hour with her new senior BFF. Megan did not tell of her plans because she wanted it to be a surprise.

It has already been a long day – the Natasha's mind has been under assault since 3:52 AM. Yesterday was no more than a lull before the heavy shelling that began the moment she opened her eyes.

Profuse sweating, shaking hands, and dilated pupils – Lady knew something was terribly wrong.

Lady recommended Sara stay home. It was as though the troubled girl had gone deaf. In a world all her own, the unresponsive Natasha went through the motions of getting ready and walked out to the car.

Sara's head hurts when she tries to resist the torrent. Arms folded, the girl staring down at her desk does not realize Megan's attempts for her attention.

Heart pounding and palms clammy, Sara feels she is being pushed out of herself. Invaded, clawed at, pulled apart, suffering assault from within.

A collision of memories trigger all five senses. Sara submits. While Mr. Colliet tells the class to open their textbooks to page 71 and Megan folds a note; Sara tastes Lady's cherry pie, hears the swing creaking, sees last night's sunset, feels her purple pillow on her face, smells the gymnasium, feels the texture of the passenger seat of Lady's car, and sees the wrinkles at the corner of John's eyes. Rocking slightly, Sara endures the overload.

Disconnected from the world, the girl who did not brush her teeth, eat breakfast, or run a brush through her hair, dares not close her eyes. Doing so only worsens her affliction.

"Psst..." Megan sounds as Mr. Colliet goes on about the human circulatory system. Sara cannot hear the Megan only a few feet away because the Megan from yesterday is so loud.

"Heather, she's not here right now, she used to be fat, but not like super-fat, only sorta-kinda fat—she's the junior who's super pale and has, like, chestnutty-auburnish-hair... anyway, she *used* to be fat and wore overalls all the time and never talked to anyone and then one day she went all anorexic or bulimic and then she lost like thirty-five pounds and started fainting all the time, and that made her all instantly super-popular somehow..." Megan's babbling rises above the clash of sounds in her mental background.

Like a backup track to Megan's spastic tutorial are the blended sounds of; a twisting bathroom doorknob, Mrs. Callahan's whistle, and pistols firing in the shooting house back at The Institute. Sara can taste Lady's Swiss steak, smell the interior of her car, and feel the smooth surface of her dresser drawers on her fingertips.

Sensory overload.

9:09 AM
The bell signals the end of first hour.

The sandy blond exits the room quickly. Unaware she is being followed, Sara, passing others as though standing still, leaves a trailing Megan behind. Lacking Sara's grace, she bumps into most everyone while struggling to catch up.

"Where are you going?! Are you mad at me?! Where are you going?!" pleads Megan in the present. This while Megan's voice from yesterday echoes the rumor of Tiffany's alleged cheating on her boyfriend Jet.

The brain gone haywire is broadsided by a memory from The Pit. Sara feels sand going down the back of her neck. Reliving the struggle to free herself from an arm-bar, she feels the back of Natasha 716's legs across her chest and face. She feels her arm snap once again.

A bolt of phantom pain.

The thunder of a breaking bone. Just another sound in the calamity of noise in Sara's head. Rubbing her right arm, the Natasha continues straight ahead.

After a sprint down an open stretch of hallway, a panting Megan catches up.

"Yeah, so I was in Ms. McCardell's algebra class for the first hour and, I swear, it was nothing but sophomores pretty much and, like, two girls from China so you know the curve is gonna be wrecked and I was like, 'Do I wanna be stuck in here for an entire semester with the cat lady and a bunch of people one year older than my sister?'—I don't think so, right? So, I was thinking 'I don't even need Algebra One because I took Mr. Corrum's Geometry class last year and you only really need a credit in one or the other." Megan grazes someone at the drinking fountain. "Unless I want to get into college, I mean, I am going to college, but I'm thinking of something like nursing school because I love helping people, but I heard that you have to change diapers or something, and I guess I could, but only if it was someone I really cared about like my mom or my dad, well, not my dad because, you know, that would be gross..."

Sara stops abruptly. Megan crashes into her.

Having gone from her seat in the back row of Mr. Colliet's classroom to almost the far end of the school, the bewildered Natasha looks around. This part of the school is not immediately familiar. Sara notices those passing each way are younger than those usually surrounding her. Disoriented, Sara turns to Megan.

Only now suspecting something could be wrong, Megan asks, "Are you okay?"

9:15 AM, 2nd Hour
Mr. Schibi's American History class

Two minutes after the bell, Sara has crashed. Mentally spent, the shell of a Natasha sits slumped at her desk.

Shoulders drooped, the girl in a stupor sits in the classroom resistant to change. A globe faded from sitting too close to the window, a pewter bust of John Adams, laminated posters of presidents and famous inventors. Mr. Schibi's desk is clear, save for a few newspapers and his dented thermos. The room is much the way he found it twenty-one years ago.

The class chuckles, but Sara does not notice.

Removed from the moment, the girl whose cheeks are a touch fuller than a couple of days ago, rests her eyes upon a random scuff in the tile. Soothing. Oddly mesmerizing. Much like the chip along the edge of the patio last night, it draws her in.

Sara has found a sort of serenity. Like a television show, she idly watches the scene playing in her mind. She sees her hands in latex gloves.

Her left hand holds a menthol cigarette while her right thumb gently presses the plunger of the 3-millimeter syringe. Three-inch, twenty-six-gauge needle. The dried tobacco absorbs the cyanide taken from the jewelry store. The much finer needle (than the one use to quickly suck up the poison) is perfect for lacing the already dangerous product. After leaking amber venom during a slow extraction, the task in complete. The Natasha notices a speck of saturation on the paper. She relives the feeling of *It will dry*. She remembers setting the cigarette down on a table. Placing the cap on the end of the syringe. Sara smells neither Mr. Schibi's cheap cigarettes nor his aftershave – only the dank odor of the unheated basement that were her quarters.

As Mr. Schibi gives an entertaining summary of America's war for independence, Sara sees a black pair of rollerblades with pink wheels laying in the passenger seat of a black Honda.

After surveilling James Allen Jones, Ruth Smith learned his habits, routines, and vices. Posing as a jogger in his suburban neighborhood, the Natasha discovered that her target living in Independence, Missouri smoked cigarettes. And returned home between 5:45 and 6:00 PM on Monday, Tuesdays, Thursdays, and Fridays.

That was all she needed to know.

At the moment Mr. Schibi wryly asks the class which president is on the ten-dollar bill, the last strand between the diverging selves breaks.

Conjoined no longer, the girl nature intended sees Twelve's past from her own perspective. Viewing the memories of another, she watches the placing of Mr. Jones' favorite brand of cigarettes in the passenger side floorboard of his unlocked car. As though standing off to the side, the girl-who-would-have-been watches Twelve carefully pull one of the cigarettes just far enough as to ensure the pack will not be thought empty.

Only one of the six cigarettes is poisoned. The Natasha knew her mark would get to that particular one soon enough.

The mind underneath does what it can to manage the rended psyche. Like a parent arbitrating between sisters, the subconscious has but a single mission – survival. Finally separate, the Natasha now wholly her own identifies as Twelve; the girl-who-would-have-been, Sara. For now, the slouching original self watches clips from a past that is not her own.

Dominating the recall is a pair of black rollerblades. Dismissed by Twelve at the time, Velcro straps and hot pink wheels prove the centerpiece of Sara's lax focus.

Surreal is the recollection. Reliving the experience of another's actions done by one's own hand. Perspective – both through her own two eyes and that of one standing by.

Though she herself was never Ruth Smith, Sara feels the asphalt under Ruth's feet as she casually flees the scene. A brisk jog through the neighborhood—ponytail swaying with each step. Sara feels herself carried away by the assassin's strides. A cognitive stowaway, Sara sees bare trees, lawns speckled with autumn leaves. Wooden fences. Halloween decorations. Children wearing coats as they play. Cars slowly passing by.

One cul-de-sac after another, Twelve's feet carry Sara out of the subdivision and to her handler's waiting car

The deluge that swept her away is now but a stream. A current running gently through the mind broken in two. Exhausted into a lethargic calm, Sara feels the chilled handle as she opens the passenger door. She relives Twelve lowering herself down into the seat. The leather seat is cold.

Her hazel eyes glued to the floor; Sara sees Twelve's first handler named John Smith. Rectangular face, thin lips, receding hair line. Uncaring eyes. She senses his volatility. As if watching from across the room, Sara watches the ill-tempered man strike Twelve with an open hand. She wants Twelve to run away, but she does not.

Sara's mind changes channels.

While Mr. Schibi talks of how the founding fathers 'bickered like cheerleaders', Sara sees a snippet of a newspaper article. *James Allen Jones, 66, of Independence, Missouri, died in a single car accident on Interstate 35.*

The article makes no reference to poison or foul play. The Russian did not know why she had to kill the retired contractor.

In the theater of her mind, Sara sees not what Twelve witnessed herself, but what Twelve expected would happen.

James Jones, a portly man with acne scars and curly gray hair, driving Northbound on Highway 35.

He removes a cigarette from the pack he does not recall dropping on the floor.

puff, puff, puff

He notices something wrong.

A curious concern slowly grows to alarm, then quickly turns to panic. James Jones tugs his collar, gulping at the air.

Sara closes her eyes. Twelve opens hers. Depleted no less than her counterpart, the Natasha remains slumped just the same.

Twelve sees through the windshield as though riding on the hood. James Jones, bursting with sweat and eyes bulging, racing for the hospital. Hair whipping, the Natasha watches with delight. Her brain no longer restrained; the Natasha now has a mind all her own. A personality. A sense of humor.

James Allen Jones turns blue. Twelve laughs.

Twelve's vantage changes to that of a car traveling closely behind. The speeding Honda Civic gradually drifts as James Jones loses consciousness. Once across the shoulder and off the road, the foreign car crumples upon hitting a culvert. Ninety-one miles per hour to zero in an instant.

10:31 AM, 3rd Hour
Mr. Godfrey's Trigonometry class
After shuffling her feet from history to math class, the zombie-of-a-person lowers into her desk. History book left behind and Trigonometry book still in her locker, the vacant one sits with her hands in her lap. So groggy as to be sleepwalking, the person too spent to be actively Sara or Twelve at the moment fails to say "Here" during attendance.

Her mind running much like a flashlight with fading batteries, not even Mr. Godfrey's usual fervor is enough to rouse her back into the present. Alternating back and forth, Twelve finds herself back at The Institute. It is unseasonably hot. Hands swollen from the pounding recoil of thousands of rounds fired in the shooting houses. Sweat and gunpowder blend. Her eyes burn.

Short is this reminiscence. Twelve's mind jumps to the time of Ester Smith, her third alias.

The basement of Raymond Smith. Twelve feels the dampness of her handler's clothes as she takes them from the washing machine.

The metal button on the fly of Raymond Smith's jeans clinks inside the dryer. This causes the perspective to switch from first-hand Twelve to third-party Sara. The original self watches the dutiful Natasha. Sara is appalled by the grimy conditions.

As the students focus on Mr. Godfrey's dry-erase board, Sara watches the operative go about a daily chore. Expressionless is the one closing the dryer.

The sound of the metal door closing kicks the memory along to a later time. Perspective shifts back to the Natasha.

Twelve feels warm water running down her body. She hears the plastic rings of the shower curtain slide.

Switch.

Sara watches the handler, holding the vinyl curtain aside. He looks Twelve up and down. He smiles.

Switch.

Twelve relives the wetness cascading down her body. The warm pressure from a showerhead pointed just below her neckline. Indifferent at the time, the memory angers the Natasha now. Being eyed by her handler as she showered was routine.

Mr. Godfrey, noticing something amiss, keeps his eye on the new student.

The runaway mind continues to roam where it will.

11:26 AM
Lunchtime

Oddly rejuvenated, but still sluggish, the girl craving sugar makes her way down the all but empty hall to the soda and candy machines near the cafeteria. Standing square in the glow of the brightly lit graphic, Sara inserts a five-dollar bill.

The girl feeling as though fresh from hibernation presses a button. A candy bar falls.

Then another.

Then a Pepsi.

Like a three-year-old, Sara proceeds to shove the chocolatey sweets into her mouth... Chomp, chomp, swallow. Chomp, chomp, swallow.

"Mmm," hums the girl with chipmunk cheeks. *Chocolate make belly happy.*

'PSSHHT!' sounds the Pepsi as two boys look on.

GULP! GULP! GULP! GULP! GULP! "Ahh." There is a rumble in her chest. *BUUUUUURP!* The boys' eyes widen at the powerful belch.

A baby burp follows. "Now, I'm hungry." Sara, mutters to no one. With chocolate at the corners of her mouth, she takes a few steps toward the cafeteria – before turning back for more candy bars.

12:25 PM, 5ᵗʰ Hour
Mr. Stuart's Government class

Like one recovering from a 24-hour bug, Sara feels a little better all the time. The mental attacks no longer seem like attacks, but movies playing in Sara's head. Like watching *Grease*. Though spacey and out of step, the world around her is becoming more real with each passing minute. Everything yet distant, it is all very much like a dream.

Sixty-eight hours and twenty-five minutes have passed since the last pill. Only trace amounts of the blue remain. At peace, and with her belly full of candy bars, Sara divides her lackadaisical attention between the high-strung Mr. Stuart and whatever memory crosses her shared mind.

While Sara hears Mr. Stuart's raspy voice explain congressional districts, she sees Twelve with a cast on her right arm in the infirmary of The Institute. She sees the run-down facility. Dingy sheets. Cyrillic writing on the building out the cracked window. Sara sees the doctor who reset Twelve's arm. He was very thin. Unfriendly.

"There are four-hundred thirty-five congressional districts, people!" says the man with the metabolism of a hummingbird.

Behind the scenes, the subconscious – the executor of the collective self – maintains a tenuous hold on the broken mind. The mind underneath does what it feels best.

Memory playing on, the nurse standing next to Twelve's doctor is smoking a cigarette. *A nurse is smoking near a patient?* Sara finds Twelve's history barbaric.

1:19 PM, 6th Hour
Mrs. Espinosa's Home Economics class

During the day that feels a week already, Sara has gone from disturbed, to vacant, to curiously content. A dreamer by nature, Sara's gaze is naturally drawn to the window. Wondrous eyes take in the world all around as the teacher with a chocolate smudge on her blouse tells of the project to come.

A nuisance once again, Russell Martin – aka "Big Ginger" – is temporarily disposed of when the crafty teacher sends him to the far end of the building to hand deliver a note. The noisy one lumbers out the door. Serenity returns.

The daydreamer doesn't realize she is being watched from three rows over. Adrian West, a soccer player with Abercrombie features and bohemian manner can't stop looking Sara's way. The guy teased by his friends for taking Home Ec instead of Woodshop, wonders how he is only now noticing the new girl eyes... *Her eyes sparkle like diamonds.*

2:06 PM 7th Hour
Mrs. Callahan's Physical Education class
Because Coach Godfrey had to leave, the girls' and boys' classes are joined today. Happy to help, Mrs. Callahan was not surprised when the boy Coach Godfrey and his wife had planned to induce tomorrow decided to come a day early. Rather than lower the dark blue partition at the half court line as she normally would when both classes share the gymnasium, Mrs. Callahan left it up for a boys-versus-girls kickball game.

Unlike yesterday, Sara does not have to worry about changing in front of the other girls. After an indirect route with no sense of urgency, the locker room was all but empty by the time she arrived. Wandering out just in time to hear her name called for attendance, Sara hears, "Cutting it close, Miss Smith," from the brawny woman with a whistle around her neck.

The boys class waits on the bleachers at the other end of the gym. The boys look at the girls, the girls pretend not to notice. Sara wishes it was volleyball today. She likes volleyball – she thinks.

Same as at lunch, the one with her head in the clouds does not notice Shelly's stare. The girl thinking about volleyball and how much she likes Pepsi has no idea how much the spike in the face has been eating at the one Mrs. Callahan calls 'Mighty Mouse'. After taking the boys' attendance, Mrs. Callahan points the boys to the outfield as she bellows, "Ladies first!". Coach Mike, knowing he would be missing a couple days, already warned all of his classes of the hell to pay should anyone cause the substitute any grief.

Tiffany and four others make their way to the bleachers. Kickball leaves no path for laps.

Air is thick with testosterone most of the boys act a little more spirited than they otherwise might.

The ladies, more demure.

After a few words from Mrs. Callahan, the impromptu game with too many players begins. Shelly kicks first because that is what Shelly does. She sends the ball booming, and burns around the bases same as she would were it a state softball championship with the game on the line.

Shelly makes it to second base. Sara, arms folded, looks on from the back of the line. *I really wish I had one of those candy bars right now. Candy bars are good. I wonder if Lady can make candy bars.* Pre-occupied and hungry, Sara is content to stay off to the side and out of the way.

The game goes on. Nobody bothers to keep track of the score.

Several times worse than what he was in Home Ec just a short time ago, Russell Martin is the loudest, most obnoxious, most rambunctious. The guy also nicknamed 'Ogre' throws around his weight with the reserve of a middle schooler. Having nothing to say does little to discourage him from talking loudly all the time. Sara pays the boy with orange freckles and yellow teeth no mind. Feeling very much out of place, she stays at the end of the line when it's her team's turn to kick.

A few of the boys seem less eager to join in the nonsense. Sara's roaming attention tends to circle back to one in particular. The sole resident of her own little La Land, she doesn't realize her tendency to look his way.

Sara curiously watches the game. For the third time now, her hazels find the same pair of blues; only this time they are looking back. Sara's heart jumps. Cheeks flush. Eyes find the floor. The strangest of sensations swells within.

The tall guy with a slender build and broad face thought the skinny girl at the end of the line was maybe looking at him. Now he knows. If Sara were still looking, she would see his smile.

Sara doesn't know why her chest is tight. Or why she is wondering if the cute boy with straight dark hair just over his ears is still looking her way. All she knows is that her heart is pounding, her palms are sweaty, and she would rather be anywhere but here right now.

Slowly, Sara's eyes rise to the third baseman with an easy stance and one hand on his hip. *Good!* She sighs with relief. *He's not looking at me!* Her face cools. *Okay, don't look at him!* the flustered girl barks at herself.

Sara doesn't *want* to look at him – she is compelled to. Which makes no sense at all. He is among the few actually not trying to draw attention to himself. A quick look, she notices a narrow gap between his perfectly straight teeth.

Her attention fluttering to him like a moth to a flame; she doesn't notice Russell's demand for everyone's attention, the red ball bouncing all around, or Shelly's shooting daggers her way. It makes Shelly angry that the person who made her angry isn't aware of just how angry she is.

Why do I keep looking at him?! wonders the girl standing as far out of the way as possible. While undeniably handsome, the third baseman does not have the angular features of a model like some of the other guys. Perhaps his effortless cool is what causes her attention to gravitate his way.

Time passes, the energy level of the gym drops. Even Russell is growing tired of his own antics. It's the boys' turn to kick and – as the rotation would have it – Sara is at shortstop. A boy from Sara's English class awaits the bouncing pitch. A hearty boot sends a red blur streaking past Sara at waist level. The ball travels far beyond before she so much as flinches.

Sara crimsons, frozen in her delayed pose. A rise of laughter gives the crimping girl her first taste of embarrassment. Each second feels like ten. *I want to disappear.*

Drowning in the moment, Sara doesn't realize that missing the ball isn't what sparked the laughter, but the entire second that passed before she even turned. That, and her expression that followed.

Relishing the moment, Shelly, sporting a smug look, goes so far as to give a slow clap.

Switch.

With Sara retreated into herself, a furious Twelve takes her place. Seething where she stands, the Natasha is not angry about the trifling kickball game or the laughter, but the loss of control. The Natasha, the killer, the Russian rolls her knuckles. Teeth grind as realization of Sara's existence takes hold. The rest of the day comes in a rush, Megan's blathering, candy bars, Shelly's snickering.

Twelve looks at the haughty brunette pulling her short ponytail tighter. *I'll get you later, bitch.*

More immediately, the Natasha with a mind all her own focuses on her intruder. Sara. Her weakness. How that weakness might be removed.

3:05 PM

The Natasha plops down into Lady's awaiting car and, with eyes forward and jaw set, growls, "Give me my blue pills!"

"Okay, dearie, they are yours, you can have them if you want them," The spy's wife acquiesces in her most soothing tone.

Twelve's awakening was unpleasant.

3:45 PM
Bedroom

Glazed eyes half open, the one laying on her belly under the ceiling fan is in a virtual coma. Lady didn't want to hand over six blues, but a potentially violent Twelve insisted. Unable to imagine what could have gotten her so worked up, Lady reluctantly placed the pills into her sweaty palm. Having worried all day, Lady was surprised she didn't get a call from the school. The way Twelve acted in the car, Lady is extra surprised she didn't get a call.

It took only a few minutes for the outer layer of the blues to take effect. Bit by bit, the one so agitated became less agitated; less agitated became calm; calm became relaxed. From lax, to loose, to limp, to catatonic.

Having an idea of what the blue pills do, Twelve is attempting to end the usurper who hijacked her body.

Staring blankly under her desk, the one still wearing her gym clothes lies, head turned, drooling on her comforter.

Sitting on the edge of the bed, Lady lightly rubs the girl's back. It feels much like petting a lioness rendered harmless from a tranquilizer dart. "What have they done to you?" she whispers, running her fingers across faded whip scars. Seven vertical lashes stain otherwise beautiful skin. Lady's heart breaks.

This isn't what Lady had in mind tonight. She planned a surprise.

9:40 PM

In a mumbling torpor, the sack-eyed girl shuffles to the bathroom.

Seeing her on her feet is a relief to Babe, who is aware of the situation. He was looking forward to another talk on the swing – and the surprise Lady had planned – but both will have to wait.

9:51 PM

Television casts a glow upon the girl propped up on pillows.

Plate of spaghetti supported by a tray, the one seeming fresh off a lobotomy slowly chews her food. Fork held in her fist; she does not notice the lock of hair trapped in the corner of her mouth.

She has said but a single word all night – "*Grease.*"

Fearing the tray will tip over, Lady stays nearby. Foregoing the urge to feed her like a baby, the lass periodically wiping red sauce from her charge's chin sighs, "What am I gonna do with you, child?"

Sara's gym shirt gets stained.

"We'll get you better," Lady promises from the bottom of her heart. "Yeah, we'll get you better."

Saturday, August 23rd, 2014

1:14 AM
Sara's bed

Consciousness at rest, the shared mind works to mend, cope, and accommodate best it can. What is done cannot be undone. No amount of the chemical comprising the core of the blue pills can turn the light back off. Two lights. The girl who was never allowed to be. And the Natasha forced into existence.

A mind broken. Split. Unable to reconcile. The original self resurrected, it is Sara who receives primacy. Sara knows not the hardship suffered during her exile. Inheriting academic knowledge and a general understanding of the world, the virtual newborn is aware of only that which she can cope. The Institute is a place she has never been.

Occupying the same realm, Twelve. Born of Necessity, tempered by pain. A product become person. Her womb was the vacuum left when the original self was put to sleep. Now with a mind – and initiative – all her own, the assassin must suffer the indignity of relegation to the shadows.

10:04 PM

Sara wakes for the first time in decade.

Sleepy eyes flutter open. Laying still, Sara looks around the room. A blink ago she was playing kickball. Now she is laying on the soft bed in her bedroom. Not only transported in time, but with full sentience. Crystal clarity. Yesterday was a hologram, a space removed, opaque. Today is life.

Sara wriggles her fingers and toes. Lips dry from the fan above; her right hand raises beneath the sheet. Fingertips travel lightly across her stomach. A tickle confirms reality. Slow breaths in and out, she watches her chest rise and fall.

Sara pulls back the sheet. She looks down at bare legs sticking out navy-blue gym shorts. *Those are my legs!*

Goosebumps.

Refreshed as having slept a month, Sara sits up. An inventory of the room; a desk, dresser, television, a closet. She remembers Lady, Babe, and arriving at the house – but it's all so hazy. Like a dream

One foot after the other, her feet touch the floor. A bit unsteady at first, Sara walks toward the door, soft carpet crushing under her bare feet.

Rounding the corner in the strangely familiar home, Sara turns to find Lady and Babe at the kitchen table. Puffiness tells Sara that Babe hasn't been awake very long himself.

"Morning sunshine," Babe welcomes warmly.

"We were wondering when you'd rise!" Lady gushes with relief. Seeing Sara up and about puts a portion of her worries to rest.

Standing at the edge of the kitchen, the girl biting her lip doesn't know what to do. It all takes a moment to process. Lady and Babe exchange a curious glance.

"You just have yourself a seat," Lady insists as she heads for the stove. "Now, I just mixed up some pancake batter in–" ... Lady stops mid-word, as though struck by a bolt. She abruptly leaves the kitchen without explanation.

Sara, yet to take a seat, looks quizzically at Babe.

"Don't look at me," says the grinning guy with his hands up. "This was her idea." Though he is a long way from well, Babe looks a little better than he did. Better color, more energy.

Shortly after stepping away, Lady is back with a gift-wrapped box. Sara is puzzled.

She is all the more puzzled when Lady places the gift in her hands. Standing with the box held out in front of her, Sara wonders if she is supposed to hand it to Babe.

The delighted couple look at her expectantly.

"Go on, open it!" insists Babe before sipping his coffee.

Wait, this present is for me?! Surprise flashes across Sara's face.

"Go ahead, open it!" Lady seconds, ushering Sara to the place already prepared for her at the table. Humming with eagerness, the rosy-cheeked lass steps back.

Sara begins opening the first gift ever given to her. Lady and Babe watch patiently. Afraid of ripping the paper, she carefully manages her thumbnail under the tape.

This is more than Lady can handle. "Oh, go on!" she bursts in encouragement. As instructed, Sara rips the paper. A shoe box. *They put my gift in a shoe box?*

Billowy white paper is seen upon the removal of the lid. She pulls the paper aside. Inside, brand-new black tennis shoes with pink on the tongue and toe. Blinking, Sara sits frozen. All she can do is stare.

Sara's chin slowly lifts. Lady and Babe look upon an astonished face. "Do you like them?" asks Lady, her hand rubbing across Babe's back.

Speechless, Sara looks back down into the box, ensuring they are not a figment of her imagination.

"Well, try them on!" urges Lady, rounding the table with sweeping steps. Soon on one knee and pulling wadded paper out of the left shoe, she lifts Sara's foot.

Astounded, Sara looks down much the way of a child while a grown-up puts on their shoe.

"We have to make sure they fit," says Lady, pushing the brand-new shoe onto a limp foot. "I was hoping that you would open them last night, but..." her soft brogue tapers, "...you were tired." *Whatever had gotten into her seems to have run its course.*

A smiling Babe looks on, taking stock of how much healthier Sara looks after only a few days. Still skinny, but no longer gaunt, he is amazed at just how rapidly she is responding to Lady's care.

"How does that feel on your foot there, young lady?!" asks a resplendent Lady.

Rendered speechless, Sara stares at the beautiful shoe. It fits perfectly. She wiggles her toes.

Hair mussed up and face still wearing deep sleep, Sara stares at the shoe at the end of her rolling ankle around as Lady puts on the other. Having only ever known boots and worn-out shoes, this feels like pillows hugging her feet.

"I wanted to get them for you on Thursday," Lady informs. "But the store only had them in a six-and-a-half." Sara looks at Babe. He loves seeing Lady so happy.

It finally dons on the girl with spaghetti stains on her t-shirt, *These shoes are mine!*

10:16 AM
Sara's run
Wearing her gym shorts and a purple t-shirt, Sara runs alongside the straight lane headed South. Staying on the grass to avoid getting dust on her new gift, she discovers a more powerful stride than she has ever known.

After the distance of seventy yards, she turns left onto the blacktop. Strong legs power up a gradual incline.

Propelled by nourished muscles, the girl with sunshine on her face runs away from the city as fast as her legs can carry.

Morning air fills Sara's lungs. Feeling like she can run forever, the girl with wind blowing in her hair races her way up the first slope. Boundless energy.

Seeing, smelling, hearing, feeling — Sara thinks of nothing aside from the beauty of the hay meadow in the distance and how good the breeze feels on her skin. Passing one house after another, driveways become farther apart.

Over railroad tracks and under drooping limbs, Sara runs with no destination in mind. Once off the blacktop, the girl who has slowed to a brisk jog approaches cows drinking from a pond. They raise their heads as Sara passes by. "Hi cows," she waves.

Grave crunches under foot.

Beginning to perspire, Sara runs past an old grain silo, under a low bridge, and away from a barking dog on a chain. Her thighs burn; she enjoys the sensation. Endorphins release as she trots past tractors, barns, pastures and other scenes remarkably picturesque. Sara wishes the horses taking bites out of a big round bale of hay weren't so far away. She wants to pet one.

Sara hops over a spotted turtle near the ditch.

After running more than six miles, a sort of euphoria sets in. Never having felt this amazing before, Sara feels she could run a hundred more.

Wiping sweat from her face; Sara enjoys the momentary shade of a stretch of trees. Temperature increasing steadily; the girl with armpits soaked through jogs past corn as tall as herself.

Maintaining a swift pace, Sara's t-shirt grows more damp by the mile. She turns at an old set of railroad tracks. Down a line abandoned long ago she goes. Stepping on patches of grass and rotting railroad ties, Sara makes her way down a path dimmed by the limbs stretching overhead. The inching forest works to reclaim land taken by the railroad company long ago.

Sara becomes smaller and smaller to the doe crossing far behind.

After running a mile – and scaring a snake sunning himself on the track – the panting girl comes upon an old bridge above a shallow river.

Huffing and puffing already; the sight takes her breath away.

Standing midway along the rustic structure, the young woman with hands on her hips and sweat streaming down her sun-reddened face is captivated. The green serenity of the wooded area all around, the lazy pace of the bending river below, flowers in bloom. Thirty feet above the water, Sara feels as though standing in the sky.

Tracks running East and West, the muddy river North and South, Sara feels the sense of standing at a crossroad. A gentle breeze soothes.

The bridge, 150 feet, a remnant from a bygone era. At one time, the grandest structure of its kind for miles – now, not worth the trouble of tearing down. Left to the elements after its service ended, the oxidized relic is but a place for birds to rest on top and roost beneath.

Surrounded by bolts and rivets, Sara stands between the two concrete pillars supporting the bulky mass.

Though the high arches on each side of the bridge were not designed for aesthetic appeal, they are pleasing to the eye.

The grainy texture turning her palms orange, the girl breathing honeysuckle spies three turtles on a log. One slides into the water.

Sara closes her eyes. So tranquil is the sound of water rippling around the moss-stained pillars.

A bush of white blossoms. A weeping willow hanging into the water after a split at its trunk. A rustling in the shrubbery. Unable to identify the creatures making the commotion, Sara assumes squirrels.

Staring into the water, a mind predisposed to drifting follows a stick along the current. Sara loses sight as it passes under the bridge. With only a few memories of her own, Sara's mind hasn't many places to go. Candy bars. The shiny apple on Mrs. Espinosa's desk. The echo of a moment in gym class… when a boy from Sara's History class suddenly got into an argument with another boy in the outfield. The attention of both classes angled the direction of the two boys nearing blows less than a minute after Mrs. Callahan stepped away from the class.

Sara relives the tension of the moment. The sense of oxygen being sucked from the gym. Fists balled. Chests puffed. Taunts shouted to the backdrop of silence.

Looking into yesterday, the girl staring into the water hears a voice crack like thunder, shattering the moment so quickly out of hand.

"Hey!" shouted the guy who had been drawing her eye. She watches him sweep in, cleanly snatching the red ball from the pitcher. "We're down by five points!" he said before rolling a smooth pitch to the next girl up to kick.

A girl with hair short on one side and long on the other boots a line drive and – just like that – the conflict evaporates into thin air. Fight averted. Life goes on.

Mrs. Callahan soon returned. It was as though nothing happened at all.

Only now does Sara stop to realize, *Our team wasn't winning. We weren't even keeping score.* Mind focused on the unremarkable situation; Sara does not stop to wonder why the memory resonates the way it does. The wistful memory passes like the clouds overhead.

Desiring shade, the girl with low-cut socks and a ponytail coming loose continues on – but not before promising to return.

Thirty-two minutes pass along during the next six miles. Passing cornfields, farmhouses, a hay meadow filled with square bales, two ponds, a slobbering dog named Brutus, and a man leveling his wife's petunias with a weed-eater while watching her run by, Sara eventually returns to the rock home on the hill. After leaving by the way of the South, she comes in from the North. Starting at the bottom of the hill, Sara walks the last seventy yards.

Hands on her hips and breathing through her nose, the pace of Sara's racehorse heart drops quickly. Every muscle from hip to knee flush and shirt soaked, a Southwest breeze cools salty skin pink from the sunshiny day. Sara interlaces her fingers atop her head as she walks through the soft grass up the mound. The stone house grows larger with each step.

Base rock of the winding drive crunching under her feet, Sara nears the chain-link gate. Upon reaching for the latch, lightning strikes her lower abdomen.

"Ugghh!" Sara groans as she buckles. The pain causes her teeth to grit as she twists to the ground. Face contorted; she cradles her torso. The stabbing within continues. "Uggghh," moans the girl clinging to the fence.

The pain abates. Confused, Sara looks around as though seeking the source of her sudden agony.

Relieved, Sara starts to stand back up... *Oh my God!* The lightning returns with a vengeance. Hanging from the fence, she holds her breath. Hunkering down, she waits out the storm. Eight long seconds pass before the next reprieve. Gradually, the tension relents. "What is happening to me?" Sara utters through tight lips.

Legs like jelly, Sara pulls herself to her feet. She notices red on her sock. Troubled eyes follow the red trail up the inside of her sweaty leg and under her baggy shorts. "What?! Seriously?!" whines an exasperated Sara ready to cry.

On cloud-nine only a minute ago, the disheartened girl looks up to see Lady alighting down the steps to the rescue. Seeing Sara grab her stomach, the mother hen knew exactly what was happening. She saw this coming.

Sara, upset and at a loss, is lead along the patio. "We'll have you right in no time, sweetheart," Lady whispers.

2:15 PM
Sara's bedroom
Heating pad on her stomach, two *Aleve*, and a bowl of ice cream, Sara is situated and watching *Grease* as though for the first time. After a shower and change into comfy clothes,

the girl with a glass of ice water on the nightstand, more ice cream in the freezer, and a remote control in her hand is feeling much better. Though somewhat edgy – and displeased at the universe for being so cruel and unfair – the girl body slammed into womanhood is as good as circumstances allow.

Legs stiff from the run, and starving despite two bowls of ice cream, she anxiously awaits the pizza bites cooking around the corner. Sara's first real day has been eventful.

Time passes. After a pile of pizza bites and a bowl of hot apple crisp with ice cream, Sara is asleep under her blanket.

8:51 PM
Sara's eyes pop open as the last bit of sun disappears over the horizon. Wide awake, she is – at least in this very moment – free of the twisting within. Needing to pee, she gets up very gently, for fear of waking the monster within.

Sara looks about the dim kitchen, wondering where Lady might be – then the front door opens.

With her usual swiftness, Lady passes through the utility room and into the kitchen. "And how are you, young lady?" she asks melodically.

Sara clears her throat, "I am better, thank you."

"You know, Babe has been up and about since 4:30!" The arching delight in Lady's voice tells this is unusual. "I'm certain he would love some company out on the patio."

Happy to oblige, Sara nods and follows Lady. Greeted by the glow of the porch light and the mugginess of an August night, Sara gingerly makes her way down the steps. The sight of Sara brings a smile to Babe's face. Cigarette between his fingers, he looks markedly better than last night.

"This is a pleasant surprise!" Babe proclaims. Not sure what to do, the slouched over Sara just stops. "Well, have a seat," he insists, patting the bench.

Taking short steps, Sara eases down onto Lady's usual spot. The swing wobbles.

"Beautiful night, isn't it?" Babe asks, a ribbon is smoke lifting from the end of his cigarette. On the ledge next to his smokes is a tall, unmarked bottle. The clear liquid inside catches a shimmer from both the porch light and the fluorescent bulbs shining atop the splintery telephone pole along the fence.

"The stars are pretty," says Sara with the timbre of one who has never seen them before.

"Did you enjoy your run?"

"Yes, I did." Sara answers, though bummed for the way her run ended.

"Good," Babe nods. "Where did you go?"

"I went East." Sara says thoughtfully. "I ran on dirt roads and um... passed farms, and fields, and... I ran down some railroad tracks they don't use anymore. I crossed over a river, too." This is the most she has ever spoken at once.

Babe notices the difference in Sara's speech. Completely different than before. Almost child-like.

He also notices the change in her appearance. Having gained a few pounds, Sara looks far healthier. Eyes bright and limbs fuller, gaining a pink glow. Cheeks no longer hollow; they seem soon to find balance with her naturally full lips.

"You crossed the river, huh?" Babe's eyebrows raise. "The Mississippi?"

"No," Sara humbly answers, "it was a small river. The bridge was very old." Telling of the serene place summons the feeling she experienced while there.

Stubbing out his cigarette, he shifts Sara's way. "What did you see?"

"I saw houses and fields," she reports. "Lots of cows." Her mind retraces the route. "I saw horses."

"Did your shoes hold up? We saw you burning rubber down the driveway."

"Yes, they were very good," Sara says. "I am very glad that I have them."

- 82 -

"You know, the first thing my Lady said, well-", Babe stops to correct himself, "*after* she said she was going to feed you, was 'I'm gonna get that girl a new pair of tennis shoes'."

Sara looks at Babe. She doesn't know what to say.

"I think she wants to throw the old ones away," he smiles.

"She can if she wants to," she replies. Babe doesn't know what to make of Sara's speech. Soft. Easy. Simple. So innocent.

"Oh now, I don't think she'll do that. You need a pair of shoes in case you decide to run in the mud." Sara brings about a grandfatherly way the old spy never knew he had.

"That sounds like a good idea," Sara passively agrees, eyes drifting to the bottle on the ledge.

Babe glances to his left. "I see my old bottle has caught your eye," he says coyly.

Biting her lip as a tiny cramp passes, the girl with curious eyes shrugs. Babe sees none of the keen awareness that defined his young charge a couple nights ago; or the slightest trace of aggression Lady spoke of last night.

"Have you ever had Vodka before?" he pries.

Sara shakes her head, suppressing a grimace as another pain passes.

Believing vodka the cure for most anything that ails, he offers, "Well, I wouldn't be much of a host if I didn't offer you a taste. Would you like some?"

After a moment of indecision, the curious girl nods her head.

"Excellent!" The swing wobbles and the dangling links jingle when Babe claps his hands. Sara takes a deep breath as John wheels his stiff body. He grabs the bottle along with the stubby glass next to it. "You'll have to forgive my only having one glass."

Feeling her pulse quicken, Sara sweeps her hair behind her ears as Babe hands her the squat glass. Anxious, she holds it between her thumb and forefinger as the man with shaky hands removes the cap from the bottle mostly full.

Babe, if only for a moment, forgets that he is ill. "You know Lady's gonna kick my hind end for this, don't you?" he informs in a hushed tone. Eyes on the tiny glass, Sara just shrugs.

Babe pours steady as he can, wetting Sara's fingers with the overflow.

"Yeah," Babe says with a celebratory tone as he places the bottle back on the ledge, "this is a big night for both of us. It's not every day an old man gets to watch a beautiful Russian woman take her first drink of vodka!"

Hazel eyes lift from the brimming glass. Sara's expression is of disbelief as she considers herself neither Russian, nor beautiful. Her first compliment causes her face to warm and body to shrink away. Blushing, she is careful not to spill her tiny drink.

After a glance between Babe and two deep breaths, she pours the libation into her mouth.

Face puckered; Sara holds it in her mouth before eventually forcing it down.

FIRE!! Sara's shouts in her head. Eyes water as the wind is sucked out of her chest.

She presses her hand to her mouth as clear lava trickles down her throat. Thrown into a coughing fit, the flush-faced girl sends the bench a-wobble and chains dancing above.

Watery eyed with her palm on her chest, the smiling Sara looks over.

"Congratulations! you are no longer a Russian child, but a Russian *woman*, now!" In Babe's glistening eyes, a rite of passage had taken place.

The white-hot flame in Sara's throat fades as the tendrils of warmth roam throughout her core. A cozy feeling, accompanied by the odd sense of pride swells within.

"What are you doing to that poor girl?!" chides Lady from the kitchen window above.

"Nothing, Dear!" he chirps unconvincingly. It's been ages since Babe let himself carry on like this.

"You don't let her have too much of that!" Lady warns, her brogue stern.

"You should grab your bottle of Scotch and come join us!" he spouts, knowing full well it's been decades since the Scotswoman has had anything more than a hot toddy. Sara's guilty look causes Babe to laugh. Babe's laugh causes Sara to laugh. Neither dare look up to the window.

They are like a couple kids! Lady shakes her head. "Are you okay child?"

"Ye-yes, I'm okay," Sara answers, sitting up straight.

Lady—less than thrilled about why the two of them are snickering and carrying on, but so glad they are—mutters something as she closes the window with a thump.

"So, what do you think?" Babe asks, peeking back over his shoulder.

An impish grin is his answer. With moths and other night bugs fluttering overhead, Sara looks around Babe to the bottle on the ledge.

"What?" Babe answers the rascally twinkle in Sara's eyes. "You want more?"

After a quick glance up to make sure Lady isn't watching, the rosy-cheeked girl gives a nod.

"Okay, you can have *one* more," Babe says, pretending to be somewhat responsible. "But under one condition: you have to throw it to the back of your throat." He motions to illustrate. "Just tilt your head back and toss it back. Gotta get it all in one glug. Got it?"

Sara nods, eager for another chance to get it right.

The sway of the swing stops while Babe's less-than-steady hand overflows the tiny glass a second time. Sara, careful not to spill, leans forward as she brings the dripping glass to her lips.

This time is completely different from the last. With the composure of one who has done it countless times, Sara tilts her head, tosses back the shot, and swallows.

No pucker, no cough, no watery eyes – only poise and shiny lips. Content with herself, Sara gives a tiny shrug as she raises a brow. Her body language asks, *Was that better?*

"I'd say you nailed it, kid," beams Babe. "I'd say you nailed it."

Little does Sara realize that Lady's wagging finger is partly the reason she likes it so much. That and the kudos from Babe.

The warmth continues to work its way throughout. Shortly after; a warm fuzziness and a glossy shine to her eyes. Cramps seeming to have retreated, Sara feels pretty good.

Babe reaches into his shirt pocket for another smoke. Hazel eyes follow the pack.

"What?" he asks with playful exasperation. "You want one of these?"

Sara's answer is a glancing check of the window.

"You are gonna get me skinned alive, kid."

Sunday, August 24th, 2014

Having gone to bed feeling wonderful, Sara wakes with a bit of a headache and the taste of ash tray. Brushing her teeth, taking a shower, and eating a pile of French toast make her feel a great deal better. Aside from tightness in her legs, dull cramps and mild hangover, Sara's first Sunday is starting off okay.

Babe is not so good. The best day he's had in a long time is followed by the worst. Venturing only to the bathroom adjoining, he and Lady's bedroom, Babe has not been seen all day.

Hoping her friend wakes soon, Sara passes the day following Lady as she does chores around the house. In between stops to fill her stomach that won't stay full, Sara helps do laundry, cook a roast, make a crust for a blackberry cobbler, tend a neglected garden, dust, vacuum, and do dishes. From 4:30 to 6:30, Sara holds down the fort while Lady goes to the grocery store. Reluctant to leave her Babe unattended, she feels peace of mind enough to step out knowing Sara is there.

Dishes, laundry, taking out the garbage—these tasks seem familiar to Sara, but the mind underneath prevents her from knowing why. At this stage, it would simply be too much.

Lady enjoys having someone to talk to. With no shortage of tales, the multi-tasking lass goes on and on about places she and Babe have lived over the years. While pulling weeds, Sara hears of Seattle; while peeling potatoes, she hears about Phoenix; while ironing shirts, she learns about Tampa.

Even though Sara likes Lady's stories, her mind still tends to wander. Inclined to roam, it does not travel far. The dog Brutus, the turtles on the log, candy bars. The bridge, the swing, gym class. Shiny red apple, her teacher Mr. Stuart, the scowling pirate painted above the exit in the gym. Every now and again, the animated opening to *Grease*.

Like a butterfly, Sara's attention just kind of goes wherever.

9:38 PM
Belly full of roast, potatoes, carrots, blackberry cobbler, two scoops of ice cream, and a handful of *Milk Duds*, Sara falls asleep with the television on.

Monday, August 25th, 2014

8:27 AM, 1st Hour
Mr. Colliet's Advanced Biology class
Before leaving to check on a package that should have arrived two days ago, Mr. Colliet told the class to divide into pairs and read pages 38-43. To Megan, who had to leave before lunch last Friday for an Orthodontist appointment, an event such as this is an answer to her prayers.

Not knowing how long she has; Megan wishes to make the most of the moment. In order to do so, she must talk a little faster than usual.

"And I heard Jake Nunley and Noah Andrews were in this super huge fight, and well, they *almost* got into a super huge fight, and it just like, totally happened out of nowhere, and nobody even knows what started it, but you don't have to be a *genius* to know that Jake used to go out with, well wait... First, I should let you know that Jake and Noah used to be really good friends, but then Jake went out with Candice Pitter – she's a senior – well, she was a junior when this happened, but she is a senior now because this was like a year ago..."

Unaware Sara was present during the incident in question, Megan's pace does not allow an opening to inform her. Content just to listen, Sara soon decides she likes Megan's version better anyway. With the hum of light conversation all around, Sara's new bestie rattles on. Megan cannot help but notice Sara's healthy new pounds; same as Sara cannot help but notice Megan periodically glancing down her front. Curious, Sara checks to see if she maybe has a stain on her shirt.

"...and Mrs. Callahan, who everyone knows is a total lesbian, was trying to break it up, but they weren't listening to her so she totally decided that she would just let it happen, or call security or something, because there was like a bunch of people holding them back, because all the guys know that they are friends because the thing with Candice happened like two years ago, so it's been forever, but you know how guys are with testosterone and having to be tough all the time, so anyway, I heard that they were getting ready to start throwing punches..."

I thought you said guys were holding them back? Sara wonders.

"...but right at the last second, Clint Fleischer, who is probably totally the most sweetest guy in the entire world, stepped in and pushed them a part..."

Clint... His name was Clint. Sara pictures his face.

10:03 AM, 3rd Hour
Mr. Godfrey's Trigonometry class
With no need for concentration on a subject she can almost do in her sleep, the girl who has gained eight pounds since arrival, thinks about whatever pops into her head. While appearing to pay attention, Sara envisions blackberry cobbler, Babe's smile, Lady's gardening gloves, a brown cow standing beside her calf in a pasture, a green tractor pulling a plow, a half dozen carp swimming just below the river's surface, a broad face, a narrow gap between gleaming teeth, and blue eyes.

Fitting a bit differently in her desk; the girl waltzing through her own personal La La Land is approached by a teacher.

"Sara," Mr. Godfrey says quietly after instructing the class to solve the odd questions, five through nine, on page 47. "Can you do question five for me?" Leaning over, he watches Sara go about the equation with ease.

"Hmm," sounds the brawny teacher with a nod. Convinced his new student can afford a few minutes away from class, he waves, "Come with me."

Wondering if she is somehow in trouble, Sara follows him toward the door. Once in the hallway, the teacher—keeping his voice low so as not to disrupt the class across the hall—takes a folded piece of paper from the breast pocket of his navy-blue button-up.

"I need you to do a favor for me, if you could."

"Sure," Sara says, relieved she isn't in trouble.

"My brother—the Mr. Godfrey who teaches weight training—doesn't answer his desk phone and can't hear the PA system because he cranks the stereo too loud," the blonde-haired teacher explains. "Could you run this down to him? I hate to ask you, but I really need him to get this pretty quick."

"Um... yeah, okay," Sara accepts the task.

Happy to help, she is soon walking past classrooms and dark blue lockers. The hallway is wide open and eerily quiet. Now at a 114 pounds, Sara has fuller thighs and more bounce in her step. Down the corridor, she continues the same route she would to seventh hour gym class.

The music her math teacher mentioned is muffled by double metal doors. Pushing one open, Bush's "Glycerine" hits Sara like a gust of wind. The sight of twenty-five girls using exercise machines and free weights stops her in her tracks. Feeling the bass through her new shoes, the girl stuck in place looks on in awe.

Like a child watching fireworks, Sara is entranced by the place of steel plates, shiny bars, cables, clamps, grunts and clanging.

She likes the music, too.

Attention funneled to the group of girls taking turns on the lat pull-down machine, the messenger does not notice the approach of the crew-cut sporting instructor.

Built as powerfully as his brother—while being a bit taller—the Godfrey with darker features can easily guess the purpose of his visitor with the folded piece of paper in her hand. The coach with a dimple in his chin deep enough to stick a finger in, yells, "Can I help you?!" over the blaring music.

Sara extends the note.

"Mr. Godfrey told me to give this to you," she says, not loud enough to be heard over the music.

Sara's attention veers away as the note is read. Captivated, she doesn't hear whatever Coach Mike said next. Realizing she just missed something, her focus snaps back.

"I said you look like a mouse in a room full of cheese!" repeats the older brother with a big smile.

Though Sara doesn't know what to make of what he said, there is no doubt it was friendly. Unsure as how to respond, the messenger just shrugs.

The stopwatch in his hand beeps, Coach Mike blows his whistle and thunders, "Switch!!"

Like soldiers, every group in the class moves to the station to their right. Sara recognizes two of the girls moving from the pull-down machine to the seated tricep machine. Devon Hailey and Michelle Decker. Members of the infamously popular group Sara has heard so much about each.

"I don't believe I have seen you around here before," Coach Mike says upon turning back. "Did you just move here?"

"Yes, I am new to here." Coach Mike has to read Sara's lips.

"You must be pretty smart if you're in one of my brother's classes," he compliments.

"Yes, I like math," Sara answers, attention divided. While one person in the group lifts, the other two wait their turn. She notices some of the girls looking back at her.

"You ever done weight training?" Coach Mike asks over Cake's "The Distance".

"No."

"Do you play any sports?"

Sara shakes her head. Though the towering man is athletic and strong from lifting weights each day, she never considers him a threat. She does not think that way.

"Well, I got to get back to class here, but feel free to take my class in the future," he invites. "But if you do, be ready to work hard!" The ring in his voice intones both a warning and a challenge.

Getting a good look before leaving, Sara turns back the way she came. *That looked like so much fun!*

11:28 AM
Lunchtime

Setting down her tray made heavy by a cheeseburger, French fries, a personal pizza, two egg rolls, and 20-ounce sports drink, Sara takes Angela's freshly vacant seat. It is only Megan, Lexi, and Karen today.

"Heeey," says Megan, eyeing Sara's tray. "Looks like you're hungry!"

Karen greets with a soft "Hello", Lexi, a little wave.

"Yes, I am very hungry," Sara answers simply.

"So, what's new with you?" Megan begins, noticing Shelly Thompson staring from across the way.

Unaware of anyone looking at her, Sara takes a bite to avoid having to answer. With nothing to say, she gives half a shrug, continuing to chew.

Lexi, the petite sophomore with straight hair made curly, asks, "Are you starting to get used to things here?"

Through a mouthful of pizza, Sara answers, "It's nice here." She thinks more about Babe and Lady's home than school.

"Me and Sara were partners today in Advanced Biology class," Megan blurts, "and *she* told *me* that she was there when Noah and Jake..."

As Megan gives details, Sara sees the boy with dark hair pushed behind his ear. She remembers how he calmly walked back to third base after defusing the situation. Off in her own little world, Sara stares at the snapshot her mind took of him standing with his hand on his hip.

"...didn't they?" Megan asks.

"I'm sorry, what?" Sara returns to the moment.

"Everybody got between them right before they started throwing punches," Megan repeats with hand motions.

"Uh..." Sara stammers. *Is she telling the same story?*

"Noah and Jake were yelling at each other and right before they started throwing punches, the other guys were pulling them apart so they wouldn't bash each other's faces in." Sara can sense Megan's neediness for corroboration. The girl with a mouth full of cheeseburger goes along with a nod.

Lexi's big brown eyes hint to something behind Sara. Sara turns to find Shelly looking her way.

Arms folded and mouth pulled to the side, the mean girl with one brow raised locks eyes with Sara as Tiffany whispers something into her ear.

Instantly freaked out, Sara turns slowly back around. Facing Megan once more, she remembers all the scary stories about Shelly beating people up.

Sara's discomfort proves contagious. Even Megan is quiet. Their side of the table facing 'The Bitches' table, Megan and Lexi can see what Sara cannot. They can tell their new friend is the topic of conversation.

Megan and Lexi look at each other, and then back at Sara. Suffering a tightness in her chest, she sits frozen, as though doing so might cause the little bully to forget she is there.

The tension ratchets like a rollercoaster, climbing its initial arch. Click, click, click, click.

Made all the more anxious by the moment, Megan feels compelled to break the silence. "Um," she scrambles for something to say, "me and Lexi and Karen were just saying how we've noticed that you've gained weight since you got here."

Lexi's eyes, already big as they are brown, grow wide as saucers. Her mouth fallen open; she turns to a Karen equally awed.

Megan has succeeded in making everyone forget about anything going on behind Sara.

After a few seconds, something like an underwater mine detonates in Megan's head. *Oh. My. God. What did I just say?* Megan looks at Lexi and Karen. Lexi and Karen look at each other. Then, all three look to Sara.

Time slows to a crawl.

Sara gasps; though not knowing why Megan's words penetrate the way they do. So deeply ingrained is her aversion to gaining weight.

Lexi and Karen look back at one another, then to Megan again. Each second an eternity, all three look to Sara once more. Emblazoned across Sara's face, a blend of shock and disbelief. The mind keeping reality at bay has also managed obliviousness to the effects of eating around the clock.

Lexi and Karen slowly lean farther and farther back so as to distance themselves from the social equivalent of an oil spill. In a tailspin, Megan scrambles.

"I was... well-" she sputters, "*we* were, um, noticing that... well, not in a bad way or anything, because it's totally not, but... anyway, we were-"

Their heads shaking, the expression on Lexi and Karen's faces say, *We want nothing to do with this conversation.*

"Like, and I can't stress this enough, this is not in a bad way... but we have kinda noticed that it looks like you might be gaining a little weight, you know, in a good way." Upper lip sweating, Megan continues to dig. "Because when you got here you were skinny. Too skinny. Like the kind of skinny guys don't even find attractive. I mean-" *God, please kill me now!* "I wish I was as skinny as you, but you are much prettier now!" Panicked, the pleading Megan would gladly give her right arm to go five minutes back in time.

Sara just looks at Megan, trying to process her sputtering words.

It's like watching someone drown, Lexi thinks to herself. She puts a French fry in her mouth the way one eats popcorn while watching a horror film.

"What I mean is," Megan tries again, "that we thought you stopped being bulimic, and *that's* the reason you gained weight!" *I hate you mouth! Why do you say such stupid things?!* thinks the girl with a pulse of 132.

"Yeah, that's way better," Lexi smothers a smirk.

"Help me out here, girls!" begs the spiraling, Megan.

"I think you're doing, fine," says Karen, eyes welling. *Do not laugh Karen. This is too terrible to be funny! Don't laugh!*

Blissfully unaware as to why she was not allowed to gain weight, the uneasy Sara just sits, watching her freefalling friend continue trying to make things better. Despite the full-length mirror in her bedroom, Sara has failed to notice the gain. Powerful is the mind underneath.

"When you got here you were so skinny you looked awful. I mean awfully thin, like you were sick or something, and…" Megan almost swallows her tongue when Sara stands up, abandons her food, and heads for the exit. Shelly, watching with a smile, assumes Sara's sudden retreat has something to do with her.

Lexi and Karen watch the repentant Megan follow Sara.

"Megan should speak at funerals," comments Lexi.

"No," Karen says thoughtfully, "I am thinking she should be a motivational speaker."

"What are those people who talk people out of jumping off buildings?" Lexi asks.

"You mean hostage negotiators?"

"No, they aren't called that," responds Lexi, deep in thought, "but I think she'd be good at that job, too."

Oh my God, oh my God, oh my God! Willing to give both arms—and maybe a foot—to make the last five minutes not happen, Megan hurries to keep pace down the mostly empty hall. Fearing Sara is going to cry or hate her, it is Megan's mission to avoid both.

Chin down and arms straight, Sara continues her b-line for the scales in the locker room.

"I'm sorry, I didn't mean it in a bad way, actually, it's a good thing," pours Megan with all her being. "I mean all of it is in your boobs and your butt, and I *wish* I had that problem. Wait, not that that's a problem... Oh my God!"

Deaf to Megan's blabbering, Sara wants to size up the damage. As though speed-walking on a level conveyer belt at an airport, Sara zips past the band room with a hyperventilating Megan a half-step behind.

"It's not like I was talking about you until right before you sat down, because that's not something I would do, you know? What we were actually doing was talking about, uh... *not* you!" Mouth dry as her armpits are wet, Megan asks, "Are you gonna be okay? I'm sorry. I'm so sorry... Please don't be mad at me!"

"I'm not mad at you," Sara speaks for the first time. "I am glad you told me." Though alarmed, Sara truly isn't angry with Megan.

Thank you for telling me?! Oh my God! She is super furious!! "Are you gonna be okay?" Megan fearfully asks.

"Yes, I am fine."

Fine? Fine?! 'Fine' is the worst way any female can ever be! Sara definitely hates me now!! Wishing she had a bridge to jump off of, Megan follows Sara into the empty locker room and around the corner to the digital scales just outside the showers.

Sara looks down. 000.

"It's not working," she says to herself.

"You have to, um, get off and then let it say zero, and then get back on." Megan says with the calmness of one standing near a bomb.

Sara does as advised. A few seconds later it reads 114.

"Ah, shit. I've gained eight pounds." Sara's first curse word tumbles out.

"You weigh 114? That's nothing. That's like half of what half the girls in this school weigh!" Megan exaggerates. "And before you were like..." she pauses when Sara steps off the scale and walks away. Assuming she is leaving, Megan rushes to follow.

"Like I was saying, you were too skinny before and eight pounds in a week isn't really all that mu-" Megan collides into Sara after an unexpected stop in front of the mirror above the sink.

Viewing from the waist up, the girl who has avoided mirrors looks at herself for what feels like the first time. She recognizes the person looking back – but doesn't.

"See," Megan points at the mirror. "You're pretty."

Brain lagging, Sara raises her right hand so as to make certain she is not the shorter girl with brown hair and glasses standing beside her. A troubled mind struggles to reconcile. "See, you're pretty." Sara's lingering mind finally hears.

Uncharacteristically quiet, Megan is puzzled by the perplexity on Sara's face. *This is so weird.*

Sara wiggles her fingers as she steps closer.

"You look great," Megan says in a small voice.

Thrift store jeans fitting tighter, sports bra digging in, dark blue t-shirt verging on snug. *How have I not noticed this until now?* Sara twists at the waist. The soft bulbs overhead cast a flattering luminance over burgeoning curves. Sara's lithe body has begun taking shape right under her very nose.

Sara steps forward, face inches from the mirror.

Pushing her hair away unveils skin turned flawless from nourishment and discontinuance of the white pills.

Cheeks approaching the fullness of her lips.

A sweeping jawline.

Bright eyes.

That cannot be. Is that me? Who is that? Sara touches her cheek.

Okay, thinks Megan, a little weirded out. *This is starting to get kinda creepy.* Sara reaches back and squeezes her behind. *Sara just squeezed her own butt!* Megan can hardly believe. *Um, yup! Definitely getting creepy!*

After a while of weirdness, Sara turns to her speechless friend and points to the mirror, "That's me."

3:30 PM
The patio
Having requested Babe, Sara now sits on the swing waiting. Able to tell something is amiss, Lady offered to help, but her help was declined. Sara wants to talk to Babe.

Swaying to and fro, she waits.

3:41 PM
Babe, roused and in route, can be heard making his way through the front door. A suction sound is made every time it opens. Tattered robe over his flannel pajamas, the man with freshly combed hair lets out a long yawn as he eases down the porch steps and around to his spot on the swing. Still waking up, he braces with both hands as he lowers down onto the weather-worn bench.

"What's up, kid?" he asks warmly.

"I've gained eight pounds," confesses Sara.

Babe waits for the rest, but that is all. "Okay. So, what did you want to tell me?"

"I've gained eight pounds," she repeats, chin down, eyes lifted.

"I believe you," Babe concedes, scratching under his chin. "I'm sure if you put your mind to it, you'll gain eight more." He chuckles.

"No," Sara says, missing his humor. "I am telling you, so you know."

"Okay." Babe tries not to laugh. "What would you like me to do?"

"I can't gain weight!!" Sara blurts.

- 99 -

"Why not?" Babe shrugs.

"Because I can't!"

"Who said?"

Babe's question stops Sara in her tracks...blank stare.

A moment passes.

"Are you afraid you will become too beautiful?" Babe asks the confounded girl.

Sara holds still as a photograph, looking at Babe as though he just fell out of a spaceship.

"Are you afraid they will suspect you're a spy because you look healthy?"

Sara doesn't understand the question.

Working to remove his robe on account of the heat, Babe notices Sara's look of bewilderment. This concerns the weary handler.

"People are looking at me!" Sara whines, having completely dismissed the spy question.

Babe bursts into laughter, then coughs. *Of course they are!* Thinks the man doubled over as he barks. *COUGH! COUGH! COUGH!* *You're getting prettier by the minute!* *COUGH! COUGH! COUGH!*

Wishing she could help, Sara can only sit by on the wobbling swing, waiting for the red-faced, teary-eyed man to recover.

Babe wipes his eyes and clears his throat. "Sorry about that," he needlessly apologizes, removing the pack of smokes from his shirt pocket. "Let me ask you this... Are you afraid this new eight pounds will interfere with your assignment?" He lights his cigarette.

"My assignments are easy. I have taken all these classes before," Sara responds innocently and without hesitation.

If Babe wasn't awake already, he would be now. *Oh shit!* His concern converts to fear. *She thinks I am talking about an assignment for school! I don't think she knows she's a spy!* A cool customer, Babe's fissured face does not betray his alarm. "Are you feeling okay?"

"My legs are a little sore, but yeah, I'm okay." Once again, Babe realizes he and his young ward are having two different conversations.

She doesn't know she is a spy. Babe brings a cigarette to his mouth. *What in the hell was in those damn pills?!*

Sara's eyes tell Babe she wants a cigarette, too.

"Oh, here you go," groans the guy who still feels bad about giving her one yesterday. *You got bigger problems than smoking, kid.*

Sara leans in for a light.

Made ten glamorous years older by the way she holds a cigarette, Sara blows smoke through barely parted lips like a starlet of the silver screen. *This tastes awful! But I like it anyway.* Distracted with impish delight, Sara's only worry now is Lady appearing in the window above.

Babe can only shake his head at Sara's innocent sophistication.

Cars zoom along the bottom of the hill. Sara enjoys her cigarette. Babe racks his brain as how to handle a spy who seems to have forgotten she's a spy.

Unsettled, and uncertain as to how long his energy will hold out, Babe circles back to the original topic of conversation.

"Well, so far as food goes, we told you when you got here you could eat whenever you wanted, and I don't see that changing anytime soon."

Wrist elegantly bent, the smoke from Sara's cigarette lifts lazily away. "Yeah, but you didn't say I would gain weight."

"Yeah," Babe huffs, trying not to smile. "I probably should've warned you that if you ate pizza and ice cream all day, every day, that you just might put on a couple pounds."

Sara nods before taking another drag.

"And who cares about your weight anyway?" Babe swats at the air. "Do you like the way you look?"

Though unable to envision her own reflection, Sara nods. She does like when people say nice things about how she looks.

"And do you like the way you feel?"

Sara is quick to nod.

"And you *do* enjoy eating, don't you?"

"Uh, huh." *I like pizza best.*

"Well, okay then." Babe states, hoping to have put the issue to rest. "If you are healthy and you are happy with the way you look, then I don't know what else to tell ya."

"People look at me though," Sara sullenly says, despite accepting Babe's logic.

"That doesn't surprise me," Babe scoffs. "I'd only be surprised if they didn't."

"But I don't want them to," mumbles the one deeply ingrained with the doctrine of invisibility.

"Hate to be the bearer of bad news kid, but you're pretty. Being looked at is just part of the deal," Babe regretfully notifies. "Comes with being ugly too."

"Some of the girls don't look at me in a nice way," Sara confides, her smile falling away. She sees Shelly's hateful green eyes peering at her. "Some girls are-" Sara trails off. "Why are some girls mean to other girls?"

"Uh..." Babe hesitates, shaking his head. "Sara, I am sixty-three years old, and..." *I am so not qualified for this.*

Sara patiently awaits the rest of his cautious answer.

"The more I learn about women, the less I know. And for that reason, I am the last guy in the world you should ask about why women do *any* of the things they do. Ever. At all." *Questions about brain surgery would be easier than this.*

Babe's humble humor and the look on his face make her smile.

Cars continue to pass along the bottom of the hill. A warm gust of wind pushes. The shade of the cloud moves away. Babe takes the cigarette butt from Sara's fingers and snubs it out for her.

"Tell me about school today."

Sara tells about the girls' weightlifting class she walked into, but doesn't tell him about how Shelly Thompson threw nasty looks her way all through gym class again. She tells about her classes, but not how she felt when she saw Clint in the hall on the way to Home Ec. She tells how Megan, Lexi, and Karen talked to her, but not how it bothers her that they were talking about her when she wasn't around.

"Sounds to me like you need to be taking weightlifting class," Babe says matter of factly.

"But I am in Trigonometry class at that time," she points out, as though there's nothing to be done.

"You can change classes, can't you? You said some of the other children were changing classes, right?"

"Well..." Sara stops to consider. "I guess so."

"Why don't you, then?" Babe urges.

The girl biting her lip smiles. "You think I should?"

"Absolutely. You *absolutely* should," Babe encourages, hands slapping his lap.

"Okay!" Sara effervesces. Breathed back to life and lit like Christmas morning, her worry is no more.

11:29 PM
Full of lasagna, wheat rolls, strawberry short cake and vanilla ice cream, Sara sleeps.

As if the idea of changing to weightlifting class wasn't enough to make her night, Sara walked into her room to find no less than nine bags from The Buckle and three shoe boxes on her bed. Lady had made a few phone calls, and with the help of the fashionista manager and a credit card, made arrangements for delivery.

Bags filled with Rock Revivals, Silvers, and Miss Me Jeans. Four bags of t-shirts, and what the manager called 'the cutest tops ever'. A couple hoodies, socks, and various undergarments.

Not only a surprise to Sara, it was a shock to Babe as well.

A lifetime of Christmases at once, the girl who couldn't stop smiling tried on every article of clothing in every combination with each pair of shoes as the luminant Lady looked on.

At least a dozen times, Lady reminded, "Now if something doesn't fit, we can take it back for a different size." When changing outfits, Sara stood in front of the full-length mirrors. Blind to her scars, the mind underneath shielded same as it did when she changed for gym class. Without knowing why, Sara discreetly changed in the bathroom stall.

Unfortunately, Lady has no such blinder. Fighting tears, she could plainly read the painful history written on Sara's skin.

Anxious to show off her new outfits, Sara raced after each change to Babe's recliner. Her beaming face proved more benefit to Babe's health than any medicine.

Now, with every article of clothing either neatly folded or hanging, Sara's body rests – the mind she shares does not.

While the body lies under a purple comforter, the mind is in a place long ago. The projector inside the unprotected psyche casts a grainy visage from the last light before the pills began.

Three weeks before leaving St. Petersburg for The Institute – four weeks before the pill regimen was supposed to begin – Natasha 712 awakens in the musky darkness of the dormitory shared by the fifteen remaining Natashas.

From under the sour-smelling blanket on her top bunk, Natasha 712 watches 708 soundlessly make her way from her bottom bunk to the latrine. Eight, the runt of the class, wears a full-length cotton gown, same as the others. Reserved and withdrawn; she has received a great deal of correction.

Sara twists and turns in her bed as the curtains billow above. Amidst her state of rest, she relives both her desire to help and guilt of not being able to do so.

Soon after the restroom door closes behind Eight, Sara hears a short yelp. Silent as a shadow, she can feel herself climb down to investigate. The metal frame cool on her hand, hard tile hard under foot, the pangs of hunger in her core.

Sleeping on her side – pillow between her knees – Sara can see the bathroom door as she nears. Ten-years-old once again, the one dragged back to the past knows what is on the other side of the door, she wants to stop. She doesn't want to go inside. But she has no choice. Carried by yesterday, the memory plays through.

She can feel the coolness of the heavy door on her palms. The thick smell of blood fills her nose. Sara looks upon Eight's horrified face once more.

Six opened her wrists in the night.

Moonlight through a high window shimmering in the crimson; the pool spreading slowly toward Eight's toes. Hand cupped over mouth, thin body recoiling, Eight is unable to take her welling eyes off the girl, slumped against the toilet.

Natasha 706; gazing down and away, hips scooched out, razor still in hand. Peacefulness.

Tuesday, August 26th, 2014

8:08 AM
Hallway

A bit sluggish from the eight pieces of French toast with peanut butter, four pieces of bacon, and banana, Sara makes her way down the buzzing hall. Feeling as though she might burst – and distracted by maple syrup burps – she doesn't notice the attention her now 116-pound body and designer clothes attract. Natashas are hyper-vigilant. Sara, not so much. Especially when her mind is occupied.

Should've put the rest of that bacon in a baggie. If I had, I could eat it later. I am so full. If I had bacon in a baggie, I would probably eat it now. I really like bacon a lot.

Unaware of the flattering effects of perfect-fitting jeans, Sara thinks only of how good the clothes feel on her skin and how pretty they looked in the mirror. Head in the clouds, the one drawing stares from girls and boys alike continues toward her locker.

Two burps later, Sara finds Megan waiting.

Megan looks like someone who may, or may not have, been up all night imagining the worst possible scenarios about how mad Sara might be. With two-and-a-half hours of sleep, three cups of coffee, and some black and

yellow pills found near the register of a gas station, Megan –
even more Megan'd up than usual – takes complimenting to
a whole new level.

"Oh my God!" she gushes. *Please don't hate me!*
"Where did you get that outfit?!" *Holy hell, she looks like a
model!* "You look amazing!" *Please give me one more
chance!*

Taken aback by Megan's outpouring, Sara stammers,
"Um, my grandmother bought them for me."

Having defaulted to the Natasha's cover, the girl
opening her locker assumes Lady to be her grandmother.
Sara simply hasn't thought about it.

*Don't say anything stupid! Don't say anything stupid!
Don't say anything stupid! Don't say anything stupid.* "Are
those jeans Diesel? They really make your butt stick out!"
Dammit! Mouth, I told you not to say anything stupid!!

"She, um..." Sara takes a quick glance back and
down. "The bags said Buckle on them but some of the
clothes came from other-"

"The Buckle?!" Megan can't help herself from
blurting, "I love the Buckle! I used to go to the Buckle every
Saturday with my-" *Shut up! Shut up Megan, shut up!* Megan
clasps her hand over her mouth.

Sara stares at Megan standing with her eyes wide
and hand cupped across her face. At the same time, both
turn to notice those looking their way.

Sara thinks the silence and stares are because of
Megan's spazzing. Designer jeans that seem custom-fitted,
along with a t-shirt made of velvet-like material, announce
Sara's recent development as though said over the PA
system. The girl wearing no makeup looks around, causing
eyes to avert and the volume to return to normal.

"Some people," Megan rolls her eyes, "just can't
mind their own business."

Wishing to be anywhere else, Sara grabs her Biology
book and turns for first hour. Knowing the destination,
Megan hurries in the lead.

Noticing more people are looking her way, Sara hides behind her textbook. The girl wearing a reddish-brown t-shirt with a black design on the front remains hot on Megan's heels –until a pair of blue eyes meet her own.

Chattering away, Megan takes ten steps before realizing Sara is no longer behind her.

Frozen in the moment, Sara stares at the guy staring back.

9:21 AM, 2nd Hour

Excused from Mr. Schibi's class, Sara is in the secretary's office, waiting to be seen by a counselor growing rather tired of trying to accommodate every clique, crush, breakup, makeup, and student who selected classes proving too difficult. Third in line, Sara doubts she will return to Mr. Schibi's class anytime soon.

Instead of looking at the boy with purple hair and a pierced lip, Sara pretends interest in the anti-smoking ad on the wall. Her mind isn't on smoking. Instead, Sara's thinking about what Megan said since interrupting her long look at Clint. After that, Megan new just what button to push.

"Clint Fleischer is the sweetest guy in the world," Sara's memory replays. "His family owns a farm outside of town like fifteen or thirty minutes away and his older brother Russ – he was a senior like two years ago, and I know Russ. Well, me not so much, but my brother Jeremy graduated last year, so he was a junior when Russ was a senior, but anyway, they were friends and they used to hang out sometimes and one time I was with my brother because my parents had to leave a basketball game early, and they couldn't find me because I was hanging out with some juniors when I was a freshman, because like I said, it was two years ago, and anyway, it was Jeremy's job to give me a ride home, and he was hanging out with Russ and Russ was hanging out with Clint because Clint is—you know—is his brother. So anyway, they were all going to some place, like to a party or something, and Jeremy was being a total jerk because Jeremy is just kind of a jerk all the time, so he was trying to get me to get a ride with someone else, but the juniors that I was hanging out with had already left and all the other people I knew didn't have a license yet. I mean, if I'd known about needing a ride before, I could have totally gotten a ride from the juniors I was hanging out with, but they were already gone by the time I even knew I needed a ride. So anyway, Clint was a sophomore and he talked my brother into not being such a jerk and letting me ride with them because, like I said, Clint is the nicest guy ever, so anyway, I rode with Jeremy, and Russ, and Clint, and I was in the backseat with Clint – but nothing happened because Clint only goes with girls from other schools, and because he hates drama even more than I do, and by the way, he works a lot on his dad's farm so he doesn't play sports, but he used to, but not anymore, but, oh my goodness, this one time..."

The Megan track continues to the backdrop of phones ringing and a copier spitting out copies. Sara sees his face. Unlike gym class, neither looked away.

The waiting area is a little cool. Sara folds her arms, causing newly acquired cleavage to rise. Not only is her blossoming bust no longer restrained by a sports bra, but is accentuated by the somewhat padded brassiere picked out by the manager who selected it upon Lady's request.

The boy with purple hair keeps looking out the office window beyond Sara's bust line.

10:05 AM, between 2nd and 3rd Hour

"You know," the math teaching Mr. Godfrey begins, his pen at the ready, "if I'd known my brother was gonna steal you from me, I'd have sent someone else to deliver the note." Though Sara has yet to get the hang of sarcasm, the teacher's smile tells her he isn't actually angry at her for switching out of his class. Even so, she still feels bad.

"There is only one girls' weightlifting class," Sara explains, as he hands her back the slip he needed to sign to seal the deal.

"That's okay," Mr. Godfrey says with his usual energy. "You just be sure to tell him that tonight, we are *all* running sprints after practice. Players *and* coaches!"

"Okay, I will tell him," promises Sara, despite the message making no sense to her.

"Now, I'm supposed to keep you in here one more day, but I think that would be a little silly, don't you?" Mr. Godfrey says as students pass by.

Not knowing what to say, Sara just shrugs.

With a signed piece of paper in her hand – and a genuine wish for good luck from Coach Ray – Sara is soon headed toward her new third hour class.

10:07 AM
The bell sounds.

10:09 AM, 3rd Hour
Coach Godfrey's Weight Training class
Sara enters through the heavy metal doors into the quiet weight room. Folded piece of paper in her hand, she approaches the teacher waiting for his class to get changed into proper weight training attire.

He assumes she is delivering another message from his brother. "You should start your own courier service!" Spouts the John Wayne of a man as Sara nears.

Sara hands him the slip.

After a quick glance, he grins. "You want to pump some iron, huh?"

"Um, yeah," answers Sara, feeling small as a mouse. "I was told we are all running sprints after practice."

Puzzled at first, Coach Mike soon makes sense of his brother's playful retaliation. "Oh, he doesn't like me stealing his best students, huh?"

Sara shrugs. Right then, a few girls emerge from the locker room. The sight of students trickling in prods the coach with a pencil behind his ear into action.

"Tell you what," he energetically directs, "you go on in and get changed and get back here as quick as you can

- 110 -

cause we have *a lot* to get done and *not* a lot of time to do it. We move pretty fast around here. Sound good to you?"

"Yes," says Sara with nervous energy.

"You're in Mrs. Callahan's class so you have gym clothes, right?"

Sara nods.

"All right then," he says with an enthusiasm that must run in the family, "hurry back!"

10:13 AM

Sara returns to blaring music and a class in full swing. *What in the world have I gotten myself into?*

The man who prefers 'Coach' or 'Coach Mike'—anything besides Mr. Godfrey—slices the air with his whistle. "Switch!"

As though a drill sergeant had barked out, each group hurries to the next station.

"I want you to join their group!" Coach shouts over the music, his finger pointing toward the leg extension machine.

Sara sucks a sharp breath. *That's Devon and Michelle!*

Wearing the t-shirt growing more snug by the day and her baggy shorts, Sara walks past Coach Mike's cluttered desk and on to the group of two that was a group of three yesterday.

Devon, with her raven hair pulled back into a ponytail, powers through her set as the less-than-intense Michelle stands by. Chin buried in her chest as her muscular legs cause the weight to rise and fall, Devon does not notice Sara's approach until seeing her black and pink shoes near the machine. Big, black eyes framed by perfectly plucked brows rise.

"Hey new girl!" grunts Devon, face twisted from strain. Right then, the whistle blows.

"Switch!"

Devon slides her lower half out of the padded machine, quickly stepping away. Michelle unenthusiastically takes her place.

A curvy blonde with dark roots slowly reaches down to move the pin, effectively cutting the weight in half. From her seated position, she watches Devon. The follower is reluctant to do or say anything until seeing what Devon does first.

"So, yeah. Hi. I'm Devon!" Welcomes the dance team captain with dimples and 'little devil' charm. Sara is struck by her friendliness.

"I'm Sara," she replies, voice drowned by the loud music. Michelle looks on, lazily riding out the clock.

"I've seen you around," says the girl with French Indian features. "Nice to finally meet you. I've been meaning to introduce myself and say hello, but you know..." Devon tilts her head and shrugs.

"Yeah," Sara says meekly, "nice to meet you, too." Not noticing Devon's name on the wall, along with all whom hold weightlifting records, Sara is taken with her graciousness and maturity. Devon strikes her as someone several years older.

"This is Michelle," Devon introduces, shifting her feet and pointing at the curvy blonde.

"Hi," Michelle gives a half-wave. She rests while Coach Mike looks away.

"Nice to meet you, too." Sara mutters. Devon and Michelle have to watch Sara's mouth to make out what she says.

"So, have you lifted weights before?!" Devon shouts over 'The Red' by Chevelle.

Sara shakes her head.

Michelle does a couple reps when Coach Mike turns her direction.

"Well, it's pretty simp-" Devon begins before the whistle blows.

"Switch!" Coach Mike thunders.

"Okay, time to go!" Devon chirps as Michelle slides out of the way. Soon situated in the machine, Sara does one rep. The weight jerks up and bounces.

"Here, wait!" Devon halts. Michelle looks on as Devon moves the pin down several holes to increase the weight. "Okay, *now* go!"

After a couple more reps, Devon moves the pin again. Then once again.

The weight moving smoothly up and down, Sara soon has the hang of things. Devon looks at Michelle with growing astonishment as the girl who claims to have never lifted weights easily does the same amount Devon struggled with.

"Uh... that's pretty good," Devon says under her breath.

Sara continues without sign of fatigue.

WHISTLE!!

"Switch!"

Devon slides into the seat for another set.

Thighs burning. Muscles pumped and flush. Sara likes the way this feels.

"You're pretty strong!" Devon yells over Limp Bizkit as she goes about her set.

"Okay!" yells Sara, still yet to get the hang of compliments.

"Do you play any sports?!"

Sara shakes her head.

Nearing the end of her set, Devon points at a big, sliding contraption along the far wall. "After this, we'll go over to the leg press!"

Sara looks across the room where a girl is currently pushing its weighted rack up and down with her feet.

WHISTLE!

"Rotate!" yells the coach.

Every group rotates to the next station. Keeping an eye on Sara, Coach Mike knows Devon will help her.

Going out of turn so she can show Sara how it's done, the girl with a widow's peak places her feet up against the textured plate.

"Go!!"

Sara and Michelle stand by as Devon does a set; palms pressing the top of her thighs to keep her shorts from falling down. The weight at the end of the rubber-coated cable goes up and down as blaring music drowns the awkward silence that might otherwise be.

WHISTLE!!

"Switch!"

Devon slides out of the machine and stands next to Sara. After taking her time to get situated, Michelle moves the pin way up to lessen the weight, then begins her set.

"Are you sure you never lifted before?!" shouts the panting Devon.

"No," Sara answers, anxious for her turn. Watching Michelle, she doesn't realize how many people are watching her.

WHISTLE!!

"Switch!"

Sara slides down into the machine as Devon adjusts the weight. She has to adjust the weight two more times before adequate resistance is found. Coach Mike rounds the bench press for a better look at what appears to be over half of the stack sliding up and down.

Distracted by surprise, his stopwatch rolls right on past the one-minute mark. "Ah, shoot!"

WHISTLE!!

"Switch!"

Caught up in the moment, Sara does two more reps before stopping. The flabbergasted Devon helps her out of the machine. More surprised than anyone, Sara blushes, smiling ear to ear.

This isn't gonna be good, thinks Michelle, standing with arms crossed. The one so fearful of a faux pas knows this will not sit well with Shelly.

10:59 AM, between 3rd and 4th Hour

Having over done it, Sara makes her way to English class very carefully. Legs like jelly, Sara knows she'll go down if either leg bends too much.

"Better take it easy if you want to walk later," Devon's words of caution echo in Sara's head. Legs all but locked straight, she walks somewhat like a toddler.

Her grace absent for a time, Sara keeps close to the wall so as not to slow traffic – and for support.

11:22 AM

Mrs. White excuses her fourth hour class for lunch.

Devon's advice proving wiser with each step, Sara has to use her hands to push up out of her desk. Stepping gently, she trails the rush out the door. *My legs are* so *stiff!*

Upon nearing the cafeteria, Sara decides to save a few steps by cutting through, rather than circling the hall to the entrance nearing the end of the a la carte line.

11:24 AM

Sara enters the dining area on unsteady legs. *Don't fall. Don't fall. Don't fall. Don't fall. Don't fall,* worries the girl no longer with a wall for support. Though the daydreamer can be less-than-perceptive at times, it would be impossible not to notice the heads turning her way. Feeling more eyes upon her with each step, Sara very much regrets not taking the long way around. Fearing her wobbly legs will give way any moment... *Don't fall. Don't fall. Don't fall. Don't fall. Don't fall.*

Sara passes the long white tables, one after another.

Chin down and eyes away, Sara, after what feels a country mile, turns down the line and out of sight of most. Were it not for her starving, she would head straight on out the doors she should have come through in the first place and leave.

Out from under the heat of the spotlight, Sara's face returns to its normal temperature. *Why in the world are people looking at me?!* Puzzled and more uncomfortable than ever, the hobbled Sara doesn't even have the option of running away.

Without warning, Megan appears as though from a cloud of smoke.

"Oh, my goodness. I have been looking for you everywhere!" Megan presses with a whisper anyone within twenty feet can hear. "Everyone is talking. *Everyone!*"

"Wait, what? Who is talking? What are they saying?!" Alarmed by Megan's urgency, Sara doesn't realize the line moving ahead of her.

"Oh gee, I don't know, let's see," begins Megan, basking in the drama, "you looked like death warmed over when you moved here, *but then* you grow boobs and a butt over the weekend, your clothes go from hand-me-down to Diesel overnight, and then you switch from nerdy math to weightlifting class and *shatter* all the records. Did you know Devon is furious with you for breaking her records?!"

"Devon is mad at me?" Sara stammers.

"Um, *yeah*, you broke- Wait...*shattered* all of her records. I heard you benched like 200 pounds!"

"We didn't even do bench press. And Devon was so nice to me -" says Sara, frazzled with worry.

"Wait! Devon talked to you?!"

"Um, yeah. I was in her weightlifting group with Michelle," answers Sara, fearing she had done something wrong.

"Michelle Decker?!" Megan confirms.

"Yeah, it was the three of us. Did Devon *say* she was mad at me?"

"Wait, okay... So, you were hanging out with Devon Hailey and Michelle Decker, and you *didn't* tell me?" Megan is flabbergasted.

Now standing by the pretzel display, Sara's mouth opens, but nothing comes out. An overloaded mind swirls. *It was only thirty minutes ago. I haven't had time to tell anyone anything. What is there to tell anyways? We didn't even test so I couldn't have broken any records. We didn't even do bench press. I looked like death warmed over? Do I want one pizza or two?*

Expressing a blend of disbelief and disappointment, Megan awaits an answer.

"What would you like?" asks the lunch lady. Sara's attention turns.

Ugh! thinks Megan, believing the interruption could not have possibly come at a worse time.

Seconds tick by slowly as Sara points to pizza, chicken strips, tater tots, egg rolls, and then a green sports drink.

Megan doesn't want food – she craves answers. Nourished by the moment, drama sustains her. "So," she pleadingly urges, following Sara. *Oh my God! Everybody is looking at us!* "What did you talk about? With Devon and Michelle, I mean."

Looking down at her tray, Sara focuses on not falling down and dumping food all over herself. Cautious steps all the way to her usual spot. Megan, right behind, notices eyes tracking Sara's huge pile of food.

Grateful to have made it without dumping her tray, the girl with creaking muscles carefully takes her place across from Lexi.

"So, what did you, Devon, and Michelle talk about?" Megan loudly projects, to notify the others of what she and Sara were discussing.

Lexi, surprised at the heap of food, takes inventory of what she guesses at least half a million calories.

Angela, who knows she will be late for class, decides, *Yeah, this is totally worth a tardy.*

"We didn't talk, not really. It was loud and we were lifting weights." Sara answers before asking, "Who told you Devon was angry with me?"

"Uh, *everybody.*" Megan answers without hesitation.

In between bites of two pizzas, three egg rolls, five chicken strips, and the tater tots, Sara repeats what little answer there is to Megan's same question asked a dozen different ways.

Look at her! seethes Shelly from across the way. "Look at all that food! She eats like a fucking pig!"

12:24 PM, 5th Hour
The ladies' room, nearest Mrs. White's class
Sara looks for answers in the mirror. Answers as to why people are looking at her; why people are talking about her. Leaning over the sink, she looks at herself for what feels like the first time again. Sara blinks. The girl in the mirror blinks. Sara sticks out her tongue. The girl in the mirror sticks out her tongue. Sara smiles, and the girl in the mirror smiles. *That's not me. It can't be me. Is that me?*

Sara touches the glass.

"Are you afraid you might be too beautiful?" Babe's voice echoes. *She is beautiful,* Sara believes of the image looking back. A mind struggles to reconcile. What Sara sees – and what she feels like she should see – could not be more different.

That isn't me. Can that be me? That's not me. Is it?

1:22 PM, 6th Hour
Mrs. Espinosa's Home Economics class
Divided into groups of four and five, the class begins the two-day process of making snickerdoodles. Today, the batter. Tomorrow, they bake.

Legs flimsy, and ready for the day to be over, Sara does what she can to stay out of the way. The problem of too much attention has been made all the worse by Russell Martin, now wanting *her* attention. For the third time, Big Ginger says something obnoxious, only to turn his pumpkin-sized head Sara's way to make sure she heard. Each time, the guy with disproportionately small teeth gives a yellow smile. *Are his teeth really yellow, or is the rest of him just so orange that it makes them look yellow?* Sara wonders.

Leaning against the counter with her unreliable legs locked, the girl wishing she was next to Babe on the swing, is filled with regret. *I really wish I had that bacon now. If I'd only just grabbed a baggie!*

Five minutes later, a girl Sara has never spoken to approaches. "Hey, um, Sara... Devon wants to talk to you."

"What?!" Sara snaps out of a daydream.

"Devon is outside. She wants to talk to you."

Sara shrugs as though helpless. "But I'm in class."

"Just take the pass and go on out," says a girl from Sara's group. "She won't care, just don't be gone too long."

"Okay." Sara whispers, scared she will get in trouble.

Mrs. Espinosa, occupied with being everywhere at once, doesn't notice Sara's hesitant steps toward the door – but Russell does. Having managed to get flour on his cheek, he gives Sara a quick look up and down while sending another yellow smile her way.

More anxious with each step, Sara is sure of it now. *Megan was right! Megan was right and Devon is mad, and now Devon is here to yell at me!*

Sara continues as if she were headed to the gallows. After a quick glance back, she grabs the pass off the ledge of the dry-erase board and dips into the hall.

Heart up in her throat, Sara finds Devon waiting. Appearing to have something important to say, Devon signals for her to follow. *Oh no! Devon wants me to follow her somewhere so she can yell at me!* Thirty feet and one turn later, Sara and the girl with a pencil holding her hair up enter the ladies' room.

Devon turns on her heel. "Okay, I just wanted to tell you that, if you can, avoid Shelly."

"What?" Sara replies, expecting something else.

"Shelly Thompson. The dark-haired little bi-" Devon bites her tongue. "You know who she is."

"Um, yeah..." Sara's pulse can be seen in her neck.

"Just, if you can," Devon repeats, talking with her hands, "just avoid her and she'll probably just let it go..." Devon's voice is hopeful, but not confident.

"Let go of what?" asks a puzzled Sara. "I thought *you* were the one who was mad at me."

"Me?!" says Devon, now befuddled herself. "What? Wait. No. Why would I be mad at you? Who said that?"

"I was told that's what 'everybody' said," Sara answers with innocent relief.

Devon shakes her head and sighs. "I hate this school."

"So why is Shelly angry with me?" Sara whispers low. "I've never even said anything to her-"

With a sigh, Devon informs, "You don't have to actually talk to Shelly in order to get her to hate you."

"Then how?"

"You don't have to say *or do* anything to Shelly to make her hate you." Devon does her best to explain. The naïve look on Sara's face makes her want to help even more.

"Here, just do this—avoid her as best you can and *just try* not to give her any excuse to, you know, act like Shelly. Okay?"

"I thought you and Shelly were friends?" a confused Sara askes in a confused voice.

Devon's chin drops, "What?"

2:12 PM, 7th Hour
Mrs. Callahan's Physical Education class

The locker room, live with chatter when Sara walked in, has been quiet ever since. A strange vibe in the air, everyone including Tiffany, hurries to change and get out. Shelly is taking her time.

Not wanting to cross Shelly's path to go change in the bathroom stall, an apprehensive Sara waits near her locker. Doing her best to heed Devon's advice, she stalls, all too willing to take a tardy. Shelly continues messing with her phone as those remaining finish changing.

"Avoid her as best you can and just try not to give her any excuse to, you know, act like Shelly." Sara hears Devon's voice. Heart racing, she pretends to be occupied with something in her locker. Girls leave through the heavy wooden door one and two at a time. Eerily quiet, it's as though there's a secret
everyone knows but her.

The last two girls leave together. Only Shelly remains. Legs cramping and pits sweating, Sara keeps her eyes in her locker. Shelly's locker shuts. Footsteps. Sara holds perfectly still, like prey hoping to go unnoticed as a predator passes by.

Shelly stops behind Sara.

"What's up new girl?" Shelly snipes. Sara turns, staring down at the glowering girl with her hip cocked. "What? Nothing to say?"

Terrified, Sara utters, "I just-"

"Shut up!" Shelly barks. "You *shut* your mouth when you talk to me!"

Eyes welling, Sara begins to tremble.

"*I* speak, *you* listen!" commands Shelly. "That's how this shit works!"

Sara's worst fear has come to pass.

"Look, I don't know who *the fuck* you think you're impressing," Shelly seethes through clenched teeth, "but you are *not* special. You are *not* a fucking snowflake. You are *not* a fucking butterfly! You understand me, bitch?!"

Fearing being struck, Sara quickly nods to the venomous girl poking a finger in her chest.

"Look, I realize that you're new and that's all cute and shit, but *you* need to realize real quick and in a mother*fucking* hurry, that you are just the newest thing and nobody is going to give two shits about you soon enough. Got it?!"

Sara nods again. A tear trickles down her cheek.

"Good."

BOOM!

Shelly's palms punch into Sara's chest. Wet noodle legs buckling as her back smacks the locker, Sara goes from standing to flat on her back in the blink of an eye.

"Know your role, bitch!" is the last thing she hears before the door is kicked opened. From the perspective of an ant, Sara watches size four shoes walk out. The door slowly drawing closed.

Coldness of the floor on her back, the ceiling goes blurry from tears. Worse than the ache in her elbow or the stabbing pain in her throat, is knowing she let Devon down.

sniff, sniff

I didn't even say anything to her.

3:14 PM
Outside the school

Sweltering, it is the hottest, muggiest day of the last two weeks. Shoulders slumped, eyes downcast, the girl standing under the maple tree wipes the sweat streaming down her face. Eyes puffy and red, Sara stares at the spot Lady *should* be. *Of all the days to be late.* Movement all around – people with places to go and things to do – Sara just knows all of their lives are *perfect*.

The girl who walked laps instead of playing volleyball doesn't know what she did wrong. *I just want to curl up in a ball and die.*

I tried to stay away from her. The sullen girl thinks for the hundredth time.

Sara looks again. Still no Lady. She sighs. *I can barely even stand up.* Sara has gone from feeling like the strongest girl in the world to the weakest. Still no Lady. Her right elbow aches. The back of her head hurts too, but only when she touches it.

I hope Devon doesn't get mad at me. Sara looks again. Still no Lady. She sighs.

Sara just laid on the concrete. After some time, she picked herself up, washed her face, changed, and joined the class. Receiving only a warning for a tardy, the girl who wished she could play volleyball, took laps around the court instead. She did her best not to look at Shelly, busy telling everybody what had happened. So delighted was the smiling viper that she didn't even care about winning.

Sara pretended not to notice those looking her way and snickering when Shelly whispered in their ear. She is tired of people looking at her.

Slipping out a few minutes early, Sara was changed, out the door, and into the heat before the rest of the class was even excused. Her face long already, realizing Lady wasn't outside didn't help.

Desperate for Lady to take her away, Sara turns a little sadder each time she looks up. Bumper-to-bumper traffic crawls as a sea of novice drivers manage their way out of the parking lot and onto their perfect lives.

Eyes glued to the ground, Sara gazes into the grass.

A stream of sweat trickles. She doesn't bother to wipe it away. *I didn't even say anything to her.*

Half of a minute passes. Sara looks up. Instead of seeing Lady, she sees Tiffany's 2014 Mercedes, and behind that, Julie's Range Rover.

Hazels lower again. *I wonder if it's too late to change my schedule so that I am not in Shelly's class anymore. How mad is Devon going to be at me for not doing a better job of avoiding Shelly? I hope people aren't still talking about me. They probably are.*

Sara remembers Shelly, up on her tippy toes, whispering in girls' ears. She remembers the expression on the listeners' faces – each time a look of surprise, followed by a snicker. At least a half-dozen times.

Zoned out once again, Sara finds relief in oblivion. A random blade of grass draws her attention same as the chip near the edge of the patio – same as the nick in the tile in Mr. Schibi's class. Wishing not to be part of the world bustling around her, she simply pushes it away.

Resigned, Sara feels as though under water. *I don't want to go to school here anymore.*

Time loses sense of itself. One minute passes – or maybe five – before eyes of green and gold eyes rise again. Like a balloon on a string, Sara's awareness lifts from the lowly blade of grass to a cherry-red fender under a thin layer of dust. The moving gleam under a cloudless sky leads her attention along the broad side of a fully restored 1959 Chevrolet Apache with a short-wide bed. The sort of pickup one usually only sees on television or a calendar. The mind underneath recognizes it from a photograph in an American studies book back at The Institute. The sad girl is soothed for reasons unknown.

Spirits lifting, her gaze crawls up the driver's side door and into the face of Clint staring back.

It's him! Sara gasps.

Having noticed her well before she noticed him, the guy looking at the girl standing in the shade doesn't realize traffic ahead is moving. A bump of a horn snaps Clint's attention forward.

And just like that, the boy with his wrist draped over the steering wheel shifts into gear and quickly pulls away – but not before looking back two times on his way out.

Just my luck, Clint thinks during a right-hand turn. *Couldn't find her anywhere and there she was.*

Lady's maroon Buick pulls along the street.

3:41 PM
Lady and Babe's bedroom
Napping after his first visit to a doctor since being diagnosed, Babe is shaken awake by Lady.

"Sara needs your help. Something is wrong with her!" Lady whispers with urgency.

"Is she hurt?" responds a groggy Babe as she helps him sit up.

"She is telling me she wants her blue pills and I..." Lady pauses. "I can't give them to her again. I just can't!"

With Lady's help, and all the strength he can muster, Babe is soon headed for the door. Stopping along the way, he points back to the nightstand. "Get that for me, would ya?"

"She doesn't need that stuff!" Lady staunchly opposes.

"It's better than those damn blue pills!" Babe snorts, grabbing his smokes.

Using the wall and everything he passes by for balance, Babe makes his way to the front door. Greeted by the heat, he descends the steps with Lady's help.

Feeling relief the moment he sits next to her, Sara is surprised when Lady sets the bottle of vodka on the ledge before heading back inside.

Though relieved Sara isn't crying, Babe can tell she has been. *Looks like we've had ourselves a bad day.*

Sara just stares down at the ground.

"Afternoon, beautiful," Babe greets the girls with a long face.

If I was beautiful, people would be nice to me, thinks Sara who says nothing back.

"Rough day today?"

"Can I have my pills please?" Sara tries not to cry. She doesn't know why she is asking for the blue pills. She just knows she wants them.

"Oh," Babe begins, his gray eyes off toward the city, "don't see how I can keep them from you. They being your property and all."

Expecting resistance, Sara turns to the man calmly looking into the distance. "Really?"

"I mean, you're a grown woman and they *are* yours. Think there are forty or so left in the bottle." Babe watches Sara from the corner of his eye. "Not sure what they cure though."

From the window above, Lady watches the old spy reach into his shirt pocket.

Though she doesn't like the sight of her Babe handing Sara a cigarette, she can't help but be reminded of the James Dean cool that caught her eye so long ago. Despite his health, she finds her husband dashing as ever. Though she wishes to oversee, Lady walks away so the two might have some privacy.

Her full lips crimped around the filter, Sara twists at the waist so Babe can light her smoke. After a puff she reaffirms, "So I can have my pills?" She is forced to wait as he lights his cigarette.

Babe blows out a chest full of smoke. "You know," he decides to sidestepping the question, "you smoke like the ladies used to in the old days. In old movies, I mean."

Sara shrugs, faintly remembering the old movies she watched in Americanization class. "I just saw other people do it, I guess."

"Well, you're a natural." Babe's smile causes Sara to smile a little, too.

Sensing a lift in her spirits, Babe allows the sway of the swing and his contagious calm to run its course. He buys time with a long drag.

"I'm not gonna ask what has you bothered. If you want to tell me, you can, but I won't ask."

Sara looks at Babe funny. She assumed he would pry.

"Because I would rather ask you about the things that make you happy. Did anything good happen today?"

Her mind kindly ushered away from what bothers; Sara recalls the joy of third hour. "I'm in weightlifting now."

"Oh, you are?!" Babe rises. "Did you lift weights today?!"

"Yes." A smile fights its way to the surface.

"Well!" Babe urges. "Are you gonna tell me about it?"

"I was able to lift more than the other girls," Sara mentions.

"That's great!" Babe slaps the tops of his thighs. "Are you making new friends?"

"There is one girl who is really nice. Her name is Devon."

"Good! Good!" Babe couldn't be happier.

"I think I did too much though. My legs are really weak now."

"I wouldn't worry about that too much," Babe assures. "They'll be fine in a couple days."

Sara turns solemn once again. "Everyone looks at me."

"Yeah, we talked about this," Babe reminds in a mentoring tone. "I need you to remember that all that matters for a spy is that no one knows they are a spy. Nothing else matters." Babe tests the waters.

Sara turns with bewilderment. "What?"

Test failed. His hope of yesterday being a fluke is gone. Any guilt he had for giving Sara a cigarette is shoved aside by urgent worry. Unshakeable, the old timer hides his concern.

The mind underneath has swatted Babe's comment away. "Can I have another cigarette, please?"

"Sure kid," he reaches for another. Noticing the way Sara eyeballs the vodka, he thinks, *Yup... she likes to smoke and drink. She's definitely Russian!*

Sara leans so Babe can light her cigarette. And just like that, she is a starlet once again. "So, can I have the pills?" she inquires after blowing smoke through pouting lips.

"Here, I'll make you a deal," Babe offers what he believes the lesser of two evils. "You can have your pills, or you can have vodka. Up to you."

Sara's expression answers for her.

"You could've at least *pretended* to think about it!" chuckles Babe. In the mood for a taste himself, he enjoys a drink alongside Sara.

"No more sour face!" Babe applauds. Sara smiles as the warmth travels down.

A bending of Sara's sore arm reminds her of how the school day ended. She yearns for the fuzzy relief she knows will come with a couple more shots.

"The clothes Lady got me are-" Sara stops to think, sweeping her thick, sandy hair behind her ear. "They're really nice and I like them, but I don't think I should wear them to school anymore."

"We've been over this, kid," Babe says, at a loss. "People are going to look at you no matter what. *Not* wearing those clothes isn't going to change that. You think that if you stop wearing the new clothes, people will stop looking at you?" His tone is that of one speaking to a child.

Sara half nods and shrugs as she extends her tiny glass again.

"Sara," Babe says as he pours. "You could dress in a burlap sack with armholes cut out and people would *still* look—especially the boys."

This brings a flash of red fenders and blue eyes.

"How do the girls treat you at school?" Babe hesitantly asks.

"Um..." Sara stalls. "Some are nice. Some aren't." With this, she tosses back a second gulp of bitterness. Sara hates the way it tastes but loves the burn.

"Hmm," sounds Babe, the situation coming into focus. "You know, my Lady used to have problems with girls when she was your age."

Sara tilts her head. "Why?"

"Oh," Babe leans back with a wistful smile, "I didn't know her until she was a little older than you are now, but trust me, Lady was a looker." Babe goes on to tell Sara of porcelain skin, auburn hair, and hourglass figure.

Having never considered Lady any other way than she is now, Sara has difficulty picturing the ravishing woman Babe describes.

Feeling warm inside—and fuzzier as time goes on—Sara learns of what Lady had to deal with during her teenage years. She never came right out and told Babe it was because she was pretty; she didn't have to.

A little defensive of the woman who has been so nice to her, Sara doesn't like the idea of anyone not being nice to Lady. Yesterday's question circles back. "Why are girls so mean to each other?"

Babe shakes his head. "You know what? I've wondered that myself."

"Are they this way in other places?"

"Put it to ya like this, kid," Babe sighs, "if there is place, and there are women there, some of them will be being mean to other ones." With this, he shrugs as to say, *I don't know what else to tell you.*

Babe can tell Sara has something to say. But when she begins to speak, nothing comes out.

"Why do you ask... if you don't mind my asking?" Babe pries only because he believes she wants him to.

"A girl pushed me down at school today," Sara mumbles.

Babe's brow raises. "A girl pushed you down, huh? Well, what'd you do to her?" he asks, posture stiffening at the notion of his girl getting bullied.

With this, something happens. A bristling. Pupils constrict. Knuckles roll. Jaw clenches. A shift. A sharp breath as hard eyes look on.

Noticing the peculiarity, Babe poses the question again. "What'd you do to her?"

"What did I do to her?" she coyly responds in Russian, coarse and low. "Nothing yet."

Babe reels. Studying from the side, he cranes around to see her face. "You feeling okay?"

"Huh?" Sara returns, innocence rushing back like water.

"You said you haven't done 'Anything yet'...in Russian!"

"Huh?" Sara repeats as though coming out of a trance.

Babe sits confounded, staring at Sara for the longest time. *That wasn't Sara,* he knows in his bones.

"Can I have one more drink?" she asks shyly.

"Yeah," Babe scoffs. "If there was ever a time for another drink, it's now."

Wednesday, August 27th, 2014

8:43 AM
Sara's bedroom
Sara wakes to an argument between her stomach and head as to which feels worse. The girl with a dreadful taste in her mouth doesn't recall Lady all but carrying her up the steps into the house. Not only hung over, but stiff and achy from lifting weights, she wouldn't move an inch if not for having to pee.

Pulling the covers from her bare legs, Sara begins her arduous trek. "Ungh," she groans as nausea, sore limbs, and a pounding headache combine for the holy trinity of awfulness. Hair pasted to her cheek by dried drool; Sara manages her legs off the side of the bed. This causes the elbow whacked on the locker to flare with pain. "Err," she grumbles, stomach churning.

Burrrp! *So gross!*

Sara musters the strength to stand. "Oww," she lowly moans, muscles feeling as though they were beaten with a stick.

The girl who will not be going to school today begins toward the bathroom. She feels betrayed by the clear liquid that was such a friend to her last night. Using the edge of the dresser for stability – then doorknob, then the wall, then another spot on the wall – Sara eventually makes her destination.

She looks into the tri-fold mirror above the sink to discover bloodshot eyes, puffiness, strands of her hair matted to her oily face, and a painful grimace looking back.

"That looks about right," Sara mutters upon the first reflection to accurately represent how she feels. *Should've just taken the pills.*

10:00 AM
Though better than she was, Sara is still a long way from good. Pulling the covers over hair still damp from a twenty-minute shower, the girl with two aspirin and six pieces of toast with marmalade in her belly, is ready to go back to sleep. Mouth minty after brushing her teeth three times, her headache is half what it was. The shower helped more than anything. Before long, Sara—skin still pink and fingers still wrinkly—is sleeping once again.

Pulling double duty, Lady has two patients today. Checking on both throughout the morning, neither are off to a good start.

Babe's chemo treatment yesterday weighs heavily on him today.

2:45 PM
Sara wakes feeling significantly better. Lady makes one waffle after another until she finally gets full and staggers away from the table. The lass clearing the table is surprised to see Sara walk into the living room rather than back to her bedroom as she usually does.

After passing by the dining table where her blood was once drawn, Sara takes a seat on the end of the couch nearest Babe sleeping in his chair.

Watching from the kitchen, Lady sees Sara rest her head on one of the decorative pillows. On her side with her knees pulled up, Sara just wants to be in there with him, even though he mostly just sleeps.

Almost back to sleep, she hears Babe's tired voice, "Feeling better, kid?"

Sara looks back and nods. She knows he is feeling terrible, so she doesn't ask the question back.

Sara lays her head back down. She doesn't want to go to school tomorrow either. She never wants to go back.

Thursday, August 28th, 2014

8:07 AM
Hallway

Sara, who did not want to come to school today—but did anyway—makes her way to her locker. Everybody is looking at her. Not Megan's "everybody", the *actual* everybody. Whereas the looks the day before were at least somewhat discreet, the stares now are as though she just stepped out of a tomb.

Chin down and wishing she had a book to hide behind, Sara wants to turn around and run. But she doesn't. *I can hardly breathe,* thinks the girl wearing a draping beige blouse.

It's like the walk across the cafeteria, only worse. So much worse.

One foot in front of the other, Sara makes her way until dipping into the nearest ladies room. Upon entering, the three girls touching up their makeup become quiet.

Were they talking about me? Sara wonders with near certainty.

A moment later, the door flies open – Megan enters. "Oh. My. God. I totally heard you moved away!"

Sara shakes her head. "What?"

- 133 -

8:24 AM, 1st Hour
Mr. Colliet's Advanced Biology class
Sara woke knowing she didn't want to come to school today, but only now can she fully appreciate just how much she didn't want to come. Having been briefed by way of a rambling Megan, Sara learned: Shelly beat her up in the bathroom for breaking Devon's weightlifting records; Sara was too injured or scared to come to school yesterday; Sara is moving back to Florida; and Devon is mad at Shelly for not letting her "handle her own business."

As if that were not enough, rumors relating to breast and butt implants, an eating disorder, and a sugar daddy are in circulation as well.

Sara gets *another* note once Mr. Colliet turns his back. *Did you go to the hospital?*

With a look of disbelief, Sara shakes her head at Megan, who immediately starts scribbling the next note. When Mr. Colliet turns his head, Sara hears, "pst..."

Sara opens the note: *Do you need me to take you to the hospital?*

Sara sighs.

9:16 AM, 2nd Hour
Secretary's office
Sara waits for Mr. Miller, hoping she can switch her schedule for seventh hour.

9:24 AM
Sara learns the cutoff time for schedule change was yesterday.

10:32 AM, 3rd Hour
Mr. Godfrey's Weight Training class
Devon pulls Sara aside and tells her how furious she is with Shelly for what she did. Though relieved that Devon isn't angry, Sara is solemn and with no idea what to do about seventh hour.

- 134 -

Sara goes through the motions as she, Devon, and Michelle move station to station. She is clueless as to the rift running through The Bitches.

11:03 AM, 4th Hour
Mrs. White's English class

Sara has successfully avoided Shelly all morning. Lingering until the halls are all but empty, then racing to barely make the next class on time has worked thus far, but does nothing but delay the inevitable. Sara still doesn't know what she will do when seventh hour arrives. Though she wants to go home, she can't bring herself to pick up the phone and ask Lady to come get her.

Living life one minute at a time, Sara hopes seventh hour somehow magically doesn't happen.

11:24 AM, Lunchtime
Library

Not hungry for breakfast, Sara is definitely hungry now, but not hungry enough to walk into the lunchroom. Rather, she waits out the lunch break in the library with a sorely used *People* magazine and six candy bars she got from the vending machine. She holds the magazine high to shield those looking her way.

5th Hour

Anxiety builds. Coach Stewart's spastic manner doesn't help.

6th Hour

Sara has anxiety – but also snickerdoodles. The group saved her share from yesterday. Russell is more obnoxious than usual, but not by much.

2:06 PM

The bell sounds the end of sixth hour.

Sara walks as though headed for the gallows.

2:12 PM, 7th Hour
Locker room

The locker room is stuffy with a blend of tension and daffodil air freshener. The class is collectively surprised at Sara's return. Shelly makes her own displeasure known. Already dressed, the one who thought she had been understood loud and clear leans against her locker – arms crossed, mouth pulled to one side. Pretending not to notice, Sara can feel Shelly's green eyes burning into her.

Shoulders rolled forward and chin down, Sara stands at her locker, turning the dial on her lock.

"I can't believe she actually came back." Someone whispers.

Just act like you didn't hear it, thinks Sara, gathering her clothes so she can change in the stall.

A couple minutes and several whispers later, Sara emerges, believing the locker room empty.

The locker room is not empty.

"You know," begins Shelly, who has been waiting patiently, "I think it's *really* big of you coming back – to school I mean." Sara wants to dart back into the stall and lock the door, but doesn't. Instead, she stands still, holding her clothes as the condescendingly snarky one slowly approaches. Holding her breath as she looks down, the petrified Sara soon sees Shelly's feet.

"Tell you what," Shelly sneers, "you just keep walking in circles with your head down and we'll get along *just* fine, got it?"

Giving a frightened nod, Sara expects another push—or worse—but nothing happens. Not realizing she had closed her eyes until she opens them, Sara discovers Shelly has gone. Feeling like she dodged a bullet, the girl with jeans and a t-shirt in her arms finally exhales.

The heavy wooden door she didn't hear open closes itself.

Heart racing like a scared bunny, Sara looks around the empty locker room. Everything is quiet now. She goes to swallow but hasn't the saliva to do so. Then it happens.

A feeling washes over her.

Heart rate begins to slow. Breathing slows and deepens. Fear fades to calm. Sara closes her eyes... then falls away like a satin robe falling off shoulders... Twelve opens her eyes.

The Natasha looks around, "Where is that little bitch?"

The assassin throws Sara's clothes in her locker and exits the locker room.

2:18 PM

Late for roll call, Twelve walks past Mrs. McCallahan.

"Need you to get out here a little sooner, Ms. Smith," notifies the teacher with a cautionary tone.

"Eat me, dyke," mutters Twelve under her breath.

"Excuse me?!" belts Mrs. McCallahan, her head whipping the direction of the girl going on to her first lap. After some deliberation, the teacher (who was the only one to hear what her student said) decides to let it go for now. Far from done with what's been a long day already, Mrs. Callahan is in no mood for teenage moodiness at the moment.

On the prowl, Twelve stalks. Circling the perimeter, the Natasha waits for her prey to leave the safety of the herd.

While she walks, the Natasha processes her counterpart's memories. Cigarettes and vodka, waffles with peanut butter, lifting weights, looking in the mirror, Shelly pushing Sara down. Twelve dwells on the push.

2:41 PM

Shelly excuses herself and makes her way toward the restroom. Twelve follows. No one notices the Natasha slip away.

The corners of Twelve's mouth rise as she enters the daffodil-laced locker room.

2:42 PM

After locking the door behind her, Twelve soundlessly rounds the corner. Squatting down, the Natasha looks under the stall. She sees the tippy toes of size-fours touching the tile.

Shoe's on the other foot, bitch, thinks the Russian to the sound of tinkling.

Flush

The locking mechanism sounds.

A stall door opens.

Shelly emerges. Initially startled, surprised eyes quickly harden at the girl blocking her way.

Feet shoulder width apart, chin down, and with a glower all her own, the Natasha has her sister's bully cornered. The only way is past.

"What the *fuck* do you want?!" Shelly hisses, her neck rolling.

Twelve says nothing. She isn't here to talk.

"I *said*," Shelly repeats through gritted teeth, fists balling. "What in the *fuck*, do *you* want?!"

Her eyes Putinesque, Twelve reaches to touch the shiny button on the noisy hand-dryer. To loud backdrop of hot air blowing, the Natasha provokes with the raising of the brow, "You just gonna stand there?"

Three hard steps later, Shelly swings.

Shelly's haymaker travels harmlessly past. The off-balance assailant receives what feels a baseball bat to her outer right thigh.

Not allowing Shelly's crumbling body to fall, Twelve uses her brute strength to wrench, lift, and slam the tiny bully onto the floor. Size fours in the air, the Russian attempts driving her *through* the tile.

The dryer muffles the sound of Shelly's back slapping flat. Green eyes bulge out of their sockets as concussive force slams her lungs shut.

Not one to leave a point unpunctuated, Twelve drives her knuckles straight downward into Shelly's chest - *SMASH!!* - right between the B-cups.

Wracked with pain, Shelly feels as though having fallen two stories onto concrete. Watery eyes filled with terror, the broken one looks into the face of mercilessness.

The dryer shuts off.

The sound of Shelly's bare legs and tennis shoes rubbing tile is the only sound as her balled body quivers; arms folded tight.

Her body broken; Shelly feels Twelve's fingers digging under her tucked chin.

Twelve seizes her throat.

Windpipe clamped. Shelly closes her eyes. She cannot bear the sight of Twelve's fury.

Veins bulge in her victim's cheeks as tears escape lids squeezed tight. Twelve lowers almost nose to nose. Grip vice-like, she gives a jostling shake. "Look at me, you little cunt!" Bloodshot eyes dare peek. Twelve drinks in Shelly's dread.

"You so much as *look* at her again and I will sneak into your house at night and cut your mother's tits off! *Do* you understand me?!" Twelve warns low and guttural.

Fearing for her life – and too shattered to form words – Shelly nods best she can. Anything to appease the Russian bearing down.

"Please," Twelve dares, digging her nails even deeper into Shelly's neck. "Please touch her again. I want to cut your mom's tits off." The broken girl cringes, expecting a strike. Instead, the Natasha releases her grip. Shelly rolls onto her side. Writhing on the cold floor, face twisted in agony, she tries to breathe, tries to scream, but nothing. Curled into fetal position, Shelly believes she is dying.

Sara, on the far side of the gymnasium, is confused. In a daze, the girl who was alone in the locker room a few seconds ago is now walking laps around the basketball court. Sara has no idea where the last thirty-six minutes have gone. Relaxed to the point of sleepy, Sara knows only that Shelly is nowhere to be seen and that she isn't scared anymore. *How come I have nail marks on my wrist?* Sara wonders upon inspection.

Lightened, the girl taking laps watches the others play. Lackadaisical, her mind wanders as it often does. *I wonder if anyone has been to the bridge since I was there... I wonder what Lady is cooking for dinner... I wonder if it would be okay if I went for another run on Saturday...*

Her peaceful recall of the horses she saw on her run is interrupted by the commotion of Mrs. Callahan and her classmates rushing into the locker room. *Huh... I wonder what's going on over there?* Sara leisurely veers across the court to see. *Peanut butter on a Snickers bar sounds like a pretty good idea...*

The girl with food on the brain pulls back the door to find a mass – lead by Tiffany – huddled around the distraught Shelly. Gushing with compassion, emoting classmates jockey for position to pat her on the back and tell her it will be okay. Little could they imagine; it took several minutes and all of Shelly's strength just to climb onto the bench.

Ding! Something like a timer goes off in Sara's head. Much the way one might remember having left the stove on; Sara remembers Shelly's breaking—kind of. Like a movie seen long ago, she can't recall details, only the basics.

So distant, so far removed is the hazy memory.

Sara looks closer at Shelly.

Holding an icepack on her leg, the girl sniffing watery snot breathes by way of short, choppy breaths. Eyes puffy, red, and downcast, the one feared by everyone is now pitied by all.

Oh, my goodness! Sara takes in the very picture of despair. *She looks like she just watched her family get eaten by a bear!*

Sara feels bad for Shelly, but not bad enough to stick around. *I'll change later,* Sara thinks, draping her Miss Me jeans and beige blouse over her arm; newest pair of shoes pinched between her fingers. *Class is pretty much over anyways.*

The door jerks open. Sara, on her way out, steps aside so that the trainer from the football team can enter.

"Is everyone decent?!" he shouts, hand over his eyes.

"Yeah," say all the girls at once. The young guy heads for the center of the fussing, fanning group. "She twisted her knee!" is the last thing Sara hears before walking out without permission. Mrs. Callahan doesn't notice.

Sara makes her way down the empty hall, leaving the drama farther behind with each step. Not a worry in the world. *I wonder if Lady would get me some ice cream?*

2:58 PM
Seeing Sara at a distance, Lady realizes just how much she is filling out. With a newly found fullness in her hips and limbs, she conveys herself even more gracefully than before. Less walking than flowing, the girl who was so glum yesterday seems light as air today.

Sara opens the door and lowers herself into the air-conditioned sedan. New clothes in her lap and shoes in the floorboard, she puts on her seatbelt.

"So," Lady pries, "how was your day?"

The look on Sara's face is answer enough, the happy girl just nods and asks, "Can we get some ice cream?"

3:27 PM
From his spot on the swing, Babe watches the car make its way slowly up the drive and into the carport. Lady and Sara emerge, each with an ice cream cone in hand. Lady's right hand holds a white paper bag with a surprise for her guy out soaking up sunshine.

Swirling her vanilla-covered tongue, Sara follows Lady along the walk.

"Hey girls!" he greets with a big smile.

"Hope you're in the mood for ice cream!" sings Lady. Babe hasn't had much of an appetite lately. Her cheeks rosy,

- 141 -

the lass with sass reaches down into the paper bag, pulling out a clear container housing a banana split with whipped cream and a cherry on top.

Placing the treat on her husband's lap, Lady takes her place on the swing as Sara pulls up a folding chair. Together, the three enjoy a cold delight on the day that is hot, but cooler than it has been. Babe and Lady enjoy the view of the city beyond the girl licking at her ice cream.

Watching Sara go about her treat, Babe is awestruck by how far her pendulum can swing. Child-like to sophisticated to whatever – or whomever – he saw for a moment last night. *It's like she's as innocent as the moment allows,* he thinks to himself. "How was school today?" Babe asks, tossing away the cherry stem.

"It went fine," Sara answers as though ten years old.

"Were the girls nice to you?" he asks, resting his hand on Lady's leg.

"They were nice," Sara answers with only Devon and Megan in mind.

"I'm glad to hear it!" Babe is relieved.

Quiet sets in before Sara asks out of the blue, "How did you two meet?"

Lady, mid-swallow of mint chocolate chip, lights up at the question. Loading with a deep inhale, she gives Babe a double pat on the thigh as to say, *You just relax. I'll answer this for both of us!*

Babe grins, knowing he will not be able to get a word in edgewise.

"More years ago than a lady cares to admit," she begins with an arching tone, "my cousin Mary and I went down through Europe on holiday. I had never left Scotland other than going to Kent to visit family, so I was *very* excited... and nervous. Mary, on the other hand... she'd been *all over* Europe with her husband—he was a doctor—but this was the first time she'd left Edinburgh since her husband took off with the hussy nurse he'd met in Belgium."

Sara leans forward, attention rapt, as a Lady even more melodious than usual, sets the stage.

Cutting a banana with a plastic spoon, Babe listens as Lady tells how Mary received a rather generous settlement in the divorce. Wishing to get away for a time, Mary, who was a few years older, decided to take Lady along.

"London, Paris, Prague, Rome, Vienna... It was the third leg of the trip when I met a 'Czechoslovakian' man..." Lady rolls her eyes at the word 'Czechoslovakian'. "...with a head of jet-black hair and sunglasses. He was wearing a t-shirt when everyone else was wearing a coat!"

"It wasn't that cold," Babe defends his younger self.

"Yes, it was," Lady corrects with a double pat.

"Maybe for a Scotsman." Babe slips in.

"What's that?" Lady turns.

"Oh, I didn't say anything, dear," Babe playfully retreats.

"Anyway," Lady resumes. "Now, I wasn't always a fat old lady," she says, referencing the padding accumulated over the years. "Matter of fact, I used to be a head turner!" Babe nods along, brows raised. Sara remembers him telling how fetching Lady was in her day.

Mint chocolate chip dripping down her fingers, Lady goes on to tell how she'd spotted the young man with gray eyes and his sleeves rolled up at the train station... and then the café... then outside her hotel.

"What was I supposed to do? She was beautiful!" Babe shrugs. He sees Lady wearing her heavy burgundy coat. As though yesterday, he remembers the way her hair blended in with the deep red brick behind. How her porcelain skin seemed to glow. Though she was not wearing lipstick, the cold made her look as if she was.

A little embarrassed, Babe hears about how his younger, more impetuous self, kept turning up everywhere Lady and her cousin went. He remembers how nervous he was. How much nerve it took to introduce himself – and the ruse he used to do so.

"He had a camera around his neck and asked if he could take my picture—told me he was a photographer!" Lady howls, tossing her head back.

"I *was* a photographer," Babe defends. "I was taking pictures of a corrupt diplomat."

"Well, he wound up taking pictures of me under a streetlight!" Lady tells Sara, clinging to her every word. "And then the photographer," she rolls her eyes, "asked me to go dancing!"

"Did you say yes?!" Sara blurts like a child.

Lady smiles fondly. "Well, I told him I would *only* consider it if he had a guy for Mary, who was still back in the room. Not like I was going to just go out *alone* with some stranger I'd just met on the street!"

"I should probably mention I was on a mission, and that I was *supposed* to be tailing a government official, not chasing-" Babe discreetly points his thumb at Lady. Babe also goes on to tell how he not only had to keep his activities hidden from the other three men on the detail, but also pay a stranger he met in a tavern to pose as his friend. The price doubled when the friend saw Lady and wanted to switch dates.

"We danced all night, even though I'd never danced before in my life!" Lady tells, smiling so hard her cheeks begin to ache.

"You danced *juuust* fine..." The words crawl through Babe's grin. "And then she gave me a *big* kiss goodnight."

"I most certainly did not!" Lady passionately refutes. A cackling Babe braces himself for a punch that may or may not come. His laughter sets the swing a-wobble.

"Well, that's how I remember it!" he follows up.

"I did *not!*" Lady turns to a Sara, hand cupping her laughter. "Tell her the truth!"

Sara enjoys the sight of Babe not being treated as though he were sick. A glimpse of how things used to be.

"No," Babe recants, "She was a perfect lady. That's why I call her 'Lady'."

Honor restored and the floor reclaimed, Lady tells of how he saw her every chance he could. Babe followed the diplomat by day and spent his evenings with Lady.

"I was *dead* tired," Babe slips in as Lady takes a breath.

"After the dance hall closed, we'd just walk around the city and drink coffee and talk all night," Lady wistfully recalls.

"I had to drink coffee to keep from falling over!" Babe tells the starry-eyed Sara.

Eventually, Lady admits to giving a peck on the cheek when she got on the train to leave. "Tell her what I told you," she insists.

After a long sigh, Babe says, "She told me that if I wanted a *real* kiss to meet her in four days' time-"

"In Vienna!" Lady slaps her lap, proud of how hard she made him work.

Drinking in the story – a story made all the better by the two of them are carrying on – Sara leans in for more.

"In Vienna," Babe seconds. "She made me go all the way to *damn* Vienna."

"I told him if he wanted to see me again that I would be at the train station in Vienna at 4:10 in the afternoon. I hoped he'd show, but I didn't think he would," Lady dismisses with a flick of her wrist.

"Was I not there?" Babe asks with an *I told you so* tone.

"Yes," she confirms, her pale eyes welling. "Yes, you were." Sara feels a pinch in her throat.

"Then what happened?" Sara asks, her eyes welling too.

"Oh!" Lady jumps as though poked with a tack. "The scarf! I almost forgot about the scarf!"

"I remember the scarf," Babe smiles.

"He gave me his scarf!"

"She *took* my scarf." Babe corrects soberly.

"He told me he wanted his scarf back, so *I told him* that if he wanted his scarf back, he'd better be in Vienna in four days."

"And a damn blizzard hit," Babe utters with despair.

"Not for me it didn't. I was in Rome!" Lady guffaws at Babe's misfortune before telling how she and Mary went all over Rome. How they visited the Vatican, the Colosseum, Caracalla's baths, The Forum, and ate all the pizza and spaghetti they could handle.

Then Babe tells his side of the story. Sara melts as she learns of him risking serious trouble by fudging his logbook, paying a paperboy to follow the corrupt official on his behalf, and living on apples and stale bread for having spent his month's wages before Lady left.

"Tell her about the blizzard!" Lady insists.

Sara hardly blinks as Babe details an unseasonably early blizzard shutting down the rail lines and how he bribed his superior with half of next month's pay for a few days' leave. "Lucky for me, I didn't make very much money!" he adds.

Brimming eyes darting back and forth between the two, Sara learns that while Babe was begging, bribing, and hitchhiking his way to Vienna, Lady's recently scorned cousin was doing her best to prepare her for the worst. For two days, the cousins were stuck in Graz while crews worked to clear the snow-piled tracks ahead. "We don't even know when we'll be in Vienna!" Mary pointed out, hoping to blunt her younger cousin's disappointment.

"The blizzard was a pain in the ass." Babe points out. "But it gave me time to get where I needed to be. I would've called her on her cellphone, but cellphones weren't invented yet!" Babe jokes.

Sara wipes her eyes as she laughs.

"Are you crying, young lady?" asks Lady, swiping away her own tears.

"No... Yes. Maybe..." stammers an embarrassed Sara, wiping her nose with the back of her hand.

"Why are you crying?" she teases.

"I don't know. Keep telling the story!" Sara flutters her hands.

"What do you wanna hear?" Babe grins. "About how I had to ride in the back of a logging truck for two hours, or how I had to steal a bicycle and a city map to make it on time?"

"He took the bicycle back," Lady exonerates.

"I kept the map." Babe laughs at Sara, fast becoming a mess.

"Then what happened?" Sara pines know. She wipes her nose with her shirt. Lady wistfully turns to the love of her life.

"There, on the platform, without a penny in his pocket and looking like Hades, he was waiting for me just like he said he'd be..."

Friday, August 29th, 2014

8:11 AM

Sara makes her way down the hall.

There is a buzz in the air. While Sara draws some looks, she isn't being gawked at like yesterday. She can hear the whispers. The chatter is all about Shelly Thompson's knee injury.

As Sara approaches the area commonly known as "Bitch Central", she sees Julie, Devon, Tiffany, and Michelle, their boyfriends and other members of the social upper echelon. Because of the game tonight, Jensen Hallowell—Shelly's boyfriend and star quarterback—wears his jersey, as does Jet Ryan, Cody Cassidy, and Russell Martin.

One brow suspiciously raised, Devon tracks Sara as she passes by. While virtually everyone swallows the twisted knee story hook, line, and sinker, Devon does not.

8:17 AM, almost 1st Hour
Mr. Colliet's Advanced Biology class

"Oh. My. God. Did you hear what happened to Shelly Thompson?" Megan begins.

Sara sighs. *This ought to be good.*

10:13 AM, 3rd Hour
Mr. Godfrey's Weight Training class

As Michelle half-heartedly does a set of leg curls, Devon shouts over the blaring music, "You know, it's really weird! Shelly goes to nationals in gymnastics every year since she was ten, never gets hurt, then gets hurt playing volleyball! Isn't that strange?!"

Sara, looking the other direction, doesn't seem to hear Devon two feet away.

tap, tap on Sara's shoulder. She turns. Devon has achieved eye contact.

"I said it's *really* strange that Shelly *hurt* herself so bad that she had to be carried to my car! Don't you think?!"

"It's really loud in here!" Sara yells as the whistle blows.

"Switch!"

"It's my turn now!" Sara turns to lay belly-down on the machine.

Okay, fine, Devon thinks to herself, *I'll wait...* She passes the minute with hands on her hips, foot tapping the floor.

When Sara's set is over, Devon not only helps Sara up, but turns her square by her shoulders so as to secure her attention. The one with long lashes and perfect brows uses hand motions in conjunction with words.

"It's funny!" Devon touches her dimples. "Shelly got *hurt*!" She runs her fingertips down her cheeks like tears. "So bad she had to be *carried*!" She does the motion of carrying a baby. "To my *car*!" She does a driving motion. "And no one *saw* it happen!!" Devon does a peek-a-boo with her hands. And shrugs her shoulders.

Sara, Devon, and Michelle all turn when Coach Mike chirps his whistle. The look on his face asks, *Why is no one in your group doing anything?*

"I think it's your turn," says the one dodging Devon's line of questioning.

"Michelle," Devon says nicely, "could you do a set really quick?"

"But it isn't my turn," Michelle whines.

"Michelle, will you *please* do a set for me?" Devon turns back to Sara. Grumbling, Michelle lays back down on the leg curl machine beside the two of them.

Sara is pretty well boxed in.

"So yeah, we were talking about Shelly," Devon continues. Michelle strains to hear over the blaring music. "Somebody – I'm not at liberty to say who – but *somebody*, said she saw Shelly walk off the basketball court totally fine!" Sara's eyes drift away. Devon brings her back with a quick shake. "So, she *must* have slipped in the bathroom, huh?!"

The corners of Sara's mouth raise.

"I knew it!" Devon flares. Guilty but proud, Sara smirks even though she barely knows what happened herself.

An exhilarated Devon, doing her best to restrain herself, grips Sara by her arms. "Okay, look! We can't talk here, but just so you know, I knew *sure as shit* that Shelly didn't hurt her knee playing volleyball!"

Sara blushes at the attention.

"Does anyone else know?!" Devon asks, looking around.

Sara shrugs.

"I want to know everything. *Everything!* Leave nothing out. I promise I won't repeat a word! Cross my hear and hope to die!" vows a giddy Devon.

WHISTLE!

"Switch!"

Devon turns for the machine as Michelle gets up – then back to Sara. "Promise me! Promise me you will tell me everything!"

Melting under rays of adulation, Sara nods.

Devon requires a pink swear. "Everything."

Soon after class begins, Devon pops her head into Mrs. White's classroom. "Can I borrow Sara for just a minute?" she requests, fingers pinched together.

"Sure," Mrs. White acquiesces to the probable valedictorian who lives three houses down from her. Devon rolls her eyes at the guys who look at Sara's derriere as she passes by.

"Only need her for a sec!" Devon says with a wave goodbye.

Speed walking, Devon leads to the nearest bathroom. Once inside, she pivots back. "Okay, spill it, sister!"

"Um, well," Sara begins to answer, only to realize she has only the faintest clue as to what happened. "Shelly, um..."

"Come on!" Devon urges, dying for details.

"Why are you so happy?" asks Sara, buying time to think.

"Because I hate Shelly, and I don't hate anyone, but I hate *her*. Everybody hates Shelly. *Jesus* hates Shelly."

Though Sara is happy that Devon is so happy, the memory of Shelly crying and broken makes her sad. Sara opens her mouth, but nothing comes out.

"I know you're new," Devon says, trying to articulate behavior so contrary to her nature, "but you haven't dealt with Shelly long enough to fully appreciate just what a mean, domineering, backstabbing snake she is. And trust me, whatever you did to her was long, *long* overdue."

Devon's intense whisper echoes about the white and blue ladies' room.

"Trust me," Devon emphatically goes on. "She had it coming. And just so you know, I wasn't kidding about carrying her. I *literally* had to *carry* her to my car and then into her house." *Why does Sara seem so oblivious?!* "And she was crying. Shelly doesn't cry!" Not getting much of a response, Devon cannot help but wonder, *Could she really have done this to Shelly? How did she do it to Shelly? None of this makes sense!*

"We got into a fight."

Devon almost swallows her tongue before sputtering, "No shit, you got into a fight! She can't even walk! Did you hit her with something?!"

Sara shakes her head. *I don't think so.*

"We're running out of time," urges an unsatisfied Devon. Though she doesn't mean to, her insistence makes Sara feel cornered and anxious. The moment suddenly becomes too much. Devon watches the apprehension on Sara's face give way to predatory keenness. A disquieting vibe resonates.

"You want to know what I did?"

Okay, officially freaked out now! Devon nods anxiously.

The Natasha's eyes gleam. "I choke-slammed the little bitch and threatened to cut her mom's tits off."

"Um, okay..." murmurs Devon. As though standing near a bomb, she slowly backs away.

11:28 AM, Lunchtime
Cafeteria
En route to her usual spot—toting a tray with two personal pizzas, a burrito, two egg rolls, fries, a juice box, and a sports drink—Sara is intercepted by Devon. Mouths gaping, Megan, Lexi, and Karen watch Sara receive what appears an imperial escort to the VIP section. Megan and her table aren't the only ones watching the new girl sit in Shelly's spot.

The reception is mixed.

Devon, Michelle, and Julie give a warm welcome, while Tiffany and Heather, who seldom comes to the cafeteria, are less welcoming. Cody (the class clown with perfect teeth) is welcoming, same as Jet Ryan—much to Tiffany's displeasure.

Feeling like the Scarecrow being pulled every which way, Sara is overwhelmed by the attention from all directions. Swept away by Devon's endorsement, Sara notices neither the stares from all around nor a crying Megan rushing toward the exit.

Unsure what to make of the all the fuss, a flattered Sara soaks up the moment.

People are being so nice to me!

12:28 PM, 5th Hour
Mr. Stuart's Government class

Sara sits with her head in the clouds once again. Yesterday feeling like forever ago, she cannot stop smiling. People looking doesn't bother her so much anymore. Actually, in a way, she is beginning to like it. Sara likes when people are nice to her. All she really hoped for was that people wouldn't be mean.

A little puzzled, Sara continues to wonder, *Why did Devon act funny after we left the bathroom?*

She isn't too worried about it; her new friend has seemed okay ever since.

1:16 PM 6th Hour
Mrs. Espinosa's Home Economics class

While the disruptive Russell Martin hand-delivers yet another message to the far end of the school, Mrs. Espinosa oversees the cupcake making process. *Everyone is being so nice to me!* Sara thinks for at least the hundredth time today.

No longer on the culinary sidelines, Sara finds herself the center of attention. Doing her best to listen to the three or four people talking to her all at once, the hour passes in the blink of an eye.

2:10 PM 7th Hour
Mrs. Callahan's Physical Education class

Mrs. Callahan – still displeased by the name Sara called her yesterday – is all the more puzzled. *How has she gone from sickliest girl in class, to that?! She is changing by the day!* In all her years as a teacher and a coach, the educator ever concerned with her students well-being has never seen such a radical change. Coach Mike has mentioned the weight she lifts in his third hour class.

Mrs. Callahan nearly chokes on a sip of tea when Sara spikes the ball like a college player on scholarship.

Hands clasped over her mouth; Sara seems surprised as anyone at her own prowess.

Having meant to talk to Sara regarding Shelly's bullying, Mrs. Callahan no longer feels the need.

2:55 PM
Locker room
Everyone is being so nice to me! Sara thinks for the two-hundredth time as the very girls who were snickering at her only yesterday are now tripping over one another to say something nice. Unaccustomed to compliments, Sara just says, "Thank you."

3:11 PM
Unable to change in front of the girls who kept wanting to talk, Sara once again walks out wearing gym clothes. The clothes she wore all day over her arm and a pair of open-toed flats pinched between her fingers, the girl with cheeks sore from smiling makes her way through the athletic department. Sara feels bad for making Lady wait—she's been trying to get away.

Nearing the heavy metal doors, she hears "Sara!" from behind.

Sara gasps. *It's him!*

With his dark hair tousled and still wet from the shower, Clint trots the distance to where Sara stands frozen. Relieved he didn't miss her again; he walks the last few steps.

"Sara, right?" Clint says, playing it cool.

"Yes," answers the girl staring into the blue eyes she has seen in her mind so many times. Sara's craned wrist floats up. A second passes before she realizes he is shaking her hand. *His hand is rough, but soft.*

The farm kid, with blue jeans frayed from work, coolly leans against the stand stuffed with pamphlets for joining the Marines.

"I'm Clint," he begins, "and you're Sara." Everything he rehearsed has abandoned him. "Nice to meet you, Sara."

"Nice to meet you, too," her words trickle into the air.

"I like the name Sara," Clint says, holding her gaze. "Way better than 'new girl'."

This makes Sara smile. Which makes Clint smile. Sara's face warms.

She's smiling, this is good! thinks Clint, who may have been tipped off by Megan that Sara was interested in him.

"You see, I uh... I've been wanting to introduce myself for a couple days now," Clint says with enamored timbre, "but I haven't been able to think of anything cool or clever to say, so... I decided to wait... and then I gave up on waiting, so here I am." Disarmed by his manner, Sara's anxiety falls away.

"Okay," breathes the enchanted one, clothes draped over her arm.

"Since you were just standing here, you know, thinking about joining the Marines," Clint jokes as though he didn't just flag her down and run the length of the Athletic Department, "I thought I would stop and tell you my name is Clint. Maybe see if you wanted to go to dinner with me." *Please say yes. Please say yes. Please say yes. Please say yes.*

Rendered speechless, Sara leaves him hanging in an awkward silence.

"I mean, it doesn't have to be dinner. We can do whatever. We can go to a movie or shoot pool or... go bowling, or..." Clint forgets he is nervous. "Or whatever, I don't care, as long it's something you want to do. I mean, we can rob a liquor store if you want, that's fine, as long as we can make a date out of it. But I would like to get something to eat first."

Sara chortles for the first time in her life. The back of her hand to her mouth, she is embarrassed by the sound she made. But she is smiling. Believing progress, Clint is cautiously encouraged.

"Okay." *Quit while you're ahead!* Clint shouts at himself as he begins stepping away. "You haven't said no, which is almost half of a yes. So, I am just gonna let you think about it."

Sara wants to say something but can't.

"If you decide you'd like to go out sometime, let me know." Clint continues backing away, giving all the space in the world. "If you decide that you *don't* want to go out with me, please think about it some more."

Yet to even process the kindness during lunch, the lagging girl stands frozen. *Oh my... is this really happening?*

"Until then, you have a good night and take care." And with that, the guy with a slight drawl and tiny gap in his grin turns and walks away.

After some time, Sara starts to breathe again.

8:20 PM
The swing

Lady could tell something was going on even before Sara made it to the car. Her face resplendent, Sara almost swallowed her tongue when the smirking gal said, "It's a boy, isn't it?" Lady wishes she would talk to her about things, but Sara only seems to want to talk to Babe about anything of importance.

Waiting for Babe to wake from his nap, Sara—belly full of pizza rolls and pie—fell asleep herself. Woken by the sound of his footrest lowering, she was already putting her shoes on when Babe poked his head in to invite her to the swing.

With much to talk about, the two fresh off naps sit side-by-side. "Pretty night," Babe thinks aloud, enjoying the scent of summer.

"Yeah," Sara pensively murmurs; her swing buddy digging a pack of smokes out of his pocket. Not knowing how to bring up what she wants to talk about, Sara nervously picks at her nails.

Babe yawns deep and long, causing his eyes to water. He looks on to what little sun remains as he hands over a smoke. "So," he begins, sensing Sara has something on her mind, "how was school today?"

"It was a *very* good day today," Sara prompts Babe to ask more.

"Anything out of the ordinary happen. Anything with Devon or Maddie?"

"Megan," Sara corrects, leaning for a light.

"Oh yes, Megan." *I swear she goes from fourteen to twenty-seven when she has a cigarette between her fingers.* "Are the other girls treating you okay?" he pries with cautious optimism.

"Yes," Sara perks, "they have become *very* nice to me – most of them, I mean."

"Really?!" says Babe, delighted at the news. "What about the girl who pushed you down?"

"She didn't come to school today," Sara's attention trails into the distance.

"Okay," Babe decides not to dig, "but you say the other girls are being nice to you, though?"

"Today we made cupcakes in Home Ec and I helped. Before I would just kinda stay out of the way, but today, everyone was really nice, and I helped a lot."

"What kind of cupcakes did you make?" *Sure are coming out of your shell, kid.*

"We didn't finish them. We just mixed up the batter. We will cook them on Monday."

"You still never told me what flavor they are," Babe nudges.

"Oh yeah, um, strawberry. Some people picked chocolate. We picked strawberry."

"Are you going to share the cupcakes with the other girls?" Babe teases the girl with the appetite of a gorilla.

"Yes!" Sara bashfully giggles.

"That's mighty nice of you," Babe stops to take a long drag. "So, I have to ask," he proceeds hesitantly, "what, uh... What happened to the girl who pushed you down?" Fresh is his memory of the steely-eyed visitor who appeared night before last.

"I heard she hurt her knee playing volleyball." The mind underneath shifts Sara's focus. "Oh, and Devon is going to go jogging with me tomorrow!"

"That's great, kiddo," Babe says, still curious about the girl who pushed her. "If I'm awake when she comes by, I'd like to meet her."

"Okay!" chimes Sara, happy to introduce the two. She takes the last drag of her cigarette and snubs out the butt on the concrete.

After a lull in the conversation, Babe breaks the silence. "So, have you met any boys at school?"

Saturday, August 30th, 2014

1:27 AM
Sara's bedroom
Sara dreams.

Standing along a busy street, Sara looks across four busy lanes of traffic to see Twelve looking back. There is no sound. No wind. No drivers in the cars.

While Sara wears designer clothes in front of a beautiful building, her sister dons ripped jeans and a stained t-shirt in front of a haunting structure of gray brick.

The TV casts a glow on Sara as she groans, kicking the comforter off sweaty legs.

Cars zip past. Sara is scared, unable to run. The cars serve as a moving barrier. Terrified, Sara knows Twelve would cross if she could.

With an understanding only available in the cognitive world beneath, Sara knows the Natasha hates her and why.

Unable to make a sound in what feels a vacuum realm, Sara mouths the words, "I'm sorry."

8:07 AM

Her blanket on the floor, Sara wakes to Lady's harmonious notice. "Sara, your friend is here!"

Huh? She thinks as she rouses. *Oh yeah! Devon's here!*

8:21 AM

Devon makes small talk with Lady while Sara brushes her teeth, pulls her hair back, and eats a muffin. Soon after, two ponytails go bouncing down the straight lane headed South. Her stride more powerful than a week ago, Sara keeps having to slow so Devon can keep up.

Nicknamed "Indian Runner" for her stamina, Devon can run – but not like this. After pushing herself hard as she could for as long as she could, the girl with legs and lungs on fire cries out, "All right! Slow down!"

Realizing she left her friend behind, the now 122-pound Sara lopes back.

"What's wrong with you?!" Devon forces in between gasps.

"Uh... I tried slowing down."

"Good God!" Devon wails. "I'd have to have a rocket up my ass to keep up with you!" Having three older brothers has somewhat affected the otherwise genteel girl.

"Maybe we should walk for a while," Sara offers.

"Either that or carry me!" Devon manages, hands on her hips.

Walking for a time, the two enjoy a morning coolness certain not to last.

Once Devon's breath returns, she gently broaches the elephant in the room. "So... You gonna tell me what happened in the locker room?"

"Tell you about what?" Sara's mind keeps working to reject the memory like a bad implant.

"Um... Shelly?" Devon utters.

Mentioning the incident sends a probe into Sara's murky recall. Curious herself, she tries pulling the hand-me-

- 160 -

down memory into focus. Devon waits patiently as Sara works to defy the mind beneath.

Why is she having so much trouble remembering? wonders Devon.

"We were in the bathroom – I mean the locker room," Sara says as though staring into the Grand Canyon. A car slowly rolls by.

"She came out and...and she tried to hit me." Sara stops, waiting for more to come to her.

"Did you punch her?" Devon asks, glad to finally be able to talk with no one around.

"No," says Sara, eyes glued to the ground. Another car crawls by. "Not at first." From a perspective of one standing in front of the hand-dryer, she sees Shelly curl up into a ball and roll onto her side. The vision is choppy. Emotionally removed, Sara sees Twelve not as identical to herself – but a faceless female form.

"Did Shelly try and punch you?" digs Devon.

"She tried to punch her." Sara answers as though in a trance.

"Her?" Devon finds Sara's wording odd.

"Yes." Sara continues her bystander's account. "Shelly tried to punch her but she moved to the side and Shelly missed." Sara sees the faceless woman step into a low defensive stance, pivoting to the outside as Shelly's punch sails past. Then throwing a wicked knee into Shelly's outer thigh. Her crumpling body being seized, lifted up, and driven back down.

"She kneed her in the leg," Sara mumbles so low Devon need lean in. "And slammed her."

"On the tile?" Devon winces.

"And punched her in the chest," Sara adds with a blend of sympathy and disgust.

"You keep saying 'she'-" points out Devon; now wanting to check Shelly's chest for a bruise.

Staring into the past, Sara's vantage changes – but not to Twelve's perspective looking down, but Shelly's point of view looking up. Sara sees smoldering rage in the face she

- 161 -

mistakes for her own. Slapped out of her stupor and into a state of fright, Sara literally runs away from the subject.

"Ah, shit," Devon grumbles before taking off after her.

"St-stop!!" Devon shouts after a quarter mile, her face twisted and her legs and lungs aflame once again. Sara stops. Veering off the blacktop, it takes all she has to keep from collapsing in the grass. Doubled over once again, the one born with a perfect tan watches her Olympian of a friend make her way back.

"Y-you're killing me," says Devon manages between huffs.

"Are you okay?" asks Sara, incapable of understanding why Devon is tired so soon.

"I should've brought a bicycle."

"It might help," Sara agrees without sarcasm.

Devon drops to one knee.

"Have we gone too far?"

"*Far* isn't the problem." Devon swipes at her eyes with her shirt. "You said that you... you said that you *jog*... *This* isn't jogging-!" Devon lowers onto the grass.

Sara scans the tree line beyond the hay meadow. The more Sara is out in nature, the deeper her love for it. She sees something moving in the distance. *It's a deer!* The ugliness of the Shelly situation shut away; Sara is at peace once again.

Squinting from the sun over Sara's shoulder, Devon points out, "You don't like answering questions, do you?"

Her focus on the deer, Sara doesn't respond.

"Okay, well," Devon says, a little dizzy, "if you *don't* want to answer, please don't run away. You're gonna give me a stroke or – or a heart attack, or – " She takes a few deep breaths. "Or *something*. Holy hell, I'm too tired to think!"

"Um, all right." Sara goes along.

"Can I ask you a question?" jokes Devon, her hand extended for help getting up.

"Yeah." Sara answers, hoisting Devon to her feet.

- 162 -

"Are you on steroids?!"

"Uh, no." Sara answers, not understanding why Devon would ask that.

Eventually, after her wind returns and dizziness passes, a curious Devon takes hold of Sara's shirt so she can't run away. "Please tell me, *how* did you grow boobs like those and a butt like that in a week and a half, because I have been trying to grow boobs – Hey! Come back here!" grunts Devon being dragged behind.

9:38 AM
On a rural road

With cars and trucks slowly rolling past—some *very* slowly—the two make their leisurely way back to the house. Having learned there are topics Sara prefers to avoid, Devon has been all too happy to fill the air with talk of her wonderful new boyfriend.

Loving any story about a relationship, Sara is all ears as her new friend goes on and on about how the 'super gorgeous' Justin from another school is tall and muscular, and how he is a football player and a wrestler, and how he is super charming and sweet. "He wrote me a poem," Devon adds as another pickup gives a double honk.

After a quick bit of silence, Devon considers asking a question. Unsure how Sara will react, the curious girl subtly reaches over for another handful of t-shirt, just in case she decides to bolt. "So, pray tell, have any of the guys at school, you know, said anything to you yet?"

Sara's blushes, but she does not run away.

"Do tell – and, before you do, know that I am the only person in school that can keep their trap shut. I won't say anything, at all, to anyone. I promise."

Sara, not sure she wants to talk about this, glances ahead not once but twice.

Fearing Sara will take off, Devon tightens her twisted grip. "I will jump on your back and you will have to carry my fat ass the whole way home if you run," jokingly threatens the girl with a prominent posterior.

- 163 -

Unlike the other questions, Sara wants to answer this one. "Clint." His name jumps out of her mouth.

"Clint Fleischer!" Devon belts in disbelief.

"Yeah," answers a jolted Sara. "Is that bad?"

"Is it bad?! Uh, yeah, it's *definitely* bad—if you're any other girl in school, it's terrible!"

"What? Why?"

"Okay, let me get this straight," Devon begins with a blend of disbelief and something bordering envy. "Clint Fleischer—the nicest, most down-to-earth guy in the entire world, the guy pretty much *every* girl has wanted to date since 9ᵗʰ grade, the guy who *only* goes out with girls from *other* schools because he doesn't want to be a 'spoke in the rumor mill-'" Devon adds air quotes. "Asked *you*, the *most* talked-about girl *in* school, on a date? Is this what I am understanding?"

Sara stares at the flabbergasted girl with her palms up. "Uhhh, yeah – " Sara says after some thought. "Wait-! People are *still* talking about me?!" Sara believed that people being nice means they stopped talking about her.

Devon, muttering to herself, struggles to process. "Okay, one thing at a time here," *And this is the same girl that beat up Shelly?*

"Okay." says Sara, confused by Devon's confusion.

"For starters," says Devon, who has reset herself. "You wonder *why* people talk about you? You are not talked about one *millionth* as much as you *would* be if people knew about the Shelly thing *or* the Clint thing. You're just lucky that it was me who figured out the Shelly thing and not someone else."

The fear of being talked about more bubbles up. "You don't think she's going to tell anyone?"

"No," Devon says with her little devil grin. "And if she was going to tell, she'd have done it by now." Under her breath, she mutters, "Little bitch wouldn't give people the satisfaction."

"So, what do you think I should tell Clint – you know, about the date?"

"You didn't say yes already?!!"

10:17 AM
Lady's kitchen
Exiting the restroom, Lady hears the front door open and close. "Look at you two!" she sounds at the sight of a sweaty Sara and a bedraggled Devon. "You two have a good run?"

"She about killed me!" blurts a Devon rejuvenated by the air conditioning.

"Must be the shoes." Lady winks at Sara as she sets the pitcher of juice down on the table.

"If that's the case I want to borrow them," comments Devon as she takes a seat. "Thank you," she adds.

No more than a bit sweaty and pink from the sun, Sara sits down too.

"Do I hear two girls in there?" calls Babe from his chair. Happy to meet any friend of Sara's, he joins the young ladies in the kitchen. He enjoys a cup of coffee while the girls cool down.

"I am glad our girl has a friend like you," Babe says not long into the conversation.

Though Devon enjoys resting, her cold drink, and conversation with Babe, she must excuse herself. The girl with a purple tongue and grape juice mustache has a plan.

10:20 AM
Devon hurries to her cherry-red Jetta for her phone. Two calls later, she has Clint's number.

10:25 AM
Devon seizes the initiative.

Clint, while working cattle with his dad, receives a call from a number he doesn't recognize. He answers while stepping away from the noise. His dad, Howard, soon wonders who is calling, and why his son is smiling like someone who just won free ice cream for life.

Hiding his surprised delight as best he can, Clint makes the girl he has known since seventh grade repeat herself, even though he heard her fine the first time. "How about 7:30?" is the last thing she says.

On her way back into the house, Devon sends texts to both Julie and Michelle. Her mission is underway.

10:31 AM

Devon closes the door to Sara's room. She begins what she has to say with, "Okay, don't freak out..."

Sara gasps. "What do you mean I have a date with Clint?! Why did you-?!"

"There's no time for questions!" interrupts Devon, who doesn't feel the slightest bit bad for the panic she's causing. "I did you a favor! We have to get you ready! You'll thank me later!"

Sara's reluctance falls on deaf ears as she is pushed into the bathroom, Devon's palms at her back. "We're gonna meet Michelle and Julie at the mall at noon and we *still* have to swing by my house!"

"But I-" voices the one watching Devon turn on the shower.

"No time for buts. Chop, chop!" Devon shuts the door behind her. "We're leaving in fifteen minutes!" *You're lucky I'm so helpful!*

The plan is to meet at Mid Rivers Mall at 12:00. Devon told Julie 12:00 but told Michelle 11:00 so that she might arrive on time. Nicknamed "Miss Bossy Pants" when she was four years old, Devon admits that she can be a bit bossy, but only when acting for the greater good.

10:44 AM
Lambert International Airport
St. Louis, MO
Lazlo Set, the bushy-bearded chemical engineer with varying degrees of culpability in bombings on three continents, clears customs with a fake passport. Rather than being taken into custody as his true identity would warrant, the man with a prosthetic leg is on his way to the baggage claim.

The forty-three-year-old Bosnian lost his leg from the knee down while building a bomb for a Pakistani client almost a decade ago. Though hobbled, he has hardly slowed. Wearing a suit, the man with a squat body and wide face looks harmless, even amiable. Accompanying him are his brother Bakir, 45, Bakir's youngest son Zvanko, 17, and their nephew Amer, 21, the middle son of Lazlo's other brother, back in Sarajevo.

Zvanko, a tall, lanky young man with thick glasses, looks around with awe. This is his first time in America.

On the other side of a pillar is the agent who has been tailing the four since their layover in Brussels.

Beyond the baggage claim, waits Lazlo's son, 23, alias Milo Adonovic, with his wife Mira, 21, who is eight months pregnant.

Speaking into their wrists, the agents confirm visual on Lazlo Set, AKA, The Beast of Belgrade.

10:44 AM
The rock house on the hill
Lady signals Sara to follow into her and Babe's bedroom, leaving Devon and Babe to talk in the living room. Trembling with excitement, Lady – standing on a short stool – takes one box after another from the top shelf of her closet, handing them down to Sara to put off to the side.

More curious by the second, Sara watches as Lady pull out a section of wall, revealing a hidden compartment. Her neckline damp from wet hair brushed back, Sara reaches up for a shoe box bowing from the weight of whatever is inside.

Lady carefully gets down. "Okay," she whispers low, "a few years ago, all the people like Babe were given fake money to spend in an effort to mess up the monetary system." Sara listens as Lady whispers. "But we felt the government was doing a good enough job of that on their own."

Sara's eyes widen when a lifting of the corner reveals layers of neatly bundled twenty-dollar bills.

"Now, this money isn't real," Lady reminds, "but it might as well be."

Not the US Treasury's most recent version of the bills, what Sara sees are the notes that were new to circulation almost twenty years ago.

Lady digs out one bundle, begins to close the lid, but then decides to grab a second. After handing the banded bundles to a shocked Sara, she climbs to put the box back in its hiding place.

Sara stands frozen in place.

"Oh, go on!" Lady fans toward the door. "If anyone asks, it's birthday money."

"What's birthday money?"

"Child..." Lady shakes her head. *Poor girl doesn't know what birthday money is.*

"We gotta get going soon!" Devon kindly reminds from the kitchen.

"Go on now! Shoo, shoo!" Lady insists. "You've got to get dressed so you can get gone to the mall!"

After squeezing into a pair of jeans fast growing snug, Sara follows Devon to her car. On it's rear, a magnetic bumper sticker stating, 'A Woman's Place Is In Control'. Radio turned up, the two are soon zooming toward the city.

Devon's daredevil driving offers the passenger wearing a pair of her sunglasses the sensation of a carnival ride.

This isn't really happening. Is it? wonders the girl looking up through an open sunroof.

Devon lowers the volume but still has to talk over the wind. "Okay, we are gonna kill a few birds with one stone today! I have been promising to go shopping with Jules for a while now, but it keeps not happening!"

"Jewels?!" Sara repeats back, her damp hair whipping wildly.

"Julie! The tall blonde!" Devon glances to her right. "Hold on!" she warns.

"Okay!"

Devon jerks the wheel as she flips the turn signal, cutting across three lanes. Nowhere near as scared as she probably should be, the smiling Sara clambers for something to grab onto. "Told you to hold on," Devon shouts to the girl slung over the console.

"Okay, so anyways!" Devon resumes with a shock of hair stuck to her lip. "I love Julie to death, but, well, she just isn't as fun as she used to be! I hate to say it, but she's kind of a drag nowadays." Sara can tell Devon is dancing around something she can't come right out and say. "And if I go without Michelle—hold on!"

Devon punches the gas to catch the end of a yellow light, then jerks the wheel to the left, pressing Sara against her door. Once settled, the laughing passenger straightens her glasses.

"If we get pulled over, you might have to show the cop your boobs! They're bigger than mine!" teases Devon.

"What?! Wait, no!" bursts Sara, glancing down at what are now C-cups.

"Just kidding... unless it's a construction zone-" Devon utters just loud enough for Sara to hear.

"Why isn't Julie fun anymore?" inquires Sara.

"Okay, I'm not one to repeat what I'm told in confidence or pass along a rumor," Devon soberly disclaims, "but it's pretty well common knowledge that something happened at a party last year..." Sara curiously awaits further explanation that doesn't come.

"Um, what happened?" Sara asks over the wind.

"Eh, if you ask around, I am sure..." Devon trails off while checking her rear view. "Anyways, I just kinda decided to wait until I had someone else to tag along." Devon doesn't have to talk as loud after turning off the interstate.

"You said Michelle is going."

"Oh yeah, if I take you and Julie and *not* Michelle, then – yeah, let's just say it will be easier to do things the way we're doing them." Entering the upscale suburban neighborhood, Devon slows to a reasonable speed.

"What about the others?"

"What others?" Devon replies, her little red car passing by perfectly manicured lawns.

"The other girls like Heather and Tiffany-"

"What about them?"

"Do you want them to go, too?"

Devon sighs as she pulls into the drive of her two-story home. "That's such an adorable thing for you to say."

Sara follows Devon through the front door leading into the house and up to her room. Looking at the pictures on the wall, she realizes Devon's parents are nearly the same age as Lady and Babe. Sara sits on the bed as Devon multi-tasks, getting ready and articulating her dislike for Tiffany at the same time.

Though Devon's room is bigger and has nicer electronics, Sara still likes her little room better.

By the time Devon is done changing clothes, doing her makeup, and putting on her earrings, Sara has learned that Devon and Tiffany were close until around 8th grade – until Tiffany transformed into the way she is now. Where Megan professes to feel sorry for Tiffany – whom she believes is persecuted for being so pretty – Devon has no such sympathies.

"Tiffany was a snobby little spoiled brat who grew into a snobby little spoiled bitch," Devon informs. Sara doesn't know what to say when Devon, fast becoming more open with her opinions, told her she is glad to see "somebody give Tiffany a run for her money."

Sara is curious as to who this person is but is too embarrassed to ask.

11:43 AM

Devon and Sara rush to the car befitting Devon's personality. Feeling like movie star upon putting them on her face, Sara slides on Devon's sunglasses as soon as she gets in. Because she wants to live, Sara puts on her seatbelt.

Within a few minutes of pulling out, Sara learns Devon doesn't know Heather very well. This surprises Sara. She thought Devon and the pouty-lipped girl with chestnut hair and an oval face were good friends. "Heather can come off a little bristly," Devon says in her candid way, "but I think it's just because she's hungry. She doesn't really say much. How she gets along with Shelly is beyond me!" Devon goes on to tell how Heather absolutely hates Tiffany.

Sara likes how Devon is so direct. She can't help but compare Devon says to what Megan told her. *And here I thought that all of them were such great friends.*

The driver of a Toyota Tundra gives Devon (who may or may not have cut him off) the finger. Devon waves. Sara laughs.

Intoxicated by the feeling of freedom and the company of someone she doesn't feel cool enough to be around, Sara forgets to be nervous about her date tonight. The song 'White Houses' comes on. Sara turns the stereo up. Then turns up the stereo some more. She loves it.

"Who sings this song?!" Sara asks over the wind and speakers. Devon thinks for a moment. "I think her name's Vanessa Carlton!" her voice cuts through the wind.

"I like this song!"

"I can tell!" Devon shouts, stomping the gas to shoot past a van doing 75.

12:02 PM
Devon and Sara arrive at Mid Rivers Mall. Julie has already arrived. Michelle, as expected, is nowhere to be found.

12:04 PM
Devon calls Michelle's phone and sighs. "Voicemail... big surprise."

Knowing better than to wait, Devon leads the trio inside.

12:17 PM
Michelle calls, claiming she will arrive in "two minutes". Devon is dubious. Believing Sara in need of a manicure, she leaves her with Julie and three nice Korean ladies for French tips while she runs a few errands.

Sara is intimidated by the Amazonian with honey-colored hair, but the mind underneath refuses her the understanding as to why. Julie, the one who used to be known as bubbly jokester, looks strikingly similar to the tall, blonde Natasha who put scars on her body and broke her arm.

Distracted by the royal treatment of the salon, the inexplicable anxiety Julie causes soon fades.

1:02 PM

On her way back from *Ladies Footlocker,* Devon gets a text from Julie: *Done here. You heard from Michelle? Where r u?*

1:03 PM

Julie receives a text from Devon: *No. Keep getting vm. Near food court. Meet me here.*

Sara, unable to stop staring at her new nails – and feeling like she can't touch anything – follows Julie to the smell of pizza.

Still unsure what to make of Sara, Julie can't help but find her complete lack of pretension endearing. Preconceived notions melt away as she spends time with the girl who seems as though she has never been in a mall before.

1:11 PM

Devon gets a call from Michelle. After a stream of excuses as to why she's late, Michelle says she is looking for a parking spot.

Because Sara is with Devon and Julie, she eats pizza with a flimsy plastic knife and fork rather than her hands. Not wanting to be thought of total pig, she eats only two huge pieces instead of three or six.

1:21 PM

Michelle arrives. The group of four moves out.

1:35 PM

Sara uses some of the money shoved down her back pocket to buy her first purse. A black leather Kate Spade cross-body bag that goes perfectly with the distressed *Silvers* and dark blue T-shirt she is wearing. Though she does her best to be discreet while paying the $175.00 plus tax, a nosy Michelle peering from around a rack sees the wad of bills in Sara's hand.

Sara puts her fingers over her lips. "Shh."

1:42 PM

As though running down a 'get Sara ready for her date' checklist, Devon says, "Hey, I want you to meet somebody."

"Who?" asks Sara, who keeps pulling back the gold zipper on her new purse, looking inside as though something may have magically found its way inside since the last time she looked.

1:50 PM

Sara enters a hair salon for the first time.

"Sara, this is Armando. Armando, this is Sara," Devon says to the man who looks like a short, chubby Ricky Martin. Devon has been looking forward to this.

2:00 PM

Laid back with her head in a big sink, Sara is having her hair washed by another person for the first time. Her eyes dart around the ceiling as though balloons were popping all around. The man who over-pronounces the "S" sound asks if she would like to try an elegant brown.

Warm water running down her scalp, Sara looks to Devon for guidance. "Um... yeah, that sounds good."

2:08 PM
Collinsville, IL.

In the rundown residence that will suffice until the baby is born, Mira slowly goes about cleaning up after the meal she spent hours preparing. Zvanko (the gangly seventeen-year-old seldom without headphones over his ears and eyes glued to his smart phone) offers to help the woman doing everything with one arm cradling her big belly, but she politely declines.

While Mira puts away dishes, her father-in-law's brother Bakir shaves the hair he grew solely for the trip; and her husband Milo speaks with his father in the bedroom at the East end of the hall. With the scent of borscht in the air, Zvanko and Amer get situated in the room they will be sharing on the opposite end of the ranch-style home.

Much like a mobile home, the small house is cramped, but will have to do.

2:17 PM
Mid Rivers Mall
Devon, called "little devil" by her dad, gets a kick out of watching Sara's first time in a stylist's chair. Head covered in cream-colored goop; she keeps turning back to look in the mirror. Even though she has nothing to do but wait for the dye to set, Sara feels like she should be doing something. Devon stifles her giggle the best she can.

2:45 PM
Feeling left out, Michelle becomes antsy as the salon grows more crowded. Knowing it will be a while, Devon puts down her magazine and leads Michelle and Julie on a time-killing walk. Armando, moving like a mongoose with frosted tips, sashays his way to Sara with scissors snipping at the air. "Are you ready for me to make you look *fabulous*?!"

2:54 PM
Sara is looking up at the ceiling once again, warm water rinsing excess dye down the drain.

3:04 PM

Sara keeps an eye on her purse, still sitting in the spot where Devon was. Underneath the vanilla-colored cape, she runs her thumbs along the glossy tops of her new nails.

Armando lifts, cuts, and snips his magic.

3:33 PM

Sara squints as the guy who keeps using the words "gorgeous" and "fantabulous," blow-dries her hair. The snippets of wet hair on the cape look black to Sara.

I hope my hair isn't black!

3:52 PM

With the flare of a Vegas showman, Armando spins Sara's chair. The girl who scarcely recognizes her reflection on a normal day stares, stunned silent by the sight of hair that cannot possibly be her own. The color of chocolate, Sara's layered style is every bit as elegant as the man with spirit fingers said it would be.

"Do you think it is fabulous, or no!?" Armando confidently asks, his hip cocked, body bent like an "S".

Sara reaches out from under the cape to touch it. *It's so soft!*

4:04 PM

Sara is soon on the way to Kelly; the cosmetologist Armando made her promise to see as soon as she could get her 'fabulous self' down there. Directed to go all the way down and take a left, Sara – the one Devon says is the "only person in the world without a phone" – walks slowly past kiosks, a coffee place, a mattress store, and a giant gumball machine. She walks slowly, as though her new hairdo might slide off if she tilts her head too much.

Same as at school, the girl with painted-on jeans and designer purse over her shoulder notices looks coming from all around. Stares bothering her far less than it did, Sara continues through the dream that has been her day.

4:07 PM

Just missing Sara – and Armando, who was only scheduled to work until 3:00 – a frustrated Devon is now in search of two people. Michelle wandered off some time ago. Now on the hunt for Sara, Devon calls Michelle and gets voicemail.

"Grrr... It's like herding cats!"

4:08 PM
Memphis, TN

Norman lays on a twin-size bed in a cheap hotel. His cellphone rings. "Yeah," he answers.

"Purple night twelve, forty-eight," is all the voice on the other end says before hanging up. Non-sensical jargon to anyone else, to Norman it means *Agent 712 has been secured, be ready to move within forty-eight hours.*

Having met three of the seven Natashas assigned to his authority, the grumpy asset believes this operation a joke. "What the fuck have you gotten me into?" he later asked his contact.

4:09 PM
Mid Rivers Mall

Pretty sure she is in the right place, Sara steps into the brightly lit boutique. Looking at overpriced purses and clutches, and a limited selection of jewelry, Sara breathes in the scent of a dozen perfumes blended into one. Stepping lightly, she approaches the cosmetic station.

"I was told to find Kelly," Sara says to a young woman from behind.

"I'm Kelly!" jumps the startled cosmetologist with green and purple hair. Pointing at a rectangular bump underneath her smock, she soon realizes her name tag is not visible. "Oh my! Where is my head today?!" Kelly reminds Sara of Megan.

"Um, Armando said to come see you."

"Armando sent you to me?! He is such a doll!" gushes the peppy woman, spinning her chair. "Have a seat why dontcha?"

Sara sits in her third chair of the day.

She holds perfectly still as the makeup artist moving with the speed of a NASCAR pit crewman does her magic.

Sara is reminded more of Megan as time goes on.

"You have the tiniest pores I have ever seen!

"What kind of toner do you use?

"You have the prettiest eyes!

"Do you know who Rebecca Romijn is? No? Your face reminds me of hers!

"What kind of cleanser do you use?" ...compliments and questions trail one after the other.

Brushes brush, pencils line, and some funny shaped thing crimps and curls eyelashes. Though Sara tries to hold still, her eyes flutter.

The girl acts like she's never had makeup on before! thinks Kelly.

Her back to the entrance, the preoccupied Sara doesn't see Julie and Michelle walk past as they look for her.

"Go like this," Kelly says, pressing her lips together. Squatting down in front, she dabs at the full lips with a wet brush. The up-tempo Kelly doesn't ask about the tiny scars she notices in Sara's eyebrows. Sara does her best not to blink as Kelly, holding her hair aside, adds just a little more eyeliner. Last touches include a swirling brush that tickles her cheeks and a little more mascara to embolden lashes all the more.

Focusing on not blinking, Sara is unaware of the stares of those passing by.

As the artist gives her canvas one last look, the words, "There you are!" arch from far behind.

"I think your friends are looking for you," Kelly says, turning the chair toward the approaching Michelle.

"We've been looking all ov-, holy shit!" Michelle is stopped in her tracks. Michelle's expression is much the same as if she were staring at something hideous.

- 177 -

"Whataya think?!" bounds Kelly, displaying her work.

"Um... Yeah," Michelle says, turning her head without taking her eyes off the impossibly glamorous Sara. "Julie!!" She bellows with the voice of one staring at a ghost.

Julie, approaches, not realizing Sara has been spotted. "Maybe she went back to the Food Cour-," she sees Sara over Michelle's head. "Oh my God!" she coughs, then more emphatically, *"Oh my God!"*

"Tiffany isn't going to like this," mutters Michelle.

"I was *just* thinking the *same* thing!" gushes Julie.

5:00 PM
Parking lot
Devon's Jetta

Her first time alone with the girl so excited at the discovery of jeggings, Devon just comes out and says what's on her mind. "Um, I think it might be better to, you know, maybe not go to school like, you know, like that." Devon – having to stop-and-go her way out of the crowded lot – can't see through the sunglasses covering half of Sara's face, but if she could, she would see pure befuddlement.

Feeling much like a little girl after a day long dress-up, Sara asks innocently, "Why not?"

Devon hardly knows how to answer. "Well, your hair is fine, but the makeup... I think might be best if you, you know, go the way you usually do."

"I thought you said it looked good," Sara says in a way that makes Devon feel a little bit sorry for her.

"Look, I have come to terms with the fact I am not the prettiest girl in the world," says the one Sara believes strikingly beautiful. "Hell, I am not even bummed about the fact that you make me feel like I should be wearing a bag over my head when I stand near you, but I promise you, you go to school like *that*..." Devon swirls her finger at Sara's face, "things will only get worse."

Why would she put a bag over her head? Make what worse? Sara doesn't know what to say.

- 178 -

"Do you understand?" Devon asks with a compassionate tone. "Yes, it sucks and it's stupid and it isn't fair, but if you go to school looking like human Photoshop, you'll just get a *whole* lot of attention that *you do* not want."

Looking into the visor, Sara considers the over-sized sunglasses more a mask than accessory. *I like the way sunglasses look. I should have bought a pair at the mall. If I wear sunglasses, people can't really see my face. I wonder if I can wear sunglasses in school...* Sara's butterfly attention has fluttered away. *My lips are shiny.*

7:30 PM
Babe and Lady's house
A '59 Chevy, fresh from a wash, eases up the lane. While Devon touches up Sara's makeup, Babe makes his way from the swing to greet the young man with a new haircut and dash of his big brother's cologne.

This is the first time Babe has been farther than the patio for weeks – other than to leave for his doctor appointment. Even though the old spy doesn't feel up to it, he wouldn't dream of sending his and Lady's girl off without meeting the boy first. "Hello there," he says, liking what he sees at first glance.

"Someone's here!" announces Lady, putting away a dish. Keeping a close eye on Babe as he nears the gate, she wants to steady him, but knows he'll want time alone with the young suitor.

Sara, having yet to worry – because she didn't actually believe Clint would show – experiences a sudden wave of anxiety. "What am I supposed to do?" she asks Devon, whom she believes knows everything.

"What do you do?" Devon balks. "It's a date! You go out and watch a movie or eat or, you know, whatever. Talk, get to know each other. Just like any other date."

Troubled eyes stare back.

Then it hits Devon. *No way!* She thinks to herself. "You *have* been on a date before, haven't you?" The longer

Sara doesn't answer, the more painful the look on Devon's face.

Sara swallows hard.

"You *haven't* been on a date before?" Devon confirms. Sara shakes her head, causing chocolate locks to sway.

"This explains a lot," Devon sighs under her breath.

While Devon scrambles to give advice, Lady looks through the window at the two men leaning over the fender of the classic pick-up. The sight of both smiling warms her heart. Though eager to meet the sharp-looking young man, she decides to give them a bit more time to get acquainted. Peeking into Sara's room, she finds the two whispering intensely.

"Well," Lady purrs, "you're not gonna keep that boy waiting all night, are you?"

The sound of the front door opening causes Babe to turn and Clint to forget whatever he was saying. Both see Sara being pushed out the door by Devon, whispering, "You'll be fine, just go!"

Wearing a lilac blouse, a pair of painted-on jeggings Devon just pulled the tag off of, and a silver necklace borrowed for the night, Sara makes her way down the steps. Escorted by Lady, Devon follows, ensuring Sara doesn't turn around and run back inside. Shy – and fearing she will stumble because of more heel than she is used to – Sara walks with her eyes on the ground.

She walks by the swing.

She passes along the short, narrow walk.

And through the gate held open by Lady.

Babe turns to the young man. "She's something, isn't she?"

Clint doesn't hear him.

Hazels rise to blues.

Lady, Babe, and Devon take collective delight at the sight of each, drinking in the vision of the other.

"Hello, Sara." *Is she really leaving here with me?!*

- 180 -

"Uh. Hi," she replies. Something about the look on Clint's face eases her worry. "You got your hair cut."

"Yeah." Seldom at a loss for words, the sight of an orange sun shining on Sara's face causes a moments delay. "Just trying to look presentable."

"You look *very* handsome." Lady steps in to shake his hand.

After a little small talk and a voluntary promise to have her back at a "decent hour," Lady, Babe, and Devon watch Clint open the passenger door and help Sara inside.

"Don't want to mess your hair up," Clint winks at Lady while rolling up Sara's window.

After a quick wave and a wish "good night," the two are on their way.

"Like Cinderella in a carriage," Lady says cheerfully.

"You sure he's a good boy?" asks Babe, scratching his chin.

"Oh, yes. A perfect gentleman," Devon assures without pause.

"He'd better be."

7:38 PM
Memphis, TN
A Diner
Norman – a block of man with short white hair combed forward – gets a text. Were one to look over his beefy shoulders and past his cauliflower ears, the text would appear no more than as a message regarding twelve used cars in Collinsville, IL. In fact, it is a coded notification as to the location of Natasha 712's first assignment.

The operative with over forty years in the field takes a bite of steak that is not good, but good enough. His short, flat teeth grind slowly; displeasure etched in his pocked face. *This is the worst goddamned idea yet!* He thinks of his employers.

In his mind, Norman sees the three Natasha's Nathan rounded up from their handlers and brought back to Tennessee. Gaunt, hollow-eyed, sickly girls. He thinks of the

- 181 -

tall blonde in particular. Finding them creepy, the look in their eyes remind him of the child-soldiers he saw in the Congo.

Preferring to stick his toe in the water rather than diving in, the guy using far more steak sauce than he would like has decided to utilize the handler already in place.

No need in working harder than you have to, he thinks to himself.

7:41 PM
Clint's pickup
"So. What would you like to do?" asks Clint, wishing the air conditioner in his old truck blew cooler air.

"I don't know," says Sara so quietly she can hardly be heard.

"Are you hungry?" he asks the girl with her purse in her lap.

"I'm always hungry." She answers slightly louder.

"You're not shy, are you?" Clint teases, his left wrist draped over the wheel.

Sara shakes her head instead of answering with words.

"I'm glad we cleared that up." he grins.

Sara likes the tiny gap between his teeth.

The city growing larger as he nears, Clint has difficulty keeping his eyes on the road.

"What are you hungry for? Italian? Chinese food? Wings?"

"I don't know. I've never had wings before."

"Really? Wait, how have you *not* had wings before?"

Sara just shrugs.

"Well, if you want wings," Clint informs, "you pretty well have two options. Either a nice, *clean* place with wings that are okay, or a really run-down, cruddy place with *great* wings. Unfortunately, those are your options."

"Why's that?" asks an inquisitive Sara.

"I don't make the rules; that's just how it works."

- 182 -

"I think that I want to try the place that's not so nice," Sara says, not knowing why she finds that option so enticing.

"For the record," Clint says as though stating a disclaimer, "I will take you *anywhere* you want to go. We don't *have* to get wings."

"No, I want wings at the one place."

"Then that's where we're goin'."

8:01 PM
Hackett's Hotwings

Clint pulls into a small parking lot; Sara looks up at the faded sign above the. One of the T's is hardly visible anymore. "Wow... It's more run-down than I remembered," says Clint, regretting bringing Sara to such an unsightly locale.

"Looks okay to me," Sara says, unable to care less about aesthetic appeal.

"You sure?" Clint offers, hoping she will change her mind. "If a bird lands, the roof it might cave in..."

Sara laughs at the vision of a tweety bird causing the tiny building to collapse. "You said they have the best wings, right?"

"Yeah." The old truck continues to idle.

"Then I want to eat here. Plus, I am really hungry."

"Then what are we waiting for?" Clint switches off the ignition. "We should probably hurry before a building inspector shows up and has the place condemned."

Sara laughs. She only thought Babe was funny.

As Clint escorts Sara to the door, he tells her, "You know, if they straighten the place up a little, it could be a haunted house." He finds Sara's laugh adorable.

"I like your hair, by the way," he says, opening the door. "Meant to tell you earlier."

"Thank you."

Is she really with me? He can't believe it.

First in, Sara looks around; four booths, two tables, and a jukebox that hasn't worked since who knows when.

She likes the old newspaper clippings and framed pictures on the walls. The smell of wings hits her hunger high note.

"Hey there, Clint!" greets the cook from behind the serving bar. Carl, who freely admits to being "uglier than a mud fence" makes it a point to remember his favorite customers by name. Clint and Sara step aside so a guy picking up his to-go order can get past. Ninety-five percent of Carl's business is carryout.

"What do you know, Carl?!" returns Clint, nearing the chest-level bar, Sara at his side.

"They are beatin' me *to death*, I tell ya!" jokingly complains the man with a saggy round body and face like a Shar-Pei. "I just got an order for three hundred wings! *Three hundred*!" Carl keeps glancing at Sara. "Don't they know this is a one-man show?!"

"If you messed up a few batches, people might not ask for so many next time," Clint smilingly advises. Sara likes the way Clint interacts with people; how they treat him.

"You know how hard it is to mess up a wing?!" the gregarious Carl booms, his eyes darting Sara's way.

"I'm sure if you put your mind to it..." offers Clint, ready to get back to his date.

"Now I *have* to ask—where did *you* find her?!"

"This poor blind girl doesn't know how pretty she is or how ugly I am, so I'm gonna keep her with me 'til somebody straightens her out."

A burst of laughter sends Carl's big belly a jiggle. "In that case, good lookin', this guy here is ugly as sin and I look like a young Robert Redford!" The flattered Sara blushes as Carl's laugh bounces about the tiny establishment once again. The man from Mississippi slides out a basket with eight teriyaki wings. "Here you go, poor blind girl. This'll get you started!"

Soon, the two are in a booth with their starter basket, and an order of Greek, Buffalo, and more teriyaki on the way.

Clint explains, "Okay, first thing you need to know about eating wings, is there is no way to do it without looking like a total pig. Okay?" Sara listens attentively. "This is not a food for etiquette or manners or civility." Though he isn't trying to be funny, his words make her smile.

It doesn't take Sara long to figure out how to eat wings.

Any initial awkwardness having passed, the two in the corner booth are so engaged as not to notice the stares of those coming and going.

One guy carrying out his order clips his shoulder on the door jamb looking back at the ravishing girl with wing sauce all over her fingers.

Time is lost as dusk turns to night. The world goes away.

Comfortable in a way she has never been, the girl who hardly ever knows what to say finds herself blurting out questions as they pop into her head. Sara is taken with anything Clint tells her about the family farm, the people on it, or the animals.

For the life of him, Clint can't see why she finds these subjects so interesting, but he's glad she does. Lost in her resplendence, he tells all there is to tell of the place simply known as "the farm".

Were it not for the location closing, neither would think to leave.

"Don't come back unless you bring her with you, you hear?" is the last thing Clint hears as he holds the door for Sara, wiping her fingers with an alcohol towelette. After a wave to Carl – and a promise to bring her back – Clint escorts the beauty to his truck as headlights pass by.

Sara nears the old Chevy a little slower than she normally would – not because her belly is full of deliciousness or because her shoes were designed for looks, not comfort – but because she does not want the night to end.

Wanting to hold Sara's hand, but lacking the nerve to reach for it, Clint looks over at lips glowing red from the spicy wings. *She's the most beautiful thing I've ever seen.* He holds the passenger door open while Sara climbs in.

Driving Sara slowly as the law will allow, the entire ride home is spent making plans for tomorrow.

10:35 PM
Home
Sara, after having been escorted to the door and wished a good night, enters the dark house. She hears the footrest of Lady's recliner fall.

Lady follows Sara to her room, rounding the corner to find a girl who could be knocked over with a feather. Sara lifts her puppy-dog eyes to Lady, who was waiting on the swing until a short time ago.

Uh oh, Lady thinks, sighing. *I know that look.* "Have you been drinking?" she teases. Sara's rosy cheeks and glassy eyes could cause one to wonder.

"No," Sara answers, soft as summer rain.

"So, what did you do?" Lady asks, sitting down alongside.

"We had chicken wings at a place called Hackett's," Sara begins as though recalling a dream, "and he told me about the farm he lives on, and how they have a horse named Leo and that no one has ridden him for a long time, but that I could ride him, and he had pictures of Leo on his phone..."

Lady remembers when she felt the way Sara does now. She herself has spoken with the same velvet tone.

"He has two brothers, Russ and Kyle, and his mom's name is Lois and his dad's name is Howard, and the farm is really big and there are ponds—I think he said three ponds—and he had pictures of those too, and the cows..."

Though Lady wishes Babe were up and enjoying Sara's telling of her evening, she is glad for the moment alone. This is the first time Sara has discussed anything with her. She usually goes to Babe.

Sunday, August 31st, 2014

12:09 AM

Lady yawns as Sara, who isn't getting tired at all, is tending to repeat herself. She wonders if this is how Mary felt on the train ride from Vienna. Unlike Sara, who has plans to be picked up by Clint after church tomorrow, Lady had to wait almost three months to see the guy who braved the elements to get to her. Having been told everything from how Clint's mom leads the music at church, to how his youngest brother Kyle is a daredevil who is always crashing things, to how his older brother Russ just got a job at the railroad, the tired Lady with a load of clothes to put in the dryer has to bid Sara adieu for the night.

Sara finds herself alone.

With nothing to do and way too much energy to do it, the girl looking for the remote to her TV knows she will not be sleeping any time soon. Sara looks at her reflection in her sliding closet door. Each time seems like the first.

She waves her hand. The reflection waves back. *That's me.*

1:53 AM

Not sleepy, Sara pictures Clint and Babe side by side with their arms folded atop the fender; sun setting behind them.

2:41 AM

Still not sleepy, Sara replays Clint confessing that the only reason he was brave enough to ask her on a date was because Megan tipped him off.

4:01 AM

Even less tired than she was at 2:41 AM, Sara sees Clint looking up from the bottom of the steps saying, "I had a really great time tonight." She sees him standing with one foot on the bottom step, hand on the rail. Blue eyes. She remembers a moth fluttering around his face, even though there wasn't one.

4:58 AM

Sara gives up on sleep.

5:11 AM

Sara falls asleep.

7:12 AM
Memphis, TN
Hotel room

An otherwise early riser, the operative with a boxy, fleshy face sleeps in. He knows it will be a long day and an even longer night. Expecting – almost hoping – for the operation to fail, he will be giving Natasha 712's current handler no prior notice. No preparation. No advance warning. Norman wants to see this Natasha perform in real time, under less-than-optimal circumstances. If she is going to fail, he wants her to do it quickly.

7:21 AM
Sara's bedroom
Sara wakes. Though she should be tired, she isn't. Still wearing what makeup didn't rub off on her pillow, Sara is instantly spry as if she already drank three cups of the coffee wafting its way around the corner.

"Good morning!" greets Lady, knowing Sara didn't sleep much.

"You look like a raccoon," Babe says, grinning behind his old, cracked mug.

"I do?" Sara says as she sits down. She picks up a butter knife to see her reflection, then laughs at her smudged mascara. Lady and Babe both love that she doesn't take herself too seriously.

"Well, I guess it's a good thing you got that date out of the way so that boy won't be coming back to bother you anymore," Babe mutters as Lady sprays the waffle iron with oil.

"What?!" blurts Sara gullibly.

"Now don't you go razzin' her," Lady wags her finger.

"The way he was looking at her, I am surprised he wasn't waiting on the porch this morning," Babe chuckles to himself. This is the most lively he has been since his chemo treatment last Tuesday.

During mouthfuls of half-chewed waffle, Sara tells Babe all about her date last night. Not one to repeat what is told in confidence, Lady told him nothing other than that the date went very well.

8:31 AM
After a post-breakfast swing and smoke, time slows to a crawl.

8:49 AM
Confident that at least thirty minutes have passed, Sara looks at the clock. *Dammit! It's only been eight minutes!*

9:30 AM

Sara rejoins Babe on the swing he never left. Babe slips her another cigarette even though he's been catching a lot of flak for doing so.

"Is she smoking?!" Lady's voice rushes from above.

"Er, uh-, no!" Babe fibs, clearing his throat. "She was just holding it for me!" Caught red-handed, the two snicker like little kids.

10:16 AM

Lady tries to teach Sara how to play Rummy at the long dining table, but Sara couldn't concentrate if her life depended on it.

11:14 AM

Devon calls the house line to ask Sara how her date went last night.

11:14 AM to 12:28 PM

Sara gabs with Devon about last night. Seventy-four minutes pass by like fifteen.

12:28 PM

Lady sings, "He's *he-ere!*"

12:29 PM

Without reservation and ready to go, Sara walks outside in light blue *Silvers*, a pink t-shirt, and the little bit of eyeliner Lady helped her apply.

Despite his hurry to beat the rest of the family home from the church dinner, Clint takes time to grab the two grocery bags bulging with sweet corn out of the back of his pickup and run them up to Lady on the porch. "Good afternoon," offers Clint in his Sunday best.

"Isn't that sweet!" Lady gushes. "Thank you!"

The boy's no fool, thinks Babe, emerging from the house. "How are you, young man?"

After a cordial exchange of thank you and goodbyes, the new couple are heading down the road, Sara's cocoa-colored hair whipping in the wind.

Keeping his eyes on the road best he can, Clint hurries with hope of beating home the family he loves dearly, but hopes to avoid. He knows he will be cutting it close.

"Sorry I took so long, preacher went fifteen minutes over," apologizes the guy with a bit of dust on his slacks.

"That's okay," replies Sara, having no idea he got less sleep than she did last night.

"Now, you're *sure* you want to go to the farm? There are a million places I can take you in the-"

"I want to see Leo!" The words jump out of Sara's mouth like a little frog.

"I feel like I should have you sign a waiver or something," says the guy slowing for a stop sign. Clint dreads not being gone before his parent's grey Impala pulls in.

Sara looks at him curiously.

"I mean..." Clint tries to explain. "They are a lot to take in. Good people, they are just... a lot." He sees a mental image of his mom, dad, and little brother fighting for Sara's attention like three puppies fighting over a rope.

Unsure what to make of what Clint is saying, Sara just smiles. She knows Clint would never take her anywhere bad. Clint can tell she's excited.

Twelve minutes after leaving her house—twelve minutes that should have taken closer to fourteen—Sara gets her first glimpse of the farm in the distance. The higher the old Chevy climbs the slope leading to the turn-off, the grander the view. *It's bea-utiful.* As though laying her eyes upon the Promised Land, the girl with her palms on the dash scans a rolling green scape. Outlined and divided by barbed wire fencing and gravel lanes; spotted with red and white cattle scattered about. The sprawling vision includes a brick home, a big tan and white shed surrounded by *John Deere* tractors, and all kinds of equipment pulled by the shiny green and yellow machines. There are tall trees, grain bins and a big shimmering pond – *But no Leo*, notices the wondrous Sara.

Once at the crest of the hill, Clint turns right onto a gravel road.

"We might have made it," says a wishful Clint, looking long ways across the pasture for his brother and parents' cars. He nears the lane leading to the brick home. "I don't see Kyle's car." Hoping against hope, he knows this means nothing as the gray Impala could be in the garage and his little brother could be anywhere.

Heading down the lane, Clint sways to dodge cow patties; Sara watches two bull calves push head-to-head. *That is so cute!* She wants to run out and pet them both.

"You ever ridden a four-wheeler before?" Clint asks.

"No." Sara says, hoping that's not a problem.

"That's okay, you can ride with me." Clint hides his grin
While waiting for a cow taking her sweet time crossing the lane. "Sometime today would be nice," he says under his breath to the cow.

The red truck continues on.

Clint and Sara drive over the cattle-guard (that keeps the livestock out of the fenced in yard) and into one of the parking spots between the house and big shed.

"The Hill" – the Grand Central Station of the farm. The house. The shed, where equipment is stored and repaired. Where Howard's hunting dogs bark in their pen. A place most always in motion – is quiet. *Quiet. Almost too quiet,* Clint jokes in his head.

The guy hopping out of his truck and heading for the shed feels lucky, but knows he isn't in the clear yet. *They could be here any minute,* he thinks with much the mindset of one amidst a prison escape.

Sara watches him push back one of the shed's two big, white sliding doors, revealing even more tractors and implements inside. Biting at her cherry-glossed lip, Sara follows. The huge machinery makes her feel tiny, like a mouse in a kitchen. She likes the smell of the motor oil and grain dust.

Off to her left, the Southeast corner of the metal building, the machine shop area. Every tool imaginable scattered about a work bench and two welding tables. Sara takes inventory as Clint makes his way to the bigger of two four-wheelers kept in the Northeast corner. Bay windows facing both the East and the South, a welder, cutting torch, an air compressor as large as a refrigerator, red *Craftsman* toolboxes stacked atop one another. She likes how everything has a place and a purpose.

VROOM!

Sara's attention snaps to the revving Big Bear 400. After clunking it into reverse, Clint backs the aptly named ATV up alongside.

"Well?" Clint invites, sitting astride the rumbling machine.

Without a moment's hesitation, Sara hops on behind. Clint thumbs the throttle just as his mom and dad's car crests the swell of a hill halfway down the lane. Like a bank robber fleeing the scene just before the cops arrive, Clint and Sara shoot past the house, over the cattle-guard and across the pasture.

"What's that thing back there in the ground?!" Sara yells over the engine, referring to the 4' x 8' rectangular grate of fat pipes buried level with the ground.

"That's called a cattle-guard!" Clint hollers over his shoulder. "The cows don't like stepping on those fat pipes running side to side! Keeps them out of the yard!"

"Okay!" Sara hollers back, her curiosity sated for now.

Arms around Clint's waist, the girl on the back of the four-wheeler twists to look at the four-door Sedan nearing the house. Looking back are a Howard and Momma Lois, hoping for a glance at the one Clint described as the prettiest girl he's ever seen.

"Lois Mae," smirks Howard, his neck craning. "I think I figured out why Clint's head has been up his ass the last few days."

"Is that Sara?" Lois asks, looking behind Howard and through the backseat window at the dark green four-wheeler kicking up dust.

"If that's *not* Sara, then whoever *is* Sara is out of a job," he replies, laughing at himself as he often does.

Once at the end of the lane dividing two 30-acre pastures, Clint drives through the open gate and takes a right. A two-story house to her left and sixty-foot sycamores to her right, Sara doesn't see Leo right away – but soon does. "Leo!"

Passing by a couple shiny grain bins, Clint pulls up to the old barn Leo calls home. The exquisitely muscular, but hardly excitable, red horse with white bolt running down the middle of his face, moseys up to greet the girl hopping off the four-wheeler yet to come to a complete stop. Hesitant at first, Sara lightly pets his face, "Your nose is so soft." Melting near the point of tears, she sees her reflection in his big black eyes.

"He likes to have his chin scratched." Clint offers, cutting the engine.

Leo, chest pressed against the wooden fence, lifts his head as curling French-tips hit just the right spot. Slumped on the ATV, one foot resting on the fender, Clint watches the girl of his dreams and his mom's old gelding have a moment. "Starting to think I should've saved Leo for last," he smiles.

"Why?"

"Same reason they save the biggest fireworks 'til the end, I suppose."

"Do you ride him?"

"I have a feeling I'm gonna start," answers the guy who'd take up knife juggling if Sara found it interesting.

"Can I ride him?" asks Sara, looking back at Clint.

"Ride him? You can *have* him," smiles Clint. "I'll just tell Mom I left the gate open, and he ran away!" The guy who knows he should've changed out of his church clothes cannot even remember being heartbroken a couple weeks ago.

"When can I ride him?" Sara bites her lip.

Clint's answer is a quick step into the feed room of the barn, followed by a swift return with a dusty halter and lead-rope found hanging on the wall.

Using the fence as a step, Sara climbs onto Leo's bare back. Clasping a handful of mane, Sara hangs on as Clint leads the docile equine around the pen.

Sara is surprised at the coarseness of Leo's mane. "What kind of horse is this?" she asks, unable to believe she's actually riding a horse.

"Leo is a quarter-horse," Clint readily informs. "They call 'em that 'cause they're good at racing a quarter-mile at a time."

Less than passionate about horses, Clint could never have imagined such enjoyment in walking Leo in circles.

After thirty minutes of doing loops in the pen—and a promise to return—Sara slides off Leo's back. Back on the four-wheeler, Clint begins the official tour. First stop, the river bottom.

Rumbling westward down a long gravel lane, Sara sees a wooded area ahead, cattle drinking from a pond to her left, and a soybean field to her right. Fences dividing every section off for its own purpose, she finds each piece of a big, beautiful puzzle.

After cruising the dusty lane – old fence to one side, shallow ditch on the other – Sara and her escort arrive at the entryway to The Bottom. Clint hops off and opens the gate.

"Alright," says Clint with an expectant look on his face. "Come on through."

Sara, sitting on the rumbling beast, stares at the guy patiently holding back the brand-new red gate. *Uh, he wants to drive this thing?!*

Clint waves in a way as to say, "It's alright, nothing to be afraid of." Sara looks at wooded area beyond, then down at the idling machine.

Nervous, she scooches up, reluctantly gripping the handlebars. A little push of the throttle with her thumb – *VROOM!* – causes her eyes to saucer as the lumbering machine jumps a few feet ahead. Spooked but exhilarated, Sara laughs at herself. A few lurches later and she is through.

Clint shuts the gate and, to Sara's surprise, hops on the back. "How about you drive?" he suggests.

"Where do I drive?" asks Sara, scanning the shaded expanse of maple, oak, and walnut trees twenty to forty feet from one another.

"I don't know," says Clint from behind, gripping the metal rack on the rear. "You're the captain."

"There are a lot of trees," she points out pensively.

"Avoid most of 'em if you can," Clint suggests over the grumbly engine.

"Any other rules?" asks Sara stalls.

"We'll just call that 'rule number one'. Stick to that and we'll probably be alright."

"Okay," says the excited driver. *VROOM!!!*

Hesitation lasting less than a minute, birds are soon frightened by the roar of Clint and Sara ripping down a bending path. "Remember rule number one!" Clint pleads over her shoulder.

Smile blazed across her face, Sara veers off the beaten path, through the pecan grove.

Clint hangs on tight. *At least if I die, I'll show up to heaven in church clothes!*

Birds are scared out of the trees, and squirrels are scared into the trees by the two racing toward the river.

Sara racing from one spot to another; her passenger hangs on. From the chat-pile (a giant mound of gravel left from by a bygone era of mining) to the junk pile (a graveyard for old appliances and other sizable items too big for the trash burner) and all along the river, Sara and her quasi-navigator criss-cross the 100 acres home to deer, raccoons, opossums, armadillos, coyotes, bobcats and squirrels.

Eventually, the girl with speckles of dried mud in her hair is back on the long, straight lane and kicking up gravel again. Sara waves at Leo as she drives by.

"Where are we going next?!" shouts the girl with windblown hair.

"Anywhere but there!" Clint points to North to The Hill.

"Why not?!" asks Sara, slowing as she drives past the empty two-story house the family used to live in.

"You'll see!" Clint answers, pointing due East. "Let's go check the fields!"

"Okay!" *VROOM!!!*

One o'clock soon turns to three, then four, then skips to almost six.

Chore time.

Her butt and hands still humming from the ATV, Sara climbs into the white ¾ ton Chevy 4X4 to accompany Clint during his evening routine.

Clint is in the driver's seat once again. Despite wanting to get gone before any family emerges from the house, he takes time for a good look at the girl with wind-blown hair. Clint believes himself the luckiest guy in the world.

6:23 PM
Collinsville, IL
With bellies full once again, all of the new arrivals – save for Lazlo, who is out shopping – are asleep. Uncle Bakir, face and head freshly shaven, has taken the bed normally shared by Milo and Mira. Amer and Zvanko share the room on the opposite end of the small home. Milo rests on the tan couch behind the coffee-table in the living room while Mira, quiet as a church-mouse, finishes putting away the dishes.

Wal Mart
23.7 miles away
Lazlo, unassuming as can be, finds one of the ingredients he needs in the pool cleaning section of the nationwide chain

that never closes. He *could* get the side-cutters, duct tape, AA batteries, wire, and other items he needs in the hardware department, but will instead spread those purchases over a number of locations.

Mostly household items, the necessities for Lazlo's bombs do not draw suspicion so long as too many aren't purchased at once.

The surveillance team continues unnoticed.

6:26 PM
Memphis, TN
Having awoken just long enough to eat, shower and go back to sleep, Norman continues to rest. Alarm set for 8:40 PM, the asset with his bags packed has a four-and-a-half-hour drive ahead of him. A ghost, a cat's paw, an instrument, a liaison – Norman is many things. Ready to cut and run should things go awry, the man on his back, fingers interlaced, is no more dedicated to the agency than they are to him.

The handler snoring loud enough to be heard through the wall would like for *Operation Dropkick* to work. With an eye for opportunity, Norman has plans of his own.

6:34 PM
The Farm
After doing chores slowly as he could, Clint carefully pulls the chore truck through the sliding doors of the shed and into its spot. Knowing zero hour is upon him, he stalls a couple extra seconds before shutting off the engine.

"This has to be done," he reminds himself.

Seeing Clint happy all day, Sara is puzzled at his somber dread.

"Last chance." Clint warns, knowing what awaits.

"Last chance for what?" Sara asks, looking forward to meeting the people he told her about last night.

"Well," Clint succumbs to circumstance, "hope you're hungry."

"I'm always hungry."

Sara follows the guy with mud-spotted church pants past the tractor he and his dad will finish fixing tomorrow, and out the big sliding doors. Sara stops to watch Clint pull them almost shut.

"Why didn't you shut the doors all the way?" asks the ever-curious Sara.

"So Dad's cats can get in and out," he answers, leading her past his red pickup and toward his mom's plum tree. *Please, God. Please don't let Mom and Dad embarrass me too much. Please?*

"That makes sense," says a content Sara, again enjoying the logic of the amazing place all around her.

At least Kyle's not here, Clint focuses on the positive.

Momma Lois watches Clint and "the prettiest girl he's ever seen" walk alongside her flower bed to the backdoor.

Clint opens the backdoor (used by everyone except Jehovah's witnesses and traveling salesmen) and leads Sara into the utility room. The utility room, AKA, "Momma Lois' anteroom". The place where the men wash up before meals, laundry gets done and extra groceries are stored. Clint opens the door leading into the living room.

Sara is greeted by the scent of vegetable soup cooking and Fox News blaring. Clint's dad in his recliner by the fireplace; his mother in the kitchen.

"Well, *there* she is!" Momma Lois bursts with delight and surprise. The woman looking like she just stepped out of a *Tide* commercial crosses the open expanse to greet her guest. "You *must* be Sara!"

This will not be over quickly. Clint mutters sullenly in his head. *You will not enjoy this.* The volume of *Fox News* plummets as his dad unreclines his recliner.

"I'm Lois," Clint's mother introduces herself with a big hug. "And Clint was right! You *are* the prettiest girl in the world!"

"Nice to meet, you too." Says Sara, receiving her first hug.

Shoot me now. "This is my mother. She has no filter."

Howard – lean, lanky and still with all the dapper panache that caught Lois's eye at the pool twenty-five years ago – takes in the sight of the girl his son has been acting so funny about. "And I'm Howard." Sara turns to the classically handsome man with ears a size too big.

"I'm Sara," she responds, a little off-center from the outpouring of attention.

"Oh, I know who you are," coos the dad wearing a pearl snap shirt. "You're the reason my boy can't remember to close a gate or shut off a water hydrant anymore."

"I'm adopted," Clint solemnly lies. Any hope of his family not embarrassing him blows away like dried leaves.

"You just have yourself a seat," Lois says, clearing the couch of newspapers and uncut coupons.

"You should've run when you had the chance," Clint murmurs.

"Are you hungry?" asks the woman with more than enough sass to handle a house full of men.

"Um, yeah," Sara admits. *Starving.*

Clint and his dad watch Lois redirect Sara from the couch to a spot at the table. Momma Lois is so happy to meet the girl who pulled her boy out of the dumps after his last girlfriend broke up with him.

Standing beside his son, the smirking Howard advises, "You might as well sit down and eat, because this is gonna take a while."

"When he came home last night," Momma Lois notifies without restraint, "and mind you, he *usually* just comes in and goes straight to his room – he stopped and told us *all* about how you two went to eat wings and he went on and on about how pretty you are and how he couldn't actually believe you were sitting across from him!"

"Mom?!" Clint attempts to stop what cannot be stopped.

"You know," Momma Lois forges on, deaf to Clint's protest, "we thought for sure he was gonna try and sneak

- 200 -

you out of here without letting us meet you, but it's a *good* thing he didn't!"

These are the nicest people! Sara thinks as Momma Lois tells what she feels needs known.

"Can't you stop her?" Clint pleads to the dad reveling in his anguish.

"Son," Howard says in a low voice, "if I could stop your mother from doing anything, don't you think I would've by now?"

"Mom... Mom!" Clint finally gets his mother's attention.

"Clint?" Her expression kindly tells him she is busy at the moment.

"She hasn't been here for five minutes." he wines.

"We're just talking." Momma Lois innocently dismisses, swatting at the air. Sara gives Clint a smile to let him know that it's okay.

"This isn't funny," groans Clint.

"It is for anyone who isn't you," Howard chuckles.

"He went out with his last girlfriend for two years and she *broke his heart*," confides Momma Lois, believing anything true is fair game for discussion.

"Mom, you're gonna make her not want to come back."

"Oh, she's okay," assures Sara, quite interested in what his mother has to say.

"You know, I don't think we're gonna be able to get any girl talkin' done in here," notifies Momma Lois, scooping a bowl full of soup for Sara. "I think I want to show you my sewing room."

Sara gives Clint a reassuring smile as his mother leads her around the corner and away.

Soon it is only Clint, his Dad, and a pot of stew big enough to feed ten people.

Clint turns with a look of disbelief. "I think we just witnessed an abduction."

"No son, I think we just witnessed an *adoption*," Howard corrects, dumping soup into his bowl.

"Should I go get her?" Clint asks, his imagination running wild with all his mother could be saying.

"Seal Team Six couldn't get that girl out." Howard scoops a bowl for Clint. "Looking at the hallway isn't gonna get her back any quicker... You're just gonna have to let this run its course. Now eat 'fore it gets cold."

"I thought *you* were gonna be the one to embarrass me," says Clint, pulling out his chair at the table.

"I would've. Your mother just beat me to it."

Clint shakes his head.

Time passes slowly.

For a while, he doesn't say anything. Take a bite, look back at the hall. Take a bite, look back at the hall. A reel of worst-case scenarios stream through his head. He can easily imagine his mother pointing at an old photo album. "And this is Clint's first time on the potty..." He shivers at the notion.

"This is your fault, you know," points out Howard.

Clint inquisitively raises an eyebrow.

"You can't come in here jabberin' like a monkey in a tree about some girl, and *not* expect your mother to take an interest."

"I know," admits Clint, painfully aware his dad is right. "She just comes on so strong."

"Lucky for you, Sara doesn't seem to mind at all," Howard reasons. "Besides, your mom isn't *trying* to embarrass you."

"She doesn't *have* to try," mutters Clint, knowing she means well.

"No, she doesn't. She's just that good. But she'll do you more good than harm, promise you," eases the guy with a better handle on things than his teenage son realizes.

It had to be done. It had to be done. It had to be done. Clint reminds himself over and over again. *There is no way to hide her from them forever.*

Twenty minutes later, a car pulling in too fast to be anyone other than Kyle bounces the cattle-guard and slides into the spot next to Clint's truck. Fourteen years old—and with the ink yet to dry on the farmer's permit – the loud and cocky little brother is the last person Clint wants to pull in the drive. *Please God. Please... Please keep her out of sight until he goes into his room.*

Kyle soon comes bopping inside, his shades pushed up into his tousled dark hair. Armed with GQ features and a grin the girls love, he is the only freshman likely to start on the varsity basketball team this year.

Having seen her baby boy pull in, Momma Lois rushes to introduce the girl she's already decided to keep. The two no more emerge from around the corner when the guy Sara recognizes from the hallway at school blurts out, "Hey, you're the new chick from school! What are you doing here?!"

"Orphans have it so easy," Clint says to himself.

9:35 PM
After three hours of what Clint has coined the "embarrassmentathon," he and the guest of honor are headed toward the door. With a plastic container of soup for Babe in her hand, Sara gets a squishing hug from Momma Lois and a "thank you for stopping by" from Howard. Sticking to his story of Sara having a ten o'clock curfew, Clint finally gets her out of the house. He wonders if it's too late to put himself up for adoption.

Unaware that today was the new best day of Sara's life—and owing Kyle twenty dollars for having vacated the scene two hours ago—Clint apologizes for his family.

"I'm sorry about all that."

"Sorry? Sorry for what?"

9:58 PM
Sara's house
After a rather quiet ride home, Clint walks Sara to her porch. One foot on the first step, and a hand on the rail, he looks up at the girl not wanting the night to end. "I had an amazing time with you today."

- 203 -

"I did, too." Sara's mind swirls. "Your family is very nice."

"I know," he admits. "They're good people. Mom isn't usually that... um, aggressive."

Sara smiles. Momma Lois reminds her of a younger Lady – if Lady had a country drawl.

"She really likes you." The porch light casts a halo. He loses himself in the sight of her. "You have a good night, Sara."

And with this soft farewell, Clint turns for the truck he left running.

"Good night." The words trickle out of Sara's mouth. She doesn't go inside until Clint's truck turns off the Southbound lane. Taillights disappear over the distant rise.

Quiet as a feather, Sara tiptoes as to not wake Lady asleep in her chair next to Babe's. Head swimming and hair a mess, the girl sitting on the edge of her bed can hardly believe the day she had. More amazing than she could have imagined, she can't focus on any moment for more than two seconds before another takes its place.

Sara knows she will not be going to sleep any time soon.

11:11 PM
"Do the cows have names?!" Sara hears herself over the ATV's squall.

"No!" she hears from over her shoulder.

"But the bull has a name!"

"Yeah!"

"So why don't the cows?!"

"I don't know, just never got around to naming-, TREE!! TREE!! TREE!!"

"Whoops!" Sara smiles at the memory of turning the handlebars so sharply the four-wheeler tilted on two wheels.

Winding up rather than down, her mind replays snippets of her amazing day.

"You are as hard as a rock!" Momma Lois proclaimed, squeezing at Sara's shoulder and leg.

"Do you know any good farmhands, Sara? I used to have a good one 'til you came along," Howard teased.

"This soup is very good." she hears herself say.

"It's easy to make. I can teach you how." Momma Lois's voice is warm.

Riding in Devon's car was fun, but not as fun as Clint's truck, the four-wheeler, or the chore truck. But Leo beats all of them added up.

11:58 PM

Sara isn't asleep. Norman nears.

Monday, September 1st, 2014

2:41 AM
Sara's bedroom

Beginning to drift, Sara rises when headlights beam her room bright as day. Looking out the window above her bed, she sees the silhouette of a car pulling up to the fence. The girl on all fours grows uneasy at the ominous sound of as base rock crunching under slowly rolling tires.

Who could it possibly be? Sara knows no one would ever be expected at this hour.

The engine shuts off, then the headlights. Seeing a man in a dark green Ford Taurus, Sara hunkers behind her pillows. Turning off the engine tells her the man parked under the light on the telephone pole isn't stopping to ask directions. Fear strikes.

Oh no! Sara ducks even lower. *He's here to take me away!*

Peeking over her pillows and through the sheer curtain, she watches the husky man reach under his seat. Guessing him to be in his late 50's, the clean-shaven man reminds Sara of the bust of Pompey sitting in Mr. Schibi's class.

He opens the door to get out. Stiff from the drive, he takes his time doing so. Growing more troubled by the second, she tracks the man with a manila envelope in his hand as he walks through the gate and along the patio toward the porch. *He has eyes like a rattlesnake!*

She loses sight of the man wearing a black button-up once he passes the swing.

Sara holds still as a scared bunny.

BAM! BAM! BAM! Sara jumps at the jarring knock. *Oh no!* She is certain he has come to take her away.

Lady's footsteps bring a measure of relief. *Lady won't let him take me,* Sara hopes. The front door opens.

Straining to listen, Sara doesn't realize she's holding her breath. Though the man's voice is louder than Lady's, Sara can understand neither.

Each second feeling like ten, the front door closes.

Breathing again, she watches him make his way through the gate and toward his car. Sara doesn't notice that the manila envelope is no longer in his hand. Lights flood her room again. The car starts and backs down the drive.

Sara hears slow steps. Her door, already ajar, is slowly pushed open by a crestfallen Lady. "Stay awake, dearie. I'll be getting Babe."

Oh, my! What's wrong?! Lady looked like she was about ready to cry!

The fingers of dread creep around Sara's neck. The walls are pushing in. Helplessness becomes her.

Sara closes her eyes... it happens again.

Twelve opens her eyes.

Throat loosens. Helplessness dissipates. Twelve's pulse slows during a deep inhale. Looking around the room she finds "frilly", the Natasha processes what has taken place since she was last awake. First, the warm and fuzzy memory of choke-slamming Shelly – which seems like two minutes ago. Then eating, jogging with Devon, eating, getting nails done, getting hair done, eating, picked up by Clint, eating with Clint, cows, horse, Momma Lois, eating, looking downward at Clint from the porch, and Lady saying, "Stay awake, dearie. I'll be getting Babe."

Dismissing the second-hand recollection of hot wings and four-wheelers, the operative hones her focus on the current situation. Twelve analyses her sister recall.

5'9", early 60s, military swagger, bad knees, probably Airborne, proven killer. One predator recognizing another, Twelve can tell the midnight visitor is a killer. Unfortunately, what Twelve sees offers more questions than answers.

The Natasha climbs off Sara's bed.

As Lady works to rouse a groggy Babe, Twelve, rather than focus on how angry she is about having gone back to "sleep", takes stock of her now 125-pound body.

Even though only four pounds have been gained since the incident with Shelly, it feels like ten. Stronger, sturdier. Stepping in front of the mirror, Twelve sees why she feels so strong. Vision geared to see well in the dark, she takes stock of powerful hips and thighs, a taut waist, and bust projecting enough to obscure her vantage looking straight down.

"Going to have to strap these bitches down," she says cupping her breasts, pressing them to her body. Lifting her gaze, the Natasha looks into a face feeling every bit as foreign to her as it does to Sara. Loving the strength, she loves the face just as much. *A pretty face is more powerful than a handgun.*

"Sara," the Russian hears the Scotswoman from around the corner. Twelve exits her borrowed domicile to find Babe and Lady at the long dining table. Looking haggard and unwell, he waits while Lady draws from a glass vial with an insulin syringe.

Both look over at Twelve, then back to one another. *That's not Sara,* the two think as though sharing a mind. The Natasha's posture, the precision of her grace, the fierceness of her countenance. Not a trace of their girl remains.

Patiently waiting while a flustered Lady gives an intravenous injection, the Natasha watches Babe suddenly come to life.

"I believe we met the other night," says Babe, the moment Lady is gone. He begins to sweat, heart beating fast from amphetamines.

"Briefly," Twelve says, coarse and low. She remembers the moment on the swing.

Wow, thinks Babe, possessing a general idea as to what is happening. *She doesn't even sound like Sara.* Facing multiple mysteries at once, the old spy spurred on by stimulants puts the disappearance of Sara on the backburner for now. Not knowing how much time before he passes out – or dies – Babe knows he hasn't a moment to waste.

"Who was he?" asks Twelve.

"He brought an assignment," Babe wipes his brow. "It's not the assignment we've been waiting for. This is something else." Twelve can see the confusion on his face.

Both can tell something is out of place. Something is wrong.

Giving himself just a minute to acclimate to the injection, Babe stares at the person who looks like Sara, but doesn't. Sharp, confident, and strong, she reminds him of a Spetzna. Relieved in the moment, the man pushing off the table to stand hopes there is a later to worry about.

"Will we be gone long?"

"I don't–" Babe stops to steady his wobbly self. Once centered, the man breathing deeply continues. "I don't think so. We aren't going far."

Believing he could keel over any second – and not caring if he does – Twelve waits for instruction.

"I need you to get dressed," he tells the one wearing Sara's t-shirt and shorts.

"Dressed how?"

"You're going to kill people in the dark-"

"Got it." Twelve turns on her heel. Babe loses sight of the stranger around the corner. Fear and relief collide. The old spy hopes the person who has taken Sara's place will be up to the challenge. *Please protect our girl,* prays the man who never prays.

Twelve flicks on the light and slides the door to Sara's closet. *Well, at least the bitch got clothes.*

With little regard for the way her sister has everything neatly folded, the Natasha helps herself to the darkest pair of jeggings she can find, a solid Navy-blue t-shirt, an old training bra, low-cut socks, and Sara's favorite pair of tennis shoes. Once dressed, Twelve walks into the bathroom, wets her hair, brushes it back and pulls it into a tight bun.

Upon returning to the living area, Twelve is signaled to follow the profusely sweating Babe into the sunroom. Lady is out of sight. The Natasha does not know Babe told her to stay in their bedroom with the door locked until they leave. Twelve follows him the length of the rectangular living area to the small room of bay windows on the Southern end of the home. A room mainly used for storage; Sara has never entered it before.

A musky scent escapes upon opening of the door. Windows turn into mirrors upon the flick of the light. The reflective glare cast from the backdrop of darkness gives Twelve a whole new appreciation for her recently acquired dimensions. Unlike Sara, Twelve likes looking at herself.

"Move that crate with the magazines," orders Babe. Twelve chooses to follow the order. "Then pull back the carpet. Get under the floorboards."

Leaning on the wall to conserve strength, Babe watches the stranger in the cramped corner of the 7'x15' addition. An area filled with totes, boxes and two chairs, there is little room to maneuver, but the Natasha manages.

Soon, carpet pulled back and with a pile of little boards beside her, Twelve lifts a metal case from its hiding spot.

"Go on," Babe urges in a tone he wouldn't use with Sara. "Open it."

Pupils dilate at the sight of two 40-caliber Glock Model 17's, two suppressors, four boxes of ammunition, and two additional magazines. She reaches down and pulls one of the pistols out of the box. It fits her strong hand perfectly.

"Bring them," Babe instructs in Russian, signaling with a nod for her to exit the sunroom first. Babe won't turn his back on the steely-eyed stranger; not until they are out of the house and away from Lady. *She glides when she walks,* thinks Babe watching Twelve walk away with the metal box under her arm. Heart racing and undershirt absorbing perspiration, Babe focuses on one step at a time. Next step—get on the road.

3:06 AM
Interstate 70 East

Twelve and her handler have been on the road for seven minutes since moving Lady's car out of the way and backing the gray 2004 Chrysler out of the white building attached to the carport. Heading toward St. Louis on 70 East, neither has said a word until now. Twelve breaks the silence.

"He's following us," she stoically observes.

"I know," replies a troubled Babe, glancing up into the rearview. *This is wrong. Everything about this entire situation is wrong.* "The man that brought the file... Did you get a look at him?"

"Yes," answers the assassin shifting in her seat. The nineteen pounds gained has changed the way she fits in the world around her. *Probably should have put on a second sports bra.*

"Have you ever seen him before?"

"The guy three cars back?" Twelve recognizes the headlights. "No. Never seen him before."

"Ever seen anyone hand deliver an assignment before?" Babe asks the passenger with two pistols in the floorboard.

"No." Fearing neither the man following nor whatever awaits at her destination, Twelve's primary concern is the driver. *Stay awake, old man.*

The brightly lit cityscape grows larger.

"Okay." Babe begins the rundown, reminding himself he is not speaking to the sweet girl who follows him out to the swing. "I was given very little information." He wipes his forehead with napkin. "Nothing but an address and a standing kill order for whoever is inside. Nobody walks away. Understood?"

"How many?" Twelve asks, confident in her abilities.

"Didn't say." Feeling he has let Sara down, Babe turns to his passenger, "I'm sorry. I thought we had more time." He hopes his girl can hear him.

Disinterested in any sentiment to her usurper, Twelve focuses on what lay ahead. With killing on her mind, she goes about checking her weapons and screwing the suppressors into the end of each barrel. No need to look back for the guy in the dark green Taurus; she knows where he is.

3:36 AM
Driving through the brightly lit city, the gray Chrysler is one of an endless line of automobiles going the same way; just another red ant passing under the cornstalks of steel and concrete looming over. Twelve sees The Arch. Though she saw it en route to John and Johanna Smith's home, it looks different now.

Though wired from the injection, Babe can hardly hold his head up as he puts the city and The Arch in his rear view. Running his hand through sopping wet hair, he hopes for nothing more than another chance. He glances over at Twelve. Though she looks like Sara, Babe does not find her beautiful.

3:49AM
Twelve sees the Collinsville exit.

3:50 AM
After getting off the exit, Babe enters a lower-middle-class neighborhood—an area where vinyl siding becomes more cracked, paint becomes more faded, and yards become more unruly the deeper one goes. Scanning her surroundings, Twelve sees houses missing numbers, vehicles

in disrepair, and porchlights mostly off or busted. A quiet night, only two have been on since the last turn.

With his police scanner on the dash, Babe slows to a crawl in front of a tan, ranch-style home. Leaning over the armrest, he cranes his neck so as to be double certain he is at the correct address. In front of the run-down residence is a late-model Honda Accord very much out of place.

Address confirmed, Babe gently pulls to the end of the street where he turns around and stops. Face blanched and looking as though he might vomit, he stares down the dreary path lit by streetlights and the moon.

Surprised he's made it this long, Twelve gives the failing man a moment to collect himself.

"I didn't see any lights. Probably means their asleep," Babe manages between huffs. He clears his throat. "When I stop, you get out. No hesitation. Speed and aggression."

Veiling her excitement, Twelve looks at her handler as though he were giving her a grocery list.

"Do a full sweep," Babe forwards the orders. "Nobody walks away." He finds the Natasha's poise disquieting. "I'll be waiting."

Twelve turns from Babe to looking straight ahead. This is her way of saying "Let's go." In gear once again, the Chrysler pulls ahead.

Shock and awe, Twelve thinks to herself. *Shock and awe.*

Drawing near the end of the walkway leading from the street to the front door, Twelve estimates twenty steps once she's rounded the rear of the car. Before coming to a complete stop, the Natasha dressed skin-tight is out the door.

Babe watches bold strides from behind as the woman with a Glock in each hand and malign sense of purpose marches her way to the door.

POP! POP! One bullet passes through the doorknob lock. The other through the deadbolt. A size seven stomp-kicks the front door wide open. The brightness of a living room light punches Twelve in the eyes.

No one is asleep.

Time stops, but only for a moment. Pupils contract. The five seated in a crescent-style swath around a coffee table (littered with bomb-making materials) register a look of shock. The Natasha opens fire.

POP! POP! Lazlo, on the left end of the couch, hears a crunch as the first bullet passes through his bushy beard, pulverizing his jawbone. The second enters below his left eye.

As though in slow-motion, the Natasha sees Lazlo's teeth jump out of his mouth like popcorn.

Holding his breath as his heart skips a beat, Babe looks helplessly on from the street. Yellow glow outlining her silhouette, Twelve can be seen inside the doorway, standing strong as the jolt of each shot passes through her. Brass shell casings flick, shimmering as they tumble. Babe is frightened for his girl.

Only four seconds have passed since the lock was shot. Amer, Zvanko, and Milo scramble to get away. Uncle Bakir – next to his dead brother on the tan couch – reaches for the 9mm on the coffee table.

POP! POP! POP!

Bakir receives three hollow points to the face and neck from less than four steps away. The contents of Bakir's skull hit the curtain behind as Amer and Zvanko make a break for the bedroom down the hall to Twelve's right. Milo to the bedroom at the end of the hall to her left.

Twelve extends her arms as though on a cross, pointing down each hallway. Eyes on the two brothers flopping and gushing red on the couch, she fires both directions.

POP! POP! POP! with her left.

POP! POP! POP! with her right. Three and half seconds have passed since Uncle Bakir's bald head burst open.

Lazlo's corpse slides off the blood-drenched couch the moment his son Milo falls. Wedged between the couch and his coffee table/workstation, the *Beast of Belgrade* flails and jolts as his son's lungs fill with blood.

Bakir is all but still as three 10mm rounds strike his youngest son.

Splitting the door while diving into the bedroom, only Amer escapes Twelve's wrath. *Grrr!* The Natasha is angry at the tall, skinny Zvanko for not falling quickly, enough, shielding the guy in front of him.

Twelve looks left at Milo. *Dead.* Looks right at the groaning Zvanko. *Wishes he was dead.* She disappears (to the right) out of the doorway. Doing so reveals the splattered crimson disaster that is the couch.

"God damn," Babe gushes with awe. Uncle Bakir lay sprawled, head sheered at the bridge of his nose. Lazlo's legs continuing to churn.

Walking calmly past the television in front of the big blacked out window, Twelve goes to see about the olive-skinned man who left the others for dead. "Don't run from me," she taunts, pistol pointed over the fallen teen and into the bedroom. "You'll only make it worse."

Twelve glances down at the moaning Zvanko; with a mangled chunk of lead lodged in his tailbone, right arm almost severed at the elbow, and his right ear sheared off by a graze. Her eyes on the door, she doesn't even look down.

POP! the boy stops groaning.

Twelve listens closely...

To provoke a response, she taunts again. "Hey... You want to come out so we can talk about this? Maybe let me shoot you?" Twelve is surprised by her new sense of humor.

Squatting down – both pistols angled upward – she listens closely. Amer's breathing gives away his position.

That is all the Natasha needs.

Twelve looks past the door, now split and hanging on its hinges, to see the bed her target had disheveled when he dove inside. *Around the corner to my left. Seven or eight feet,* the Natasha calculates while pulling off one of Zvanko's sandals. *He's jumpy.*

Cat and mouse.

"I'm gonna come in," Twelve announces as though talking to a child. "One. Two. Three!" She tosses the sandal about head level.

KA-BOOM!!!

A twelve-gauge blasts a hole through the door and out the side of the house, sending splinters and dust into the air.

"Sara!" Babe cries at the obliterated wood, insulation, and vinyl siding exploding from the side of the house. Silence has been broken.

Time slows for Twelve as she waits and listens.

SCHLICK The first action of reloading another shell. In a sliver of a moment – the blink's worth of time between pumps of the slide – Amer registers only a glimpse of the phantom amidst a cloud of dust and wood chips still falling.

POP! POP!

The first bullet strikes the trim along the closet. The second enters the closet by way of his mouth and out the back of his head. Shotgun falling from his hands, the nephew of the infamous Lazlo Set crumples like a marionette with the strings cut.

Assuming the shotgun blast has cops on their way, Twelve; hops over Zvanko, walks briskly through the bloody living area and through to the immaculately clean kitchen.

A glimpse of Twelve passing through the doorway allows Babe to breathe again. *Just come on!* He thinks, no longer caring about the mission.

"Nobody walks away." The Natasha recalls, approaching Milo, face down and hemorrhaging. His head near the open bedroom door; his body blocking the entry way to the small bathroom with its door closed. Wheezing, gurgling breaths clutter the air.

POP! Milo is silent.

Twelve hears whimpering coming through the bathroom door. She identifies the sound as female. She

- 216 -

touches the barrel of her Glock to the door at torso level. Order is to kill everyone. Something stays her hand.

"Are you armed?" Twelve demands.

"No!" Mira sobs. "I have a baby." Sitting on the lid of the toilet – arms around her belly – she shields her unborn.

The bathroom door bursts open. Before Mira can scream, a Natasha is lording over her; two warm barrels pressed against her neck. Her trembling hands up, the blubbering mother-to-be begs in her native language.

Something narrowly convinces Twelve to spare the cringing woman.

Her eyes clamped tight; Mira can see neither the monster standing over nor her murdered husband just outside the door. By the time she opens them, the Natasha is gone. Mira sees Milo and screams.

Twelve hears the pregnant woman's anguish as she exits the home, flicking off the light on her way out.

Relieved at the sight of her once again, Babe – and all the curious folks who've come out since the shotgun blast—watches Twelve glide down the steps and make her way along the concrete strip leading to the street. Police scanner squawking, he knows the cops are on their way.

Shades lift and doors open as more neighbors rouse to the commotion. Pistols held close to her body; the Natasha discreetly approaches the vehicle. Nearing the end of the walk, Twelve tucks the 40-calibur in her right hand under her left armpit in order to free a hand to open the passenger door.

Panic strikes Babe when a pregnant woman with a pistol appears from the darkened doorway.

"Sara!" Babe shouts as a bang sends the unsuspecting Twelve twisting to the ground. Whirling around while the crack of the 9mm still echoes, the buckling Natasha fires back.

POP! *POP!*

Falling into the grass along the sidewalk, Twelve hears the sound of her first shot hitting vinyl siding as the woman with bullet in her lung tumbles back into the darkness.

Porchlights pop on one after the other as half of the neighborhood peers to see what's going on. Spectators look on as the white-haired driver lends aid to the woman pressing her hand to her side. He can be seen picking something up off the concrete as she staggers to her feet. They watch the wounded woman refuse help. Both drag themselves to their side of the car. Babe and Twelve fall into their seats.

The dome light turned off; the car is lit by the streetlights overhead. The tint of fluorescence causes the blood coating Twelve's fingers to appear black. *Fuck! That's liver blood!* fears the Natasha.

"How bad is it?!" pouring sweat, Babe straightens up in his seat.

"Just drive!" Twelve grinds, laying her seat back. Headlights turn on, causing those ahead to squint as the Chrysler drops into gear.

The gray car speeds away.

The searing pain under Twelve's pressing hands pales in comparison to her blazing rage at having spared the pregnant woman in the first place.

"How bad is it?!" Babe hollers again. Flipping on the dome light reveals saturated cloth and hands slicked in cherry-red blood. Not black.

"It's not my liver," says Twelve with relief. *Thought for sure that was black*, thinks the Natasha with a dime-sized hole just above her right hip. She lifts her drenched shirt to inspect.

Lot of blood... worries Babe, with a bit of relief as to the location of the wound. He turns off the light. Driving past houses and under streetlights, the inside of the car alternates from bright to dim. Each passing flash illuminates Twelve's bloody hands.

"You're gonna be alright, Sara! I'm getting you to a hospital!"

"No!" Twelve roars; both rejecting the hospital and the name Sara. "I *deserve* to die for a fuck-up like that!" Pressing down causes warm wetness to squish between her fingers. "Should've killed that bitch when I had a chance!"

"You *need* a hospital," Babe insists as he turns onto the street leading back to the interstate.

"I said *No!*" Unwilling to suffer the indignance of capture, the one now believing her wound less than mortal grits her teeth, embracing the wage of stupidity. *Should've killed that bitch when I had a chance! Should've killed that bitch when I had a chance! Should've killed that bitch when I had a chance!* She repeats in her head.

"Where did she come from?" asks Babe, trying to make sense of what happened.

"Not now, old man," spits Twelve.

Babe keeps his hands on the wheel and eyes straight ahead as a police car with its lights on and sirens blaring passes in route to the scene they just fled. Stressed and soaking wet, the over-taxed man wipes his burning eyes and forehead.

Two miles later he turns onto the highway. Eyes darting between the road and the one breathing long and slow, Babe wants to turn on the dome light − but feels it better not to disturb the Natasha with her eyes closed.

Five quiet minutes pass. Babe can see the city in the distance.

Feeling 100% responsible for what has taken place, he hesitantly asks, "Has the bleeding stopped?"

"Mostly," answers Twelve without opening her eyes.

"How bad does it hurt?"

"I don't think I'm going to die," she answers serenely.

"We're gonna get you taken care of," Babe promises. "You sure you don't want me to take you to the hospital?"

Twelve doesn't answer.

Neither speak as an eighteen-wheeler rumbles past.

"They're all dead," Twelve calmly debriefs, her eyes still closed.

"I figured," Babe replies, not caring about them. He wonders if Sara is still in there.

Not another word is said as Babe, in need of medical attention himself, drives through the city and toward St. Charles. The cool air from the vents has turned Twelve's blood to a sticky brown paste, swelling has mounted a bulge along her side.

After an eternity of forty-three minutes, Babe arrives at the winding driveway of home. Each bump and divot is felt as Babe climbs the unpaved drive gently as he can. Twelve curls her toes, hissing through clenched teeth as her body lightly jostles.

"I'm sorry," Babe apologizes. Headlights shine on his wife rushing through the gate. "I'm so sorry...."

The car comes to a stop.

Twelve opens her eyes to Lady's lifting of the locked door handle. A rapid knocking at the tinted window follows.

"Anything she does is to help you," the fading man says. "You understand this?"

"Yes," answers the assassin, recognizing his tone from the night she had her blood drawn. He turns the engine off; Lady continues to knock.

"You won't hurt her, right? Cause..." an impatient Lady lifts at the handle again. "Cause she's about to go ape-shit."

"I won't hurt her," Twelve, weak from blood-loss, reassures.

"Good," Babe unlocks Sara's door. "Cause here she comes."

Twelve's door opens. The dome light reveals her hands and torso drenched with blood. Lady screams.

Knowing his girl to be in good hands, Babe allows himself to collapse. "I'm sorry, kid... I'm sorry."

"Goodness, gracious!!" bemoans Lady, shaken to her core. Initially fearing the passenger dead, she is relieved when Twelve opens her eyes.

Woozy — and far too weak to refuse help — Twelve is hoisted out of her seat by the stout lass telling her

"Everything is going to be okay" time and time again. All but carried toward the house, the dizzy Natasha uses her free hand to apply pressure to her leaking wound

Red-faced and panting, Lady leads the Natasha into the house and on to the bathroom.

Twelve props herself on the blood-smeared sink while Lady grabs towels and starts the bath. The sound of water rushing fills the otherwise quiet space. "Alright," Lady sounds far calmer than she really is. "Let's get you out of these bloody clothes!"

In the quiet of the night, a spent Babe lays back in his seat. Heart racing. Breathing shallow. Chalk-white and with eyes half open, the man covered in goosebumps feels he has used up the six months his doctor gave him three months ago. *Just give me one more chance,* Babe begs the universe. *Just give me one more chance.*

To the sound of a faucet gushing full blast, Twelve feels Lady's heavy-duty kitchen scissors run down each of her legs. She leans against the countertop as the stretchy, blood-soaked material is pulled away. Disgusted with herself, she doesn't look into the mirror as the scissors slice off the shirt with two holes – one front, one back.

"Good heavens!" sounds Lady at the sight of blood gushing from the exit wound. She bends to look at the front. "You've been shot!"

"I know," Twelve groans, as the pads of Lady's fingertips press lightly along her bruised and bulging lower back.

"I don't think it hit anything vital," says Lady with a pained look on her face. Sad eyes roam about the Natasha's smoothly healed scars and whip marks.

"Just get me in the tub," Twelve sneers. Down to her socks, sports bra, and bloody underwear, the Natasha smears gooey prints along the cream-colored tub as Lady lowers her down into the churning water. The patient bends her knees as she slides down... the warmth hits the wound.

"Grr..." twisting a handful of Lady's blouse, Twelve emits a guttural growl.

"I know it hurts, child," a pained Lady says.

Relaxing in phases, Twelve ignores the fact she was just called "child." Wormy strands and tiny globs of coagulated blood float to the rippling surface.

"That just looks awful," says Lady, catching her breath. *Four or five inches to the left and it would've hit that girl's spine.* The worried lass cannot take her pale eyes off the half-moon bulging from Sara's side; deep purple and leaking.

Lady shuts off the faucet, causing the bathroom to go silent. Hands on her hips, she looks down at the person with her eyes closed and weight shifted onto her left hip. The Natasha appears to be sleeping.

"I'll be right back," says Lady. Assuming she is leaving to check on Babe, Twelve is surprised at the sound of digging in Babe's pill basket. Swift, footsteps near once again.

Twelve opens her eyes to Lady standing with three hydrocodone in one hand and a glass of water in the other.

"Here you go," offers the woman with a husband possibly dying outside. The Natasha opens her mouth. Lady places them inside.

CRUNCH! CRUNCH! CRUNCH! CRUNCH!

Twelve grinds the chalky pills, maintaining a challenging gaze all the while. Lady extends the glass of water. Rather than reach for it, the patient slides down just enough for a mouthful of tub water.

GULP, GULP, GULP Twelve knows Lady doesn't like her – but doesn't care. She runs her tongue about her mouth, sweeping the bitter, grainy pieces out from her gums. Then closes her eyes, dismissing Lady.

"I'm going to get you an IV," she says with a tone of obligation. "But first, I am going to see to my husband. Are you okay for now?"

Twelve answers with a slight nod. The woman she considers "Sara's caretaker" walks away. *Finally.* Glad for the help; the Natasha is glad she is gone.

Very carefully, Twelve raises her hand to her hair. A pull at her scrunchy releases the pressure of her bun. *Ahh, that feels nice.* Assuming a Zen-like manner, she tries to focus on anything besides the white-hot sensation in both the front and back of her side. *Suck it up bitch,* Twelve chides herself. *You deserve this.*

Outside

Initially feared dead, Babe responds when Lady rubs his legs.

"I'm okay, dear," he mumbles, too week to stand. "How is she?"

Lady looks toward the bedroom window. "I don't know," she answers solemnly, more thinking about the girl's mental state.

"What?!" Babe jerks.

"No, no!" Lady soothes, palm pressing upon Babe's chest. "She'll heal," she clarifies, "I just don't know about..."

"Lady," Babe says between labored breaths, "that person in there saved our girl." He closes his eyes. "Sara ain't cut out for this."

"Well, I don't like it. I don't like any of it one bit!" Lady spits in a harsh whisper. Most always sugary-sweet, the lass with a fiery side makes no effort to veil her contempt at the situation.

Harnessing her anger, Lady uses the last of her strength getting the 165-pound Babe from the driver's seat of the Chrysler to his recliner.

Huffing and puffing, the light-headed gal turns back for the bathroom. Walking past Twelve's bloody handprint on the wall, she finds the Natasha tranquil and with droopy eyes. Three hydrocodone on an empty stomach have taken effect.

"How are you getting along?" asks Lady, her hair a mess.

"Well..." Twelve casually points out, "I was shot."

"I see that," Lady leans on the blood-smudged counter. Her usual sweetness is gone.

"How's the old man?" Twelve irreverently inquires.

So, this is who you really are? thinks Lady.

Within thirty minutes, Twelve is under Sara's blanket with the bedroom door closed.

Lady doesn't know what's going on – only that she wants the Natasha out of her home.

5:10 AM

Physically and emotionally sacked, Lady sits in her recliner by Babe.

She thinks she hears something... she turns down the volume. Barely audible at first, the low, muffled moan soon becomes a sobbing cry. Lady springs from her chair, rushing to the pitiful sound.

Upon entering the room lit by a nightlight, Lady finds Sara confused and crying. Consumed with pain, she looks around for the cause of her agony. Crying turns into bawling.

"Shh, child," Lady calms with an arm wrapped around. "You're safe. You're going to be okay," Lady repeats, her heart melting. "I'll get you some more pills for the pain."

"What happened?!" wails Sara, her most recent memory being of Lady opening her bedroom door and saying, "Stay awake, dearie... I'll be getting Babe." Now she is in excruciating pain. She doesn't realize the IV in her arm.

"You..." Lady pauses, unsure of what to say. "You were shot."

"Shot?!" Sara whines as though seven years old. "Why did somebody shoot me?!"

Eyes watering at her girl's agony, Lady pulls Sara close.

"It hurts so bad!!" the distraught girl's words are muffled by Lady's bosom. "It hurts so ba-baad!!!"

"I know it does," Lady rocks her. "I know." The broken girl weeps.

10:19 AM

Lady's kitchen

Far too restless to sleep, Lady busies herself with cleaning that needn't be done.

Babe's been talking in his sleep. Mainly mumbles of alarm. He keeps saying the word "don't", his head rolling side to side. She would rather he be in his bed, but she can neither wake, nor move him in his condition. He drinks when she puts a straw in his mouth. She is thankful for that.

Nodding in and out, Lady checks on her patients several times per hour. She is giving Sara antibiotics through her IV. One of Babe's more potent prescriptions was required to calm the distraught girl and relieve her pain. Wanting to take both of them to the hospital, the woman who cleaned the tub and burnt the bloody clothes knows she can't.

Too tired and wired to think, Lady cannot help but wonder, *What in the world is going on in that girl's head?*

10:24 AM
Hotel room
O'Fallon, MO
Norman, back stiff from spending most of the day in a car, and stomach still not right after two pieces of convenient store pizza, can't sleep. He is still trying to wrap his mind around what he saw through his binoculars. His vantage – looking in between houses from the next street over – gave intimate witness to the slaughter. He can still see the sanguine disaster framed by the doorway. *They don't normally kick that much,* he thought, watching Lazlo after his face was shot inside-out.

Even more impressive to him were the shots fired back at Mira. "Should stayed your ass in the house," Norman chuckled as the pregnant woman fell back into the darkness.

With sudden regard for *Operation Dropkick,* Norman has two plaguing wonders – *Are all these Natasha bitches that good? Why wasn't 712 scrawny like the others?*

10:31 AM
Lady hears whimpering coming from Sara's room. After turning her yellow cleaning gloves inside-out as she pulled them off, Lady pushes open the door. Sara – tangled hair

draped across her face, and chin crinkled up – cries as she pulls at the sheet stuck to her side.

"Child?!" blurts Lady rushing to help. "Let me help you!" She uses her fingertips to lift the discolored cloth from the bled-through bandage. She holds out as long as she can. The innocent one has no idea how she came to be in such a terrible state. "Ayeeyahh!" Sara shrieks. Lady's heart breaks again.

Five minutes pass.

All quiet again, save for light sobbing – relief is on its way. Two of Babe's Percocet are sure to blunt the stabbing, throbbing pain. Sitting on the side of the bed, Lady lightly rubs her back while they wait. "Are you hungry, dear?" Lady asks.

Sniff "Nooo," Sara cries. "But I gotta p-pee."

Hmm, thinks Lady, knowing it will be a painful trip.

Lady gently gets up, leaves for a minute, and returns pushing a mobile commode narrowly fitting through the doorway. Sara frowns at what is essentially a frame with a bucket.

"I'm not gonna pee in that!" She whines, resuming the cry that waned for a time.

"Alright, child," sighs Lady. "Let's get you in the bathroom."

12:21 PM
The school secretary notifies Sara Smith's grandmother she was absent from school today. Sara's "grandmother" informs the school that Sara underwent an emergency appendectomy in the night and will be missing school for an indefinite period of time. The student assistant sitting next to the secretary sees the message and tells one person.

12:46 PM
Many people know of Sara's alleged surgery.

12:49 PM

Clint Fleischer hears the news and notifies his Building Trades teacher he is leaving class.

1:08 PM

The '59 Chevy pickup climbs the winding driveway from the North. Clint is not his usual cool self. After an impatient knock and the sight of Sara sleeping, he is given multiple assurances from Lady she will be okay.

Clint leaves a note before heading back to school. Lady knows how he feels about Sara. She knows how Sara feels about him. She feels sorry for both.

3:12 PM

Sara wakes to the smell of pizza bites and a folded letter beside her:

Stopped in to check on you but you were asleep. Was worried about you. Will come back later. I hope bouncing around on the four-wheeler didn't make it worse. Get well soon.

-Clint

Tears fill Sara's eyes, but not from the throbbing ache in her side. *That is so sweet.*

3:18 PM

Spacey from the pills, Sara calls a greatly relieved Clint. His promise to swing by as soon as chores are done causes her to smile for the first time all day. "I'd come before chores, but I don't trust myself to leave before dark," he tells her. She wants him with her now.

3:21 PM

Her belly full of Percocet and pizza bites, Sara looks up to see Devon in her doorway. Groggily watching TV, she didn't notice her friend knock.

"Hey," Devon softly says to her glassy-eyed friend propped on pillows. "How you feeling?"

"I don't use that," the loopy Sara declares, her finger pointing toward the embarrassing piece of furniture behind her TV. Devon looks over at the commode and laughs.

"Heard you had a pretty rough night."

"I yam okaay." Sara drags her words.

"You look comfortable," says Devon, noting the root beer with a bendy straw and heaping pile of pizza bites.

There is a lag for the stoned girl with a blanket pulled to her waist. "I'm will be pretty good," she jumbles her words.

"Everybody knows you had surgery," says Devon, leaning on Sara's waist-high dresser. "Word spread pretty fast."

Sara shrugs. She doesn't care what people at school might be thinking or saying.

Devon gently takes a seat in the chair otherwise tucked under Sara's vanity. She goes on to tell how Shelly came to school with a brace on her leg and how she has been really quiet, hardly talking to anyone. She then goes on to tell the friend slowly chewing pizza bites about the Saturday night she had with Justin, AKA, Mr. Wonderful.

Lady remains close by, in case Sara slips up and tells the truth about what happened. Little does she realize; Sara has bought the appendicitis story herself. Instead of hearing about wanton murder or getting shot, the eavesdropping caretaker hears a slurred telling of a Saturday night of chicken wings, and a Sunday afternoon of riding Leo and the four-wheeler with Clint.

Devon slips out after Sara falls asleep in the middle of a sentence.

4:32 PM

Clint swings by to find Sara sleeping once again. Preferring not to wake her, he passes time visiting with Lady in the kitchen. At the little round table, Clint gives his account of Saturday night and Sunday over two pieces of peach cobbler.

Lady laughs as Clint tells of Sara barely missing trees on the four-wheeler and how his mother has already put her on the Christmas list. Though dead tired, Lady is glad to finally have somebody to talk to.

6:01 PM
Sara opens her eyes to a dream.

"Evenin' gorgeous." Clint says low. She reaches out to see if he is really there. Her fingers touch denim, she smiles. Everything is okay now.

"*Hey...*" Sara exhales, looking up from her bed.

In each other's company once again, the two who were so chatty all Saturday and Sunday, lay quietly side by side while *Footloose* plays on VHS. Halfway through the movie, Clint takes Sara's hand. Sara likes holding hands.

8:50 PM
After a number of sneaked looks back and forth, Sara drifts away.

Before turning to leave, Clint gently pushes chocolate locks aside for a last look at the girl he believes an angel. Glad for whatever brought Sara to him, he leans down for the tiniest kiss on her forehead. "I'll be back tomorrow," he whispers.

Tuesday, September 2nd, 2014

9:13 AM
Sara's bedroom
While Lady waters her flowers outside, an unsteady Sara manages herself out of bed. At painful expense, she steps tenderly into the living room to see Babe.

Babe's hooded eyes open at the sound of carpet crushing under foot. "Mornin', kiddo," he warmly smiles.

"Hey," Sara softly smiles back through her pain. She steps toward the couch, but Babe wants her to sit in Lady's chair.

"No, over here," he insists, pointing his curved finger to Lady's recliner alongside his.

The girl with glassy eyes takes short steps around the front of him and eases down. It wounds him to see her in such pain.

"I would ask how you are feeling, but..." Babe trails off.

"How are *you* feeling?" Sara asks, more concerned for him. "I am..." Babe stops to think. "I am worried."

"About what?" Sara asks, shifting in search of relief.

"For you. I am worried about you," he answers somberly.

Confused, Sara looks at the man resting his head in the dent along the top of his chair. Having fully adopted the appendix story, Sara has no recollection of the massacre.

"Sara." Babe hesitates. "Gladys and I had a child once—a little girl. Her name was Petra."

Sara, puzzled for a moment, is surprised at hearing Lady's first name.

"A beautiful little baby girl; seven pounds, four ounces. Beautiful." Babe's voice cracks as his eyes moisten. "She was perfect in every way, except her heart. Her heart was not strong."

Babe needs a moment. Hazel eyes pool.

"We lost her," he continues, "after a long stay in the hospital. She never saw the bedroom Lady and I had waiting for her." Sara wipes her eyes. "Because of this... Because we lost our Petra, Gladys and I never had another child. It was just too much."

A moment of silence follows. Sara's throat clamps.

"Sara... When Lady and I learned we were to receive a Natasha, I was not happy. I am sick, I am dying and... I just wanted peace during what little time I have left with my Lady."

The reality of her own truth and Babe's condition collide. The mind underneath rushes to cope.

"When you arrived on our doorstep, my Lady and I both felt... We both had the strangest feeling that our Petra had come back to us. Neither one of us said it until later, but we both... We could not save our little Petra—but maybe we can save you."

"Save me how?" Sara whispers.

"Maybe," he shrugs, "maybe you did not survive your injury. You were shot." The weary man challenges her denial. "Do you remember what happened?"

Denial pressed and memory jostled, Sara is haunted by a rush of glimpses; shooting through a lock, kicking open a door, five surprised men scrambling, walking down a short hall, Zvanko face-down – *CHA-BOOM!!!* – an explosion of splinters and dust in front of her face, falling down to the grass, opening the car door, falling into the passenger seat, her blood-covered hands, looking up through a windshield at streetlights passing overhead.

Life seems to drain from the already sullen girl.

"You okay, kiddo?"

Sara despondently shakes her head.

"I don't want to talk to you about this... not right now... especially feeling as bad as you do."

Sara looks to the man feeling no better than she does.

"But we don't have a lot of time."

Painfully disillusioned, Sara's gaze lowers to the carpet.

"Lady thinks that you think you really had surgery." Babe gently asks, "Do you believe that you really had surgery?"

Sara hears the bang of the 9mm. She shakes her head. "I got shot." The pain in the back of her throat rivals her side.

"Maybe..." Babe offer, "Maybe you didn't survive." Sara looks at him.

"Will they believe you?" Sara asks, soberly aware in the moment.

"Without a body? Probably not." Babe sighs. "But what are they going to do? Shoot me? They would be doing me a favor."

"What do you mean?" She combats reality. "You're taking medicine..."

"Sara, I have pancreatic cancer. About the worst kind of cancer there is." Babe painfully informs.

"But you took medicine last Tuesday," Sara clambers for hope. It's all too much.

"Just buying time, kiddo. Just buying time."

"Can I hide?" Sara asks, imagining herself living in the old white shed outside where no one can find her. "I can-"

"You must *run*." Babe's answer falls hard. "You must run, and not look back. It's the only way."

Chocolate locks sway as Sara shakes her head.

"We can give you money," Babe adds. "I have a friend in Dallas-"

"What about Clint and Momma Lo-"

"No." Babe says definitively. "You must run and *not* look back. Maybe you can run with Lady, but you can't stay here. Here is the only place you *can't* be."

"Here is the only place I want to be," Sara says in a small voice. Her side flares. Heavy tears stream.

"I'm sorry, kid," says Babe, wishing he had the strength to get up and put his arms around the wilting girl. Powerless to help, he gives her a moment.

Unlike the hurt confined to her side, Babe's words injure the entirety of her. No Clint, no farm, no Momma Lois, no Devon, no Howard, no school, no Leo, no Megan, no weightlifting class—none of any of the wonders that are her life. Reeling at the notion, Sara is wounded anew.

"I have heard much about Natashas, but I have never heard of an old Natasha—"

"I'm not a Natasha!" Sara lashes out like an angry child, instantly crimping from the strain of her outburst.

Enjoying this conversation no more than Sara, Babe forges on as she sobs. "Sweetheart, it hurts me to say it, but I've met her."

Though her understanding is limited, Sara knows who "her" is.

"I don't know what's going on inside of there," Babe points his finger to Sara's head. "But I do believe she can keep you safe."

Sara looks at Babe like he is crazy. The mind underneath scrambles to smother her realization.

"But even *she* can't keep you safe *here*." Babe's somber words summon flashes; red exploding out the back of a bald head, a hollow-point pulverizing Lazlo's jaw, shards of Zvanko's skull bursting open when Twelve finished him off.

SYSTEM OVERLOAD.

Sara's eyes roll back as she faints into Lady's chair.

"Sara!" Babe cries out, "SARA!!"

9:50 AM

Sara sleeps in Lady's chair; Babe continues wondering: *What in the hell is going on?* At his all-time weakest, the man who watched Lady drape a blanket over Sara wonders if he could have handled a mess like this on his best day. *Nothing makes sense. Everything is wrong. Everything.*

Babe mulls over the last few days, beginning with the last message received from Moscow. *Your new superior will contact you.* The old spy expected another call from Moscow, not a knock on the door in the middle of the night.

Babe sees Sara's face. Then Twelve's face. Then Sara's face again. Feeling unworthy of the challenge, he asks any deity that may be listening for strength. *Just enough to see Sara safe, not a drop more. Please help me help this girl. Please.*

2:08 PM

Sara wakes up in her bedroom she doesn't remember being helped to. Fuzzy from the Oxycontin, she remembers only that *something* worrisome took place in the living room. In the moment, comfortably numb, she doesn't care.

Walking past Sara's open door, Lady notices her patient is awake. "You feeling any better, young one?"

"Huh?" answers the floating girl. "Err, yeah." Warm in her opioid cocoon, Sara closes her eyes. She mutters something. Then drifts back to sleep.

"Poor thing," Lady whispers low. Hands on her hips, the woman shaking her head cannot reconcile what she has seen with what she knows. Babe hasn't talked about what happened, but the news has. 'The Collinsville Massacre' they call it.

Beyond exhaustion, Lady doesn't know what to think.

9:49 PM

After spending the entire evening at Sara's groggy side, the guy who brought flowers in a vase, a get-well card, a little stuffed bear, and plate of Momma Lois' chicken and dumplings covered in foil, has to say goodbye.

"I'll be back tomorrow," he promises.

Though Lady likes the young man, she wishes he would stay away.

Unaware he let the stock tank overflow, again, Clint can think only of seeing Sara tomorrow. Willing to give most anything to go back inside – to twirl her soft hair with his fingers just a little longer – he knows he has to go.

The cherry-red Chevy revs to life.

Wednesday, September 3rd, 2014 – Thursday, September 4th, 2014

Because of genetic alteration, Sara heals approximately one and a half times faster than a healthy person her age might normally. Because her alteration includes increased pain suppression, Sara *could* get by with smaller doses. But opiates simply make life easier. For this reason, Sara has decided Oxycontin and Dilaudid are her new best friends.

Pizza rolls, fruit snacks, and re-runs of *Friends* on TBS help pass the lulls of semi-lucidity in between Clint's visits. The girl who doesn't want to think about anything likes her pills. In the pill bottle, there are no Natashas, no handlers, no worries.

Next to wilting lilies on the dresser stands, a get-well card signed by all the Fleischers. Next to Sara, the stuffed bear named *Clint*. Bear-Clint keeps her company until real Clint returns. Incapable of much, the girl who refuses to look at her wound while Lady changes her bandages, uses her French-tips to lightly scratch her side. It itches more all the time.

Able to get out of the bed on her own by Wednesday – and almost standing straight up by Thursday – Sara promises Clint she'll be at school on Friday.

Her side constantly seeping, the swelling is a little less each day.

Friday, September 5th, 2014

8:11 AM
Hallway
Hand in hand, Clint escorts the girl with droopy eyes to her locker. Aside from a little pull in her side, Sara feels no pain. Sara is happy.

Blind to the stares and deaf to whispers. Clint escorts his slow-going lady on to her first class.

Clint gets a tardy. He's okay with that.

8:16 AM
Mr. Colliet's Advanced Biology Class
Feeling used and abandoned, a sulking Megan stares at a Sara spacing off. *After ditching me Friday at lunch so she can sit with The Bitches, she goes on a shopping spree with Devon and Michelle and Julie, and doesn't invite me or even call me. I gave her my cell phone number, so she totally has it, and she had surgery and didn't even call me! She could've totally died, and I am her best friend, and she starts dating Clint, who I totally her up with, and she doesn't even call me. Probably because they told her not to, and-.*

Oh My God! I wonder if she really did have boob and butt implants! I mean holy flippin' heck!! She has a butt like a girl in a rap video and... Well, I know she didn't have boobs put in because I actually watched her go from super skinny to how she is now. Wait! What if she was stuffing her bra so people would only think they were getting bigger?

Why won't she even look at me?! She is just staring off like she doesn't even know I am here! I wonder if The Bitches told her not to talk to me—I hope not! Oh My God! I wonder what else they say about me!

Why didn't Sara invite me on the shopping trip? Why isn't she wearing makeup like people say she did when she went to the mall? Does she dress up everywhere else but school?! Why would she do that?! How does she keep getting prettier?! Is she getting lip injections?! No! Her lips were already like that when she got here! Her lips were the only thing that's stayed the same since she got here! Her hair looked better the other way... No, it didn't! It looks way better this way.

Oh my God, I hope she's still my friend. I don't care if she really had a boob job, I just don't want her to lie to me!

I wonder when she and Clint got together? What does he say about me? I hope he doesn't say anything bad. Clint wouldn't say anything bad about me 'cause he is super nice.

I can't believe how much she has changed. Sara totally looks like a college girl, like a senior in college, but implants wouldn't make the rest of her like that though, right? No way!

Her mind racing, Megan thinks of the guy who snapped a picture of Sara with his phone after she'd passed.

Chewing at her thumbnails – and unable to take her eyes off the pharmaceutically aloof Sara – Megan is dying to know what her hopefully-still best friend is thinking.

Looking through Mr. Colliet's dry-erase board, the girl feeling as though her bones are made of rubber thinks, *I want French fries... I want French fries really bad. French fries, and Clint with French fries. That's what I want. French fries. And Clint. That would be good.*

8:18 AM
Two minutes and eighteen seconds into a silent treatment, Megan decides Sara has suffered enough.

"Pst!" Sara's head slowly turns. "Hey! How are you doing?" Megan whispers loud enough for those in the front row to hear.

"He-ey Megun," slurs Sara to her friend.

Officially acknowledged, Megan feels 100% better.

8:41 AM

Sara notices Devon in the doorway, waving her out. Slowly, she makes her way around the back of the class and into the hallway to see what the animated Devon has to say.

"*What* are you doing at school?!" Devon whispers forcefully.

"I, uh... I didn't want to miss more school," answers the quasi-cogent one.

"You should be at home, *in bed,*" charges Devon, realizing how bloodshot and glassy Sara's eyes are. "Besides, you're more stoned than the art teacher! What did you take?!"

"Uh... Whut?"

"Exactly. You should be at home." As Devon's benevolent chiding continues, Sara drifts.

French fries, with chili on them. Cheese would be good, too.

9:00 AM

After being summoned back inside by Mr. Colliet, Sara notices something sticking out of her textbook. *Clint left me a note!* Feeling even warmer and fuzzier than a moment ago, Sara reads...

Roses are red, violets are blue, get well soon, so you can help me do chores.

Sorry didn't rhyme.

-Clint

A sucker for sweetness, Sara's vision blurs as she thinks of giving Leo a big coffee can full of oats... helping carry buckets of ground up feed to the heifers in a pen... jumping out of the chore truck to open gates. If Sara knew where Clint was, she'd walk out of class right now.

Breast and butt implant speculation having pretty well defaulted to fact, the most recent rumor to gain traction involves a hidden camera reality show that "all the teachers know about." Also – among the freshman and sophomores – a love triangle involving little brother Kyle. Kyle's official position, neither confirming nor denying, only serves to fan the flames.

Shelly is oddly silent on all matters. Her "blown out" knee healing without surgery, the tiny titan refuses to so much as say Sara's name.

9:27 AM, 2nd hour
Mr. Schibi's American History class
Escorted by Clint (who left his first class early in order to be waiting outside Mr. Colliet's door before the bell rang), Sara sits comfortably at her desk. Somewhat in class, but mostly in La La Land, she stares out the window as Mr. Schibi talks about something that happened a long time ago. Absolutely starving, Sara eats another eight milligrams of Dilaudid to hold her over till lunch.

Normally given to daydreaming, the self-medicating Sara has rendered herself incapable of even doing that. Eating schedule one opioids as though they are M&M's, Sara does well not to drool on herself.

10:07 – 10:57 AM, 3rd hour
Mr. Godfrey's Weightlifting class
The newly appointed 'Secretary of Weightlifting,' Mr. Godfrey has posted Sara behind his desk until she is well enough to participate again. Coach Mike told Sara she is welcome to the jellybeans in his top drawer.

"Now my brother can't complain about no one answering the phone anymore!" he shouts over a *Jock Jams* CD.

Sara, mouth full of jellybeans, smiles.

Soon, Coach Mike has no jellybeans.

11:24 AM
Hallway
Feeling no pain – and moving more freely than she should – Sara walks past Russell Martin. He notices her. She does not notice him back. He wishes she would notice him back.

Seeing her with a "skinny twerp" like Clint Fleischer gets under his bespeckled skin.

11:33 AM
Sara sits with Megan, Lexi, Karen, the huge pile of food and the two sports drinks Megan helped her carry. Three personal pizzas, two egg rolls, chili fries, and two orders of regular fries do little to hinder the rumors of an eating disorder. Mouth full of food, Sara answers Megan's questions with nods and shakes of her head.

Waiting for Clint, whose class is dismissed for lunch second to last, the girl pushing an egg roll into her mouth will return to fourth hour when she is ready.

2:18 PM, 7th hour
Mrs. Callahan's Gym class
Roll has been taken and the last day of volleyball is underway. Sara, unable to walk laps – and Shelly, still wearing a knee brace to support her story – find themselves side by side on the pullout bench.

Sara turns to the slumped girl with her eyes low. "Twisted your knee playing volleyball, huh?"

"Yup."

Twenty second's pass.

"Had your appendix taken out, huh?"

"Yup."

5:20 PM – 6:11 PM
The Babe and Lady's house
After going home, doing chores, and loading his dad's weed-eater into the back of his pick-up, Clint headed to Sara's house.

Puzzled at first, Lady shut the oven door and went to check on the sound of trimming along the side of the house. Insisting he not bother, the grinning farm kid pretended not to hear. Appreciating the kind gesture – but preferring he stay away – Lady said nothing as she watched him help Sara up into his truck so he could take her to the farm.

Knowing this only serves to complicate matters, the troubled lass hasn't the slightest clue as what to do about it.

6:12 PM
The Hill
Sore from having overdone it throughout the day, and not taking a pill since learning Clint was going to pick her up, Sara carefully lifts her foot onto the single step leading from the utility room into the living room. Ever the gentleman, Clint holds the door with one hand while helping steady his paramour with the other.

Sara winces at the sight of Momma Lois coming in for a hug.

"She's pretty tender, Mom," cautions Clint.

"Aww, shush," Momma Lois swats at the air. "How's our girl?!" In lieu of the usual, Sara gets a tiny, gentle hug.

"I'm okay," answers the girl wearing pink Victoria's Secret pajama sweats. Having returned to the farm, Sara feels the best she has since the last time she was here. Clint helps ease his tensing girl down into "Mom's spot" on the couch.

"We sure have missed you," gushes Momma Lois, taking a seat alongside.

"I have missed you too," says Sara feeling so much at home.

"Howard has been teasing Clint to no end lately."

Here she goes, thinks Clint, bracing himself for whatever his filter-free mother might say.

"Said he's gonna sell two tractors and put Clint through nursing school since he seems to like doctoring you so much!" Clint doesn't know his mother put Sara on the prayer list in the bulletin at church this week.

That's so sweet, Sara looks to Clint. She loves the look on his face when his mother embarrasses him.

6:42 PM

As much as Clint would like to take Sara to the basement, or his room, or anywhere else – he can't. Feet propped up, a blanket across her lap, a drink on the little end table between the couch and Howard's chair, she might as well be glued in place. Momma Lois has done everything short of putting a thermometer in Sara's mouth and a bandage on her head.

Having seen Sara through the shed window, Howard and Kyle are soon on the scene.

Ever the blushing center of attention, the stationary Sara is treated like royalty by Howard and Momma Lois as Kyle continues his quest of getting her attention.

"You know she's just using you to get to me!" Kyle wishfully snarks.

"You know I have that picture of you in the dress, right?" Clint coolly retorts.

"There is no picture of me in a dress!" Kyle denies.

"Are you the one who took that picture out of my album?!" Momma Lois blurts.

"I sure did." Clint confirms with eyes locked on his smarmy brother. "And thank you, mother."

"I was seven!" Kyle defends.

"You were twelve," big brother corrects. Kyle gets quiet for a while.

The evening goes on.

8:21 PM

Without a knock – because no one ever knocks – the oldest brother Russ enters through the back door. Sara recognizes him from the pictures in the hall.

Tall and unconventionally handsome, Russ, the 'world-class wise-ass,' leans on the entertainment center with one hand on his hip. "So, you must be Sara," he says with an approving grin.

Suddenly shy, Sara just nods.

Russ continues to stare as his mother pulls him down a hug around his neck.

"Mom," Russ grunts, "you're... you're hurting me."

Sara laughs.

"If you came by more often, I wouldn't have to do it so hard," says Momma Lois, on her toes.

And how are you gonna add to this menagerie? wonders Clint, after finally shutting Kyle up. Russ, known for his ribbing and dry wit, is liable to say anything.

"Damn little brother," Russ mutters with disbelief.

"She's pretty!" chimes Momma Lois.

"Yeah, Mom, I figured that part out on my own," says the slouching guy. "What I'm trying to figure out is what *she,*" pointing his finger at Sara, "is doing with him-" now pointing at Clint. Sara can't help but smile. She loves the way the guys torment and tease each other.

Kyle tries to chime in, "I think-"

"Nobody asked you." Russ has a lot of practice telling Kyle to shut up. Under his arm, Momma Lois continues squeezing her oldest and tallest "baby" around his ribs.

"Sara," Clint says, "I would like you to meet my adopted brother, Russ."

"Yeah – Russ, Russ Rockefeller – and I am definitely adopted," the older brother plays along. "I barely even know these people."

"How come *you* never brought one like her home?" Howard asks, from his chair by the fireplace.

"Well, Dad," Russ says thoughtfully, "for starters, I've never seen one that looks like her in person, and *if I did,* I could confidently wager she'd have sense enough not to even talk to me."

Sara, more prone to blushing all the time, cups her hands over her face. It's too much, but she loves it.

"Once again," Russ says, takes two long steps to Sara and gently shakes her hand, "my name is Russ and like Clint said, I am secretly a Rockefeller and I have a trust fund they don't know about, and I can take you away from all this." Sara finds Russ's manner much like Howard's. "I'll even help you to the car."

"Kyle's got a head start on you; he's been trying to steal her away since she first showed up!" Howard informs.

"Oh," Momma Lois defends her other two sons. "Howard's just kidding. They wouldn't try and steal you away!"

"I would!" Kyle spouts.

"I would too," Russ seconds. "Now, shut up Kyle."

As much as Sara loves the way Clint's brother's bicker and banter, she likes it better when Howard joins in the mix. And the way Momma Lois runs the show with equal parts warmth and sass. Sara loves the way things just roll off each other's backs. How no one gets angry. It's just what they do. To her, the Fleischer boys – and Howard, too – seem like puppies wrestling. Laughing makes her side hurt.

Sara eventually gains a reprieve when the conversation steers away from her and towards Russ's new job with the railroad. But that only lasts a little while.

The patriarch, so glad to have all three of his sons under his roof at the same time, asks Russ, "Son, could you ask around the railyard for anyone looking to work on a farm? Because Clint got a job a full-time nurse."

"Well Dad, can you blame him?" Russ defends of his little brother.

"Nope," Howard raises his brows. "Never said that I did."

Sara doesn't want to leave. Ever. She takes hold of Clint's hand under the blanket.

9:55 PM
Clint finally has Sara back to himself. Having no idea how much she enjoys his family, he apologizes for them once again.

"Your family's really great."

Saturday, September 6th, 2014

10:04 AM
Babe and Lady's swing

Lady requested Sara not leave before talking to Babe, who's been bedridden most of the week. The man digging for a smoke is not looking forward to this conversation – but it must be done. Sara senses something is wrong

His first time on the swing since last Sunday, Babe hands Sara a smoke.

Sara lights up; Lady looks on from above.

Much has changed since the last time she watched the two swaying back and forth. Likening Sara to a dangerous animal, the woman with dark circles under her eyes wants the troubled girl gone. Plagued with mixed feelings, Lady's fear grows at the same rate Sara heals.

The decision Lady has made gnaws at her terribly. *Damned if we do, damned if we don't.*

"We've made arrangements." Babe tells. "My Lady and I have made arrangements... for you."

A hazy recollection of their terrible conversation from yesterday surfaces. Sara's face falls with gloom.

Babe delicately continues. "David, a very old and trusted friend of mine, is ready whenever you are..." Sara's head begins shaking side to side. "He will take care of you. He's an American. He's a good man."

The truth leaks in. *You are a spy. You were shot. You're a Natasha. They aren't your real grandparents...* Sara wants her pain pills.

"He has a daughter your age. One a few years older, too. I think they would be good friends with you."

I am a spy. I was shot. But I am not a spy. They think you are a spy. Somebody else is the spy. I'm not a spy. Am I? He wants you to leave. But I'm not a spy. But they think I am.

"Sara?" Babe bends to the path of her 1000-yard stare. The sad girl is a statue. "Sara?" You're not gonna faint again, are you?" He pats her leg. "Sara?"

"*When I stop, you get out,*" Sara hears Babe's directive to Twelve inside the car. "*No hesitation. Speed and aggression. Nobody walks away.*" Sara sees the pistols firing in her hands. Amer's brain and bits of spinal column blasting into the closet. Waist deep in the swamp of her reality, Sara begins to cry.

Babe puts his hand on her shoulder.

"I didn't do those things!" Sara cries through her hands. "That wasn't me!"

"I know, kiddo. I know." Babe puts an arm around her. "But the bad people don't know that. They don't understand–"

"Just tell 'em!" Sara begs, her side burning terribly. Babe notices a change in her speech once again. She sounds younger, maybe nine or ten years old.

"Kid," Babe says helplessly. "I don't even know who *they* are!" He wishes Lady hadn't refused his plan of taking Sara away and leaving him behind.

"What will you and Lady do?" Sara asks in a small voice.

"We'll have to leave, too."

"Will you go with me?" pleads a Sara, already in emotional freefall.

"No," Babe says with a heavy heart. "No, we'll have to go someplace else." *You don't want to see me finish getting sick, kid.* "Maybe you and Lady can meet up later, but not for a while. Not until it is safe."

"When it is safe, can I come back here?" She asks hopefully.

"No, I'm sorry," answers a struggling Babe. "You will never be able to come back here. Here will never be safe." His words hurt worse than her side.

A vision of Clint's face throws Sara into panic. *I can hardly breathe!* Sara clutches her chest. Shock registers. Breathing deeply – one hand on her chest, the other holding her side – she is given a moment. Too sad to cry, the solemn girl wilts.

Sara somewhat recovers. Babe has no choice but to continue. "He is very wealthy. He has a very nice house outside of the city."

"What city?" Sara is, still gathering her bearings.

"Dallas. David lives outside of Dallas."

Babe wants a man to take me away. Sara grumbles in her head. In addition to feeling helpless, she now feels unwanted as well. "When do you want me to go?"

"Soon as you are ready," Babe injects false enthusiasm. "He can be here in the morning."

"But *you're* sick." Sara sadly points out.

"Sara," Babe half chuckles, "I'm gonna be sick no matter where I am. As long as I know you're safe..." He stops to catch his breath. "As long as I know you are safe, I will be able to die happy. If I know you're safe, I will leave this world with a big smile on my face."

His selflessness only makes things harder. The girl with pulsing fire in her side and a lump in her throat asks, "You can leave at any time, right?"

"Yes. We are ready as soon as you are," Babe is quick to confirm.

"Then we will wait. When we have to go, *then* we will go."

Exasperated, Babe drops his head and sighs. Sara sees this as a reasonable compromise.

While the mulling man reaches for another smoke, Sara's mind underneath drags her most painful awareness back below the surface. What need be known for survival is allowed – nothing more. *How in the hell do I make both women happy?* Wonders the guy lighting a cigarette.

Sara waves off the cigarette she is offered.

I've gotta buy some time with Lady. "So, you're agreeing to go, right?"

Sara nods, but with less commitment than Babe would like.

"Well, the time for faking you being dead is past, but I am sure they know you've been shot." Sara, realizing she's getting her way, nods along. "So, they *shouldn't* be asking you to do anything for a while." Babe lets out a deep sigh. "Until we go, though... I think it might be best if, uh... if maybe you stop seeing that boy."

Without a word, Sara pushes herself off the wobbly bench and, hunkering over like Igor, rounds her way toward the steps.

Ah, hell! thinks Babe, hoping he didn't just take a long step backwards.

Just before disappearing around the corner, Sara turns back. "We'll leave when we have to leave." She says, bold as a woman twice her age. Babe hears the door open and close.

"Could've gone better." he takes in a long drag. "Then again, could've gone worse."

5:05 PM – 6:21 PM
The farm
Chore time.

Having squashed this morning's ugliness with thirty milligrams of Oxycontin, the girl back on cloud nine rides along in the chore truck.

Her tolerance building, it takes more to cope with the varied pains assailing her. The pain in her side. The pain of knowing Babe will soon die. The pain of leaving her wonderful life behind. Her denial strained; the mind underneath welcomes the numbing help.

Using Babe's bounty of pills, Lady aims to dope the demon into oblivion until it leaves. Lady loves Sara. Torn is the woman with no one to turn.

Sara doesn't like that Clint is driving at a snail's pace on her behalf, but she thinks it's sweet. Slowly rolling from here to there, chores take three times longer than they should.

Clint doesn't mind. The longer chores take, the longer he has Sara to himself.

Terribly bummed she can't help, Sara enjoys watching Clint open and close gates, pour five-gallon buckets of ground feed into long feeders, fill stock tanks, making sure everything is as it should be. Stretching their time alone, Clint drives from one field to another, checking on the crops he and his dad planted—corn, soybeans, and wheat.

Sara loves the way he goes about getting things done, how he always seems to know what to do. *Clint would never let anyone hurt me.*

Before heading to the house, Clint pulls the truck alongside Leo's pen so that Sara can say "good night". She reaches out to pet his nose. Leo raises his head so his new favorite person can use her fingernails to scratch under his chin. "Oh, I wish I could ride you."

9:58 PM
Halfway between the farm and Sara's house
After another night of sharing Sara with the family, Clint drives her home. Something is bothering him. Having meant to ask for a couple days now, he comes right out and asks, "Why don't you ever talk about your parents?"

"Um," begins Sara, caught off guard, "my parents live in Florida." *Right? No, wait. I don't have parents. I'm a spy. I am not a spy.* Her dam of delusion sprouting leaks, Sara reaches for the pills in her purse.

"You moved up here from Florida, but you never talk about your family... or Florida, or anything about yourself, come to think of it," Clint points out.

Sara shrugs, her consciousness battles itself. She's gone too long without a pill. Being around Clint makes her forget to take them.

"I don't want to pry," Clint treads lightly. "I mean if that's something you don't want to talk about—well, that's up to you, I just..." He trails off. "I just don't want you to tell me that it's time to go home one day and—you, know, up and leave." The thought turns him somber.

"I don't ever want to leave." Sara says, words dripping with sincerity. "And I can promise you that I am very happy here... With Lady and Babe, with you... At the farm... I don't want to leave. I don't *ever* want to leave this place." Looking Clint's way all night, Sara says with eyes straight ahead.

Why won't she look at me? wonders Clint, disquieted despite hearing what has to be the best possible answer.

Sara discretely slips a pill during a look out the window.

"So, you got plans in the morning?" asks Clint, glad to move the conversation along.

"No. Why?" she asks, knowing he has church in the morning.

"Well... I was wondering if you would want to go to church with me—and the family." Clint feels obligated to let Sara know whenever the family might be part of the equation.

"I've never been to church before," answers Sara, at a loss. "But yes, I would love to go to church with you."

"You've never been to church before?" asks the guy who's only missed a handful of Sundays in his life.

"Nuh-uh." Sara shakes her head, a little embarrassed.

Feeling sad for her, yet honored to be the first to escort her to church, Clint smiles Sara's favorite smile. "We'll have to remedy that now, won't we?"

"Okay," Sara smiles back... and just like that, the world is perfect once again.

Sunday, September 7th, 2014

11:10 AM
Smithfield Christian Church
Arriving just before services began, Sara knew she liked church right away. Finding the sanctuary of the small country church beautiful, she felt both a sense of old and new. Established in 1881, the current structure is but seven years old. The Fleischer family lead the charge in rebuilding the house of worship after it was destroyed by a tornado in 2007.

Momma Lois leads the music; Howard opens with prayer.

Sara was shocked to see her name on the Prayer List.

Having only seen church on TV, Sara expected a grandiose expanse of thousands—a colorful choir, clapping and swaying in purple robes. She was relieved at the much more mild, intimate setting of seventy or so. Blushing at the outpouring of kindness and wishes for a speedy recovery, no one needed to ask Sara's name. Snugly seated in between Clint and Momma Lois – who'd already sung Sara's praises to anyone who would listen – she eats another piece of candy from "Mom's purse of 1000 items." Russ claims his mother's purse contains everything from office supplies to type O-negative blood.

Sara enjoyed watching Clint and Howard serve communion to the congregation. It's strange for her to see Howard – always teasing and smiling – being so reverent and reserved. Except for when he reaches behind Lois, gives Sara's hair a little tug, only to innocently look away.

Sara likes the music. After a while, she joins in the singing. The girl with a mouthful of *Twix* bites holds Clint's hand—except for when she needs to take off another wrapper.

A warm, peaceful place, the church is but an extension of the farm. Like Momma Lois's house, Sara feels at home.

12:34 PM
The Hill

After the post-sermon pleasantries, well wishes for a speedy recovery, insistence she return next Sunday, and a short drive back to the farm, Sara finds herself next to Clint at the kitchen table. Heads bowed around the feast Momma Lois prepares every Sunday, Howard thanks the Lord for another day, the food they are about to eat, and the time they have together.

"Amen."

5:21 PM
The basement

During her third game of pool – and some playful taunts by a little brother looking to show off – Momma Lois comes down the stairs.

"Sara, hun, your grandmother is here."

A puzzled Sara turns from the shot she was lining up in the side pocket. "My grandmother?" Sara's nose crinkles. *Oh, Lady! What's Lady doing here?* A swell of worry takes hold. *Something is wrong... Oh no, something is wrong! What's wrong?!*

5:24 PM – 5:37 PM
Lady's Buick
Deeply bothered, Lady is only willing to say, "Babe is okay," and, "We had a visitor," during the rushed ride home.

Lady didn't even do her hair, notices Sara, reaching for her pills. *This must be really, really bad!*

5:38 PM
Home
Her side hurting from walking too quickly, Sara finds Babe waiting for her at the small table in the kitchen. The sallow look on his face causes her to worry even more. "What's going on?" asks Sara, easing down into a chair. "Who came to visit?"

"It's time," Babe says with finality.

"But who was it? What did they say?" Sara begins crying.

"We've waited as long as we can. We have to leave tonight." As much as it pains him, Babe knows he must be firm, bordering on cold.

"Was it the same guy that came by the other day? I mean, the other night?!" Sara's voice cracks.

"You should at least tell her," Lady asserts from across the kitchen. "It might make things easier."

"Make what easier?!" Shouts the girl regressing once again. Sara assumes the manner of one approximately fourteen years of age. Watching Sara closely, Lady fears the return of the one she calls "the demon."

Hardly able to sit upright, Babe tries to calm the shaking girl. "Sara, do you know what the CIA is?"

"Yes. I mean, no. Wait... Yes." Sara's mind chases understanding like a dog running after a darting rabbit. "I mean, yeah." The mind underneath allows only as much knowing as one might get from watching movies.

"The CIA has relieved me of my duties. I am not your handler anymore," Babe says defeatedly.

"The CIA!" Sara reels. "What does the CIA want with-*?*" Saying the word CIA causes a wave of realization.

Lady and Babe wait, careful not to rush a Sara paused in thought.

Sara remembers Lady sticking a needle in her arm. Stuffing a blonde wig, sunglasses, and a plastic bag into a trash can. The Collinsville exit. Truth seeps through the partition. Sara's face registers awareness. Maturity returns

Babe looks to Lady. They can tell Sara knows.

"Did he say he was CIA?" Sara asks somberly.

"No. No, he didn't," Babe answers calmly. "He didn't have to. I have been at this a long time. I know CIA when I see them. He was *definitely* CIA." Babe can see Norman's pock-marked skin and venomous eyes.

"But I'm Russian." Sara states, shocked at the words escaping her mouth. A battle rages behind troubled eyes. "I mean, *I'm* not Russian." Sara's pendulum of awareness swings back and forth.

"Sara," Babe leans on his elbows, "do you realize that sometimes you turn into someone else?"

Sara just stares. She doesn't know *what* she knows.

"Sara, me and Lady have seen the other girl. The Natasha. She is not you. She is somebody else. Not you." Babe sooths in a cautious tone.

The pendulum of knowing swings. *Look at me, you little cunt!* Sara reels at Twelve's vicious tone. *I will sneak into your house at night and cut your mother's tits off!* She bursts into tears.

Her big heart torn; Lady looks to Babe.

"Tell them!" erupts Sara, her OxyContin beginning to kick in. "Tell them that I am not her and that I want *nothing* to do with this! Any of this!" Lady tenses, fearing the demon could surface any moment.

"Child!" Babe charges, hoping firmness will reign the raging girl. "Things are *much* worse than I could have imagined." "I think the program—the *Natasha* program—was stolen by the CIA!"

"What?!" asks Sara as though she'd been slapped. "The CIA stole what?! What do you mean?!" Frightened eyes search Babe's face for answers.

"The Natasha program," Babe says deliberately low, "the program that sent you to me and Lady, has been either bought or stolen, I think."

"You think?" Sara's understanding recedes. "How does-? Wait, I'm a Natasha. How does someone steal a program?"

"My guess... And this is only a guess," he hesitates, "is that my former superior sold it to the Americans or maybe his superior."

"Sold how?" Sara pleads to know.

"How? And remember, I know nothing for certain, but I bet he sent whatever intel he had to the CIA."

Suddenly with the bearing of an executive, Sara asks, "Then why haven't the Feds raided the house?"

"That's a *real* good question." Babe answers a Sara far more mature than he has ever known. *It's like she's thirty all the sudden.*

"Will the Russians come looking for me?"

"If I am right," Babe looks at Lady, "then, no. Who's going to miss a secret program on its way out?"

"If the Americans were going to kick in the door, they'd have done it by now. Right?" Sara points out keenly.

"Yeah," Babe concurs, his energy fading. "Yeah, if that's what they wanted to do, they'd of probably been here by now."

Sara clings to her understanding, calculating how she might get what she wants. "So, you're not my handler anymore? Am I supposed to go live with him now?" Sara's poise puts Lady on edge.

You're a mess, kid. Babe sighs. "No, he wants you to stay here with us until he calls you. He left a cellphone to reach you."

"He left a phone for me?" Sara repeats back. Babe is coming to believe Sara's mature version equally difficult to reason with.

"Yes," Babe admits. "He wants to deal directly with you." This causes Sara's head to tilt.

"So, it's my decision?" asks the curiously empowered Sara.

"I'm afraid it is," Babe sighs. "You've been controlled every minute of your life," the last of his energy draining away. "We're trying to put an end to that. I must lay down." Lady rushes around to help Babe from the table to his chair.

Sara watches the closest person she's ever had to a father shuffle away.

All is silent.

Her hollow victory fast fleeting, Sara feels much the way one does in tug-of-war when the other side lets go of the rope. *He's trying to help you!* She shouts at herself, a cloud of guilt looming overhead. *"We could not save our little Petra, but maybe we can save you... As long as I know you are safe, I will be able to die happy... If I know you are safe, I will leave this world with a smile on my face."* Sara marinates in her selfishness. *The only reason I even have a life is because of Babe and Lady,* believes Sara. *It's the least I can do.*

Knowing she's most of the reason Babe is still holding on, Sara decides to put her own happiness aside so that Babe might receive the peace he deserves. *It was good while it lasted.* On some level, she doesn't feel she deserves that kind of happiness anyways.

Feeling as though she weighs a thousand pounds, Sara drags around the front of Babe's recliner.

"Okay," says the girl too sad to cry. "I'll go, but I have to say goodbye to him. I have to say goodbye."

"I'm sorry, kid." Babe hears Sara's bedroom door close.

Time passes.

Lady packs bags and suitcases for a midnight departure while Babe gets what rest he can. Sara collects her things.

Only a few hours remain.

With most everything she owns in piles on her bed, the girl moving as though in zero gravity slowly folds and stacks each article of clothing. A step apart from her lagging self, Sara feels hollow. Dead inside.

Socks and undergarments in one pile; shampoo, conditioner, and body wash in another; a necklace she forgot to give back to Devon, the note Clint left her the day he came by to check on her, and her school ID. On its side rests the plug-in air freshener; Sara means to take the scent of her cozy little room with her.

Sara has yet to call Clint. That would make the nightmare real.

Her hair still pinned up from church, she knows she needs to call Clint – and she will. Just not yet.

9:01 PM
Babe and Lady's driveway

Under the blue luminance of the telephone pole, a sliver of moon, and a sky full of stars, Clint and Sara sit in his truck.

"What is it? What's got you bothered?" Clint asks for the third time. He knows Sara is upset about Babe, but he knows there is something else.

Sara turns, studying his face so that she might take the vision with her. Gazing into blue eyes, she notices flecks of green. His chin. His nose. His lips. Top lip slightly thinner than the bottom. Sara loves the way his hair is always a little messed up.

"Has Babe taken a turn for the worst?" Clint asks.

"He is going to die." Sara admits aloud.

"I'm sorry..." Clint consoles. "I don't know him as well as I would like to, but I know he's the kind of guy the world needs more of."

"He is," Sara says, her vision falling to Clint's hand. She loves his hands.

"Are you sure you don't want to tell me what's upsetting you?" he asks the girl living solely in the moment.

I am never going to see him again, Sara's realizes. From downtrodden to breaking down, the girl who stole Clint's heart falls to pieces.

Out of his seat and to her side, Clint opens the passenger door. The sobbing Sara falls into his arms. He pulls her close.

"Whatever it is, it'll be alright," he soothes. "Whatever it is, we'll get through it together."

Sara doesn't want to cry in front of Clint, but she does anyways. The feeling of his chin atop her head helps.

Saying nothing for a time, he allows her hurt to pour out. Sara breathes in his scent as she sways in his rocking embrace.

"I don't want to go!" Her words spill out.

Clint straightens his arms so as to look into Sara's watery eyes. "Then don't."

"What?" Sara lifts her chin.

"Don't leave," Clint says with simple firmness. "Stay here... with me... forever." His words push Sara's sadness aside. He gives her strength. Everything suddenly becomes simple.

"Kiss me," urges Sara.

Not needing to be told twice, Clint kisses lips even softer than he imagined they would be.

Time stops, and the world goes away.

Nothing is solved, but nothing else matters.

Sara's behind slides off the edge of the seat. Leaning into Clint, his right arm around her waist, left hand cradling her face, she stands on feet she cannot feel touching the ground. Though her eyes are closed, Sara can still see the stars.

Nothing is wrong. Everything is okay. Sara's first kiss continues, and then continues some more.

Cars zoom along the bottom of the hill. Clint's fingers run through chocolate locks. Sara makes a decision.

I will endure what I must; die if I have to. Happy tears wash away the sad. Sara pulls back just far enough to say,

"I'm not going to leave." She sniffs. "I'm gonna stay... I'm gonna stay."

Sara has accepted her fate.

11:41 PM
Sara's bed
Of all places, Sara finds herself in the middle of Mr. Stuart's empty classroom.

Surrounded by twenty-nine empty desks, Sara waits — but for what? Eerily still is the scene, without a single person outside the window, no cars passing by.

Sara has no idea why she is here. All she knows is that she wants to leave, but can't. As though glued in her seat, she is stuck in place.

Her anxiety rises as footsteps near. Sara gasps when her sister enters the room.

Twelve is not happy.

An imposing figure, the Natasha wears combat boots, camouflage pants, and a skin-tight black t-shirt. Her bun pulled tightly and wearing heavy eyeliner, the killer with teeth clenched marches up to Sara's desk.

SLAM!

Twelve's palms crash on the wooden desk. "What the fuck, cupcake?!" she shouts, hot breath in Sara's face. "You're gonna stick around?!"

Sara cringes under the lording Natasha.

"You're sticking around because of a crush on some skinny farm kid?!" rages Twelve. Sara winces. "What's your plan, genius?! You gonna get married and become a fucking farmer?! Huh?! Maybe shit out a couple kids and join the goddamn PTA?! Is that your brilliant plan?!"

Sara dares not look her sister in the eye.

"You gonna run the show now, Princess?" Twelve condescendingly inquires. "You gonna put on your big girl pants next time shit hits the fan? No! You're gonna run and hide just like you always do! You couldn't even handle Shelly!"

Sara absorbs Twelve's berating.

"Yeah! And *by the way*, thanks a *fucking* lot for stepping in for the pregnant bitch. Big help!!" Sara trembles. "Half a step to the right and you'd be shitting in a bag, STUPID!!!"

BANG

Drenched in sweat, Sara launches out of bed to the sound of Mira's pistol ringing in her head. Heart racing, her eyes dart about for the haunting presence she can feel, but not see. Throat bone dry, Sara begins to cry from the pain in her side. *It was only a dream,* she tells herself, *it was only a dream.*

Her wits coming back, Sara tries to remember what the dream was.

For the life of her, she cannot recall.

Monday, September 8th, 2014 – Tuesday, September 23rd, 2014

Regretting what they believe to be a foolish change of heart – but unwilling to force Sara to do anything – Babe and Lady hope for whatever the best might be.

Sara walks out the door each morning to the shiny red truck waiting in the drive. Ugly thoughts pushed down deeper than the cell phone in her *Kate Spade* bag, the girl who eats six milligrams of Dilaudid with breakfast chooses to dwell on what makes her happy.

Her mind stained by yesterday (because too much was realized for too long) Sara knows she's a spy. That Babe and Lady want a man to come take her away. That a dangerous situation is brewing. And that sometimes bad things happen that she cannot remember.

Sara lives in the moment and nowhere else.

All but formally adopted by the Fleischers, Sara spends most of her non-sleeping, non-school time at the farm. With Babe's health declining, she stays home most of the day on Saturdays and has Clint bring her home early on nights when he is awake.

Though Sara is content to stay on the farm, Clint insists on taking her for a night on the town at least once a week so that he might have her to himself. Other than chore time, or whenever he can sneak her away to the basement, Clint feels like just another puppy fighting over the rope.

The only person allowed to sit in 'Dad's chair,' Sara is routinely teased by Russ, hit on by Kyle, catered to by Howard, and mothered by Lois.

Helping Momma Lois with whatever she is doing at any time, Sara enjoys being an assistant to the brassy gal running a house full of men. A hold-over from generations past, Momma Lois, former city girl herself, is not only the head cook, seamstress, laundress, nurse, and counselor – she is also half of what Russ calls the *Howard and Lois show.* Trading shots back and forth to the amusement of lookers-on, no one could imagine how sweet they are to one another when there are no witnesses.

As much as Sara enjoys her time with the family, she enjoys her time alone with Clint more. Doing chores, checking cows, driving the tractor, fixing fences – kissing.

Sara likes to kiss. Clint likes that Sara likes to kiss.

Healing quickly, Sara is able to do more all the time. Soon able to drive the chore truck, hopping out and opening the gates shortly thereafter. Clint is soon unable to stop her from filling and carrying buckets of feed to the mooing cows she insists on naming.

Infinitely curious, Sara is always asking questions. Questions leading to more questions. And more questions yet. Each evening passes too quickly. By the time she is healed, Sara knows how to drive a stick shift, a tractor, a skid loader, and help repair the wall of a shed from the time her foot slipped off the clutch of a tractor.

Despite her full recovery, Sara medicates just the same... if not more.

Six milligrams of Dilaudid before school (and two more milligrams after lunch) provide the warm, fuzzy buffer Sara needs to muffle her nagging worries and keep emotional pain at bay. No pills are needed once Sara is holding hands with Clint on the way to his truck after school.

From time to time, Sara and Babe make it to the swing, but more often than not, their time together is in the sunroom. The room reeking of cigarette smoke, they have the occasional drink, and talk about school and the farm. Babe promises to visit the farm, should he feel well enough one day.

Sometimes Babe and Sara just sit and watch the robins and redbirds through the big windows.

As Babe loses weight, Sara continues to gain until leveling off around 135 pounds. Sara uses her strength to help Babe out of his chair on his weaker days. A conflicted Lady appreciates the help.

Ever exhausted, dreading the inevitable with Babe and fearing 'the demon' lurking beneath, Lady grows more resentful by the day. Wishing Sara would just leave, Lady is civil for Babe's sake.

Due to the fog Sara keeps herself in when at home, she hardly notices Lady's coolness.

Her attendance less than stellar, the girl who misses every Tuesday to help get Babe to his chemo treatments can scarcely remember the time when she concerned herself with what anyone at school thought or said. Focusing on weightlifting, quick smooches with Clint, and lunch, Sara is blind to the fact that she is talked about now more than ever.

The girl Devon knows to be "at least a little fucked up all the time", is considered uppity and aloof by those who don't know any better.

Fact of the matter, Sara simply has too much on her mind, and too much reality to deny, to concern herself with things that do not matter. Were it not for Clint and the cream cheese Danishes in the a-la-carte line, Sara would not come to school.

Continually outgrowing her jeans, Sara apologizes to Clint for her butt sticking out too far.

"This is not a problem." Clint explains from the very depths of his being. "Seriously Sara, it's okay. I am okay with this. This is not a problem."

"But my jeans don't fit anymore."

"They make bigger jeans."

Despite Clint's affirmation, the girl described as being "built like a brick shithouse", decides to ease up in weightlifting for fear of bulking up more than she already has.

Sara – always reaching into her purse for fruit snacks – alternates between lunch with Devon and Megan. Devon likes when Sara sits with her because it keeps Tiffany and Shelly away. Megan likes when Sara sits with her because it increases her prestige among her growing clique of Freshman and Sophomore followers. Young gossips in training, they thirst for the latest headline from the *Megan Press*: *Tiffany Refuses to Stand Side-by-Side to Sara Who 'Took Her Title.'*

Much like the *Jordan vs Lebron* argument, the *Tiffany or Sara* debate is argued by the boys. All in all, it's about a 50-50 split.

The weather changes. The climate of St. Charles High School changes as well.

Heather Dawn has gained an unusual sort of notoriety. Never admitting to posing for a graphic novel last Christmas, the girl who spent an afternoon holding fake pistols and a scowl finds herself the recipient of nerd worship as the independent title *Paradigm* enjoys unexpected success.

Her oval face and pouty lips showcased on the cover of issue #1—and hair drawn an even deeper shade of red – Heather throws kicks, shoots bad guys and holds provocative poses the whole way through.

Now, with her own collection of sycophants and fans, the pseudo star wants nothing but distance from Shelly, Tiffany, and the others. Except Michelle. Heather has decided to keep Michelle.

The group recently known as 'The Bitches' has all but ceased to be.

Devon – between dating Justin, AKA Mr. Wonderful, drill team, cheerleading and competing for valedictorian – has little time for anything else.

After dumping Jet Ryan, who was benched for averaging 2.2 yards per carry, Tiffany is all about her new 23-year-old musician boyfriend who has a song on iTunes.

Shelly, a vestige of her old self, is a chief without a tribe. Boyfriend-less since the night the head coach of the Missouri Tigers visited Jensen Halowell and his parents at their house, Shelly has since resorted to reaching out to Michelle and Julie for conversation.

Nice for the sake of being nice, Julie has little to say to Shelly. Her focus is on real estate in lieu of college.

Life goes on.

Wednesday, September 24th, 2014

1:22 PM, 6th Hour
Mrs. Espinosa's Home Economics class
After countless glances Sara's way in Home Ec, the hallway, and the lunchroom, Russell Martin finally gathers the nerve to turn around and ask, "So, you gonna go out with me after you wise up and dump Fleischer?" The attention of all within range of Big Ginger's snark funnels to Sara's response.

Unable to produce words, Sara's expression speaks for her. *Are you talking to me? Why are you talking to me? Holy shit, you're stupid. Never talk to me again.* Bewilderment. Disgust. Repulsion. In that order.

Face red and blotchy from embarrassment, the guy sliding down into his seat regrets his reckless attempt. Russell's ears glow like coals.

Thursday, September 25th, 2014

12:20 PM, between 4th and 5th hour
Hallway
Hurrying to catch Sara in between her English and Government classes, Clint feels the grating of a boot rake down his Achilles tendon. "Err!" he growls, whipping around.

"Sorry about that, Fleischer."

It takes but a glance at Russell Martin's smirking face to tell this was no accident. Russell's two cronies snicker. Clint seethes.

"I'll keep a better eye out next time," Russell scoffs.

Heat escaping his collar, Clint glares into Russell's smug, freckled face. *I want to sock you in the nose, but getting clobbered in the hallway probably isn't gonna make my heel feel any better,* thinks a Clint constrained by reason.

"What?!" blurts Russell, his smirk widening into a smile. "I said I was sorry!"

"No, you didn't." Clint's lips hardly move.

"Come on! Are you *really* gonna get butt-hurt over me stepping on your foot?!" Russell says loud enough for all to hear. "Here!" he extends his meaty palm. "Friends?"

Not sharing in Russell's jovial mood, Clint resists the urge to punch Russell in his yellow teeth. "You have yourself a good day," he utters before walking away.

"Yeah! We'll just *both* have to be more careful next time!" Russell bellows loud enough for everyone to hear.

With a layer of skin sheared off his heel, and hair on the back of his neck standing straight up, a steaming Clint puts distance between himself and the situation. Feeling he should have seen this coming; he grows angrier with each step.

I knew it! Clint hisses, thinking of the dirty looks and snarky comments from Russell as of late. He suspected Russell might have a problem with him, now he knows for sure.

2:12 PM, 7th hour
Mr. Godfrey's Physical Education class, boys' locker room
"I'm lucky Fleischer didn't kick my ass today!" Russell's voice booms.

Bristling, Clint wishes for a claw-hammer and an understanding prosecutor. Ignoring the shirtless ogre and the few guys who think he's funny, Clint calmly goes about changing. *Please, God. Please shut his big, stupid, loudmouth.* Setting his wadded-up jeans atop his tennis shoes, he shuts his locker.

"Ain't that right?" Russell antagonizes. "You were about to kick my ass, weren't ya?!" All other conversations cease as the focus of the dozen or so people still in the locker room turns to Clint. Other than Russell's buddies, no one likes the idea of him giving Clint a hard time.

"Nope," Clint replies dryly. "I like you too much for that."

Russell isn't getting the response he was hoping for. "No," presses the jock, "you were pissed!" Standing in his boxers and socks, the guy with orange-red freckles covering his chest and shoulders, hopes to get Clint riled.

Veiling his fury, the farm kid four inches shorter and most of a hundred pounds lighter, counters by keeping the

- 271 -

moment light. "Accidents happen. Not like you did it on purpose."

"But if I did, you'd kick my ass, right?!" Russell does what he can to make Clint look small.

"You know," Clint answers in a conciliatory tone, "you being so much bigger and stronger than me, I probably wouldn't do a damn thing. But I know you're not asshole enough to pick on someone half your size, so I don't think we have to worry about it."

Mouth gaping, the guy left with no comeback stands speechless as Clint slips by and out the door. Though glad to have put Clint on the spot – proving himself the bigger man – it burns the All-State wrestler to see the girl who won't even talk to him with a guy he believes so inferior.

Russell itches for a chance to put Clint in his place.

Friday, September 26th, 2014

2:17 PM, 7th hour
Mr. Godfrey's Physical Education class
Many students have never played dodgeball. Some have only played with foam balls that are squishy, incapable of causing blistering pain upon impact. Those individuals are incapable of understanding dodgeball on an intimate level. They have not experienced the sting – both physical and emotional – of a properly inflated red rubber ball thrown with whistling velocity. They have been cheated.

Dodgeball teaches what cannot be learned from a book. Dodgeball separates the weak from the strong. Dodgeball turns boys into men. A 70 MPH dodgeball hitting boy-flesh has been known to kickstart puberty, ushering lagging youths into manhood.

These are the beliefs of the man known as Coach Mike.

Coach Mike, eater of barely cooked steaks and chopper of his own firewood. Coach Mike, a man who'd sooner wear a dress to the hardware store he frequents than allow another man to change the oil on his Chevrolet pickup. Coach Mike, giver of the gift that is dodgeball.

After walking into a store that wasn't Walmart, the man with a freshly leveled flat top took money from the wallet housing his deer tags and NRA membership card and bought eight of the only balls that should ever be used for the sacred game.

Voit. Not only a name brand, but the gold standard.

Bright red and scientifically designed for biting traction, the rubber ball textured with etching is the Swiss Army Knife of all things gym.

Coach Mike knows this.

Across the half-court line there is a row of the red rubber balls. Inflated just the right amount – not too little, not too much – a stockpile of ammunition for the game that puts hair on a young man's chest. If thrown with enough speed, and at the and at the proper angle, they can take hair right off a young man's chest. Like giant cherries, they are alluringly placed an equal distance between the two bands of adolescents randomly assigned. With the mindset of warring tribes, each team eyes the other. Some choose to remove their shirts. These are the bravest. Also, the most foolish.

Coach Mike, the overseer of the contest, the man who ensures each member of both factions is earnestly touching the wall previous to the whistle – eyes for anyone looking to dishonor the game with a head start. Scratched-up whistle between his crooked teeth, the coach with coffee breath allows a moment of silence... the gymnasium is quiet as a church.

The trill of Coach Mike's whistle slices through the air.

The boldest from each side race toward half-court.

Clint, quick-footed and elusive, is soon backpedaling like a quarterback cocked and loaded. Preferring to pick his shot, the skinny guy with a whip for an arm scans the opposition.

Every gym class has 'that one guy.' Every gym class has that one guy with a Dan Marino accuracy and a release so whippingly crisp as to compromise the shape of the red sphere in flight. That one guy everyone keeps an eye on – whether on his team or not. In coach Mike's seventh hour physical education class, 'that one guy' is Clint Fleischer.

Red balls fly all around. Some throw. Some try and dodge what is thrown. Clint zips the ball lengthwise across the court to hit a guy who doesn't see it coming. Grinning is the farm kid who didn't throw nearly as hard as he could've.

Both sides suffer heavy losses early – almost thirty percent are out within the first thirty seconds. The fat, slow of foot and uncoordinated are harvested early, the game slows. Dodgeball fodder take their place along the bench.

A shirtless Russell charges to the line, launching the ball at Clint's head with all his might.

Dipping to his left, he feels the wind of the cheap attempt whizzing by. Anger overriding common sense, Clint gives Russell a hard look daring him to try it again.

Sipping cold coffee, Coach Mike, the man who believes stitches build character, keeps an eye on his star lineman. He can tell something isn't right between Russell and Clint, but he doesn't interfere—not yet. Coach Mike, the man who believes running laps cures concussions, will only get involved should necessity require.

Both Clint and the guy who called himself "Orange Crush" for a time, have a ball in hand.

Russell curls his lip.

Clint just shakes his head. *Alright. You want it, now you're gonna get it!*

The cream-colored gorilla winds up over three long strides and fires Clint's head once again. Ducking under the red blur soaring over, Clint charges back. The unarmed Russell retreats.

PLANK!! ...when thrown hard enough, the sound of a *Voit* ball slapping sweaty flesh has a signature sound all its own. Often accompanied with a howl, it contains what might be described as a metallic reverberation.

"AAARGH, FUCK!!" shouts Russell through his twisted mouth.

"HEY!!!" Coach Mike thunders a warning; the entire class hissing a low "eeew." Coach Mike, the man who cries at the end of 'Old Yeller,' but never any other time, will *not* tolerate foul language in his class.

Nostrils flaring, the guy with a red welt quickly rising between his shoulder blades sends an *'I'm gonna kill you'* look Clint's way.

Consequence be damned, Clint shouts "Knock it off or I'll burn you again!" Russell's jaws clench.

Forty second's pass. Someone on Russell's team catches a ball. Russell goes back in the game, even though it isn't his turn. Everyone's attention angles at what has become a game of one-on-one.

The scowling giant with a throbbing circle on the middle of his back – and retribution on his mind – leers at his target. Russell picks up a ball up and heads straight for Clint again. In his haste, Russell releases a fast, but inaccurate throw.

Clint shakes his head as to say, *I warned you, asshole!* And blisters Russell again – *PLANK!!* – this time in the shoulder. Spectators wince as Russell's stifled shriek blends with the sound emanating from the hit.

"I can do this all day!" Clint barks, shocking those unaware of his fiery side.

His ego bruised, Russell he trudges back to the bench. Were it not for Coach Mike, the hulk with a second welt rising would charge across the court and beat Clint to a bloody pulp. Coach Mike knows this. For this reason, the guy who would like to freshen his coffee stays close.

Another game is soon underway.

The guy with his farmer's tanned arms and much paler legs stares at the bully too proud to put on a shirt.

Thirsting for payback – while fearing another hit – a Russell with speckled welts takes hesitant steps. His lily-white skin sporting perfectly round circles, Big Ginger throws and misses.

Clint returns fire.

PLANK!!

Russell gets a stinger on his left peck. "AAARGH!!"

Trotting backwards, Clint is unable to hide his delight. "It's like throwing at a barn–," he mutters to teammate nearby. His teammate, laughing at the sulking ogre trudging back to the bench, notifies Clint, "You know he's gonna kill you, right?"

"He might kill me later," Clint responds, cool as the other side of a pillow. "But not before I finish what I'm doing now."

Angry nearing tears, Russell plops down on the bench. His teammates keep their looks discreet and snickering restrained. All expect the giant to snap at any moment.

Not one to disrupt a life lesson in progress, Coach Mike keeps an eye out as Russell continues down the path he chose.

PLANK!! Left thigh. The Clint and Russell show goes on.

PLANK!! Upper left side of belly. Perspiration amplifies the sound reverberating throughout the gymnasium.

Humiliated but resilient, the big guy with bloodshot eyes and glowing red patches all over his body can't seem to get back into each the game quickly enough... A teammate catches a ball, Russell rushes back in even though it isn't his turn to do so.

PLANK!!

"AAARGH!!!"

That's gonna leave a mark! Coach Mike grimaces at the sight of a ball thrown with a little something extra. Unable to hear Russell cursing under his breath, Coach is surprised his right tackle/defensive end is handling the situation as well as he is.

Another game begins.

The whistle blows, but Clint doesn't run for a ball. By now, his teammates are all too happy to hand him theirs. One in each hand, the Wyatt Earp of the hour makes his way toward center court. Sporting a smirk of his own, Clint shrugs at Russell as if to ask, "Are you done?"

Prodded by pride, the polka-dotted juggernaut timidly inches forward, ball in hand.

"Really?!" Clint says loud enough for everyone to hear. "I'd feel sorry for him if he wasn't such an asshole," he follows up just quiet enough for Coach Mike not to hear.

Russell curls his lip and mouths, "Fuck you."

"Okay!" Clint shouts taunts. "Time's running out, dummy!"

Not sure if the charging Russell coming to throw the ball – or a punch – Clint crouches.

Russell stops at the half court, heaving the ball with all his might... so much so that he loses his balance, stepping across the center court line. Overextended, arms down, face up, Russell glimpses Clint stepping into this hardest throw of the day.

Time stops for Coach Mike who realizes he let things go too far... "Ohhhh, shit!" The man who once shook Pete Rose's hand watches Russell eat Clint's worst at point blank range.

SMACK!!!

"AAAAAARGH!!!! FUCK!!!!"

"Everyone to the locker room!" erupts Coach Mike over Russell's muffled howl. Stunned boys stand frozen at the sight of Russell clasping his stinging face.

His eyes teary from pain and rage, Russell gains but two steps toward Clint before Coach Mike is chest-to-chest and breathing *Maxwell House* in his glowing cheeks.

"I said everyone get to the locker room!" Coach Mike thunders again, not taking his eyes off the fuming lad.

Rubbernecking back at the action, the class shuffles their way out.

Face pulsing with his pounding heart, Russell tries to look at Clint over Coach Mike's shoulder, but the man of granite is having none of it. "No, you look at me!" he orders.

"I can go get changed, too," offers Clint.

"Yeah, I think that might be best," Coach answers, eyes boring into Russell.

Needing told only once, Clint swings a wide route around the two much larger guys. Coach Mike waits for him to be gone.

"Now you listen to me, and you listen good!" Coach demands. "I don't know what the problem is between you and Fleischer, but I'll bet anything *you* started-"

"But I—"

"Shut up!" Chops Coach Mike. "I'll give you a chance to talk, but for right now you're gonna listen to what I have to say!" Russell sulks. "Now, I know Clint isn't the kinda kid who goes around starting trouble. And if he was, he sure as hell wouldn't start it with someone twice his size."

Unable to deny, a pouting Russell looks down and away.

"Look at me!" Coach commands.

Russell's does as ordered.

"I don't know if you realize it or not, but right now is an opportunity for you – a real *big* opportunity!"

In addition to being trembling mad, Russell is now confused as well.

"You have a choice-!" Coach Mike says intensely low. "You can either be a man about this and go on with life, *or* you can be a little punk and handle this like a chickenshit." Russell has never heard the man who leads the team in prayer talk like this.

Russell sighs and rolls his eyes. Coach Mike pretends not to notice.

"Look-!" Coach Mike snaps as though talking to his own son. "I don't know *what* has been going on between you two, but whatever it is, it's gonna stop, you understand me?!"

"Mm hmm," Russell murmurs.

"I don't want and 'mm hmm'! I want a 'Yes' or I want a 'No'!" demands the man who had sauerkraut for lunch.

"Yes!" Russell huffs, his face and red patches throbbing.

"Good, that's *real* good. 'Cause if I find out you went out and scuffed up that boy, I'll have you playing Left Out Guard Tackle – you'll be left out of the game, guarding the water jug and told to tackle anyone who comes near it." Coach's granite face cracks a smile as he tries to lighten the mood a bit. "You got me?"

"Yeah."

"You mean *yes*," Coach corrects. "I'm counting on you here. And don't think for one second that I won't find out if you go whip up on Fleischer – and I *will* find out! You got that?"

"Yes."

"Okay then," Coach Mike extends a hand. "That means we have a deal."

Whether committed or not, Russell shakes Coach's hand.

"All right, now you go and get changed out and don't forget what I said."

"I won't..." Russell groans.

Watching the one the coaches call "man-child" lumber away, Coach Mike hopes, *Please don't do anything stupid...*

Walking to the truck – fingers interlaced with Sara's – the guy who saw no sense in hanging around does his best to keep from grinning.

"What is it?" a smiling Sara pries.

"Hun–" Clint says coyly. "I would tell you, but I don't think I could tell the story as good as anyone who was there..."

9:21 PM
Shake's Ice Cream Shop

Clint and Sara sit at one of a dozen tables in front of the walk-up ice cream shop. Even though the building is new, it has the look and feel of a long time ago. Business slow on the rather cool night, the two seated near the street feel as though they have the entire place to themselves. Hazel eyes catch the shine of headlights passing by.

As they share their second banana split, the girl who doesn't get full tells Clint how Russell is always looking at her and what he said in Home Ec. yesterday. Having thought nothing of it at the time, she regrets not saying something sooner.

Clint isn't thinking about Russell or gym class as Sara's luscious lips skim thin layers of vanilla ice cream off her spoon.

"Things are too good..." blurts Clint lost in thought.

"Huh?" Sara tilts her head. "How can things be *too* good?"

"Just..." Clint stops to think of how to say what he means. "In life, when something is really, *really* good, it tends to not last too long."

A befuddled Sara continues skimming ice cream off her spoon.

"And the way things have been going – which is great – it just... you know, seems too good to last."

Still not knowing how to respond, Sara takes afresh spoonful.

"You love the farm, and I love that you love the farm, I just..." Clint looks away briefly, then back. "I just worry that maybe one day you might not love it so much."

"Uhhh... what?" Sara drags slowly in surprise. "Why would I stop loving the farm?"

"Well, I mean, it's a big world out there," Clint reasons. "And you're young, and you can do anything...You can go anywhere..." Silence falls as Clint leaves an opening for Sara to speak.

She doesn't. A cool breeze blows a few strands of hair across her face.

"The farm is *my* dream. It wasn't Russ's dream. And Kyle's dream is to smoke weed behind the shed and make three-pointers so people clap for him. Not that there's anything wrong with that," Clint concedes. "But my point is that one day you might realize there is a big world out there and... you know, my world is here. I'm always going to be here. I mean, I can go anywhere in the world I want to go –

you know, as long as I am back by chore time." Clint's little joke makes Sara smile.

"I told you I don't want to leave the farm," Sara clarifies, not understanding the need to address the matter again.

"I know you did," Clint follows up with a cautious cheer. And you saying that makes me happier than you can imagine – its just..." he takes a bite of ice cream to buy a moment to think. "It's just that you haven't been on the farm very long... you haven't had a chance to get tired of it yet–"

Sara, with a bit of vanilla on her lip, looks at Clint as though he is crazy.

"The farm is a huge place—when you're on a four-wheeler—but at the end of the day, it's just a speck. A tiny bubble where not a lot changes. Granted, every day is different, but all in all, every day is pretty much the same..."

"Okay... soo? You think that I might change my mind and want to go someplace else?" Sara cannot wrap her mind around the idea. *I don't want anything to change.*

"Maybe someday..." Clint says sadly.

"You don't have to worry," Sara's words are like velvet. "I like the bubble. I don't ever want to leave it."

His worry assuaged for the moment, "I love you," tumbles out.

"What-?" Sara gasps.

"I said, I love you." Clint's words hang in the air.

Eyes glistening, Sara soon finds her voice. "I love you, too."

Saturday, September 27th, 2014

9:16 AM
The swing
With fewer "good" days all the time, Babe enjoys his best day in a while on the swing with the girl who got in late from her date last night. Face still puffy from sleep, he sits bundled in a coat meant for a much colder day. Enjoying a cigarette and a gentle sway, Babe listens to Sara talk about last night and Clint saying, "I love you." Suffering something resembling dementia from the chemo and pain medication, Babe sometimes believes Sara to be the daughter he lost. Sometimes unaware of the dark cloud looming, Babe is happy to see his beautiful Petra smile. Weak fingers tremble as he lifts his cigarette to his mouth.

10:41 AM
As per the Saturday routine, Sara helps around the house. The garden and flowers having falling victim to the changing season, and the lawn having been mowed by Clint last Wednesday, the list outside is pretty short. Fresh out of Dilaudid, the girl with 40 milligrams of OxyContin in her belly goes about the indoor tasks. Clint's old MP3 player around her arm, a Sara feeling no pain; dusts to Steve Miller Band, wipes windows to .38 Special, vacuums to Stevie Ray Vaughn

and cleans the tub to Kansas, all with tonight's fishing trip on her mind.

Tonight, after Sara helps situate the sunroom, she and Clint are going fishing with Russ and a friend of his from the railroad. The sunroom must be re-arranged for the hospital bed arriving Monday morning.

Worn out and almost ten pounds lighter than a month ago, Lady continues her battle against the inevitable. Everything having taken its toll; she's forgone dyeing the silver out of her hair now held tight with a wrap. It's been weeks since Lady has said much to the one she believes robbing Babe of peace.

Though bitter at Sara's broken promise, the woman taking a nap in her chair is conflicted. Believing Sara is the reason her Babe is still hanging on, Lady wants Sara to leave so the man she loves can die in peace – but she doesn't want him to let go. Were this not enough, there is the memory of Twelve. The headline 'Collinsville Massacre' plastered across her television screen. Lady has looked at Sara so many times, wondering if she is no more than a mask for the demon.

A prisoner to her plight, Lady forges on.

4:23 PM
The sunroom
Though she has spent a fair amount of time in the sunroom, Sara remains unaware of what lies beneath the hardwood slats under the milk crate filled with old magazines. To her, this room is the place where she and Babe visit and smoke cigarettes when he doesn't feel well enough to go outside – not the place where two .40 caliber pistols, suppressors, and ammunition are hidden.

Using what Clint calls her "horse strength," Sara moves what needs moved in the room with a wide view of leaves beginning to change color. Without conversation, Sara and Lady make room for the adjustable bed. The bed plus a chair from the dining room and the end table from Babe and Lady's bedroom.

5:20 PM

Sara sees Clint's gleaming red Chevy and is out the door like a rocket.

Wearing what Clint calls her "Daisy Dukes" — even though Sara doesn't know who Daisy Duke is — Sara walks along the patio with a pair of blue jeans in a bag to protect from the weeds and briars.

The red truck heads out the Southbound lane.

With Russ and his buddy seeing to the beer, it is left to Clint and Sara to pick up ice, snacks, and mosquito repellent.

Sitting in the middle, one leg on either side of the shifter, Sara goes through the gears while Clint works the clutch. This allows him to keep his arm around her while he drives.

A quick stop at Sonny's Pump N' Go and they will be set for the night.

5:35 PM

Sonny's Pump N' Go

Sonny's, one of the oldest convenience stores around, is also the easiest place for teenagers to buy beer. So long as Chris is running the register, pretty much any ID will work.

Chris wasn't all that popular when he attended St. Charles High School, but has gained the status of "super cool" since.

Always ready to "do a bro a solid," the sleepy-eyed guy rocking a blonde, peach fuzz mustache can most always be found leaning against the counter behind the register. Arms folded, St. Louis Rams hat on backwards, bowling shirt untucked. Chris is the virtual owner of the gas station that his uncle actually owns. A one stop shop for obscure knowledge of movies, music, and conspiracies, he greets every customer with a "Sup–?" and a nod. This is how Chris rolls.

Clint and Sara enter the tiny establishment stuffed with a little of everything and the scent of fried food.

Chris says, "Sup–?"

Trailing Clint through the all but empty store, Sara grabs chips, a box of Milk Duds, another bag of candy and a package of Starbursts. "Don't forget ice!" she reminds. Bug spray, lighter fluid, and a package or D batteries in his hands, Clint follows his girl to the register.

Sara grabs a bag of gummy worms along the way and dumps her cradled load onto the counter. She knocks over a container of Slim Jims. "Oops!" the embarrassed girl fumbles to catch it.

"Ah, that's cool," Chris casually dismisses as Sara goes about putting things back in place.

Blushing at her clumsiness, she then knocks over a few lighters while setting the tall, cylindrical container with a faded image of Macho Man Randy Savage. "Soorrry."

"Nah, really, it's cool. Happens all the time," Chris tries not look down Sara's shirt because her guy is with her.

As Chris rings up the pile of items, a convoy pulls into the parking lot that was all but empty only a moment ago. Those going to Chad Winters' party are making a last-minute stop for beer and booze so long as Chris is working. Several of the passengers – including Russell Martin who is standing in the back seat of "Jet" Ryan's Jeep with the top down – have a head start on the drinking. Celebrations from last night's game have carried over.

Four vehicles slide into parking spaces. Among them, "Jet" Ryan, Michelle Decker, Nathan Halowell's little brother Riley, two junior cheerleaders, Marquis Jackson (the guy who took "Jet" Ryan's starting job at tailback) and four offensive lineman. The Suburban carrying Jensen Halowell and his new girlfriend pulls up to the pump.

Sara notices the string of cars through the store's tinted windows. She thinks nothing of it until seeing Russell, his hands on the rollbar, standing like a bear on its hind legs. She can see him eyeing Clint's unmistakable truck. Sara squeezes Clint's arm.

Clint looks out the window. "Ahh shit," he groans. "I just wanna go fishing..." Though he doesn't let it show, the guy wishing Chris would hurry up becomes nervous.

Nervous herself, Sara can see the scowl on Russell's face through the smudged and scratched up door. Having been told the basics of what happened in gym class yesterday, she fears for the man she loves.

Russell hops out of the 4x4 with the mud splattered fender. The squished down frame to raises three inches before his size 15 sandals land on the asphalt. He marches to the store's tinted window, cupping his hands to either side of his face. Russell peers through the glass. He spots Clint.

Feeling the four beers he chugged one after another, the tipsy guy with yesterday fresh on his mind lumbers toward the entrance as Clint and Sara walk out.

Forgetting the ice, Clint walks swiftly towards his truck.

"Hey! There's that skinny, shit-kickin' faggot!"

"Let's just go," Sara pulls Clint faster.

"That's the idea," Clint mutters under his breath.

Neither look back as they open their doors, toss in the bulging bags and waste no time getting in.

A couple classmates have pulled out their phones; Russell's trudging Clint's direction is being recorded from multiple angles. Forearms swinging and mouth tense, he arrives at Clint's door as eight cylinders fire to life.

BOOM! Russell's palms punch the driver's side, rocking the truck. "Get out, bitch!"

"Let's just go!" cries Sara.

So angry that he is calm, Clint turns to the girl he loves, then to Russell's massive head looming just outside his window. The engine idles.

BOOM! Russell sends the truck rocking again. "Where you going, bitch?!!" Red faced and working himself into more rage, the big guy with an audience is spoiling for a fight.

Clenching his teeth, Clint bristles.

"Just go!!" Sara begs. Terrified upon realizing, *Oh my God! He's not gonna leave!* Sara's eyes spring with tears.

"Get the–!" *BOOM!* "–fuck out of the truck you little bitch!" Russell taunts. "Fucking faggot!!"

Looking down at the dash, Clint switches off the engine. "I'm sorry," he tells Sara clutching, his arm. *One way or another, this ends now.*

BOOM! The truck rocks again.

Clint turns to the enormous head his window. "I can't get out, unless you move."

"What?!" Russell leans in to hear Clint's grinding words.

"I can't get out—" he states louder, clearly enunciating each word, *"unless you move."*

"All right! Yeah!" Russell steps back, throwing his arms into the air. "Let's do this motherfucker! Yeah, we're gonna do this!" Savoring the revenge to come, the guy with glassy eyes wants everyone to know they are in for a show.

Watching through the store's window, Chris thinks to himself, W*oah dude... Somebody should call the cops.*

"Don't do this!" Sara shouts as Clint steps out of the truck, shutting the door behind.

"You can't run, and Coach Mike isn't here to save your little bitch ass!" Russell taunts, rolling his shoulders like a professional wrestler.

Phones recording from four angles capture Clint squaring with his back to the door of his truck, and Sara begging him to get back inside.

"You're gonna take it like a man, huh? I like that!" Russell huffs.

"Look!" Clint begins with his jaw set. "If you're still pissed about gym class, I'm sor—"

This is all Clint can say before a shove by Russell bounces him off the truck door and back at the brawny guy with his chin stuck out.

POW!

Blood splatters when Clint's overhand right crushes Russell's nose, along with two of his knuckles. Those looking on are taken aback by the sight of Russell staggering, blood gushing down his chin and bare chest.

Rounding the rear fender, Sara watches Clint rush the stunned giant −*POW*− the second punch puts Russell on his back.

Disoriented, it takes him a moment to even realize Clint is standing over, raining down punches.

Left. Right. Left. Right. Right. Right. Left. Right. Right. Right. Right... Covering his face, the squealing Russell tries desperately to get away. Clint is scared to let Russell up. Right. Left. Right. Left. Right. Right. Right.

Some punches come from above. Some from the hip. But none land as hard or as square at the first. "Get him off me!" Shrieks the guy curled on his side, covering his head.

"Let's go, Clint!!" Sara screams. He does not hear.

When Russell covers his face, he gets punched in the side of the head. When he covers the side of his head, he gets punched in the face. The guy who wanted to fight so bad is a blubbering mess by the time Jet pulls Clint off of him. Riding a tidal wave of adrenaline, Clint wheels around, ready to fight any of Russell's friends looking for trouble too. His bloody dukes up, Clint takes a hard step toward Jet.

"No, man!" Jet shouts with his arms straight out. "I'm just tryin' to keep you from killin' him! We're cool, man! We're cool!"

Still primed, a Clint on fire turns to the pitiful sight that is Russell. Unable to tell up from down, the punched-stupid colossus crawls like a baby on the dirty asphalt.

Phones continue recording as two guys strain to lift Russell to his feet. Knots and bumps rising all over his face and head, his left ear is purple, right is candy apple red.

Done with Russell – who is being helped back into Jet's Jeep – Clint looks around with disgust at those who were all too happy to sit back and relax as he got clobbered. "I didn't start this," he makes known between deep breaths. "This isn't what I wanted."

And with that, Clint gets back into this truck, turns the ignition, and pulls away.

Eight minutes later
The Hill

Right hand in the air and white t-shirt soaked with sweat and blood, Clint enters the house with Sara close behind. Howard and Lois are alarmed.

"Goodness gracious!" Lois gushes as Howard bellows, "What. In. The. Hell?!" Both are out of their chairs and trailing Sara and Clint to the kitchen sink.

Fox News blaring in the background, Howard and Lois close in for a look at Clint's hands under the running faucet. "What did you do to yourself?!" and "What in the hell happened?!" is asked at the same time as Sara opens the freezer to get ice.

"I hit it on something stupid," grumbles Clint, cold water cascading over both hands. The right is so swollen the left goes unnoticed.

"Where's it bleedin'?!" Momma Lois grabs Clint's hands, pulling them close for inspection.

Howard soon pieces things together. Rather than focusing on his obviously broken right hand, he checks about his son's face, neck, and body. *I wonder what the other fella looks like...* wonders the smirking dad.

"What did you hit it on?" Clint's mother asks, squeezing his swollen knuckles.

"Lois Mae, I think you're gonna have to wash that shirt twice. Little extra bleach, maybe," smirks Howard. Though still concerned, he is no longer worried.

"He got in a fight," informs Sara.

Momma Lois' attention turns from Clint's hand to his face. "Did somebody hurt you!?" She demands to know. Seizing Clint by his cheeks with her wet hands, she wrenches his head side to side during a less-than-gentle inspection. "Who hurt you?! Did someone hurt you?!" the frantic mother is ready to administer justice herself.

"Somebody's working on hurting him!" Howard laughs, fearing his wife might pull Clint's head off his shoulders.

"Who'd you get in a fight with?" Momma Lois follows up.

"It was Russ Martin," Sara answers for him. "Clint didn't want to fight, but–"

"Russ Martin?!" Howard blurts out, remembering the over-grown teenager from a football game last year.

"Why didn't you use a hammer?!"

"Because I didn't *have* a hammer," mutters Clint as his mother, on her tippy toes, pulls his blood-smattered t-shirt off at an awkward angle. "You're not helping, Mom," he groaningly protests, the wet collar raking across his ear.

"Yes, I am," she spouts back. "You're just being difficult."

"That hand's broken, Clint." Howard states the obvious.

"You think so, doctor?" Clint smarts. Adrenaline having worn off, his hand pounds with each thump of his heart. Angry, excited, wired and still a little shaken, the guy with a possibly broken left hand as well would appreciate a little space.

"You didn't kill 'em, did ya, boy?" Howard asks, a bit proud of his son for having felled the Goliath.

"He was alive last time I saw him," Clint replies, easing his puffy hand down into the big bowl of ice Sara sat beside him on the counter.

"I guess we're not going fishing," Sara says with her hand on Clint's back.

"I can cast with my left."

"Not very good, you can't," chimes Howard heading back to his chair. *You need to stay in the cool and let Sara play nurse.*

As Howard pulls the lever for his footrest, he hears a vehicle drive over the cattle-guard. Without having to look, the dad who knows the sound of each son's approach bellows, "Lois! Russ is here!"

- 291 -

9:48 PM

By the time the oldest Fleischer brother and his friend left for the river – about 8:30 or so – every joke; about Clint being "handy-capped," all the things Sara would have to help do *for* him, what Sara's nurse uniform would look like and how Clint couldn't whip Russell Martin again in 999 tries, had been made. Feeling a bit like Muhammad Ali after the Sonny Liston fight makes Clint feel better. So does the hydrocodone left over from his mother's root canal. But neither feel as good as his left hand on Sara's leg under the blanket.

Mom and Dad having gone to bed a bit ago, Clint and his "nurse" are finally alone.

"I was worried," Sara whispers to Clint, his hand in the ice.

"Worried about what?" replies the guy somewhat under the influence. "Worried he was gonna beat me to death in front of everybody?"

Long pause. "Yeah..."

"You know I hate to admit it, but my brother was right," Clint sighs. "If we fought a thousand times, he would whip my ass nine hundred and ninety-nine of 'em." Sara likes Clint's blend of humble and cocky.

"You think so?" she responds softly, as though no other outcome were possible.

"Yup," he affirms. "But you know what? I'd rather be lucky than good any day." Clint grins.

"I can't believe you weren't scared," Sara says in Clint's ear.

"I wasn't?" he answers with surprise. "Could've fooled me." Clint never realized how well he hid his fear.

"So, what do we do now?" Sara asks, her fingers in Clint's hair.

Worn out after a long day of work and an eventful evening, the wounded warrior gives Sara's question a moment of consideration. "How 'bout you stay here with me tonight?"

"Um, okay," Sara responds with surprised. "I'd like that."

Sunday, September 28th, 2014

5:30 AM

Up at her usual time, Momma Lois walks down the hall and into the open expanse that is her kitchen to the left and living room to the right. On the couch is the young couple, same as she last saw them – Clint reclining with his arm around Sara, her head resting on his chest.

Pain pill having worn off and needing to pee, Clint refuses to wake the angel snoring softly.

Old-fashioned in many ways, Momma Lois wouldn't normally allow a sleepover, but made an exception last night.

7:38 AM

Howard invites Sara to help with morning chores. Enjoying his first ever one-on-one time with her, he gains not only a better understanding of what happened last night, but the events leading up to it. One to tease Clint when he's around – and brag about him when he is not – Howard is proud of the way his son stood his ground.

9:41 AM

Holding Clint's wrist, instead of his hand, Sara walks into the small country church in the jeans she planned to go fishing in and a lilac blouse borrowed from Momma Lois. Sara has been looking forward to church all week. With a piece of butterscotch candy in her mouth, the girl who was awakened by Kyle staggering in at 2:08 AM takes a seat next to her man.

Sara leans over to whisper in Clint's ear, "Hey."

Clint whispers back, "Hey what?"

"I love you."

"More than bacon?" he curiously follows up.

"Only a bit more than bacon, but yeah," Sara giggles. Clint smiles. He loves the smell of her hair.

"That's quite a bit," Clint puts his arm around his girl.

"You know what?" he says back into her ear.

"What?" Sara feels like a couple of little kids swapping secrets.

"I love you just as much..." Clint's words tickle her ear.

"I know."

Kyle finds their lovey-doveyness nauseating.

12:31 PM

Howard says grace before Sunday dinner.

Sara fixes Clint a plate.

The Howard & Lois Show gets underway.

Kyle becomes extra Kyle. Envious of all the hoopla surrounding Clint – not only at home, but on Facebook as well – the guy who is used to being the center of attention turns up the dial. A little louder than usual, he leads the jokes regarding Clint's newly acquired dependence on Sara.

"I like taking care of him," Sara says with a wink.

"It's a good thing," Howard adds," 'cause you got about six weeks of it."

Sara is promoted to 'Foreman.' Clint is demoted to 'Sara's Assistant.'

5:34 PM

The tables have turned. Now Clint is the injured one who has to ride along while Sara runs the show. With plans to go to the doctor in the morning, he can hardly lift a door handle with either hand. From the passenger seat, he watches his Foreman climb over the fence and onto Leo's back.

8:21 PM
Babe and Lady's living room
"You don't look so good," Norman says, looking down at Babe in his chair.

Less than pleased that a CIA asset is standing in his living room, the man rudely woken replies, "That's because I'm *not* so good."

"Your girl isn't answering her phone," informs the man who brushed past Lady when he let himself in. "She at her boyfriend's house?"

"Probably," Babe answers reluctantly. Fearing for Lady, he knows lying about Sara's whereabouts could be dangerous. *He already knows where she is anyways.*

"I'm gonna need to use your phone."

8:24 PM
The Hill
RING! RING! Momma Lois gets up to answer the landline.

"Sara!" she says, bringing the cordless. "It's your grandmother." Suddenly nervous, Sara takes the phone.

Lady never calls unless something is wrong! She worries while saying, "Hello?"

"Why the fuck did your phone go to voicemail?!" Norman's gravelly voice jars the girl expecting a soft, rolling brogue.

"Is something wrong?" asks Momma Lois, alarmed by the look on Sara's face... Sara does not answer. By the time Momma Lois finishes her question, Sara has is gone.

"The phone in her purse is dead." Twelve explains, displeased at Sara's poor attention to detail. Clint looks at her funny. He notices a difference in her voice. "I'll be there within twenty minutes."

8:43 PM

Clint drives Twelve to Sara's house. Eyes forward, his usually chatty passenger hasn't said a single word since telling him she needed to go home. Unsettled by behavior so unlike Sara, he is all the more bothered by the white-haired guy parked in his usual spot.

"Are you sure you don't want me to come in?" Clint double checks.

Twelve gets out of the truck, walking away as though she didn't hear him.

What in the world has gotten into her? Clint sadly wonders. *She doesn't even walk the same.*

Twelve heads into the house without looking back.

Worried to the bone, Clint wants to follow her inside. Find out the identity of the conspicuous guy in the car. Fix whatever is wrong so life can get back to being as great as it was less than an hour ago... but he doesn't.

Instead, Clint respects her wishes, hoping whatever black cloud suddenly appeared might soon pass.

A bit dejected – and really wishing he had gotten a kiss goodbye – Clint continues out the South lane for home. *Please be okay, hun... please be okay.*

10:00 PM
Interstate 70 West

Both hands on the steering wheel, Twelve's new handler is personally escorting her to her next assignment.

Her seat belt fastened, the unarmed passenger traveling at 68 miles per hour is ready to jerk the wheel should Norman so much as even begin to reach for his gun.

He might be taking me somewhere to kill me, was Twelve's concern when told she was leaving with him. Though the assassin hasn't ruled it out, she sees little logic in killing her previous to her assignment. Setting her anger (at having been thrust back into the darkness once again) aside, the Natasha commits her awareness to staying alive. Unarmed and alone, she knows she is with a dangerous man.

The guy with deep wrinkles in his forehead and snarling disdain for his passenger feels no need to tell where they are going, how long it will take to get there, or what is expected of her upon arrival. Already hating Norman, Twelve wouldn't hate him any less if he did tell her.

I hate you. I want to murder you, the Natasha with Babe's amphetamines in her pocket thinks to herself. Not trusting her stoutly built handler any further than she could throw him, Twelve will not be going to sleep at any point while in his presence.

11:35 PM

Twelve breaks the long-standing silence by asking, "What's my assignment?"

Norman sighs. "You remember your last assignment?"

"Yes."

Norman offers no further explanation. A condescending silence follows.

I hate you. I want to murder you.

...three minutes pass.

"And try not to get shot this time," Norman scoffs.

Twelve considers jerking the wheel, letting the chips fall where they may. *That'd wipe that smug look off your face.* She can envision his jowls jiggling as the car rolls down the grassy slope.

Two miles under the speed limit, the dark green Taurus heads straight through the night. Growing thirsty and needing to use the restroom, Twelve refuses her handler the joy of knowing and telling her "Too bad."

If I need to go bad enough, I'll just piss in your seat.

Monday, September 29th, 2014

12:10 AM
Norman and Twelve enter Kansas City, MO.

3:15 AM
Nearing Hays, KS.

After weighing the pros and cons of murdering Norman, Twelve decides to wait and see how things play out. Parched, starving, and *really* needing to pee, she is also fatigued from Sara having only gotten a few hours of sleep last night. On the verge of telling Norman to "Pull over or get piss in your seat," she is relieved when he taps the brake, disengaging the cruise control. Flipping his turn signal, the guy with a stiff back and heartburn veers onto the Hays exit.

Sensing it is time, Twelve scrounges up enough saliva to swallow the tiny white capsule she pulls from her pocket.

"Taking your pills, I see," Norman says, his coal-black eyes straight ahead.

Twelve is surprised he noticed. The driver never took his eyes off the road.

"You're not gonna melt down like the others, are you?" Norman patronizes.

"Melt down?" Twelve repeats back. The dark green car eases along the off ramp.

"Yeah. Once your pills run out—"

"John Smith stopped giving me pills." *John Smith. Babe. Whatever.*

There is a pause. "So that white pill wasn't a Halotestin?" Norman follows up.

"What's Halotestin?"

"Halotestin. The steroid." Norman snarks as though Twelve is stupid. "You don't even know what you were taking?"

The Natasha shoots Norman a "fuck you" look. She does not like being talked down to. *I am definitely going to kill you one day.* The car turns at the light, heading into the small college town. Streetlights shine through the windshield. The inconspicuous sedan passes one 'CLOSED' business after another.

"So, you're off the pills now?"

"Yup." Twelve snips.

"What did you just take?" Norman pries.

"Something to keep me awake." Twelve can feel her heart picking up. Energy rising.

"Are you sleepy?" Norman snorts.

"Not now." Twelve says, eyes dilating. *Holy shit!* she thinks as the stimulant gains traction. *This stuff is awesome!* The Natasha rides the climbing rush. She soon feels as though her entire body is crawling blue electricity.

"I don't give a fuck what you do," Norman grumbles. "As long as you do your job." The guy checking his mirrors treats Twelve like a nuisance.

What does he mean, 'melt down'? wonders Twelve, her senses and perception more vibrant. The tiny hairs on her arms rise. The Natasha feels more than human. A goddess. *Are all the Natashas 'melting down'? Is what happened to me considered 'melting down'?* she pushes the question aside.

Ahead, Twelve spies an oasis of light in the otherwise desert of darkness.

3:20 AM

The Ford Taurus pulls into the gas station and up to the pump.

"Go do whatever you need to do, but don't take long," says Norman, pulling his black baseball cap low.

All too happy to put distance between herself and the guy she wants to shoot in the face, the suddenly sweating Twelve steps into the cool night air. *Ahh, that feels nice,* thinks the one drawing looks from the customers. Those eyeing the killer body wrapped in dark-colored jeans and a thin black hoodie assume her a college student.

Paying no mind to those goggling her, the Natasha uses the reflection off the back-glass of an SUV to keep an eye on Norman still at the pump. A good Samaritan holds the door for the hot chick walking inside. Twelve does not say "thank you."

His Natasha heading inside, Norman goes about wiping the windshield with a squeegee. Though it appears he is simply washing the windshield, the seasoned asset is, in fact, discreetly looking in every which way for anything amiss. He detects nothing out of the ordinary. He likes this time, early morning, very little movement. More difficult for anyone following to maintain cover.

Satisfied all is well, a stiff Norman heads inside to use the restroom and buy a drink. Dressed in slacks and a draping button-up, he pulls his baseball cap even lower over his blocky head to shield surveillance cameras.

Norman makes it a point to have never been anywhere.

3:37 AM

Norman pulls into a recently developed subdivision. Middle-class residences, none much more or less valuable than another. Split-level homes. Two-car garages. Above-ground pools. Bermuda grass. Cedar decks. Backyards enclosed with wooden or chain link fence.

Unlike the site of Twelve's last assignment, this neighborhood appears quaint, perfect for families with Labrador retrievers and SUV's. Everyone indoors and every light (save for porch and floodlights) off, it seems as though the entire neighborhood is asleep. Wary from last time, Twelve refuses to make assumptions.

Keeping Norman in the corner of her eye, Twelve scans the suburban scene. Bicycles laying in the manicured lawns, neatly trimmed bushes, 'My kid is on the honor roll' bumper stickers. She wonders how the names were selected for the streets intersecting into dead ends and cul-de-sacs... Daisy Pocket Lane, Myrtleberry Circle, Delaney Court.

No GPS, no map. Norman committed the maze of a subdivision to memory before leaving his extended stay hotel in O'Fallon, MO. After three turns and a straightaway, the handler navigating as though having been here a hundred times enters a cul-de-sac. He pulls in front of 2043 Lauren Court. A residence hardly distinguishable from the others, Twelve sees a late-model Subaru next to a red work truck with an aluminum toolbox and the tailgate down.

"That's it," Norman points out, circling an island of grass with a streetlight in the center. "No one survives." The Taurus nears the stop sign exiting the cul-de-sac.

Looking through the rear glass, Twelve notices something. "Stop," she orders Norman, as he begins pulling away from the sign.

The Natasha, twisting at the waist, looks back. From this angle – along the edge of neighbor's nearly identical home – she can see the target's back deck. *Hmmm.* Twelve smiles at the sight of a propane grill.

"What are you looking at?" grumbles Norman.

Rolling her window down with the push of her finger, the amped-up Russian ignores the guy ever in her periphery. *A gas meter. Good.*

"What are you looking at?" Norman gripes louder.

"No survivors?" repeats the Natasha spying outdoor chairs, a portable fire pit and a bright green beach towel draped over the railing of a deep, red deck.

"Did I stutter the first ti–?" ...before Norman can finish, the Natasha is out the door.

THUMP! Shutting her doorway harder than necessary is Twelve's way of saying "fuck you."

"You forgot your guns, ya dumb bitch!" Twelve ignores Norman's muffled words. She makes her way to the house.

Hair twisted into a bun and hoodie up, the Natasha passes like a specter under fluorescence shining down. A lioness on the prowl, Twelve stops at the mailbox with the flag up. *Who am I killing?* she wonders.

"What in the fuck is she doing?" Norman mumbles, watching Twelve rifle through the target's mail. The surly driver impatiently waits for her to double back for her weapons.

The return address on the electric bill: Adam Lambrecht. *Hmmm.* Twelve puts the mail back. *Guess I'll be killing Adam Lambrecht tonight.* The Natasha disappears into the darkness around the corner. She sees the dryer vent six feet off the ground. *Perfect!*

Baking beneath her hoodie, the killer with a bad case of cottonmouth and pupils twice their usual size walks to the corner of the chain-link fence. Left hand atop the rounded cap of the corner post, the Natasha throws her legs over the chest-high barrier, landing softly as a cat.

Walking past a tricycle, doggy toys and a kiddie pool, Twelve makes her way through the grass and on to the concrete pad leading to the deck. Careful not to step on the plastic scoop in a pail, the soccer ball, or the brightly colored sprinkler attachment along the way, she soundlessly makes her way up the cedar steps.

Oddly, the neighbor's motion light comes on, but not the one directly overhead.

Knelt beside the stainless-steel grill just outside the sliding glass door, Twelve makes sure the refillable propane tank is turned off before unhooking it from the six-burner grill with a deep-fryer attachment. A few twists of her wrist, and the threaded fitting at the end of the rubber hose is free. Using both hands, she carefully eases the half-full container up and out, making hardly any noise at all.

Securing the end of the hose in her left hand, Twelve lugs the cream-colored tank down the steps... along the patio... and out the gate.

Fuck, its hot! thinks the assassin sweating her thin hoodie through. She drops the tank in the grass below the dryer vent. Hands finally free, she unzips the damp, clingy top and strips it off.

Cool night air raises goosebumps.

Fuck that feels nice! Her navy-blue t-shirt drenched, she tosses the inside-out hoodie atop of the central heat and air unit.

Using her newly acquired strength, Twelve jerks the fitting out of the end of the black rubber hose hanging from the tank... *Need to bring a knife next time.*

To remedy the dilemma of the dryer vent being twice as high as the black hose is long, Twelve borrows a bicycle from the next yard over. *There we go,* thinks the Natasha resting the tank atop the bike propped below the vent.

Not to be impeded by the brittle plastic grate just inside the dryer vent —*SNAP!*— Twelve breaks the dried plastic piece along with two of Sara's French tips. *Ha ha ha!* The Natasha smiles. *Pretty pretty princess isn't going to like that!* Twelve's amusement soon gives way to another dilemma – fat vent, skinny hose. Undeterred, the pragmatist removes her t-shirt. Standing on her tippy toes, the Russian wearing a black sports bra stuffs the damp cloth alongside the skinny hose to hold it in place.

A couple quick turns of the valve and *psssshhhhh...*

Stepping back, the operative in designer jeans admires her ingenuity. Hissing like a snake, the black hose rushes combustible gas into the residence.

A bit chilly by now – and confident the hose will stay in place – Twelve manages her arms back into the sleeves. Zipper catching halfway up, the Natasha pulls up her hood as she runs out of the shadows and into the light. Looking like a jogger, she trots her way back to the waiting car.

Body humming with adrenaline, Twelve looks back at the house from whence she came...so peaceful, so serene with its neatly trimmed bushes and Red Maple sapling. Anticipating a show, she wonders how long it will be.

Parked along the street crossing Lauren Court, Norman has looked away just long enough to miss Twelve's approach.

The passenger door opens quickly, startling the grouchy handler. The assassin who moves like liquid is soon beside him again.

"You forget something, genius?" scoffs Norman; as Twelve fidgets with her stuck zipper.

Refusing to dignify Norman's remark with a response, she ignores him. His eyes lower to her cleavage – but only for a moment.

"Why are you *inside* the fucking car instead of *out there* doing your job–?" Norman boils.

"Just wait for it," ...*you fat piece of shit.* Heart galloping, skin oily and cheeks flushed, she hopes it happens soon.

"Wait for what?!" Norman's face reddens.

Heavy fumes spew... down the stairs... into the basement... nearer the pilot light in the water heater.

KA-BOOM!!!

Both Norman and Twelve's heads whip to the yellow-orange explosion causing the home to bulge and windows to burst. A blistering gust singes the lawn as the roof partially lifts from the structure.

Norman's face awash in a golden cast, he watches a billowing cloud plume into the sky. Watching Norman rather than the house, Twelve enjoys the sight of his mouth hanging open.

In awe, Norman turns to find Twelve's left brow raised. He has no words.

"Want to check for survivors?" asks Twelve. *I'm a goddess, bitch. Know that.*

Speechless, Norman gives Twelve's chest a quick glance. "Nice tits." He turns the key.

As Norman shifts into drive, Twelve declares, "I want my guns." The handle half lifted, the look on her face says, "*I will bolt right now if I don't get my way.*"

"What?" Norman sounds annoyed.

"My guns. I want them," repeats a Twelve in no mood for compromise.

Norman sighs as the car idles. "Why do you want your guns?"

"Because they are mine." *Don't challenge me, asshole.*

"You don't need 'em." The car starts to move.

Twelve opens her door.

The car stops. "God damnit." Norman grumbles. "Would you like to get your pistols out of the trunk *here,* in front of everyone, or would you rather get them around the corner, *away* from the house you just blew up?" Porch lights flip on as Twelve deliberates.

"Go," she allows, but only after consideration.

"Thank you for your permission," spits Norman to the sound of her door closing.

4:02 AM
Norman exits the neighborhood.

4:04 AM
Norman waits on the shoulder of the road while Twelve retrieves her pistols from the trunk – one still with crusty with dried blood.

THUMP! The trunk closes. An armed Twelve returns to her seat and shuts her door.

"Anything happens to me," Norman warns, "and your little boyfriend won't make it to church next week."

"Lucky for me, I don't have a boyfriend," Twelve states indifferently. "You may go now."

The handler pulls back onto the road. *This job changes things,* he realizes. *She knows her worth... Fuck!*

Pleased with herself — and Norman's dismay — Twelve continues to assert her authority by turning up the air conditioning, turning on the radio, and requiring he stop two times in the first ninety minutes.

The operatives keep an eye on one another as Norman makes his way to Interstate 70 East. Twelve uses her thumbnail to scratch crusty blood from her trigger guard.

If you weren't one of the only functioning Natashas... sulks Norman. He doesn't like taking guff from anyone, especially a woman.

7 hours and 13 minutes until back in St. Charles.

The Natasha has 7 hours and 13 minutes to be alive? She gets home... then what? Fall back into darkness? Still enjoying the blended high of amphetamines and killing, Twelve would gladly take on another assignment right now if it assured her a while yet among the living.

Amped up, the one feeling superhuman recalls Norman's threat about Clint and his family. She laughs to herself. *I don't give a shit about him.*

Strangely, the passenger feels both brand new, *and* as though she has been alive for twenty years. The world around her seems familiar — but not. Emerged fully formed as though from creation's pool, Twelve hates Sara for displacing her. An apex predator, the Natasha believes the strongest of the two belongs at the helm.

Brake lights ahead, headlights behind, mile markers pass one after another.

Enjoying the first semi-peaceful moments of her existence, Twelve reflects on the differences between this assignment and last.

First mission — fast. Action and reaction. Bullets. Thrill of the kill. This mission — slow. Calculating and methodical. Fire. Different kind of thrill. Last time began loud. This time, quiet.

Sweltering, but with only a black sports bra underneath, Twelve unzips partway and leans into her vent. *Ahhhh, that feels nice.* Twelve would strip down to her underwear were it not for Norman. Norman has been quiet since being put in his place back in Hays.

Brand new to the notion of daydreaming, Twelve pictures Shelly's face when Sara returned to the locker room after the fight. The shattered look. Her hands trembling. Smeared tears streaming. Twelve smiles.

Physical pain, emotional pain – one's as good as the other. The Natasha looks down at Sara's broken fingernails. *She is not going to like that!* Twelve smiles at the idea of Sara crying.

Norman drives. Twelve ponders. Time Passes.

Nearing Salina, KS, Twelve makes a connection between Sara's inability to cope with fear and gaining sudden control of the body. Twelve hates Norman but identifies him as a sufficient source of the type of stress required to put herself in the driver's seat. This makes her hate him marginally less.

Soon thereafter, Norman farts in the car. Twelve returns to previous level of hate.

Seven miles before the Salina exit, Twelve, smoldering pit-stained hoodie, says, "Fuck it," and goes about peeling it off. She tosses it in the backseat. Feels so much better. Down to her sports bra, the Natasha expects a snide remark from Norman, but hears nothing – for a while.

Driving past a Salina exit, Norman points to a billboard for the strip club Wild Wild West. "You looking for a second job?" he snarks.

I hate you so much. Twelve imagines Norman's brains splattering all over the driver's side window. Fortunately, there is nothing Norman can do to bring her down at the moment. Having just taken another one of Babe's little white pills – and feeling paramount as a result – Twelve dwells upon the mystery of gaining permanent control.

She recalls her initial attempt of drowning Sara with an overload of blue pills. Not yet even fully formed, the Natasha was already attempting to strangle her twin in the womb. Not knowing when – if ever – she will have the chance again, the Russian knows she must figure out something fast.

The one who will shoot Norman if he touches her goes through Sara's memories the way one fingers through an old filing cabinet.

By the time the dark green Ford nears Manhattan, Twelve has decided she's grateful for Clint, because she believes he can protect the one she calls 'Pretty Pretty Princess.' She smiles at the memory of blood exploding from Russell Martin's nose.

Twelve continues to reminisce.

Twenty-one miles past Lawrence, KS, Twelve announces, "I need to piss."

Norman sighs. "...God dammit."

Two minutes later

With hazards blinking, Norman looks through the open passenger side window and into Twelve face – as she squats down to pee just outside her door. He can hear stream hitting pavement, but cannot see the pistol pointed at him through the door. As cars zip by, Norman rings out, "Everyone can see your ass!"

"But you can't!" shouts Twelve over the Toyota Tacoma rushing by. Hardly concerned with cars passing, the less-than-proper Twelve doesn't worry that one of them might put a bullet in her head if given the chance.

"I thought you Natasha's were housebroke!" A gust of wind off another passing car rocks the Taurus.

"Nope!" Twelve maintains eye contact while pulling up her jeans.

You're my least favorite Natasha, thinks Norman as he turns off his hazard lights.

The return trip continues.

Thoughts veering between takeover and recollection, Twelve realizes just how much she enjoys looking back. She savors the memory of the "Collinsville Massacre." The bearded man's teeth bursting out. The top half of a bald head sheering off above the nose. Young men fleeing her wrath. As Norman switches lanes, she revisits the vision of the pregnant woman flying backwards into the doorway as though yanked by a rope.

Twelve took getting shot very personal.

With a wistful look on her face, the Natasha recalls Shelly crumpled on the floor, gasping for breath, wracked with pain greater than she could have imagined.

Noticing the smile, Norman eyes his passenger with suspicion. *What's that crazy bitch thinking?*

6:38 AM

The sun peeks over the horizon. Yawning, Norman is tired. Twelve is not.

85 miles from Kansas City, MO, the Natasha feeling like a prisoner on furlough is still flying high. Surging from what is basically methamphetamine, she is all the more stoked by what she believes a brilliant plan... *Only one way to test this theory!*

Twelve slips another white pill in her mouth.

I was in control until I went to sleep, reasons Twelve, remembering being helped to Sara's bed. *If I don't go to sleep, she can't take over. If I stay awake long enough, maybe she goes away forever...* Brimming with optimism, the Natasha is glad for an excuse to take more meth.

Amplified, Twelve feels immortal.

11:20 AM
Babe and Lady's home

Low on fuel, the Ford Taurus climbs the drive from the North.

Skin blotchy and flushed, Twelve wants away from Norman and into a shower. And grape juice. She wants grape juice too.

Twelve reaches back for her wadded-up hoodie as the car pulls to the fence.

Looking tired, Norman turns to the passenger lifting her door handle. "You did well," he grudgingly admits. "You didn't get shot this time."

- 310 -

Twelve's response is a snarl. *Are you done? 'Cause I want to go.*

"I don't know the next time I'll need you. Might be soon, might not. Keep your phone on you..." Norman's black eyes drift down to Twelve's breasts pushing out the top of her sports bra. With regards to how some handlers treat their Natashas, he kindly informs, "Don't worry, I won't be fucking you."

"I could've told you that—" Twelve flatly retorts. Norman dismisses the attitude from the woman with a loaded gun in her hand.

"Now, you don't have to stay with these people," he points at the house. "The man, John, he won't last much longer. I don't give a shit where you stay, as long as you let me know where you are and don't go too far. Got it?"

Twelve placates with a nod.

"Keep your phone *on you*, you got that?"

Twelve nods again.

"All right then." Norman gruffly adjourns. "Now get the fuck out of my car." All too happy to do so, Twelve exits the vehicle. One pistol in her hand, the other pushed down the front of her jeans, the Natasha holding a balled-up hoodie watches Norman pull out and away. She's not about to turn her back on him.

Pistol under her armpit to free a hand, Twelve lifts the latch on the gate. *Fuck! I feel gross!* thinks the woman yearning for eye drops and a shower. Despite feeling icky, the Natasha passing Babe's swing enjoys the sensation of supremacy.

Wooziness sets in as Twelve nears the porch. *What the fuck?* Dizziness. Disorientation worsens.

The Glock falls from her hand. Then the hoodie. Knees go weak as the world begins to spin. The Natasha collapses on the steps... Sara, who was next to Clint on the couch at Momma Lois' house only a moment ago, awakens to what feels like a hurricane passing over.

Lady rushes to the sound of crying.

One gun still shoved down the front of her jeans, Sara dry heaves while crying. The girl with nothing in her stomach to throw up hasn't the slightest idea how she came to such a pitiful state.

The front door jerks open above. "What in the world?!" hollers a Lady aghast. Careful not to step on the gun on the first step, the frazzled lass squats down to check for bullet holes and blood. *Why are you all but naked from the waist up?!* She assumes the worst.

Hysterically, Sara isn't aware of Lady's presence until feeling her hand on her shoulder. She clutches a handful of Lady's blouse while screaming "They're here!"

"Who's here, child?! Who's here?!" Startled, Lady looks every direction but sees nothing.

Delirious, the wild-eyed Sara sees... dozens of scary men wearing crawling up the hill with long knives in their teeth. "Oh, no!" Sara buries her face against Lady's chest. "They are gonna bite my fingers! They are gonna bite my fingers!!"

"What happened to your shirt!" says a hushed Lady trying not to wake Babe. "And no one is here! No one is going to bite you!"

"Yes they are!" sobs Sara, frightened beyond reasoning. "Yes, they are! And they might bite my piggies, too!"

"Your piggies?!" Lady struggles to lift the limp girl to her feet. *Oh, wait – she means her toes.* "Let's get you in here!" Lady whispers hard. "They can't get in if you're quiet!"

"Ooh-kay..." says Sara in a little girl's voice. Scared to the bone, but feeling much safer once inside, the girl being helped through the utility room has hardly enough strength to stand.

"Don't your legs work, child–?" whispers Lady, all but carrying Sara through the kitchen.

A bolt shoots through two of Sara's fingertips upon steadying herself along the wall. "Ow!" she yelps.

"Shhh!" Lady hushes, getting Sara into her room quickly as possible.

"They broke my fingers! Look Lady! They broke my fingers!" Sara cries. Arms around Sara's torso, Lady shuts the door with a backwards kick. She notices the broken nails and bruises on Sara's middle and index fingers on her right hand.

"I don't think they are broken, child—" Lady is light-headed from exertion.

"Yes they are!" Sara bellows. Lady heaves her on the bed, "Yes they are!!"

"If you don't be quiet, they are gonna know you're in here!" hisses Lady, who is not in the mood for this. She has never wished Sara away more than now.

"I'm gonna hide under the bed!" blurts Sara.

"No child, no!" Lady uses her body weight to hold Sara in place.

"You're squishin' me, Lady!" grunts Sara trying to squirm free. "You're squishin' me!"

"If you don't be quiet and hold still, they are going to come in here and *bite* your toes!" threatens Lady, desperate to calm the hallucinating girl.

And just like that, Sara freezes in place. Dread emblazoned across her face, she looks up into, pale greens and whispers, "...ohh-kay" in the tiniest voice. Only now does Lady realize how dilated and bloodshot her eyes are.

What in Hades is she on?! wonders Lady. Sara tries to look out the window above her head. A lightbulb goes off. Lady remembers Twelve demanding Babe's bottle of uppers. *That explains it.* The gal still lain across Sara doesn't bother asking any more questions.

Having gained a measure of control, Lady presses on.

"Now, do you want them to come in here and get you?" Lady asks in a spooky voice.

Her chin buried; Sara shakes her head.

Not knowing how Babe has managed to stay asleep during the noise, the whispering Lady continues. *"If you stay perfectly still while I go get something, I promise they won't be able to get you."* Sara wears the expression of a scared six-year-old. Lady can tell her words are finding their mark. "Okay... now don't move... I'll be *riiight baaack.*"

Her eyes shiny eyes, Sara nods her head slowly up and down.

Slowly at first, Lady eases off the pouty-lipped girl and disappears around the corner into the kitchen.

As long as I hold perfectly still, they can't get me. As long as I hold perfectly still, they won't get me. As long as I hold perfectly still, they won't get me, Sara reassures herself. She looks at her bruised fingertips and broken nails. "My fingers are broken—" she whines long and low.

Suspecting Norman drugged and violated Sara, the Lady at the end of her rope digs through Babe's pill basket in search of something to counter the stimulants. Lady dumps six of Sara's blue pills, three Xanax, one OxyContin and one Ambien into her palm. Still winded from dragging the girl who feels like she is made out of lead, Lady takes the pills and glass of water to Sara. Knowing she has helped herself to Babe's pill basket, Lady is fairly certain she won't overdose.

Anxious to do whatever Lady tells her – so the mean people outside don't come in and bite her fingers and toes – Sara gulps down the pills.

Why didn't you just leave when you had the chance, child? Lady shakes her head.
Fifteen minutes pass, each minute sheering another layer of fear – along with a layer of comprehension. Same as the last time she took multiple blue pills, Sara's brain shuts down. Unlike last time, she has untold amounts of pharmaceutical grade amphetamines refusing to allow unconsciousness.

Though her mind is offline, her body keeps on going.

Eleven minutes later.

Sara basically, a 5'6" two-year-old, is lead to the tub. "Don't drown," instructs Lady, shutting the door on her way out.

Blissfully incoherent, Sara enjoys the tub. Fortunately, Lady returns to check before it overflows. So far gone is Sara's awareness that she fails to recognize the agitation on Lady's face. The exasperated lass walks away.

Sara continues to play in the tub.

Forty-two minutes later
Lady returns to find Sara her teeth chattering. The tub has gone cold. Lady helps put clothes on the girl who has forgotten how to dress herself. Her eyes vacant, Sara looks through Lady.

May have overdone it on the pills, the simmered gal regrets. "Stick out your arm." The human Barbie puts her arm through the shirt.

Eventually, after getting Sara dressed and brushing out her wet hair, Lady asks, "Are you hungry?"

Sara shakes her head.

"Are you thirsty?"

Sara nods her head.

"Can you say words?" Lady challenges.

Sara nods again.

"Ahhh Hades," Lady sighs. "I drugged you simple." Soon, Sara is situated in front of the TV on her bed with a bowl of popsicles and a covered drink with a straw.

A tired Lady shuffles to her recliner, falling asleep soon after.

57 minutes later
Lady wakes to the sound of a babbling Sara – stripped down to her underwear – taking all of the items out of cabinets and setting them on the counter. The lights are on, but nobody's home.

"What in the world?!" Lady throws her hands up. "And where are your clothes I helped you put on?!"

"Hot." Sara answers while retrieving the crock-pot out from the bottom cabinet. Lady soon leads her back to her room by her arm.

Believing it very important everything be taken out and placed on the counter tops, Sara cannot understand why Lady is not happy about her help. What Sara was doing makes perfect sense – to her. She believes it crucial she finish what she started.

"I swear, child," Lady says to the girl with her bottom lip sticking out. "You're like having a pet monkey in the house."

Sara's brain is too numb to respond.

"You want to watch *Aladdin*?" Lady asks the girl with skin still flushed and eyes blankly staring.

Sitting slumped on the edge of her bed, Sara just shrugs.

"You are whacked out of your head," Lady points out, feeling all the worse for rashly giving her so many pills.

"Hot." Sara says again pointing to her arm. Lady touches her skin reddened by stimulants. Lady checks her pulse. Pulse racing.

"Let's get you back in the tub—" Lady sighs. *I wish you had an 'off' switch, child.*

Thirty minutes later
Aside from Sara being somewhat able to dress herself – and being able to say "hot" and "hurt" – this bath is same as the last.

Fearing brain damage, Lady gets the walking disaster situated once again.

"Okay," Lady says with a bargaining tone. "If I put in *Aladdin,* will you sit still and watch it?"

Sara nods, vacant eyes shining.

"You promise?"

Sara nods again.

"Can you use your words to promise me—?"

Sara nods again.

"I believe you've cooked your brain, child," Lady mutters as she hits play. "You sure you're not hungry?"

Wet hair sways as she shakes her head.

Never thought you'd turn away food... "I need to go check on Babe—and, if possible, get some sleep. It was a long night last night. If I get you some more popsicles, do you promise to stay in your bed and not get off of it?" *It's like bargaining with a mute five-year-old.*

Sara nods.

Hesitant at best, Lady brings Sara six popsicles and leaves her to her own devices. *...at least the smoke alarms will let me know if she starts a fire...* The weathered caretaker checks on Babe and returns to her chair.

Ninety minutes pass.

Sara, who's been meaning to get back to her project in the kitchen, has concluded that *Aladdin* is the single greatest film of all time.

3:28 PM

The credits rolling, Sara, who has by now regained enough cognizance to hit 'Rewind', waits for the tape to return to the beginning so she can watch it again.... *KNOCK, KNOCK, KNOCK* From happy as a lark to scared stiff, the girl with her mouth stained purple from popsicles panics, *Oh no! Someone's here to get me?!* Sara calms herself with Lady's whispered words. *If you stay right here and hold perfectly still, they won't be able to get to you.*

Sara listens as Lady makes her way to the door.

...she hears talking but can't hear what Lady and the male voice are saying. Her imagination running wild, Sara fears the dog catcher is here to take her away. Sara doesn't consider the possibility of Clint swinging by to check on her.

Believing it best Clint not see Sara like this, Lady tells him Sara is gone but will be back soon.

Deeply unsettled, Clint has no choice but to head on home and wait.

I wasn't kidding, Lady thinks, envisioning the blank look in Sara's eyes. *She isn't here. The Sara you know is far, far away.* Lady feels bad about lying, but knows it necessary.

Sara looks at Lady now in her doorway. "Is the dog catcher gone?!"

"What-?" Lady balks. "Wait — yeah. Yeah, the mean dog catcher is gone." *At least you're using words now.* "Are you okay in here? You wanna watch another movie?"

"No! I wanna watch *Aladdin* again!" It is plain to see her worry of the kidnapping dog catcher has passed. And that Sara is not getting tired – at all.

"Well, you didn't burn the house down last time, so... *yawwwwwwn* ...so I guess you're doing okay." Lady's schedule is catching up with her. "Are you hungry yet?"

"Nope!" peps the girls excited about more *Aladdin*.

Lady hits play and walks away.

Ninety more minutes pass.

Awakened twice by Sara singing along loudly to '*A Whole New World*' and '*Ain't never had a friend like me*', Lady simply sniffs the air for smoke and goes back to sleep. Tired to the bone and hanging on by a thread, the woman who's hardly left the house in months has never felt so run down.

...Rewind... Play. Sara tiptoes into the kitchen for the rest of the popsicles. *Oh yeah!* she remembers, looking around at the stuff she pulled from the cabinets earlier, *I need to finish this job! After Aladdin's over, though.* The popsicle bandit sneaks back into her room.

...Some time later, Sara's voice burst from her room in song, "A whole new world!! A new *fantastic* point of view!!" Against all odds, neither Lady nor Babe are awakened by Sara's unrestrained singing.

"No one to tell us no, or where to go!" ...by the third chorus, Sara decides to legally change her name to Jasmine.

5:07 PM

By the time Sara is hitting 'Rewind' again, the Xanax and Ambien have mostly worn off. The OxyContin never did anything because of her tolerance. But the brain deadening blue pills are still going strong. Roughly 75%. This, while the amphetamines remain in full swing. Sara has decided *Aladdin* is her new favorite thing ever – "You ain't never had a friend like me!" Lady wakes up this time.

Maybe we can put her up for adoption.

6:40 PM

Suddenly motivated, Sara decides to reorganize her closet.

As though divinely inspired, Sara sets about her task. Soon, every article of clothing is in a heaping pile on her bed. "I can show you the world!" she sings, dividing the big pile into smaller piles. Each pile has to be perfect.

7:50 PM

Lady checks in on Sara to find her restacking her clothes for the fourth time. Not wanting to disturb the girl so quietly keeping to herself, Lady returns everything Sara placed on the counters to its rightful place.

As Lady's night drags on, Sara's night flies by.

Sara's mind, usually jumping from one thought to the next, is with laser focus on her task. Needing her closet to be perfect, she tries really, really hard – until deciding the closet doesn't matter and abandons her project for something else.

9:50 PM

Sara enters the kitchen. She notices everything back in its rightful place. Hands on her hips, she shakes her head. *After I went through all that trouble.* Sara is none-too-pleased with Lady undoing all her hard work.

Physically unimpaired, Sara re-undertakes her previous objective. Why? Because doing so makes perfect sense.

As Clint worries on the farm, Sara finishes piling every appliance, dish, canned good, spice, utensil and Tupperware into a rather impressively arranged pyramid on the kitchen floor. Mind swimming with chemicals and sense of accomplishment, Sara congratulates herself. *Good job, Sara! Good job!* The girl still in her underwear sees the top of Lady's head over the back of her chair. *Lady is going to be so surprised when she wakes up!*

10:16 PM

Sara has her best idea yet! For reasons that make super-great sense to her, she stands over the tub, dumping shampoo, conditioner, liquid hand soap, mouthwash, three tubes of toothpaste, a container of bodywash, and a half a bottle of cocoa butter. *I am really getting stuff done today!* Sara nods contently. Tub slick with a pool of multi-colored goop, the girl with a mute look in her eyes dumps the waste basket in as well. *Good job, Sara. Good job.*

While congratulating herself, a lightning bolt strikes – *I GOTTA GO SEE CLINT!*

Like a fireman rushing to an emergency, Sara heads into her room, puts on shorts, a t-shirt and shoes (with no socks) runs into the forty-three-degree night.

GOTTA SEE CLINT! GOTTA SEE CLINT! GOTTA SEE CLINT! Burning to see Clint, Sara runs down the Southbound lane as fast as her legs will carry.

10:27 PM

Sara turns for the farm... *GOTTA SEE CLINT! GOTTA SEE CLINT! GOTTA SEE CLINT!* Hardly having slept in two days and eaten nothing but popsicles in the last twenty-eight hours, the dehydrated – but fully charged – Sara races through the chilly night. "A whole new world!" her voice carries in the crisp air. "A new *FANTASTIC* point of view!"

Happy as can be, the girl with a runny nose is oblivious to the cold... "No one to tell us NO, or WHERE TO GO! Or that we're only dreaming! A WHOLE NEW WORLD!!"

11:38 PM

Seventy-one minutes and fourteen miles later, Sara catches her t-shirt on the barbed wire along the North forty fence line. Sara cuts across the pasture. Not minding the hole ripped in her sweated-through shirt, she continues her dash for Clint's window. Fueled by desire, and the collection of chemicals, Sara runs around cow-patties and over fallen branches. The brick house in the distance grows larger with every bounding stride. Legs burning and heart on fire, she soon feels gravel crunching under her feet. The cows, watch Sara hop over the cattle guard, run under the willow tree and up to Clint's bedroom window.

Clint, already awake, hears *tap, tap, tap* on the glass. Sara melts at the sight of her love in the window. *"Heeeey,"* whispers the girl with cherry red cheeks and lips. Clint, unable to believe his eyes, slides the window up.

"What are you–?! How did you–?! *What are you doing here?!"* Clint gushes low. He can tell by Sara's face that something is way out of the ordinary.

"I came to see you!" a panting Sara whispers way too loud.

"Shhhh–! You're get me killed!" Clint shushes with a whisper. "How did you get here? And why aren't you wearing a coat?" he follows up. Lost in Clint's face, Sara enjoys the warmth coming through the screen.

"I came to see you!" Sara blissfully whispers.

"How'd you get here?!"

"Um... I ran really fast!" she beams, proud of her sweaty self. Standing still for the first time, the night air cools the dampness on her skin. Sara begins to shiver.

"Where have you been?!" asks the guy wanting to ask ten questions at once. He stops himself. "Wait – I'm coming out!" Her heart a-flutter, Sara watches her love disappear into the hall.

While Sara waits Clint, sneaks through the house and into the utility room. He opens the backdoor to find no Sara.

"Where in the hell–?" mutters the guy wearing a t-shirt and boxers. Only after rounding two corners does Clint locate Sara, still looking through his bedroom window. *"Hey!"* he whispers. Sara's beaming face whips around.

Clint is almost knocked down when the girl with ice-cold skin jumps into his arms.

His breath squeezed out of him – and Sara's freezing nose pressed to his cheek – Clint is kissed with all of Sara's passion.

"Where have you been?" he manages.

"I don't know." Nothing matters. Sara's in Clint's arms. The cows look on.

"You don't know where you were?" grunts a disturbed Clint.

"Nuh, uh—" Sara dismisses, resuming her kiss. Clint's worry overwhelming, he forces separation.

"Did you *run* from home to here?"

"Yeah!" Sara pulls Clint back in. But the guy with a cast on his hand holds strong.

"Whyyy?" He asks in two long syllables.

"Because I wanted to see you—" ...Sara's face turns sad that Clint doesn't seem happy to see her.

Too troubled to express his delight, he asks, "Why did you run here in the middle of the night?"

Sara stares into blue eyes brimming with worry... saying nothing, she begins to shake.

"Let's get you inside—" Clint relents.

Silently – and totally expecting his mother to appear out of nowhere – Clint escorts his peculiar acting love to the dark basement. Relieved and worried at the same time, the guy still chilly from being outside for only a short time turns the adjustable dial for just enough light to see.

Through the dim, Clint leads Sara to the couch halfway between the stairs and the pool table. Teeth chattering, Sara watches him round up every quilt, blanket, and sheet in the basement. She sits perfectly still as he wraps them around one after the other. Sara likes when Clint takes care of her.

With layers bunched under her chin, Sara looks up adoringly.

"Okay, now," knelt down in front of Sara, Clint quietly restarts his line of questioning. "Where have you been, and why are you so... not yourself?"

"*I love you*," Sara just has to say it.

"Shhh!"

"Oh yeah," Sara giggles, hands clasping over her mouth. "*I love you*," she whispers much quieter.

"I love you, too. Now where were you?" ...Sara's face goes blank once again. Clint cups his warm hands on her cold cheeks.

"...I love you," she can think of nothing else to say. Nothing else matters.

Frustrated, Clint drops his head.

Why isn't he happy to see me? wonders Sara, *I came all this way to see him.* Aware only of how glad she is to be in front of the man she loves, Sara leans in for a kiss he cannot deny.

Her lips are so soft and her nose is so cold, thinks a momentarily faltering Clint. *Snap out of it! Something is wrong! Figure it out!* barks the voice in his head. "Look, you just ran *fifteen* miles, in shorts and a t-shirt, in the middle of an awfully chilly night after..."

Sara silences Clint with another kiss. Reaching up from under the layers, she pulls him close.

Though it takes a while – and all his resolve to do so – he pulls away once again.

Smiling like she just got away with something, Sara *sniffs* her runny nose and licks her glistening lips. Hazel eyes blaze.

She didn't come here to talk, Clint senses. Hair wind-blown, cheeks flush, pupils wide. Sara is primal. Feral energy. Emanating desire. All she knows is want.

Sara pulls at Clint – he resists. "You're not yourself. There's something wrong with–" he is silenced by soft lips once again. Attempting the good fight, his resistance crumbles.

"Nothing is wrong," Sara breathes, her lips touching his. Rising to her feet, the seductress pulls the blankets away. As easy as leading Leo with a handful of oats, she places Clint on his back along the couch. One knee on the cushion, a foot on the floor, a Sara with draping hair lords over.

"I only want to do this if–" Clint half-heartedly protests.

"Shut up." Sara will not be denied. "This is what I want... I've wanted it for a while now."

She's right, Clint. Shut up. Straddled. Dangling hair tickles his face. Hot breath on his neck. His calloused palms run atop prickled skin.

Sara isn't cold anymore. She gives herself to Clint.

<u>Tuesday, September 30th, 2014</u>

12:45 AM

Under a sheet, nestled between Clint and the back of the couch, Sara lays with an arm and leg across. Neither yet to speak, they lay in dim silence, reeling at what has transpired. Things are different now. Her head on his chest, Sara is lulled by the rhythm in his chest.

Clint sniffs... *Her hair smells like coconut.*

Yawning, Sara is not sleepy. She's at peace.

1:01 AM

"I'm hungry," Sara whispers, Clint's fingertip grazing up and down her arm.

"Okay, I'll get you something to eat," he whispers back, "But I gotta get up..."

"I'm not that hungry–"

1:22 AM

"How long has it been since you've eaten?"

"It's been a while," answers Sara, her mind clear.

"Well," responds Clint, only able to address one issue at a time. "I've got to get something for this hand anyways..." Sara reluctantly allows her man from beneath her. Naked beneath the sheet, the girl with chocolate hair a mess watches her love tiptoe up the stairs.

Expecting his mother to be awaiting him in the kitchen, Clint allays his fear by rationalizing... *Everybody's gotta die some time.*

Braced for consequence, he is relieved to find no Momma Lois laying in wait. Like a cat burglar, Clint gets a pill for his aching hand and makes Sara a heaping plate of leftovers.

1:37 AM

Three cold pork chops and some fried potatoes later, Sara is out like a light. Finally having crashed, she sleeps atop a Clint in disbelief... *We need to do this a lot.*

Sara lightly snores. Clint, who can't stop smiling, thinks to himself, *Even if they do come down here, what are they gonna do? Chew me out?... I've been chewed out before.* He lightly rubs his lover's back through the sheet... *Better not go to sleep,* Clint warns himself. He is haunted by the notion of waking up to his mother looking down... *Better not go to sleep...*

1:59 AM

Clint is wide awake, confident he can stay up all night.

2:15 AM

Twirling Sara's hair makes Clint's eyelids dangerously heavy. He knows he should wake her up and get her out of the house, but can't bring himself to do so. Besides, he doesn't want to move. *They can't actually kill me,* Clint reminds himself. *And even if they could, they wouldn't do it in front of Sara, because they like her.* Breathing on his chest, Sara murmurs in her sleep.

2:51 AM

Clint doses off.

4:28 AM

Clint jerks awake. *Holy hell! I just fell asleep!* He panics, but with instant relief. Fearing the wrath of his mother, Clint makes the executive decision. *That's it! No more pushing my luck!* ...Clint wiggles a little, trying to rouse Sara lightly as possible.

Nothing.

"Hey," he whispers, "We gotta go, so we need to get up."

"Mmnaymgrhm..." replies Sara, still asleep.

4:42 AM

Wearing her t-shirt inside out and shorts that took forever to find in the dark, a groggy but glowing Sara follows Clint quietly up the stairs. Halfway across the living room, she doubles back to the kitchen for the last pork chop. Swallowed by Russ's old Carhartt coat Clint grabbed in the utility room, Sara is escorted into the chilly night. Chewing on a porkchop, the girl with goosebumps down her bare legs is surprised when the guy holding her hand leads past his red pick-up and into Kyle's white, 2004 Dodge Intrepid.

"This is Kyle's car," Sara innocently points out.

"I know."

"Won't he get mad if you take his car?" The two get inside, shutting the doors so gently that they don't latch all the way. "Won't Kyle get made if you take his car?" Sara asks once again.

Clint turns with a funny look on his face. "You think he'd hesitate to take mine if he needed it?" Right hand out of commission, he has to reach across to turn the ignition with his left. "Besides," he adds with a wry smile. "I wouldn't take my truck the route we're going..." Sara's pearly whites shine. She loves the mischievous look on Clint's face.

Her hair a mess and butt cold on a cloth seat, sneaking around with her guy (who doesn't normally do such a thing) is the cherry on top of the best night of Sara's life.

Rather than going out the normal way – right past Mom and Dad's bedroom window – Clint rounds the North side of the big shed, headlights off.

"Where are we going?" Sara whispers, still in 'sneaky mode'.

"A route that would probably be better with a four-wheeler," Clint answers with a cavalier calm. As they pass by the grain bins, Sara leans over and kisses his cheek. Clint loves Sara's little kisses.

Only upon facing West – and being on the other side of the shed – does Clint turn on the headlights. Pulled up to the fence running behind the grain bins, they near an old gate.

"I'll get it!" says Sara, out of the car in a flash. In the shine of low beams, she undoes the chain and swings the galvanized gate.

"Isn't she something," Clint says to himself as he drives from the golf course-like edge of the yard into the rough, tough ground of cow tracks and weeds. Tiny acorns and twigs crunch beneath the tires of the borrowed car as he pulls through. "Go ahead and leave it open, doll," Clint says through the passenger window.

"Okay," chirps Sara, glad to do whatever. She gets back in. Clint turns the headlights off. "Why'd you turn the lights off?" she asks.

"Cause I only turned 'em on to look at your legs," he confesses.

Sara playfully lifts the bottom of the oversized coat so Clint can see her legs in the glowing luminance of Kyle's CD player.

"...you're not making this any easier, you know."

"So what do you want to do?" asks Sara as the car begins along the clearing.

"Hun," Clint leans over to confide. "What I want to do, and what we're gonna do, are two different things..."

Sara giggles.

"I *want* to take you back to the basement, board up the doors, and never come out," Clint says mater-of-factly.

They roll slowly down the tree line. "But what I'm *gonna* do is take you home and *try* to slip back in before Mom and Dad wake up."

"What about Kyle's car?" asks Sara as Clint makes no effort to avoid sticks or cow pies.

"I'm not worried about that right now..." Clint thinks of all the times his little brother has used his stuff without permission and returned it in poor condition.

After 1200 yards of bouncing over less than suitable terrain without headlights on, Clint arrives at the end of the lane, then turns up the dirt road leading to the highway.

5:01 AM

Having taken longer than planned to get on the highway, Clint must now make up for lost time. Once on blacktop, he punches the gas.

Thrown back in her seat, Sara feels a thrill as though being chased by the cops. "You don't usually drive like this!" she exclaims, hanging onto Clint's arm above the cast.

"It's okay, this car is used to it." Preferring to test his luck with the highway patrol rather than his mother, he races Sara home. He can hear his mother now... *I don't want you corrupting that poor girl!*

Clint is pretty sure the "she made me do it" defense won't fly.

5:14 AM
Sara's house

Her legs sticking out the bottom of Russ's tattered old coat, Sara watches Clint race away – but only after a quick kiss, an "I love you" and another quick kiss. Feeling much the way she did upon her first swallow of vodka without making a face, she watches the taillights of his commandeered automobile until they disappear. Wishing to still be sleeping atop him in the basement, the yawning girl walks across the patio, onto the porch and through the door she didn't latch on her way out.

5:16 AM

Sara takes a curious look around the kitchen. *Why would Lady take everything out of the cabinets and pile it in the middle of the kitchen floor?* ...she finds this odd.

Tired, but in a good way, she decides to brush her teeth and go to bed. Upon entering the bathroom... *Why did Lady dump shampoo, bodywash and trash in the tub?!*

5:44 AM

After burning down the highway and retracing his route along the fence line, Clint pulls into Kyle's spot with the headlights off. Walking away from the car smeared green with weeds and cow pies, he creeps in through the back door. Quickly stripping back down to his t-shirt and boxers (in case he runs into anyone in the hall), Clint tiptoes through the living area and into the hall. Bedroom. Victory.

5:47 AM

Feeling like the smoothest criminal in the world, the guy who will have to pay someone to chisel the grin off his face slides under the covers. *This is the part where I wake up and realize it was all a dream,* thinks Clint.

His first opportunity to reflect; the young man with a blanket pulled over his head tries to wrap his head around what just happened. *Did Sara really just show up in the middle of the night and force me to have sex with her? I think she did.*

6:00 AM

Clint hears the alarm clock from his parent's room. Playing opossum, there is no reason for anyone to suspect anything other than a wholesome night's rest. Clint knows Kyle won't snitch on the brother with so much dirt on him. The only thing left is to straighten up the basement.

6:03 AM

Clint hears footsteps toward the bathroom in the hall. *Be cool. Be cool. Be cool. Be cool.*

7:12 AM

Kitchen Table

At the head of the table, Howard sits with the entertainment center not far behind. Clint to his left. Lois to his right. And Kyle at the opposite end of the table big enough for six. The morning seems same as any other... except it's not.

Clint, who is not good at eating with his left hand, is a bit quieter than usual.

"Clint, did you hear any coyotes last night?" Howard asks curiously.

"No," Clint answers, not looking up. "Didn't hear any coyotes."

Howard, who usually spends his mornings philosophizing or complaining about liberals, seems fixated on whatever last night's sound might have been.

Kyle pays no mind as he wolfs down biscuits and gravy, three eggs over-easy, and four pieces of bacon. He can't get out the door quickly enough.

"I don't know, Clint... Something had the cows stirring in the middle of the night..."

Shit. Dad knows. "I don't know, I was asleep." *Shit. Shit. Shit. Shit. Shit. Dad knows!*

"I thought for *sure*," Howard spouts, "that I heard *some* kind of sound coming from – well, I don't rightly know... the river bottom maybe?" Howard sips his coffee. "Kyle, you hear anything?"

"Nope," answers a Kyle with an unusually clear conscience.

A sheepish glance at his dad, and Clint knows: *The old man is enjoying this.*

Aside from the sounds of eating and Momma Lois peeling apples for a pie, the breakfast table is silent for a while.

Maybe he is gonna let this go and not torment me about it with Mom right here.

"You know what, Clint?"

Nope. He's definitely not gonna let this go. Clint sighs. "What?"

"I couldn't get back to sleep last night for the sound of whatever *it* was..."

Please stop. Clint begs with an upward look.

"Now I can sleep through the sound of your mother's snoring..."

"Can't hear me from the couch–" Momma Lois smarts without so much as looking up.

"Yeah, the chainsaw sound of your mother's snoring is something I've gotten used to..." Howard rolls on undeterred. "But I just couldn't get back to sleep last night. Not with that noise. Did you hear anything, Lois?"

"If I said 'yes', would you be quiet?" She casually sasses.

"Probably not," Howard answers, without missing a beat. "I think I might just go ahead and check the vents... it might've been coming through the vents. Maybe it was coming from the basement–" Howard bumps Clint's foot under the table.

"Don't know what to tell ya. I was sleeping. So sound I musta missed it." *Shut up. Shut up. Shut up. Shut up!!*

"Once I shut the vent it seemed to die down a little..." Howard, cat. Clint, mouse.

Are you trying to get me killed, old man? Clint wonders, realizing the vent in the far corner of the basement is under his parents' room. He didn't think of that.

"Maybe it was cats fighting," continues Howard, known for belaboring points and wringing every last drop of funny out of a joke. "You know the sound – don't ya, Clint? The sound of two cats really going at it?"

"Maybe it *was* cats." Clint pretends to dismiss... *Well, better him know than Mom,* believes the guy biting counting his blessings. Fortunately, Momma Lois is paying his father no mind.

"Did you tell Dad what happened at school?" Kyle weighs in. Clint has never been so happy to hear his little brother speak.

"What happened at school?" concerned, Momma Lois jumps into the conversation.

"Russell apologized."

"No, kiddin'," Howard says with a raise of both brows.

"You kicked *his* ass, and *he* apologized to *you*? Sounds like you punched a little Jesus into him."

"Yeah," Clint is delighted to be talking about anything else. "He said he was wrong and that he was sorry for starting trouble."

"How'd he look?" asks Howard.

"I think I ruined picture day." Clint allows himself to smile.

"Well, I am glad you two are friends now," jokes the smirking dad.

"Yeah, we're best pals," Clint mutters.

"Sounds to me like you tricked Russell into thinking you're tougher than he is," Howard prods.

"Russ says that the only way for Russell Martin to get dumber is for him to get bigger!" Kyle quotes his older brother as he gets up from the table.

"So long as he doesn't wise up before graduation, I might still have some summer help!" The patriarch laughs at his own jokes whether anyone else does or not. "Can you drive a tractor in a body cast, Clint?"

"I am practicing one body part at a time," Clint says, holding up his right hand.

"That's good thinkin'," says Howard, nodding as he leans back in his chair. "You've got *Russ Martin* tricked into thinking you're tougher than him and you've got *Sara* tricked into thinking you're good enough for her...you should play professional poker."

"Don't underestimate a good bluff," Clint says through a smile.

"Speaking, of Sara..."

Here we go again, Clint drops his head.

"She didn't come over last night. When's the last time you saw her?"

...here we go again.

6:04 PM
Sara's bed

Having slept like a rock over twelve hours, Sara opens her eyes. Face down, the girl with dry-mouth and a headache pushes herself up... dehydrated muscles creak. *What in the hell?* Thinks Sara, having never felt this particular brand of terrible. Feeling whispers from every injury her body has ever known, she is both starving and dying of thirst. Sara drags her stiff self past her perfectly stacked clothes on the floor.

She means to ask Lady why she emptied her closet and did that... but first, gotta pee.

Sara scans her memory for why she feels so awful, but her recall goes back only so far Clint's bedroom window.

Sara reaches for the doorknob to the bathroom – "Ouch!" *What the hell?!* She looks down at two broken nails on her right hand. *WHAT THE HELL?!!* She touches her thumb to painful tips... *ouch, ouch, ouch.*

Sara walks into the bathroom, surprised once again at the mess... *Oh yeah, Lady dumped all the shampoo and stuff in the tub. What has gotten into her?*

Sara removes the garbage and worst of the multi-colored goop before turning on the shower. Careful not to slip in the soapy tub, the girl thinking naughty thoughts from last night hopes Clint will want to do that again soon.

6:22 PM
Kitchen

Going into the kitchen for food, Sara finds Lady. She can tell she is *not* happy.

"Good morning," Sara timidly greets.

"Clint came by," Lady coldly informs of yesterday. "I told him you were asleep." This is all she says before walking away and disappearing into her bedroom.

Why is Lady being mean to me? Sara is puzzled. Confused – and missing a day – she thinks today is Monday.

After pouring herself a glass of juice, Sara turns to check on Babe. With a purple juice mustache – and pajama bottoms and t-shirt adhered to her from not drying off well enough – Sara is delighted to find her smoking buddy awake.

"Heey!" she says with a smile that brightens his day.

"Well, hello there, kiddo–" says Babe during a hug. Sara has become a hugger since meeting the Fleischers.

Though happy to see Babe, it's the first time she's seen him in a while without OxyContin or Dilaudid as a cushion. He looks terrible. Sara's chest tightens. Her eyes well. She goes to speak, but no words come out.

"How's my girl?"

"I'm okay," Sara squeaks. *He's so sick, yet he is worried about me.*

"Lady said you slept all day," says Babe. "You feeling okay?"

"Yes, I'm..." Stabbing pain in her chest. "No, I'm fine... I am really good." Forcing a smile, the sight of Babe decline is a knife twisting in her chest.

"Oh, now..." Babe reaches for Sara's hand, "it's gonna be all right... it's gonna be all right." Tears run down cheeks still rosy from the shower.

"I know," Sara doesn't know what else to say. Squeezing his hand, she wonders if he knows she's her, or if he thinks she Petra. She swipes at her cheeks. *Babe is sick. He is dying. He is hurting. He's gonna die soon. I don't see him enough. I don't help enough. I'm gonna lose him forever. Babe is gonna die soon.*

Gazing up proudly, Babe knows who's at his side.

"I don't want you to be sick." This is simply too much. Babe is the first person she ever loved.

"I don't want to be sick," Babe would do anything to assuage her pain, "but it's something we just have to deal with."

Who am I gonna tell things to now? Wonders Sara, her chin crinkled. She doesn't want Babe to see her cry, but she can't hide it. The girl beside the bed feels powerless. "Can I do anything to help–? Is there anything I can do?"

"Yeah," Babe says. "Yeah, there is... pull up a chair."

Sara pulls up the stool from the corner. "Okay, what can I do?"

"Just talk to me..." Babe says softly. "Tell me what's going on with my girl. Tell me... tell me how you feel."

A little cautious at first, Sara opens up to the man who's been too ill lately for their usual talks. Without over-reaction or judgment, Babe just listens. His hooded, gray eyes twinkling, Babe hears all about Leo, Russ, and Kyle. Momma Lois, Howard, and Mrs. Espinosa's class. Shooting pool in the basement, riding the four-wheeler, driving the chore truck, and riding the tractor with Clint.

Babe enjoys the story of Clint beating up Russell Martin... "I told you that boy would take care of you–"

"I know," Sara says, crying again. *Why do I keep tearing up?!* wonders the girl who hates to cry.

Eventually – more than a little embarrassed and leaving out the details – she tells about last night. Worried Babe would be disappointed, she is relieved to see the only father she's ever known chuckle.

"Can't say I didn't see that one coming." Sara is glad to see Babe smile, whatever the reason.

Looking at the beautiful, strong young lady before him, Babe sees; the scrawny girl who showed up on his porch, Sara's twisted face during her first shot of vodka, eating ice cream as Lady told the tale of their meeting in Prague, her walking along the patio for her and Clint's first date. Sara's happiness is his reward.

The girl he helped become strong has chosen her path.   Sara *sniffs* her watery nose.

"Are you gonna tell him?" Babe alludes to the elephant in the living room.

"I don't know," Sara looks away. "I don't even know what I know to tell."

"You, uh–" Babe hesitates. "You know you're a spy, right?"

...Sara just stares at the side of the bed.

"Sara?" He wiggles her hand. The girl with eyes always forward is forced to face the monster just over her shoulder.

"Yeah," she answers as though in a trance. "I know."

"Do you know where you went the night before last?"

Sara sees the gas station. A line of brake lights. Orange flames lighting up the night. "He took her," the sullen girl realizes in real time. "She did something bad." With this, Babe believes Sara knows enough.

"Well, kiddo..." Babe hesitates. "If things were turned around, what would you want *him* to do?"

"I'd want him to tell me." Sara says in a small voice.

"Okay, then," Babe shrugs as though it were just that simple. "But only tell what needs to be told... you might want to do this in parts... little more as time goes on."

Sara nods her head. "All I know is parts–" she says helplessly.

"For better or worse," Babe says soberly, "you and that boy are a pair. Like me and... and me and Lady... and..." Babe trails off, his energy waning.

Wanting to hear what her mentor has to say, Sara gives his hand a wiggle...

"Lady and that boy..." Babe rattles awake, but only for a bewildered second. Left hanging, Sara loses him to sleep. She was afraid this might happen.

"Babe...?" Sara squeaks. "Babe–?!" Sara realizes he is gone, at least for now. This preview of the inevitable sends streams down her cheeks. "I love you, Babe. I love you."

At peace in the moment, Babe rests.

7:30 PM
The Farm
A gray Chrysler with dried blood inside the passenger seat over the cattle-guard with its brights on. Rather than parking alongside Clint's truck and walking into the house, Sara pulls onto the concrete pad in front of the big metal shed and enters through the walk-in door. She knows Clint will follow.

Sara loves the smell of diesel and grease. Gasoline and grain dust. Once inside she flicks on the light. Having absolutely no idea what she is going to say, she shakes – a little from the cold, but mostly from *Oh my God! What am I going to tell him?!*

Clint emerges from the back door. The sight of him somehow causes Sara to become more relaxed and more anxious at the same time. Tension climbs as he passes along Momma Lois's flower bed, his truck, the spot where Kyle's car would be if he were home, the chore truck. Sara loses sight of Clint as he approaches the heavy, aluminum walk-in door. She feels like her skeleton could run away and leave the rest of her behind.

The door opens.

"Hey Dollface!" smiles Clint, pulling it closed behind him. He can tell by the look on Sara's face that something is wrong.

"Okay, stop right there–" halts the girl standing in front of large Craftsman toolboxes. Clint pauses with a funny look on his face.

"Ohh-kayyy," *Was gonna get a hug and a kiss but guess not.* Obviously nervous, Sara looks as though doing math in her head.

This is weird, thinks Clint. *Really weird.* "Did you steal that car?" He tries to lighten the mood. Sara, wearing jeans, a t-shirt and no coat on a chilly evening, points to a spot ten feet in front of her.

"Stand over there–"

"Okay," Clint goes along. He walks around to the spot between a welding table and the rear tire of a John

Deere 4840. To anyone looking in through the East bay window, Clint can be seen, but not Sara.

"You weren't at school today..." Clint breaks the silence.

"I know."

"Or yesterday–"

"I know." Sara further acknowledges, waiting for her courage to arrive. The two OxyContin she took on the way over are not helping at all.

"Why aren't you wearing a coat–?" Clint gets cut off.

"Turn around," she orders.

"What?"

"Turn around... and please don't look until I tell you to, okay?"

"Okay."

"Promise me."

"I promise," *As if things weren't weird enough already...* thinks Clint as he turns around. Four-wheelers directly in front and an enormous John Deere combine off to his left, the guy who hasn't slept much the last couple nights wonders what this is all about. *zip* Clint's ears perk at the sound of a zipper coming undone... and what sounds like a shirt coming off... then jeans. *Okay... sounds like the situation is improving.* "Uh, can I turn around now?" He hears jeans slipping off.

"No, not yet." Sara denies. Clint hears what crumpled clothes being sat up the edge of the welding table nearest her.

"Is anyone coming?" Sara asks.

"No," answers the guy starting to shake a little himself. "All clear–" *Don't come home, Kyle. Don't come home, Kyle. Don't come home, Kyle.*

All right, thinks Sara, ready as she'll ever be. Save for her lacey pink bra, white panties and low-cut socks now dirty on the bottoms, the trembling girl is naked. With only a general idea as to how she even came about her scars, she stands unveiled... "Okay, turn around."

Clint turns to find his love's glorious body on display. Struck into a stupor, he just stares – and then stares for longer.

Oh my God, he isn't saying anything! What if he thinks they're ugly?! What if he thinks I'm ugly now?! Terrified, Sara holds her breath. And continues to hold her breath. "So... what do you think?" Sara dares inquire.

"I–" stutters Clint in awe. "I think you look amazing."

What?! Sara turns quizzical. "My scars are amazing?"

"Your scars?" asks Clint, after staring for nearly ten seconds. He looks closer. "Holy shit!" exclaims the guy blinded by beauty. "You've got scars!" Eyes darting from here to there, Clint, now up close and on one knee, examines what initially escaped notice. "How did you–? Why are there–? Where did you get–?" sputters the guy running his fingertips along the crystalline traces of her past. *She's got scars all over!*

Having never felt so vulnerable, Sara remains still.

Blue eyes trail the laceration across her abdomen. The swooping scrape on her left hip. The textured abrasion running up her right side. *I thought the skin along her ribs felt a little rough last night,* thinks the guy who could see nothing last night. Here, there, and everywhere, a collage of scratches, scrapes, and cuts. Long since healed (save for one), the marks on otherwise flawless skin tell tales of pain. Like hieroglyphs, each blemish a story all its own. One scar, the size of a dime, stands boldly along Sara's taut oblique.

It takes a moment to register, but eventually, "Oh my God, that's a bullet wound! Is that a bullet wound?! That's a *bullet wound!*"

Sara looks up and around, "Yeeeeah," she draggingly admits.

He turns her body. "And it went out the back!"

"I know–" an embarrassed Sara wants to cry. *Now he doesn't think I'm pretty anymore–*

"Who shot you–? Wait–!" he pulls the corner of her panties in search of an appendectomy scar. "Where's your surgery scar?"

Sara only shakes her head.

Looking at her back again, he notices whip marks peeking from under her hair. "Hollllly hell, those are whip marks!" Ready to kill whoever's responsible, Clint demands "Who did this to you?!"

"Which thing–?" Sara shrugs.

"Any of it!" Clint belts. "Who shot you?!"

"I...I..."–only somewhat aware herself, Sara stammers.

"*Who* shot you?" Clint repeats low. Suddenly donning on him that Sara is cold, he hands her clothes. She buys a bit of time putting them on while a very anxious Clint awaits an answer.

"Sooo," Clint drags long with expectation.

"You don't think I'm pretty anymore," Sara mumbles under her breath.

"Huh?" Clint balks. "You think that what?!"

"You don't think I'm pretty anymore?" Hazel eyes moisten.

"I don't think you are any less pretty now than I did ten minutes ago," a baffled Clint clarifies. "I want to know why I *thought* you had surgery when you'd really been shot–" he passionately follows up.

"I don't know–" Sara says semi-honestly.

"You don't know *how* you got *shot*?!" Clint desperately pries.

Standing silent, Sara wants a hug from the man she loves – but dares not reach out. Fearing he doesn't love her anymore; she waits to be told to leave.

"Why can't you tell me?" a scared Clint urges. Though calmer, he is no less intent on finding out who hurt the girl he loves.

"I can't tell you because... because I don't really know... and because I can't."

"Which is it?" presses Clint, shaking from a blend of nerves and the cold. "Because you *don't know* or because you aren't allowed?"

"I won't lie to you–" says a dejected Sara.

"Okay, then don't. Just tell me the truth," Clint states simply. Sara sees an orange explosion, a pregnant woman sobbing with gun barrels pressed under her chin and Norman's reptilian smile.

"I can't." *My life is over.* "I just can't." *I just ruined everything...*

No less in love with Sara than he was, Clint asks "Are you from Florida?"

A forlorn Sara shakes her head.

"Are Babe and Lady really your grandparents?"

Sara shakes her head again.

"Do you really love me?"

Sniff Shimmering eyes lift. Sara nods.

"Then come here—" Sara throws her arms around, around Clint, pulling him tighter than she ever has before. Tired of denying. Tired of being strong. Just plain tired. Sara lets go. A muffled cry echoes in the big tin shed.

His chin on her head, swaying side to side, Clint knows the girl he loves is hurting. He knows that whatever is going on – whatever has happened – was not by her choice. He knows nothing will be figured out or fixed right now.

"You're here now. That's all that matters."

"Sara looks up as though surprise. "What?"

"I love you." Clint kisses Sara's forehead and pulls her into his chest.

"You do?"

"Yeah... Yeah, I do." He reassures. Sara sniffles.

"As much as before—?" she asks, half afraid.

"Would you believe me if I told you *more* than before?" Clint asks, puzzled himself.

"It wouldn't make any sense," *sniff!*

"It's not supposed to make sense, hun... it's not supposed to."

Wednesday, October 1st, 2014 – Wednesday, November 12th, 2014

Clint begrudgingly accepts a lack of answers in lieu of lies for two reasons: the pain the truth causes Sara, and the lack of alternative. Jarred by what has been revealed – and worried to the bone by whatever has not – he promises patience under the condition he cannot keep his head in the sand forever. What few answers he has gotten have done little to blunt his fears.

"Is the person who shot you still a threat?"

"No. He's dead."

"What about the person who whipped you?"

"I don't know who did that. That was a long time ago."

"Do Lady and Babe know?"

"They know some stuff, but not much."

Fortunate for Sara, Clint loves her more than he hates the situation.

Privy only to hints of the truth herself, Sara doesn't wish to bring ugliness to the place she holds dear. The farm, her sanctuary, a realm hidden away from all things bad.

Too much in love for logic to have a say, Clint and Sara have chosen whatever fate together over the safety of being apart.

Autumn arrives.

Babe's health failing as the leaves fall, Sara stays home from school more often to help care for him. Her brawn is needed to lift the 120-pound Babe from his bed into the motorized chair recently brought for him. Once situated, he steers himself through the rearranged living room to the restroom. Lady sees to him from there. He uses the railing Clint mounted into the studs to help steady between the toilet and bath.

Numbed by the pills, Sara watches Westerns with Babe on the TV she brought from her room. He calls her Petra more often than not.

Sometimes warmer than others, Lady's disposition parallels her level of exhaustion. Having lost almost twenty-five pounds, she is afraid to rest, certain something bad will happen to moment she closes her eyes. What little rest Lady does allow comes by way of twenty-minute naps in her chair. Even after a nurse begins staying between 2:00 PM and 10:00 PM, Lady will not leave the house. Groceries and medication are delivered.

Whether she goes to school or not, Sara's evenings are at the farm.

Leo's coat gets thicker as the temperature drops; and Sara gets a coat of her own. When Howard handed her the chore coat he bought her, he asks, "Do you know any orphans needing to keep warm?"

He could have said, "Here's a present," or "I thought of you while I was at Tractor Supply today..." But he didn't. That just wouldn't be his style.

As the days get shorter, the routine changes, but not a lot. Clint and Sara bring in wood for the fireplace. Howard stokes the coals. Momma Lois opens windows. The *Howard & Lois Show* plays on.

Howard: sweltering.

Momma Lois: arctic.

The banter drives Clint nuts, but makes Sara laugh.

Russ' twenty-minute visits on his way to work. Kyle's being told to slow down when he pulls into the driveway. Momma Lois stealing Sara into the sewing room. Howard's blend of philosophizing, political commentary, and playful torment. Routine offers a sense of normalcy.

While work somewhat distracts, the worry of "What's next?" weighs heavy – at least for Clint. Sara, ever with a pill at the ready, seems without a worry in the world. Far more interested in doing more of what they did in the basement that night, Sara has, at times, caused Clint to wonder if the moment in the shed really happened at all. Her scars remind him that it did.

Days pass.

At school, Clint takes his notoriety of "bad-ass" with a grin. Having never officially commented on the matter, the guy with a cast on his hand believes the multiple angles of cellphone footage say enough. Clint laughed when the wrestling coach threw an arm around him and asked him if he'd ever thought about "hitting the mat."

Because of Babe's health, the Fleischers bump Thanksgiving up a month.

Thursday, October 23rd, 2014

Clint, Russ, and Kyle take Howard's Silverado to Sara's house. The three young men help Lady transport Babe – frail but smiling – from the sunroom to the farm for Thanksgiving dinner.

Having only spoken on the phone, Lady finally meets Momma Lois. It takes no time at all for her to see why Sara feels the way she does about Clint's family.

Sitting in Howard's chair, Babe enjoys the fireplace that has everyone else sweating. Though from backgrounds that couldn't be more different, Howard and Babe get on like old friends. Babe's energy is good as anyone could have hoped.

Finding a kindred spirit in Momma Lois, Lady enjoys the family that reminds her so much of her own family back in Scotland. The pale-eyed lass wonders what might have come of those she lost touch with so long ago. Lady looks at Clint and Sara side-by-side on the couch. *They do make a cute couple;* she thinks during a sip of Momma Lois's sweet tea.

Howard comments on Lady's brogue. And Momma Lois invites her to one of Kyle's basketball games coming up. Lady gladly accepts the invitation but doubts she will be able to attend.

Despite being cockier than Babe ever was, Kyle reminds Lady of him when he was young. With his "I'm up to something" grin and chiseled features, Lady thinks Kyle is "dashing as can be." The woman who's dealt with so much alone is grateful beyond measure for the Fleischers making Babe's last Thanksgiving so special.

Upon returning home, Lady notifies Sara of her plan after Babe passes. She will be returning to Scotland, leaving Sara to stay in the rented rock home if she wishes. The lease has been paid through December 31st, 2015.

Lady doubts Babe will make it to Christmas.

Friday, October 31st, 2014

Clint and Russ take Sara trick-or-treating. Sara as Cat Woman, Clint as Joker, and Russ as Robin. After to swinging by Momma Lois's for caramel popcorn balls and two handfuls of candy, the three go into the city for haunted houses. Russ's costume grows uncomfortable as green tights ride high and pointy green shoes prove less than ideal for walking on hard surfaces all night.

Friday, November 7th, 2014 – Wednesday, November 12th, 2014

Kyle gets his first Varsity start. Relegated to Junior Varsity all football season, the 6'2" Kyle proves white men can not only jump, but also throw up twenty-one points, get seven rebounds, three assists, and do three games worth of taunting and trash talking by halftime.

Seated between Clint – who is less than amused with what he calls "Kyle's bullshit" – and Momma Lois, Sara gets jerked and jostled every time Momma Lois's "baby boy" gets the ball.

Sara likes watching Kyle play basketball. Much like a little brother – albeit a little brother who is always hitting on her – Kyle is like a little brother, nonetheless.

In the third quarter, Kyle gets ejected from the game for fighting. Soon with two cheerleaders and a 24-pack of Pabst Blue Ribbon, the skinny freshman looks forward to seeing his name in the paper tomorrow. He is quite pleased with himself.

Clint's cast comes off. Howard reminds him that Sara is still his foreman. And if he works really hard and does a great job, she will still be his boss.

"What happens if I don't work really hard and do a bad job?"

"Then Sara gets a new assistant."

Sara laughs.

Days pass...Clint does his best to ignore, deny, and distract himself from the dark cloud looming. Sometimes a low-level hum, other times like nails on a chalkboard, the worry of "What's next?" is ever present. It weighs on him, though it doesn't seem to bother Sara. At times, he wonders if it even crosses her mind.

An escapism artist, Sara continues to help herself to Babe's prescriptions, rides Leo no matter the weather and check on the cows with Clint. The river bottom, way back where even the cows seldom go, the star-crossed couple engage in their favorite pastime.

Howard wonders what takes them so long...

Thursday, November 13th, 2014

11:03AM, 4th Hour
Mrs. White's English class

yawwwnnn Sara wonders what Momma Lois is doing right now. In Mrs. White's class, the girl with eight milligrams of Dilaudid in her tummy thinks about cooking with Momma Lois. So proud of herself, Sara made dinner without any help the day Momma Lois got stuck in traffic on her way home.

No one noticing that it was *her* who made dinner instead of Momma Lois was the biggest compliment she could have gotten. Like an art forger replacing the work of the masters, Sara has learned to copy the cook who doesn't use measuring cups. Momma Lois uses "pinches" and "dashes" and "heaps."

Unable to care less about whatever 19th century poet Mrs. White is talking about, Sara thinks of Leo. Worried her big buddy didn't have a warm enough place to sleep, Sara busted three bales of hay to make him a soft, warm bed to lie down in at night.

When Clint saw it, he smiled. He didn't have the heart to tell her horses sleep standing up.

Leo has since eaten his bed.

The queen of La La Land hears a cell phone chirp. Then chirp again. The attention of the class turns her way.

Looking side to side, Sara wonders whose phone it might be... still wondering, still wondering. Like a pinch on her behind, she suddenly realizes the sound is coming from her. Blushing, she reaches into her purse while mouthing, "Sorrryyy," with a pained expression.

After a disapproving shake of her head, Mrs. White goes back to her lesson.

"One new message" – Sara's pulse quickens. She checks the text.

'North entrance. Now.' A fluttering of hazel eyes later, Twelve is looking down at the message – then around at a bunch of teenagers she immediately decides she hates.

Woozy from Sara's pills, it takes a bit for Twelve's fuzzy brain to update. Once it does, the Natasha realizes just how miserably her plan to maintain control had failed.

Last memory... approaching the porch with a wadded-up hoodie and a pistol in her hand... Twelve looks up at Mrs. White's dry-erase board. The date is November 13th. She realizes over six weeks have passed.

"Fuck!" Twelve slams her hands on the desk. Stunned silent, students and teacher alike watch the girl they believe to be Sara punch the pencil sharpener off as she storms out.

Mrs. White's mouth hanging open, everyone looks around with the expression of *Did you just see that*?!"

Walking unsteadily, the Natasha without her sister's opioid tolerance makes her way down the hall, past the secretary's office, and out the heavy metal and glass doors. Though hazy, the pissed off Twelve is aware of what has transpired over the last forty-three days – except for Clint and Sara's new favorite activity.

Fuming mad and suffering vertigo, Twelve grinds her numb teeth. She nears the dark green Taurus parked along the street. Having gone from on top of the world (what seemed only minutes ago) to feeling as though she just stepped off a carnival ride, the Natasha wonders *How does this bitch function?!*

Noticing the scowl on her face, Norman mutters, "At least she's in a good mood."

The dizzy Twelve gets into the car and shuts her door.

Car idling, Norman turns to the grumpy assassin. "What's the matter? You on your period?"

Extra pissed off from feeling as though she just saw Norman five minutes ago, Twelve snarls, "No. I am not on my period."

"Oh..." Norman huffs, shifting the car into drive. "So, you're always a bitch..."

I hate you so much.

12:11 PM – 12:26 PM

Norman drives Twelve to her residence.

12:26 PM – 12:37 PM

Norman waits for Twelve to get what he told her she will need for this assignment. He told her she will not be needing her pistols. Sara grabs one of her pistols anyway, should she decide to shoot Norman.

Norman watches Twelve make her way along the patio. With a bulging backpack over her shoulder, the Natasha wearing the black and gray sweat suit Devon called "super cute" is ready to go. Displeased with her sister, Twelve left Sara's room a mess.

The back passenger door opens. Twelve tosses Sara's backpack in the back seat. Back door closes.

Passenger door opens. Passenger door closes. Norman turns to the Natasha with a pistol in her lap.

"What's the matter?" Norman snarks at Twelve's sweats. "Your ass get too big for your jeans?"

"Just drive," Twelve replies with disdain.

"You keep eating..." Norman pats his belly. "You'll wind up like me." Twelve rolls her eyes.

Taking a little white pill to counter Sara's downers, the Natasha is revved once again.

From the kitchen window, Lady watches the dark green car roll down the drive and pull away. Lady's pendulum swings Sara's way. *Be careful, child.*

Soon on 270 South, the ride is quiet for a time. Twelve hopes it stays this way.

"Did you see your last job on the news?"

Shit. He's talking. "No."

"Really?" Norman sounds surprised.

"No." *Dumb bitch Sara doesn't watch the news,* Twelve hisses in her head.

"You don't know who you blew up..." he mumbles under his breath.

Adam Lambrecht. I killed Adam Lambrecht. The assassin who checked the mail knows who she killed. But Norman doesn't need to know she knows.

"You remember that other little spy program they ran alongside yours? The one with the half-colored girls?" Norman inquires after a few minutes of silence.

Funny you should say "they", Twelve recalls Babe saying Norman was CIA. She nods.

"What are they called?" Norman asks, knowing full well.

Twelve pictures the building in St. Petersburg, the girls who were darker-complected than the Natashas... "Shannons."

"Ah, yes – the Shannons," says Norman, scanning for emotion.

"What about them?" Twelve asks indifferently.

"I guess you could say they are being 'recalled'."

Twelve realizes she is being briefed. "What does this have to do with me?"

"You have any qualms killing your little school friends?"

"No," she answers coldly.

"You know what Shannons do?" Norman asks while changing lanes.

"No, but I bet you're gonna tell me," smarts Twelve.

"While you crazy bitches have been running around killing people," Norman sneers, "the Shannons have been doing shit that takes brains." *Yeah, I don't like you either you little cunt.*

Keeping Norman in her peripherals, the Natasha with dilated pupils and quickened pulse imagines how fun it would be to shoot Norman's flat, wide teeth out the back of his head... this, while a four-year-old boy makes a fish face at her through the window of a white Chevy Tahoe.

"Corporations," Norman condescendingly forges on. "*That's* where the wars are now. *That's* where the Shannons are. *That's* why they shit-canned your program. You and the rest of those little psychos might as well be a bunch of muskets."

"Guess you don't need me then," Twelve scratches her left eye with her middle finger.

"But I do," Norman replies with a quick wag of his stubby finger. "I *do* need you... to go up into the Shannon's office, kill the bitch, and bring me her laptop."

"Sounds simple enough."

"Simple, huh?" Norman scoffs. "Killing the half-colored chick might be simple. Getting the laptop might be simple. Getting out... may not be so simple."

The Natasha sighs. Downers help Sara cope with seeing Babe's illness. Uppers help Twelve tolerate Norman. "So, you gonna tell me where we're going?"

"Western Spec," Norman answers.

"What do they do there?"

"Well, pretty-face," Norman says as though Twelve were stupid, "they speculate."

Twelve wonders how deep a .40 caliber bullet would go inside Norman's fat body.

Norman continues. "This company gathers information that effects futures and commodities and a bunch of other shit you know nothing about. Got it?"

"Yeah," Twelve flutters her eyes sarcastically. "I got it." Sara has been learning sarcasm, therefore Twelve has been learning sarcasm.

"No, you don't, but that's okay because you don't need to know. You just need to go in, do what you need to do, and get out. And by the way," he adds, "you're gonna have to do it without your little peashooter there. That's why I told you not to bring it."

Peashooter, huh? Twelve recalls her .40 cal splattering brains. "Yeah, well I like my pea-shooter."

Norman grumbles. "You'll need to pass through a metal detector, go up to Western Spec's offices, eliminate the target — I forgot her name, it's in the file — get the laptop in her office, and get out of the building before they lock it down. Got it?"

"What's not to get?" asks the Natasha with an *'I'm a fucking goddess'* attitude.

"This isn't like holding up a liquor store, you *cocky little bitch!*" Norman gripes.

Little? I was fat a minute ago, Twelve smarts in her head.

"Western Spec doesn't welcome visitors." Norman's voice turns to gravel. "You've got security to deal with and sixteen floors to get back down before they seal off the building—unless you plan on flying out the window."

"If it's so secure, why don't I hit her at home?" Twelve asks. Norman repeating himself is getting on her nerves.

"You see, this is why I do the thinking!"

Grrr...

"Because the employees don't take their laptops home at night... so it's gotta be *in* the building."

Neither says anything for a while. Norman turns onto Interstate 44 West.

"I suggest not using the elevator on the way out," he warns. "And don't think I won't leave you behind."

"What am I supposed to wear?" Twelve moves the conversation along.

"I brought you an outfit just for the occasion..."

Twelve envisions a Hooters outfit.

"...but you'll have to fit into it... Didn't plan on you ballooning up."

I've gained six pounds dick! Twelve roars in her head. Fact of the matter, Sara has gained a little since resuming her weight training.

"Brought along some goodies. Shit that will pass through a metal detector."

"So where is this place?" *Please be close. Please be close. Please be close.*

"Houston."

"Fuck." *Houston is so fucking far!*

Friday, November 14th, 2014

1:29 AM
Houston, TX
After hours of conversation-free travel, Norman pulls in the parking lot of a Ramada Inn.

1:36 AM
Backpack over her shoulder. The dossier Norman gave her in her left hand. Her duffle bag in her right. Glock under her armpit. Twelve enters room 221 alone.

Norman goes to room 124.

Pistol laying on the waist-high dresser and everything else on the spare bed; Twelve switches the air on 'high' and looks out her window. A bit warm under black and gray top, she peels it off, tossing it onto the round table in front of the window. The Natasha looks around the room with two queen-sized beds, a large mirror over the dresser and larger mirror over the double sinks just outside the small bathroom.

Though curious about the "goodies" in the duffel bag, Twelve sees to security first.

Not trusting Norman — or anyone for that matter — she braces the door with one of the two heavy, wooden chairs from under the table. Then, with the burgundy shades drawn, she hoists the heavy nightstand (from in between the beds) atop the round table in front of the window – should anyone wish to shoot her heat signature through the window.

Defensive measures having been taken, the Natasha switches on the TV and dumps the tightly packed duffel bag onto the bed. The dossier – blueprints, documents, pictures of the target – lay under the pile. Jacked from a little white pill, Twelve looks down at a wrinkled, cream-colored pantsuit. A wadded-up black blouse. A matching cotton blend skirt. A pair of size seven flats that match the pantsuit. A large, bulging rectangular purse that matches the pantsuit. And a blonde wig. Twelve lifts the pre-styled wig up and away, dropping it as though it were a dead mouse.

After years of being beaten by Natasha 716, Twelve does not care for blondes.

The Natasha empties the over-sized purse the way a child dumps a Christmas stocking. Out spill a large pair of dark *Prada* sunglasses, a small aluminum spray bottle from *Bath and Body Works*, lipstick, mascara, a compact, a wallet with nothing in it, a ten-inch-long eyeliner pencil with screw threading on the unsharpened end, and what appears a screwdriver handle with a hole.

Scratching at the tip of what is in fact carbon-fiber strong as steel, Twelve screws the threaded end into the handle... *That's clever.* The Natasha stabs what is essentially an icepick into the surface of dresser, burying the tip into the wood.

"Good luck, metal detector," Twelve smiles. She loves her new toy.

A double-check of the bag reveals a tightly coiled, very thick, industrial strength zip-tie. An eighth of an inch wide and long enough to slip over a basketball, it has a handle wide enough for three fingers. Twelve imagines looping it over Norman's neck and zipping it tight. The mental image of his pitted face turning purple causes the corners of her mouth to rise.

Tossing the zip-tie aside, she picks up the shiny little bottle labeled 'cinnamon' and shakes her head. "...I don't think you're *really* air fresher." 99.9% certain its cyanide, Twelve sets the liquid death on the dresser.

Delighted with the goodies Norman gave her, Twelve decides to look through the blueprints later. Needing a shower, she first jerks the mirror from the wall and sets it so that she can see the entrance from inside the shower.

Nobody is sneaking up on me, thinks the woman stepping out of her sweatpants... t-shirt, bra, underwear, then socks.

Twelve turns on the water.

Curtain pulled back and bathroom door wide open, the Natasha with her .40 cal on the lid of the toilet can keep an eye on the entrance.

Water cascades down Twelve's body.

Enjoying her first shower, Twelve – in between glances at the door – looks down at her recently healed, but still discolored wound. Seeing it makes her angry. *It'll fade,* she reminds herself.

Pulling her right breast aside, she sees skin textured and two shades darker along her ribs. Twelve can remember her foot slipping during a rock-climbing exercise. Falling. The rope around her waist raking up her side. While painful, it saved her from plunging another forty feet and dying the same way Natasha 715 would three weeks later.

The tip of her middle finger traces the laceration across her midsection. She recalls how this one came about as well.

Preferring to drip dry rather than use a towel, Twelve wrings her hair with twisting fists before stepping out. Leaving footprints on carpet, the Natasha rounding the corner for her backpack on the bed stops, turning as though tapped on the shoulder. Twelve sees a striking reflection; hair slicked back, skin shiny with wetness, exquisite curves glowing pink from the heat. Twelve has never seen herself like this because Sara has never looked at herself like this. *Hmmm,* she tilts her head.

Towels hang neatly from the silver rack to her right. An assortment of soaps to her left. Lights shine warmly from ahead and above. Twelve steps forward until the cold edge of counter-top presses across her hips.

I'm beautiful, her lips move along with her thought.

Body turning slowly, she takes an inventory of her remarkable form. *Holy hell, I do have a huge ass!* Twelve likes what she sees. *I should be in a rap video;* she jokes in her head. In awe of flesh that cannot possibly be her own, the Natasha lightly squeezes her breasts.

Turning back to see herself straight on, she tenses the muscles in her arms, then legs. Recalling how thin she used to be, Twelve loves her new strength. The power and beauty of the body she is forced to share makes the Natasha want full ownership all the more. Bright eyes rise to the face she was told looks like Rebecca Romijn. Twelve smiles the way she knows people like to see... "What a lovely mask you have," she purrs, then smiling for real. The Natasha knows her smile is far more deadly than the handgun laying a few steps away.

A surge passes through the assassin feeling powerful as a 280-pound lioness, yet light as a feather. Reveling in the memory of stalking the guy who tried to kill her with a shotgun, Twelve decides she enjoyed the walk down the short hallway more than actually killing him.

High from her pills and the anticipation of killing again, Twelve – who loves each one of her scars – never wants to come down.

Surging, the woman who feels she could explode slams her palms down on the edge of the sink. "Fuck you!" she curses Sara for stealing her body.

"Fuck you!" she curses Mira and all of those who've tried to kill her.

"Fuck you!" she curses everyone who's imposed control over her.

"Fuck you!" she curses anyone who may challenge her.

Aching for battle, the chance to inflict her supremacy once again, the Natasha must wait. "Grrrr!!"

3:50 AM

After watching a number of 24-hour news channels (and wishing Sara watched the news or read a newspaper from time to time) Twelve reviews the file for tomorrow. Her hair tangled, the assassin wearing only panties spreads pictures, blueprints, and papers with Western Spec's company letterhead all over the second bed. Like a house cat staring at a goldfish in its bowl, she looks at an 8x10 picture of her mark. "Hmmm... pretty." *Too bad I gotta kill ya, bitch.*

Denise Jackson, a Shannon with green eyes, is attractive by any standard. Pristinely professional, the twenty-six-year-old operative projects the bearing of one bound for success. Twelve looks to see if she recognizes Denise Jackson from her time in St. Petersburg – then remembers she doesn't care and stops looking.

Moving on, she studies the blueprint of the 16th floor. The location of Denise Jackson's office. Denise Jackson's boss's office. The breakroom. The conference room. Approximately how many steps between locations.

Television on in the background, Twelve decides she wants the entire cast of *Jersey Shore* to die screaming – except for 'The Situation'. She wants to drown him in a lagoon of horse piss.

The Natasha reads memos pertaining to security.

In addition to the security maintained by the greater structure, Western Spec – same as several other businesses under lease – contract with private firms for additional security.

Like several companies in the twenty-two-story building, Western Spec is completely off-limits to the general public. Furthermore, no laptops, cellphones or data storage devices of any kind are allowed beyond the lobby without expressed and verified clearance.

Metal detectors and an x-ray machine at the only entrance, multiple security firms working in concert, and surveillance cameras covering every square inch (save for janitors' closets and restrooms) "Simple, huh?" Twelve recalls Norman's scoffing taunt.

"Fuck you, Norman," Twelve says aloud. *He wants me to fail.* Vowing to deny him the pleasure, she studies photographs of the interior.

The white sandstone lobby, the front desk, fountain, elevators, the stairwell. There are no pictures from within Western Spec, only a picture of the foyer and the receptionist sitting at her desk. A very thin lady with jet-black hair and glasses low across her nose. Twelve guesses her approximately sixty-five years of age.

Though appreciating the difficulty of her mission, the dossier does not alarm the Russian reading on. Twelve unfolds a piece of paper with the words 'Denise Jackson's lunch period.' 11:30 crossed out and 11:45 written underneath.

Once all the germane information is committed to memory, Twelve haphazardly stacks the pages and pictures, and closes the folder. Tossing the file aside, she turns to watch more *Ridiculousness*. She likes watching people get hurt.

3:20 AM
Twelve sees Ariana Grande on TV. "Uh... I think I might be a lesbian."

4:24 AM
Knowing the clothes Norman brought need ironed, Twelve calls the front desk. "I'm sorry, ma'am, we don't have a 'clothes ironing' service."
"Your hotel sucks."

5:05 AM
Twelve irons. Poorly. *Norman should have to do this shit.*

Going about the task she feels below her, Twelve's mind, still blazing from her second pill, hopscotches from memory to memory.

Triangle-choking Natasha 702 unconscious in the sandpit.

Executing the prisoner in the showers.

The sight of her second handler, Thomas Smith, smoking a pipe on his front porch.

With a peculiar sense of nostalgia, Twelve recalls being held over a desk – hand across the back of her neck – and beaten with a plastic rod. She knows it was a part of what made her strong. Her only regret is having eventually screamed.

7:00 AM
Norman calls her room.

"Hello?"

"Didn't run off, did you?"

Twelve hangs up on Norman.

The plan is to leave at 10:45 AM. Arrive at Western Spec at 11:15 AM. Twelve has plenty of time. Propped on pillows, the Natasha watches a *Friends* marathon on TBS.

7:09 AM
Norman goes down to the continental breakfast.

9:00 AM
Twelve washes down another white pill with a gulp of sink water. Even more amped, the Russian feels she could shoot lightning bolts from her eyes and fingertips.

9:11 AM
Twelve hops in the shower.

After jerking tangles out of her hair, the Natasha standing naked as a jaybird is soon poking her thick hair underneath the nylon cap tight on her scalp.

With all but a few renegade strands tucked under, she puts on the wig that regained its form after hanging on the doorknob for a while. "Holy shit," says the Natasha, pushing platinum bangs aside. "I hardly recognize myself."

9:43 AM

Benefiting from Sara's practice, Twelve applies makeup for the first time.

10:00 AM

Sure to bring along two sports bras, Twelve cinches down her bust; and pulls up the black skirt she will wear underneath her pantsuit. With some wiggling, squirming, and bouncing on the bed, she manages her lower half into the cream-colored bottoms. With absolutely no chance of hooking the clasp on the pants, Twelve buttons the tight-fitting top and turns to the mirror.

Not about to tell Norman he did a good job picking out her wig and clothes, Twelve would call the style 'sexy realtor'. She fears a seam might burst at any moment.

10:14 AM

With everything ready to go and time to kill, the Natasha turns the television to *Jerry Springer*. Twelve loves a good raucous.

10:24 AM

Twelve flips through the channels, stopping on *Nancy Grace*. She watches forty seconds before yelling "What a cunt!"

10:25 AM

Twelve stops on *Jerry Springer* again. Two very large women are fighting. *This show needs me to watch it.*

10:28 AM

Twelve looks around the room. Beds not made. Nightstand atop the round table in front of the window. Towels on the floor. Wall damaged from ripping off the mirror. Mirror still propped against the wall outside the bathroom... "And that's what maids are for."

10:41 AM

The blonde wearing over-sized sunglasses, exits room 221. Backpack over her shoulder, duffle bag in one hand, big handbag in the other, the assassin with a dossier under her armpit feels like a pack mule. She enters the lobby.

Unrecognized by Norman at first, she walks past him and out the automatic doors.

"Can I help you with our bags, ma'am?" offers a man in a cowboy hat.

"Can you fuck off?" Twelve snipes without so much as turning her head.

Norman chuckles as he tosses his cup in a wastebasket. Following out the exit, he stops beside the baffled young gentleman. "You know," he says leaning in, "it's a good thing you caught her on a good day. Sometimes, she can be a reeeal bitch."

11:08 AM

Pulling into the parking area of Western Spec, Norman begins to speak – but cuts him off.

"You don't have to talk if you don't want to," Twelve smarts curtly. Norman scowls.

"I've got more of you, you know?" he notifies. "More Natashas, I mean."

Twelve doesn't respond. Instead, she eyes those coming and going from the grandiose structure. The shrubbery in between the six massive stones lined in front. The manned booth at the entrance of the sub-level parking. The sea of cars. The heavy double doors leading inside. Black and tinted, the building is essentially a twenty-two-story mirror.

Norman and Twelve sit. Waiting.

11:28 AM

Twelve exits the car two minutes early, leaving Norman – who was mid-sentence – to wait. Just in case she doesn't make it out, the Natasha wanted to agitate him one last time. As much as the grouchy handler despises his young operative, he can't help but enjoy watching her walk away.

Scratching the itch caused by the skirt tucked up under her bra, Twelve makes her way past rows of late model cars until reaching a sidewalk. After waiting for a car to pass, she crosses the street, confidently stepping onto the smooth gray path leading to the entrance/exit of the building. The platinum Natasha passes two women and three men leaving for lunch. All five take notice of the stunner heading inside. Sweating from the Houston heat, Twelve feels shrink-wrapped in the chic pants suit.

A man on his way out opens the door for Twelve. For appearances sake, she gives the friendliest, "Thank you!"

"You're welcome, ma'am–" says the guy sucking in his gut as the pretty lady passes. Twelve is greeted by air conditioning and two guards looking her up and down.

Men are so stupid; she snickers to herself. This thought turns her fake smile into a real one.

"Afternoon, ma'am," greets the taller, more robust of the guards. His name tag says 'Bob,' same as the much smaller Bob.

"Hello," beams Twelve as she lays her bag on the moving belt. *You look like the 'Pen and Teller' of guards*, she thinks to the soothing sound of water trickling down the smooth stones of the fountain in the center of the lobby. The professionally perky receptionist answering the phone at the welcoming desk off to the side. And elevators dinging.

"Any cellphones, blackberry, cameras, or recording devices of any kind?" asks the smaller Bob – same as he's asked every other person who has passed through.

"No."

"Any weapons, exotic animals, fruits, ungerminated seeds, germinated seeds, liquids in unsecured containers, lighters or potentially explosive devices of any kind?" he follows up.

Feigning dismay, Twelve charmingly shakes her head. "Ungerminated seeds?! I would never!"

The Bobs chuckle.

"Have you recently visited the Philippines, East Africa, Uruguay, Uzbekistan, or any country adjacent to Uzbekistan?"

Twelve shakes her head.

"They make me ask," smiles the smaller Bob, his dentures shining.

"You come right on this way, Miss," waves the bigger Bob, gesturing for Twelve to walk through the metal detector.

Twelve passes through without a sound.

"Arms up like you're gonna fly away," Big Bob politely instructs. He runs the hand-held wand over and around Twelve's body and outstretched limbs.

Because of her access to Sara's memories, the big man waving the metal detector wand reminds her of Hoss from the television show, *Bonanza*. Twelve puts down her arms.

"Looks like you're all set to go!" says the bear of a man, hands on his hips.

The smaller Bob hands Twelve her bag. "Here you go, ma'am."

There's that "ma'am" again, she grumbles in her head while saying, "You two have a nice day."

The woman who never removed her sunglasses slips her arm through the straps of her oversized bag and heads for the elevator.

"Gal's got an ass like the back step on an ice truck," Big Bob comments.

"Of all the days for me to leave my glasses on the dash of the car," huffs the smaller Bob, squinting hard.

11:36 AM

Twelve enters one of six elevators and pushes the number '16'. The number now glowing, she feels the upward bump of the elevator in motion.

Nine minutes to kill, Twelve thinks to herself. *I should probably take a piss first.*

Ding! She arrives at the 16th floor.

The Natasha heads to the ladies' room.

The most upscale restroom she's ever entered, Twelve takes notice of the blended earth tones – deep red and browns – large ceramic tiles covering the floor. She glances herself in the mirror above the marble counter and four porcelain sinks. Behind the Natasha is four stalls, the one on the end larger than the others.

Sitting in the far stall, Twelve multitasks. After scratching her itching scalp, she screws the threaded end of the carbon-fiber 'eyeliner' pencil into the handle, twisting until tight. Placing her stabbing tool into the purse, she retrieves the small, shiny bottle since confirmed to be cyanide. With a couple quick pumps to get air out of the line, she saturates a tiny spot on the roll of tissue paper, holding her breath while doing so.

Almost ready, the Natasha makes a hoop out of her over-sized zip-tie and places it back into her purse as well. *This should be interesting*, thinks the one excited about the mayhem soon to come.

Done with her business, Twelve, with some effort, manages her pants back up. Glad Norman doesn't know of her difficulty, she can hear his smarmy voice in her head— *"Did your ass get fatter since you put them on?"*

Fuck you, Twelve says to imaginary Norman.

11:41 AM

Twelve exits the stall. She likes that no one has entered during the few minutes she has been inside. Low traffic.

Not one to bother washing her hands, the Natasha stops to look in the mirror with a heavy, Greek-style, pewter border. The assassin who knows she's beautiful. She adjusts her sunglasses.

Twelve exits the bathroom; she soon expects to return soon.

At the midway point between the lobby of Western Spec and the restroom, she waits.

Her plan, should Denise Jackson not pop into the restroom on her way to the elevator, is to lure her in. Should

Denise Jackson fail to follow, Twelve's plan is to take her by force.

11:46 AM
Right on time. Denise Jackson, wearing an azure blouse and dark pants, exits the Western Spec lobby. She heads the Natasha's way. Appearing to be enjoying the view through the window, Twelve tracks her target out of the corner of her eye.

"Yup. That's you." Once the Shannon is past, Twelve follows. Ladies' room upcoming on the left.

Ready to ask for assistance that would require Denise follow her into the restroom, Twelve realizes there is no need. Denise enters on her own. *Bad move, Buttercup,* thinks the operative trailing behind. *Bad move.*

Eerily reminiscent of the time she followed Shelly into the locker room, Twelve locks the door.

Now, same as then, she squats down to see the feet of an unsuspecting victim under the stall. Approaching a state of euphoria, the Natasha takes her position at the middle sink; zip-tie at the ready in her upright standing bag. Twelve primps to pass the time.

The automatic toilet flushes. A door painted deep-red opens. The Shannon emerges.

Wiping along the side of her nose, the Natasha can't help but think, *Holy shit, my skin is oily!* Denise – with perfect makeup and shiny, straight hair – steps up to the sink alongside Twelve.

Ready to get the show on the road, the Natasha kicks off her flats. *Well, time to kill this bitch.*

In the blink of an eye, Twelve loops the zip-tie over the Shannon's head and around her neck. Cinching it tight with a sharp pull.

ZIIIP!

Eyes bulging, Denise claws at the plastic strip imbedded in her skin. She makes a panicked dash for the door.

Where the fuck you think you're going?! With an arm around her waist, Twelve drags the Shannon unable to scream toward the far stall.

Kicking and clambering, the flailing operative is dragged into the far stall like a zebra pulled into a river by a crocodile.

Denise loses a shoe.

No match for Twelve's strength, the Shannon is slung down into the space between the handicap toilet and wall. Wedged in the narrow gap, the beet-red Shannon grasps the railing.

SMASH! Twelve breaks three of Denise's teeth with a punch. The automatic toilet flushes as her victim crumples down into the confined space. Gripping the railing for leverage, the Natasha raises her foot high.

STOMP! STOMP! STOMP!

Unthrottled viciousness, Twelve disfigures the one gone limp.

STOMP! STOMP! STOMP!

The last snaps Denise's neck.

Twelve hears a light knocking... "Occupied!" she sings congenially.

"Oh, okay—" a woman's voice muffles through the door. The Natasha knows it's time to go.

After snatching Denise Jackson's ID badge from around her neck and straightening her wig, Twelve glances down at the crotch of her pants. *How did they not rip during that?!* she wonders. She looks back at Denise.

"What a shame," she whispers to the face undone by her heel. "You used to be so pretty."

After dragging the Shannon's body so as not to be seen, the Natasha locks the door and slides out underneath.

Noticing the swerving black streaks left by Denise's scaping heels, Twelve first uses her thumb nail to try and scratch them off. *Wow. That shit's really on there.*

On her hands and knees, she then uses a damp soapy hand towel to scrub the marks as best she can. "It's always something," she grumbles under her breath.

Someone lightly knocks on the door again.

"Oh, fuck," Twelve mutters. "Occupied!" Already frustrated by Denise's mess, the Natasha does not need extra hassle right now.

Twenty seconds later, Twelve looks down at her clean-up job. *Looks like shit, but it's better than it was.* Knowing it's time to go, Twelve slips on her shoes, gives herself a quick look, straightens her pantsuit, grabs her purse, and heads for the door. Upon exiting, she finds a round-faced woman waiting. *Oh, so you're the bitch who's been knocking.*

"You been waiting out here?" Twelve asks in her nicest tone.

The nervously reserved woman nods.

"Yeah? Well, the toilet on the end is broken so...probably want to use one of the others."

"Oh, thank you for telling me!" says the cheery stranger.

Twelve takes two steps toward Western Spec, only to turn back. "No, really," she tells the woman heading in, "you *really* want to use one of the first two. If you don't, you'll probably overflow and get shit all over the floor." The Natasha speaks with the tact of a New Jersey construction worker.

"Oh, dear!" says the woman, disconcerted at the thought.

"Better yet..." Twelve takes the gullible woman by the shoulders to lead her away. "You might want to use a different bathroom. That one's pretty fucked up."

Taken aback by Twelve's language, the deeply uneasy woman shuffles toward the elevator. "Maybe maintenance should be notified," she says.

"They'll know soon enough," Twelve says while waving. *Just get the fuck out already.*

Once the woman Twelve assumes owns at least six cats is on the elevator, she turns around and heads on. *If it's not one thing, it's another...*

Twenty-two steps and a right turn later, the Russian passes through the glass door with a gold plate bearing the words "Western Spec" in Gothic lettering.

Surrounded by the décor and scent of a law office, Twelve (not realizing she has blood droplets up the calf of her right pant leg) sees the receptionist's desk to her left – but the lady usually sitting behind is under it at the moment. "I'll be right with you!" a frail but friendly voice says, heels visible around the bottom of the mahogany station. "Just have to plug this in..."

Unable to believe her luck, the Natasha steps out of her flats and passes like a ghost behind the woman carefully backing out from under. Twelve soundlessly hurries toward the seventh office on the right.

Scratching her shoulder, she raises her elbow high, so as to block her face while passing by the break room smelling of Chinese food.

Twelve arrives at Denise Jackson's office.

She swipes Denise's badge.

Green light.

The Natasha enters the office.

Knowing she hasn't much time, Twelve rounds the desk, jerks the cords out of the laptop, and closes it. After removing the shiny bottle and her stabbing weapon from her purse, she slides the laptop inside. Noticing an external hard drive with a Post-it note saying 'GST', she shoves it alongside.

Quickly sliding the tiny bottle down her cleavage – and the stabbing tool down the front of her unfastened pants – Twelve exits the office with the blocky purse under her arm. Composed but in a hurry, she walks through the waft of beef lo mien once again, passing one office after another.

Ahead of her, the ninety-pound receptionist she snuck past rounds the corner. She squares her bony body so as not to allow the intruder past.

"Ma'am! Ma'am! You *must* stop!" says the grandmother of eight, her reading glasses dangling by their chain. Twelve does not stop.

CRUNCH!! Crushing knuckles level the receptionist. Driving dental work down into her throat, Twelve shatters bones made frail by time. Choking on her own blood, the woman sees Twelve stepping over.

Heads poke out of two offices and break room to find their beloved coworker quivering on the tile as the Russian agent continues on.

"Hey, you!" shouts Rick Thurman, a junior advisor in fossil energies. Seeing the blonde with a bulging bag turn the corner for the foyer, he gives chase. Racing down the hall, the thirty-four-year-old with a fleshy body rounds the corner to a Natasha waiting.

STAB! STAB!

Twelves shank plunges into his left eye and throat.

To the siren of Mr. Thurman screaming on the floor, she passes through the lobby out of and out the door.

You're lucky I'm in a hurry, Twelve hisses in her head at the man now blind in one eye and choking on his own blood.

Sprinting down the hallway toward the stairwell, a hefty woman wanders out of the elevator and into Twelve's path.

WHAM! The Natasha with a full head of steam sends papers flying and the large woman spinning to the floor. After but a stumble, Twelve continues on like a running back, cradling her purse like a football. The woman with a split lip and no idea what hit her turns in time to see the door to the stairwell closing.

Racing down the steps, Twelve pulls off her wig and nylon cap. Struggling out of her jacket, she has to stop just long enough to remove her blood-stained pants. Not noticing the gash across her knuckles from the secretary's teeth, the barefooted Russian rushes down the stairs, her black skirt now freely hanging down.

No longer constricted by the cream-colored pantsuit, the suspect now with dark brown hair is much freer to move. Left hand sliding along the railing, the Natasha takes the stairs three and four at a time.

Stabbing point jutting out the bottom of her hand and rectangular-shaped purse under her arm, Twelve descends the 12th floor.

11th floor.

10th floor.

9th floor.

8th floor.

Rounding the 7th floor – *SMACK* – the oaken door opened by security officer Mendez was not meant to knock Twelve into the wall.

Fearing having injured someone, the former football player with a barrel of a body, military haircut, and two-inch height advantage over Twelve quickly realizes he has encountered the suspect. He reaches for the radio at his left shoulder.

The crouched Natasha lunges. *STAB! STAB!*

"ARRGGHAA!" he howls as the tip of Twelve's shank enters his wrist – then sinks straight down behind his collarbone, near his shoulder. "ARRGGHAA!" Face contorted; Officer Mendez sounds a guttural howl.

Pulling back to stab him again, the Natasha's hand slips off the handle slick with blood. Buried deep, the carbon-fiber shaft is wedged between two bones.

Oh shit! Twelve turns to bolt back up the stairs. Snarling, Officer Mendez catches a handful of hair and jerks the Natasha backward.

Twisting back around like a cat on a leash, Twelve sinks her teeth into his hand before (shifting her feet and) throwing a sharp knee into the side of his meaty thigh. Her eyes wild, she torques the handle sticking up and out. "AAAARGH!!" Officer Mendez roars in agony.

Adrenaline surging, Officer Mendez tackles Twelve – *CRACK!* – smashing her body between his driving shoulder and the stairs.

"UNNGH!" Fearing it was her back that broke – Twelve, pinned to the stairs with the wind smashed out of her – has never been hurt like this. Despite wracking pain, the Natasha (unable to breathe) maintains focus. *Can't allow separation! Keep him close! Don't let him touch his radio!* Twelve scissors the thick man's torso, pulling him intimately close. *Gotta get my little bottle!*

Clinging for her life, Twelve gets smashed two more times while digging for the shiny bottle... she raises it to his face... *psshht! psshht!* Thick mist wets the brute's nose and mouth.

Further enraged by the acrid taste, Officer Mendez drives his weight once again – *CRACK!* – something else breaks.

"URRGH!" The assassin would vomit were anything in her stomach. Feeling shattered inside, the Natasha with veins bulging in her neck and face fights on.

Eyes burning and anchored by the suspect latched underneath, the officer can neither reach his radio, nor get to his feet. Too proud to yell for help, he tries to stand once again – his foot slips.

"UNNGH!" Twelve gets landed on.

He's turning blue! Twelve realizes. *He's turning blue!* His panic is her pleasure. Terror registers in the gasping man's face. His mass bearing down, Officer Mendez swipes as though something were covering his mouth. Abandoning any attempt at apprehension, the man with the handle of Twelve's shank nearly touching his cheek wishes only to get away.

"Oh, no you don't motherfucker!" Twelve forces hot breath in his ear. The edge of the second step digs into her lower back. Hardly able to breathe herself, Twelve sips at the air while the brawny bruiser struggles to escape her clutches.

"You're gonna die today!" she taunts, savoring the fright in his eyes. The sound of a door bursting open, and men's voices can be heard from the floor above.

Time to go! thinks Twelve while spitting the words, "You're already dead!" She releases the man between her legs, bucking him off to the side.

Officer Mendez rolls onto his back, hitting his head along the wall.

Dizzy and disorientated, the fallen officer doesn't resist when Twelve wrenches her stabbing weapon free. Bloody shank in one hand, she picks up his radio with the other. "She's on the roof!" Twelve misdirects. "She's on the roof!"

"Diane? Is that you?!" the radio squawks back. Twelve ignores.

"You should've left me alone," grinds the Natasha, veins bulging in her neck and face.

Officer Mendes pleads, "No" with a shaking of his head. Defenseless – and only partially aware – he can barely raise his right hand to refuse the Natasha with her shank held high.

"Medical personnel required on the sixteenth floor!" the radio squawks.

"Puh-please..." Officer Mendez faintly wheezes before—

STAB! STAB! STAB! STAB! to his face and thick neck.

Closed casket, mother fucker! Twelve hears in her head. The wet sounds of puncture. The tip of her shank hitting and skipping off bone. Knowing time is up, Twelve turns away from the man gurgling bubbles through holes and reaches for the fire alarm.

RIIIING!!

Knowing the liability of public safety trumps security in America, the piercing sound of the fire alarm is music to the Natasha's ears.

Big purse over her shoulder, the broken Natasha hobbles down the stairs like a limping hunchback. Alarm slicing through the air, the stairwell fills with staff members as Twelve makes it from the fourth floor to the third.

Screams come from above. *Must've found him*, thinks the one with lungs unwilling to open. Twelve believes she might be dying. Assisted by some among the flowing mass, the Natasha falters down the last couple floors and into the lobby. People rush to join the crowded mass at the exit. *How in the hell did all these people get here so fast?!* she wonders as the Bobs scan those leaving the building one and two at a time. *Shit! This is not good!* thinks the Natasha barely able to stand.

To make matters worse, Twelve gets her bare foot stepped on.

Hardly able to breathe, the injured Natasha knows she is too weak to fight her way through the crowd. Hopelessness. Then an idea strikes.

Pulling her hair across her face, Twelve turns to a robust Latino man wearing a custodian's uniform. "I'm pregnant!" she cries out with what little breath she has.

Appearing in his early forties, the stoutly built man with a push broom mustache and the name 'Hector' stitched into his uniform is quick to aid to the woman with a torn blouse and blood on her face.

"What happened?!" he asks, leaning down to her.

"I was attacked by a man!" Twelve is drowned by the alarm and people all around. "And I'm pregnant! I am pregnant!"

Like a knight in shining armor, Hector scoops up the woman who is heavier than expected and heads for the exit.

"Clear a path!" he shouts with a Spanish accent. "Clear a path! I've got a pregnant lady here and she's injured!!"

The bulky purse between her curled body and Hector's chest – her face buried in his shoulder – Twelve can feel herself moving through the air.

"Clear a path!" Hector shouts, forehead beading from strain. "I've got a pregnant lady! She is injured!" All Twelve can do is hope. Hope the Bobs don't stop Hector. Hope Hector doesn't drop her. Hope her lung isn't punctured.

Arms around Hector's neck, Twelve hides her face behind a curtain of hair pulled across her blood-sticky cheek.

"Clear a path! Clear a path!" Such reverence for expectant mothers, even those elbowing in the chaos step out of the good Samaritan's path.

To the sounds of grunting in her ear, the Natasha feels a change of temperature and sunlight on her skin. *Holy fucking shit! We're out!*

For whatever reason – the Bobs looking for someone by another description, regard for women with child, the fact it was a staff member carrying her – Twelve is on her way toward the crescent-shaped mass along the street. Emergency vehicles and squad cars arriving one after the other, the Natasha is carried past two uniformed policemen running for the entrance.

The people in the crowd, most of whom with either their cell phone to their ear or held up recording the excitement at the entrance, watch an exhausted Hector shuffle to the curb. Sliding down his front, the bottoms of Twelve's feet touch warm sidewalk. "I'll get you an ambulance–" says Hector, looking like he could use an ambulance himself.

HONK! HONK! Bystanders step clear when the dark green Taurus pulls alongside. The passenger door is pushed open from the inside, almost hitting the squatting Natasha in the head.

Hector, confused and panting with his hands on his knees, watches the injured woman crawl in the car.

"What the fuck happened?!" Hector hears the driver say as the sedan pulls away; the woman's legs not even fully inside.

"Maybe that was her father–" says Hector, hoping the young lady is okay. Pulling away quickly at first, the getaway car soon slows as the passenger door closes. The dark green Ford passes an ambulance and a firetruck as it exits the lot.

Writhing, the Natasha digs her nails into the center console. This is more painful than being shot.

"Wow," Norman says with a hint of compassion. "You're pretty fucked up..."

Trembling and gritting her teeth, the Natasha twists in search of relief.

Looking down at the laptop sticking out of the purse on the floorboard, Norman asks "Is she dead?"

Hair stuck to her blood-speckled cheek, the assassin with what feels like shattered ribs doesn't hear the question.

"I'll do what I can for you," says Norman, giving up on a response. "But we got to ditch this car first."

Minutes pass. Each stop, each acceleration, each turn is agony for the one balled in her seat.

Endorphins and adrenaline ebbing, Twelve's body stiffens and swells. Excruciation.

"I'm hurt..." manages the Natasha. "I'm hurt bad."

"I can see that," Norman is surprised at his lack of pleasure at her pain. *I wanted to see you get fucked up, but not this bad...*

Norman flips his blinker for the Walmart ahead.

Feeling as though she has fallen three floors onto pavement is only part of Twelve's pain. Being vulnerable to Norman is a suffering all its own. The quivering Natasha knows he could strangle her to death if he so chooses.

Norman pulls into the busy parking lot.

Twelve doesn't notice pulling to the lot, or parking – only Norman's grunting exit from the still running car and popping of the trunk.

Standing at the rear of the car, the broad-backed handler digs a black satchel out of one of his travel bags. The satchel includes syringes of morphine, same as would be found in a combat medic's supply bag.

Twelve hears the trunk thump shut. Her door opens. She feels her skirt lift, but not the needle darting into her backside. Seconds pass...a calming wave runs over her body. The screaming pain within her core melts away. A warm pleasure takes its place. Eyes rolling back, she goes lax within seconds.

"What happened?" asks Norman, kneeling down in the space of the open door. He leans Twelve's seat back. Her body lays with it.

"Whaaat?" murmurs a passenger lost to euphoria.

After tugging her skirt decently down, Norman pulls out the external hard drive.

GST? What the fuck does that mean? he wonders, setting it down before shutting her door.

Fear and anxiety gone; Sara feels as though riding a raft down a rolling river of delightfulness. Oblivious to matters going on, she watches Norman pull his baseball cap low and make his way toward a man loading groceries into the rear of a white Chevy Blazer in the row straight across.

Drugged silly, the scene through the windshield is like a movie to the girl peering over the dash. Norman approaches a tall, thin – seemingly affable – man. Norman leans close. The man's knees buckle. As the unconscious man falls, Norman catches him. Vacantly curious, Sara watches Norman heave the limp man atop the groceries, retrieve a small object from his waistband. Norman checks to make sure no one is looking, then presses the small object to the man's temple.

A turn of Norman's thick body blocks Sara's view of whatever causes the man's legs to jolt. Higher than she has ever been, Sara watches Norman casually removes keys from the man's front pocket. She watches Norman close the rear of the SUV and round to the driver's side calmly as if his name were on the title.

This is...where is...? Is the guy from?... Her mind bathing in morphine, Sara believes she is at school and Norman is a bus driver.

The rear lights of the Chevy Blazer begin to glow. Exiting the idling SUV, a winded Norman looks side to side before heading back to the dark green Ford for the last time.

He is ugly! Sara thinks in the voice of a child. The ugly man soon opens her door.

"I need you to get up," he says in a rush.

"Whaat?" Sara tries to get up. She can't.

- 381 -

"Oh, fuck," Norman grumbles. Sara floats up from her seat to the sound of a low grunt. "Goddamn, you're heavy!" he strains. Though she doesn't hurt, it is hard to breathe.

Sara moves her legs as best she can. "Wherrrre yar are we going?"

"Shut up," grunts the man escorting her with an arm wrapped around.

"Yurrrr mean," she slurs as they wait for a Toyota Camry to pass.

"Use your legs!" Norman growls in Sara's ear.

"Ohh-kayay," she says in a sweet voice. Together they get her jelly body to the passenger side. Norman opens the door and hoists Sara up inside. Red-faced and huffing, the brutishly strong Norman shuts the door—*THUMP*

Completely gassed, Norman makes his way around the front of the vehicle. "Fuck, I'm getting old!" he gushes low. Soon in the driver's seat, he pulls his new ride around to the rear of the Ford Taurus.

Glad the grumpy man is gone; Sara turns on the radio. *Nickelback* plays while Norman transfers the contents of one automobile to another.

*Wow...*thinks the girl feeling as though floating in a warm pudding... *this band suuuucks...*

Assuming law enforcement is searching for the Taurus now, Norman splashes the inside with ammonia.

Ke$ha comes on the radio. This makes Sara happy.

Norman bids adieu to the car that has served him so well. On his way to the driver's seat, he peeks through tinted glass at the dead man atop the groceries on his way to the driver's side.

"Wherr we gunnah go nooow?" Sara asks the guy climbing inside.

"Home if you shut up," Norman huffs.

"...You're meeean," Sara informs with a frowny face.

Norman looks at his out-of-character Natasha. *Must be the drugs...*

"I yam thirsteee...can I get something to driiiink?"

- 382 -

Norman reaches back. He recalls seeing a cup in a holder behind the center console. He hands Sara a McDonald's cup half full of something warm. "Here."

"Yuck!" Sara whines. "Iz warm! Pop's nah sup-oz-abee warm!" Norman changes the radio station.

"Why for did you chanjuh thuh ranio sashun?!"

Looking at the unhappy camper, Norman, who didn't think Twelve had a snowball's chance in hell of making it out of the building, begrudgingly relents. "I guess you earned it,"

Sara surfs the channels. She runs across *White Houses* by Vanessa Carlton.

"Yaaaay," Sara says, long and soft. "I loooove this zong." Though having to arch her back to breathe, Sara is in opioid heaven.

Norman turns Northbound onto the interstate.

Within an hour, the morphine begins to wane – both the pain and Twelve return.

"Fuuuck—" the Natasha groans, shifting in her reclined seat. Discomfort growing by the second, she hardly remembers switching vehicles. Everything hazy since Walmart, Twelve knows Sara took her place for a time.

"What did you do to yourself, anyways?" Norman asks a Twelve now stirring.

"I got in a fight," the wincing Russian grinds.

"Looks to me like you lost," Norman jibes.

"Tell that to the other guy—" says the Natasha, remembering Officer Mendez on his back, with blood gushing out half a dozen holes.

"I need more."

"More already?" Norman raises his brow. "I've only got two more and we still have eleven or twelve hours to go. You just got that an hour ago."

Knowing her ribs are fractured, Twelve wishes she had a pillow under her back.

"...and we still have to switch cars."

"Grrr!" *I wish I had Sara's purse!* Twelve regrets, knowing how helpful her sister's Dilaudid and OxyContin would be right now.

I'll get you some over-the-counter medicine if you want," Norman offers with unusual kindness. "Maybe some whiskey."

"Vodka," Twelve corrects. To the agonizing Natasha, Norman being nice is somehow worse than his usual self. "Fuck it. Give me half a shot... and some vodka" She groans through a grimace. "That'll stretch it."

"Works for me," says Norman switching on his blinker for the next exit.

Parked outside the truck stop, Norman injects half a dose into Twelve's thigh... relief comes with the push of a plunger. The Natasha with three broken ribs, a cracked lumbar and bruised sternum sinks into her seat. "Ahhhh."

Norman heads inside. The Natasha waits.

With two plastic bags in one hand and a paper bag in the other, Norman returns to the glossy-eyed spy. Though mellow, he does not see the shimmer of innocence he did before.

"I got you Ibuprofen, vodka, and water," he says soaking a handful of napkins. So docile is Twelve, she allows Norman to wipe her sweaty, blood-smeared face. The dampness feels nice.

"Evun though yurr be-yun nice tuh-me...I still hate youuu—" Twelve wants her caretaker to know.

"Well," Norman softly returns the honesty, "if you weren't so good at what you do, I'd smother you right now and leave you face-down in a ditch somewhere."

"Least we unerstan one anuther..."

Time passes.

At a salvage yard North of Dallas, Norman and a guy named Jimbo help Twelve out of the SUV and into a gray 2008 Lincoln.

Sips of vodka between partial injections blunt otherwise intolerable pain. Having somewhat come to terms with her vulnerability, Twelve knows that if Norman was going to kill her, he'd have done it by now.

Feeling like she'd been hit by a bus, the one who believed herself a goddess only this morning feels very mortal at the moment. Every mile feeling like five, the Natasha endures.

Saturday, November 15th, 2014

11:24 AM
Sara's Bedroom

Sara wakes to the worst pain she has ever known – pain made all the worse with a hangover and dreadful taste in her mouth. Flat on her back, arms at her side, her last lucid memory was sitting in the back of Mrs. White's English class.

Toes wiggling under the sheet, tears running down, Sara yelps, "Lady–"

She waits.

"Lady!" she cries at painful expense. Breathing shallow, the girl with what feels like a boulder on her chest waits.

...after what feels an eternity, Sara hears footsteps. *Oh good!* Sara twists at the sheets. *Lady is coming!*

Expecting gushing compassion, Sara is surprised at the stern expression of someone beyond fed up.

"So, it's 'Lady' now?" she huffs, hands on her hips. "Last time I checked it was 'Fat Ass' or 'Dipshit'!"

"What?" mutters Sara, legs pumping under the sheet. "I never—"

"Don't feed me that rubbish!" Lady snaps low.

"What are you...?" Sara says through twisted lips. "...talking...?" Enveloped in anguish, she can hardly talk.

"Let me guess," Lady says in her rolling brogue. "You want me to 'shut my whore mouth' and 'get you your F'n pills'?" With this, Lady disappears from the doorway, heading for the cabinet where she keeps Babe's medication.

Blinded by pain and confusion, Sara is unaware of the exchange between Lady and a rather hostile Twelve around 3:30 AM. Eyes squeezed tight, Sara doesn't realize Lady's return until her right leg is being swabbed with alcohol. A little pinch when the needle goes in...Sara wiggles as she waits.

Relief comes in waves, eventually turning her to jelly.

"...and now you're wetting the bed," Lady sighs. "That's great."

"Huh?"

Not in the mood to deal with this now, Lady puts the cap over the needle and walks away. The bedraggled Scotswoman can hardly separate the venom-spewing demon she helped carry in the middle of the night and the girl now looking about as though glowing butterflies were fluttering all around.

Once returned to her chair, Lady resumes watching coverage of the shooting at Western Spec. Gun control is the topic. Domestic terrorism is the narrative. Lady has a feeling the one lying in a pool of her own urine is responsible in some way.

Face sunken and worn from sleeplessness; Lady simply does not know how much more she can take.

1:49 PM

Lady gasps at her first sight of Sara's back and ribs. "Child! You might have a broken back!" gushes the woman who helped Norman carry her in. Aghast at the bruising and swelling, Lady has never seen anything so terrible. Sara's entire torso is black and blue.

Lady medicates Sara to the point of painlessness once again. "One of these times, you aren't going to make it back."

2:40 PM

Sitting in a chair at the dining room table, the nurse who comes by to check on Babe wraps Sara from waist to armpits with a long, stretchy, flesh colored band.

Four-wheeler accident is the story.

Only somewhat lucid – hardly able to recall anything since Thursday at noon – the girl staring vacantly into the floor realizes a yearning to hear Clint's voice. "Can I use the phone?" she asks in a small voice.

Lady sighs, knowing who Sara wants to call. *If it wasn't for that boy, she'd be gone...*

Sara doesn't know Clint has been by the house three times since Thursday afternoon and called at least a dozen times.

3:38PM

Clint, after cutting across the pasture and racing to Sara's house in the chore truck, walks through the house and into Sara's room. Worried sick since hearing of the outburst in Mrs. White's class, he rushes to her bedside.

"Sara!" Clint sounds with a blend of relief and alarm. On bended knee – clasping her hand – he takes in the sight of his battered and bruised love.

"Whaaat happened?!"

"I don't know," says Sara, so glad to see him. Clint lifts the sheet to make sure she's not missing any parts. "I love you."

"I love you, too–" Clint says in a rush. "Have you been shot?"

"Whaaat?"

"I asked if you've been shot again!" overwhelmed, Clint's fear and frustration bursts.

"No," Lady answers from the doorway. "But she does have some broken ribs – probably a broken back."

"A broken back?! Is she paralyzed?!" Clint jolts with panic.

"No." Lady says calmly, "Not this time."

"Not *this* time?!" Clint blurts before turning back to Sara. "What happened?!" ...the girl fresh off another shot stares blankly.

"She doesn't know," a tired Lady offers. "As much morphine as she's on right now, I'm surprised she even knows who *you* are."

"How does she *not* know how she has *broken ribs*?!" Clint boils over. "Who keeps hurting her?!"

"Well, it's *not* me doing it so I suggest you *watch* your tone!" fires the weary gal.

"I'm sorry!" Clint is quick to pull back. "I didn't mean that towards you—"

"I know!" Lady counters sharply. "And I'm sorry too! I'm sorry you got yourself caught up in all this." Her tone softening with each word. "Now, you're a fine young man and I hate to say it, but you have absolutely no idea *what* you've hitched your wagon to."

Clint looks back and down at Sara. Her head swimming, she currently wonders if there is any vanilla ice cream or bacon nearby.

"Talk to me. Level with me. Please!" Clint pleads. "Whatever the truth is, just tell me, I can handle it. Trust me, nothing can be worse than being kept in the dark." The guy with tears in his eyes desperately wishes to know.

"I don't know the truth," Lady says somberly, "but I do know that you are wrong. The truth, what little I know, is much worse than not knowing. I'm sorry."

"Does Babe know?"

"Babe..." Lady's throat tightens. "Sometimes Babe doesn't know whether I am his wife or his sister he hasn't seen for over twenty years."

"I'm sorry," Clint offers, able to see the toll everything has taken on someone he thinks so much of. "I just..." he turns back to Sara, who is pawing at his leg. "I want to help. I want to keep this from happening again."

"Are you willing to say 'goodbye' to her?" Lady asks. "Are you willing to let her go?"

"No…no, I'm not."

"Then you're not willing to do what has to be done to save her…" With this, Lady walks away, leaving a speechless Clink in her wake.

"What's going on, Sara?" he asks the girl with a warm, but hollow, stare. "What is going on?"

5:57 PM

Once again, Sara awakens to the feeling of being crushed. After a few shallow breaths, she eeks, "Laaadeeee–" She soon hears footsteps.

"Where's Clint?!" she asks loudly as her pain allows. It is as though he disappeared during a blink.

"He had to go home for a bit. He'll be back shortly," Lady informs her, taking the cap off a 23-gague needle.

"You sure?" whispers Sara through tense lips. Lady gives her another shot.

"I'm not giving you morphine this time. I don't want to use any more of that than we absolutely have to." Silence enters as they wait for the injection to take effect. Feeling bad for how short she was earlier; Lady sounds more like her usual self. Once again – as is routine – a vacancy washes over Sara's face as the pain fades.

"Babe would like to speak with you once you're able."

"Okay," complies Sara, willing to do anything Babe asks. Her effort to rise brings dizziness, taking her breath away.

"Once you're able," repeats Lady to Sara, sinking back down into her mattress. *She doesn't realize how hurt she is.*

Pain and frustration cause Sara's eyes to water. She thought she was done with being injured. *This is worse than being shot.* Confused and helpless once again, Sara begins to sob. Hating when people see her cry, she covers her face.

"Ohhh, child..." says the torn lass, her sternness converting to sympathy. *She really isn't the other person.* For the first time, Lady considers the possibility that Sara and the "demon" are completely separate people.

Sara's muffled cry fills the room.

"You know, I used to think all that 'multiple personalities' stuff was just a bunch of malarkey. Something criminals could use as an excuse to get out of trouble, but..." she trails off. A sniffing Sara peeks out from in between her fingers.

Multiple personalities? Sara never thought of it in those terms.

"...but I just don't know...I just don't know." *If she is faking it, she's awfully damn convincing!*

Sara just listens.

These last few months have been hard, real hard. They've also had some good times, too. Lady thinks of eating ice cream on the porch with Babe and Sara. Watching Sara open up her new shoes. Every smile Sara has put on Babe's face.

Looking up at a Lady lost in thought, Sara winces at a spasm in her back.

"I've just had trouble believing..." Lady can hardly believe she's saying this, "trouble believing you really *weren't* her. And now, after all I've seen, I think...ah, Hades, I don't know *what* I think." In her heart of hearts, she doesn't believe Sara and the "demon" who told her to "Shut her whore mouth!" are one and the same.

A little taken aback, Sara can hardly remember the last time Lady was so gentle toward her. "I'm sorry..."

Lady coughs out a laugh. Fatigued near delirium, she lets go. "I don't even know what you have to be sorry for." *Poor girl woke up in this mess once those damned pills stopped.*

"What's she like?" Sara dares ask. She tugs at the stretchy wrap in search of breath.

"Now I don't make it a practice to speak ill of people," Lady disclaims. "But 'Twelve', as she calls herself, is a total bitch."

Sara's eyes pop open. She's never heard Lady sound so un-Lady like before. "What is she like?"

"Well, for starters, she has mouth like sailor and all the charm of chainsaw," Lady reports.

Forced to arch her back to breathe, Sara listens like a child being told of a scary monster.

"She's the kind of person who'd drink a gallon of gasoline just to piss on your campfire–" adds Lady with brows raised.

Sara envisions a monster woman with fangs and metal fingernails.

"She–" Lady stops... mercifully deciding to spare further details, she softly summarizes. "She is nothing like you."

Right or wrong, Lady has made up her mind.

7:20 PM

Sara is dreaming. Or maybe not. She isn't sure. She's under water. The bottom of the sea. Clint is sitting beside her. Little fish swimming around. Even though he is under water, his voice is clear, and his clothes are dry. Sitting on a rock, Sara can't get up. Her hair is floating all around.

"I love you," she says as a little fishy tries to swim into her mouth.

"I was afraid I'd lost you," Clint says...a fish that's actually a *Pop-Tart* swimming behind him.

"You won't–" Sara tries to tell Clint he'll never lose her, but little fish tries to swim in her mouth again. She crimps her lips tight.

"What?" Clint says leaning in.

"I said–" Sara slaps her hand over her mouth. Persistent little fish. Clint sighs.

"Lady thinks your back may be broken–"

But Sara hears, 'Lady stinks. Your cat was stolen.' This makes Sara very sad, even though she doesn't have a cat. Sara starts to cry. Everything makes sense in dream world.

"Why are you crying?" Clint asks.

"My cat was stolen."

"What? You don't have a cat."

"Not *now*!" The Sara under water whines. "He was stolen" – and then another little fish tries to swim into her mouth.

...Sara's eyes open to find Clint laying alongside. She doesn't know how long she was out, only that he is gently rubbing her leg now.

Ceiling fan swirling, television off, light rounding in from the kitchen, Sara stares for the longest time... "I love you."

"I love you too, hun–" Clint touches her cheek. "I love you, too."

Sunday, November 16th, 2014

12:04 PM

Sara is helped to the sunroom so she can see Babe. She sits in the chair pulled alongside his bed.

"Heeey," says the girl hurting despite her Oxycontin. She wishes she could stand but can't.

"Hi there, pretty girl," Babe smiles for the first time in days. "How you doing?"

"I'm okay," Sara weakly fibs. *He looks so terrible.* Throat crimping, she tries not to cry. "How are you feeling?"

Each take in the sight of the other. Though Sara's bruises are hidden under a baggy top, the look on her face and slow movements give her away. The feeling of a railroad spike digging into the base of her spine – and breathing stifled by the wraps – are nothing to the wrenching hurt of knowing Babe will never rise from his bed again. Nearly pale as the sheet draped across him, he is but a skin and bone vestige of himself from a few months ago.

"I'm better now that you're here," Babe hopes truth will alleviate Sara's sadness.

Sara sniffs her running nose. So many things she wants to say. Years worth. Time is slipping away.

"What is it, kiddo–?"

Babe is gonna die, Sara hears in her head. Tears stream down her cheeks... "I need you to tell me about her—" the words tumble out. So strange. Twelve is the *only* thing she wasn't thinking about. Sara sees flashes; an orange explosion, cords being jerked out of a laptop, a blonde beauty looking back in a mirror. Sara sulks.

"Well," Babe stalls, thinking of the best way to answer such a query. "Why don't we, uh – why don't we start by you telling me what you know already..." Sara shrinks in her chair.

"I know she hurts people," Babe hears after a waiting patiently.

"Yeah," Babe agrees, nodding his head. "Yeah, she does. How much can you...how much can you remember?" asks the man struggling to focus.

"Only bits and pieces...I remember a woman in a bathroom...she shot me and I fell down." Babe remembers the pistol wielding woman emerging from the darkness. "And she killed her. Twelve killed her." Sara says in a trance of sadness.

"I saw it happen," Babe tries to ease. "She shot you first. I mean—" he is quick to correct himself, "the woman shot *Twelve* first...yeah, she shot her *first*."

"Why'd she shoot her?" asks Sara. "Why'd the woman shoot Twelve?"

"I was outside in the car," he dodges the question.

"Have you talked to her?" Sara asks, gaze shamefully down and away.

"No more than I had to—" chuckles Babe, trying to lighten the mood. It doesn't work. "Twelve isn't much for conversation." Silence falls again.

Sara wishes she either knew everything or nothing at all. "Why can't I remember?"

"Because *she* isn't *you*," Babe answers boldly. "And you are not her...you are not a Natasha." His strength seeping, Babe feels light-headedness coming on.

"Natashas—" Sara beings.

"Are *spies*." Babe steps in. "They are…" His eyes grow heavy. "They are not sweet girls like you–" Sara can see he is fading.

Driving the railroad spike deeper into her spine, Sara forces herself to her feet. Easing to Babe's bedside, she takes his hand.

Embarrassed at having drifted, Babe's eyes pop open. "I'm sorry kiddo – I'm up."

"It's okay," Sara calms. "It's okay." Using her free hand, she brings the plastic straw of his water bottle to his parched mouth.

Babe takes three long gulps – "ahhh!" and smiles.

Bending her knees, Sara endures the hurt of lowering herself for a little kiss on Babe's forehead.

"My Petra," he says with a raptured glow. "My Petra."

"Yeah," answers Sara. *Maybe I am.*

Monday, November 17^{th,} 2014-
Tuesday, November 25th, 2014

In the days following Western Spec, Norman learns the Shannons attacked by his, Patrick's and Nathan's Natashas were seven of twelve total – and one Shannon managed to survive. Though multiple Natashas are malfunctioning, all proved capable of executing their assignment. Oddly, Sixteen, the only Natasha without issue, is the only one to fail her assignment. Because of dramatic collateral damage, Twelve and Sixteen made national news. The others received far less coverage. Cover-ups and disinformation on all.

Norman fears both Patrick and Nathan are breaking rule number one. With seven Natashas between he and his two partners, the lead handler is left wondering who's running the other five.

Clint takes life one day at a time. Doing chores without his partner has proven drudgery for the young man who becomes a nurse once the animals have been seen to. A paper-thin story of "Sara fell down the steps" is the blame for her injury. Fortunately, the time of year makes for light duty around the farm; allowing Clint to spend every night at

Sara's house, helping care for her and Babe. Clint's muscles come in handy with both patients.

Having had a change of heart even before Clint's coming over every day, Lady has come to believe Sara's blue-eyed guy a god send. Relief for a woman running on fumes, she even allows herself to go into her own bedroom for a nap because she knows Clint is there taking care of things. Lady, same as Clint, lives one moment to the next. As much as she wishes Sara wasn't hurt, the weary lass is glad for the time Babe has with her. No longer oscillating between Sara *or* Petra, the ailing Babe has come to see the beautiful young lady who sits with him as one and the same. Most days cloudy, Sara is Babe's sunshine.

Though watching the last of his life dripping away hurts, she wishes to be no other place than by his side.

While Clint is at school, Sara and Babe watch game shows in the morning and Westerns in the afternoon.

Growing a little stronger everyday herself, Babe slips at the same rate. Sara fears he will pass in her sleep, that she won't have a chance to say goodbye. The nurses – now hospice – go from one shift per day, to two, to 24 hours. One nurse, a girl with a heart-shaped face and southern accent, rewraps Sara every time she comes by. Healing time and a half faster than a person normally would, Sara is getting around with a walker after about a week. Victory is achieved one small task at a time. Sara is, albeit verrry carefully, able to brush her teeth...then raise her arms to shoulder level...then wash her face. She relies on Clint to help her in and out of bed, chairs, and her baggy plaid pajamas. Every movement beckons varying degrees of pain.

The highlight of Sara's every day is when Clint scratches her back once the wrap has come off. Sara's back is an ever-changing collage of purples, yellows, and greens.

Her mind ever more stained by increasing awareness, Sara blunts her pain with pills working less all the time. What was once achieved with two milligrams of Dilaudid now requires eight. Fifteen milligrams of Oxycontin, now forty-five.

Same as they would for family, friend or neighbor, both Howard and Lois come to visit every few days. Finding it sad that Lady and Babe don't have family in the area, Lois brings something delicious and talks to Lady on the swing as Howard speaks with Babe. Though he has never been a religious man, Babe appreciates Howard putting a hand on his shoulder when he prays for him.

Lady is surprised one afternoon when Russ and Kyle swing by to visit on their way into the city. Reminded once again of what kind of people Clint comes from, it does Lady's heart good to know her Babe will not pass un-mourned.

Days go by.

Wednesday, November 26th, 2014

9:17 PM
The Sunroom

Holding Babe's hand, Sara knows the day has come. Unlike every other time, she doesn't fight the tears running down her cheeks.

At peace, Babe is ready. He looks up at the young woman he and his Lady brought into this world. *"We did good kid...we did good."* Sara's chin crinkles at words thick with pride. The warm smile across his face somehow makes her sadder.

Knees wobbly, cheeks red, throat pinched; all Sara can do is cry. It's too much.

"Noo...no, it's okay. It's okay. I'm ready. This..." Babe takes a few raspy breaths... "this is the best we could have...hoped for."

"I don't want you to die," Sara eeks, stroking Babe's hair. She has heard about people coming back to visit in dreams. "If you can... if you can come back and t-talk to–"

"Oh, believe me, kiddo," Babe picks up after Sara's voice is stolen away. "If there is a way for me to come back and...and talk to you...I'll do it." Babe wishes he could offer his girl a measure of the peace she has given him.

"Promise?" *sniff*

"You betcha," Babe flashes a ragged smile. The smallest relief enters – the possibility of a connection one day – but only for a moment. Soon follows a wave a guilt. "I'm so sorry," she cries.

"Sorry...sorry for what?" Babe gives Sara's trembling hand a squeeze.

"For not leaving like a I said I would..."

"Sara–" Babe shakes his head. "Don't be sorry for that...because if you left...you wouldn't be here now..." A teardrop splashes on Babe's wrist. "We all make chuh-choices, kiddo..." he says between labored breaths. "Me and Lady...we made our choices...and you made yours...you love that boy and...and he loves you." Sara wipes her nose. "I would've done the same thing if...if I were..." Babe's focus fades, but soon returns.

"I'm glad I'm here now," Sara says in a small voice.

"Me too, kiddo, m-me too. If you weren't here, I'd be worried...then I'd re-really be in a pickle." Sara coughs out a laugh, smiling, but only for a moment. Her smile brings a twinkle to tired eyes.

He's dying and he's worried about me, Sara's mind cries out.

"Every...everything happens for a reason, kiddo...you are..." slowly goes the adoring Babe, "right where you need...need to be. You need to be with that...that boy."

"He's here now," Sara reminds.

"I know that," Babe nods gratefully. "Wherever you are...that's where...where he is gonna be." Sara rubs Babe's hands. "You take care of him...and, and he takes care of you..."

"I know," Sara ignores the pain in her back. "Like you and–" Sara's words are snatched away once again.

"You know..." Babe sighs, "you really are... suh-something special..."

"I love you," the words spill out. Sara wants to say it a million times. She wants him to understand what she cannot put into words. A love that comes from her very bones. A love she hardly understands herself.

"I love you too, kiddo," says the grateful man. "I need two fav...favors from you."

"Anything!" Sara blurts, sending a shock of hurt through her torso.

"I...I want you to leave...those cigarettes alone," Babe says regretfully. "I nuh-never shoulda given you...one."

"Okay," Sara vows to never touch a cigarette again.

"And I want you to...reach down..." Babe points to the stand beneath the TV, "and get into that cabinet...there." Sara lets go of Babe's hand long enough to get the almost empty bottle and two tiny glasses. The tears that slowed for a moment rush freely once again.

"Are you sh-sure?" Sara asks, her chest aching from the choppy breaths.

"Sure as I've...ever been about anything," Babe grins.

What am I going to do without him? wonders Sara, trying to steady her hand as she pours the first glass. "I don't think the nurse is gonna like this," she whispers.

"Just don't tell on me...till tomorrow," Babe whispers with a grin. "There's that preh-pretty smile...again."

A touch of a button raises Babe's bed as the last drops fall into the brimming second glass.

Nearly full the first time she saw it, the bottle is now empty.

Babe and Sara, neither much steadier than the other, raise a dripping glass.

Babe, pausing to count his blessings, takes a long look at the cherry on top of an otherwise wonderful life. "I'd a taken the deal..." he says.

"What?" Sara asks, her voice unsteady.

"If..." Babe explains, glass held in salute. "If I had been offered this...this life as a young man...Lady...you...all the happiness..." Sara feels a rise within her. "I'd have taken the deal. Cheers, kiddo—" Babe and Sara's last drinks go down.

"Ahhh!" Babe beams, savoring both the flavor and the moment. Sara cries.

"What do I do?" she asks, fearing a world without Babe in it.

"Just..." Babe takes her hand, "just live your life...live your li-life one day at a...at a time...and enjoy every minute...every minute of..."

Sara gives Babe's hand a wiggle.

Oh, no! His eyes rolling, she fears he is dying right in front of her. "Babe?!"

"...little things...that boy loves...you love..." Babe's eyes close. "...each other...care of...of itself—"

"I love you!" Sara rushes. "I love you!"

"I love you, too...kid..." Babe mumbles while slipping under. "I love...you...I love...you, I love..."

"I love you!" Sobbing and shuddering, Sara falls upon her father. Not knowing if he has passed, or merely asleep, she cries "I love you," over and over, wishing he take her love with him upon his travel ahead.

I love you too, kid. I love you, too.

Thursday, November 27th, 2014

12:21 AM
Sunroom
> Babe passes.

Monday, December 1st, 2014

St. Louis Post Dispatch, Monday, December 1st, 2014

In the early hours of Thanksgiving morning, John "Babe" Smith passed after a long illness. 63 years of age, he was a resident of St. Charles, Missouri for six years.

He is survived by his wife Johanna and granddaughter Sara Smith.

A small service will be held at Smithfield Christian Church on Tuesday, December 2nd at 10:00 AM.

Pallbearers will include Clint Fleischer, Russ Fleischer, Kyle Fleischer, and Howard Fleischer.

Tuesday, December 2nd, 2014

2:04PM
Lady's Kitchen

It is quiet after the funeral service Babe never expected. Everyone has left since the dinner following the burial, Lady and Sara are alone for the first time in a while.

Lady, hair perfect and still wearing her black dress, sits at the little round table. Sara stands at the sink drying dishes. There is nothing else to do. Everything is different now.

Grateful beyond words, Lady can hardly believe the way Clint's family saw to everything. Howard organizing and leading the service. Lois cooking, arranging the flowers, and notifying the newspaper. The Fleischer boys dressed in suits, serving as pallbearers. Though only the Fleischer family had known Babe, many of the members of the church family came to pay their respects and support Sara during the difficult time.

Those offering Lady their condolences found no shortage of kind words for her granddaughter.

At least a dozen times, Lady has told Momma Lois that she doesn't know what she would've done without her family. Lady cried as Clint's mother sang during the small, but lovely service.

Through the day has been sad, it is not without relief. So many of Lady's fears; Babe's leaving this world with no one besides herself to mourn him, no funeral service, grieving alone, are no more. What's done is done; and what came to be was much more than Lady could've hoped. There is solace in knowing she did her best.

Emotionally spent – and far from fully comprehending the man she loves is really gone – Lady is restless, clinging to the comfort of knowing Babe isn't hurting anymore. She can still feel him.

"Sara," Lady says after a long exhale. A wave of her hand invites her to take a seat.

After drying her hands on the frayed dish towel hanging from the refrigerator door, Sara sits across from the woman newly a widow. Lady breaks the silence.

"It was a lovely service."

"Yes," replies Sara at the compliment to the Fleischers. "It's what they do..."

"Lois has the prettiest voice...He really would've liked that."

"Yeah," Sara agrees, her mind drifting back to times on the swing. She remembers the heat. How Babe's eyes would between her face and the sunset. "She sings at church every Sunday."

The kitchen is quiet. Eerie is the silence during a time a Western would usually play.

"I'm sorry..." says Lady.

Sara's eyes rise quickly to the woman with hair a darker, more chestnut color than before. Though Sara's lips say nothing, the look on her face says, "What?"

"I understand why you didn't go." Lady's words fall like raindrops. "If I were in your shoes, I'd have done the exact same thing...and Babe would've, too." Lady laughs at herself.

Her face quizzical, Sara hasn't seen Lady laugh for the longest time.

"I married a spy!" Lady's teary eyes shine. "And here I was telling you to–"... and just like that, the laughter stops. Her smile fades away. From hysterical to solemn in a snap, she sighs. "And I'll suppose that boy will marry a spy, too...history just keeps..." Lady trails off. "I'm sure me and Babe weren't the first."

Sara's face falls flat.

"I didn't mean to..." Lady regrets broaching the subject of spies.

Though reminded of Twelve every time she takes a deep breath, mentioning her curse makes it real. Sara can only shrug.

"I'm glad you found Clint...I'm glad you were here when Babe passed...and I'm sorry I treated you...I didn't understand."

"It doesn't matter now. It's over." Sara says forlornly.

"I didn't..." Lady hesitates. "I didn't understand. I still don't understand. I just want you to know I'm sorry...you're a sweet girl and a good–"

"It's okay," Sara interrupts. She doesn't want to discuss this. Especially not now.

"No, it's not." Lady doesn't cut herself any slack. "It made me angry that I didn't understand – and you know what Babe told me?"

Sara's attention salutes the mention of Babe's name.

"When I told him I didn't know what to make of all your..." Lady sees no reason to elaborate. "He told me understanding that I *don't* understand is half the battle... guess I didn't handle not understanding as well as he did." The lass with fingers interlaced regrets the stubbornness that accompanies her passion.

Sara just listens.

"Even though I don't know everything, I do know he died happy. I know how proud he was of you." Tears well in hazel eyes. "You know, he never did want you to go..."

Sara's head tilts. "How do you know that?"

"Well, you know, I *did* sleep next to the man almost every night for thirty-five years," Lady points out. She hesitates before going on. "He believed you were our little Petra come back to us. The *last* thing he wanted was for you to leave."

Sara's brows raise at the mention of Petra's name. Lady has never mentioned the child she lost. "Do you believe that?" she asks cautiously.

"Me? No," Lady swats at the air with her hand. "But he did, and that made him happy. And his being happy made me happy...and, at times, maybe a little jealous."

Jealous? What?! Sara's balks with surprise. "Why would you be jealous of me?"

Lady, embarrassed at the pettiness so unlike her, shakes her head. "Oh, I don't know...you helped in a way I couldn't. Maybe that's it. You always made him smile." Still yet to get a good night's sleep – worn to the brink of delirium – Lady's words hardly make sense to even herself. "And–" she changes topics without warning, "he was thankful for *her*. Even though he hated her, he was *thankful* for her."

"Her who?" Sara asks, realizing half a second later, *Oh, yeah, Twelve.* Her mood shifts. Body stiffens.

"Yeah, I don't like her, either–" Lady agrees.

Sara stands to walk away.

"But she'll keep you safe–" Lady relays Babe's sentiment.

"She's doing a *bang-up* job so far!" snaps Sara, remembering the bullet passing through, the sound of ribs breaking.

"He said she is strong–" Lady's words lasso a Sara walking away. "He said she moves like nothing he's ever seen."

After a pause, Sara continues on toward her room.

"Babe left you something," Lady adds. "A couple of things, actually." Sara turns. "You remember the money in the closet?"

"Yeah," answers Sara, hardly thinking of money at the moment.

"Well, he wants you to have that."

"Okay."

"And there is something else," Lady says, getting up from her chair. She walks toward the half-eaten cobbler on the counter.

Curious, Sara watches Lady reach into the cabinet, retrieving a thick, manilla envelope from the back of the middle shelf. Corners worn and with stamps from a number of countries, it is crinkled and smudged. Holding it as though it were a bomb, Lady sets the roughly handled package on the counter.

Sara's stomach twists.

"Now, I don't know how he got this or who gave it to him," Lady says forebodingly. "All I know is that he called in favors from 'old friends' as he put it..." Lady returns to her seat; Sara picks up the envelope.

Peeking inside the tightly stuffed envelope, Sara sees a mixed and matched stack of what appears to be government documents and medical records, all written in Cyrillic. Her fingers crawling through the pages, she searches for anything in English.

"He said to burn it," Lady states with a thud.

Jolted, Sara's looks up.

"Well," the widow relents, "he said he *hoped* you would burn it. He wanted to burn it. But he said it wasn't his, so..." Honoring Babe's wishes, Lady defers the matter to Sara.

A heaviness flooding her heart, Sara sits in Babe's seat. Sitting at the place he took his coffee every morning, she feels his presence... *He's still looking out for me.*

Wednesday, December 3rd, 2014- Friday, December 19th, 2014

As it always does, life goes on.

Physical recovery is simple. Sara's back and ribs heal steadily. Recovering from the loss of Babe is complicated. Sometimes it makes her smile to think of him. Sometimes it makes her cry. Either way, hardly a stretch of time passes without him crossing her mind. Everything reminds her of Babe in one way or another.

Through Sara doesn't know what happens after people pass, she hears his voice throughout each day. Babe visits in her dreams; she's always sure to get a hug before waking.

Sometimes it's hard to breathe when she thinks of him. It's hardest at night, right before she goes to sleep.

Her heart heavy, Sara finds comfort in the man who promised Babe he would look after her. When not at school, she spends most every waking hour on the farm. With Lady gone more than she is home, Clint and Sara often have the rock house all to themselves.

Things are different between Sara and Lady, who now makes her way to the farm most every day herself. An honorary member of the Fleischer family, it is soon unusual to not see the lass between Kyle and Momma Lois at dinner time.

Lady enjoys cooking with Lois and attending Kyle's basketball games. Believing Kyle the cockiest young man she has ever seen, Lady gets no less carried away than Lois when Kyle gets the ball. She likes when the dashing young man stirs trouble and taunts the other team.

She has told Howard that Kyle should take his looks to Hollywood and become a movie star.

"...Well, don't tell *him* that," Howard replied. "He already thinks he's cute enough."

Attending school again, Sara seeks routine, a new normal; doing what work she can on the farm, dragging Clint to Kyle's home games, holding her man's hand at church. Everything helps a little, but nothing helps as much as Clint's arms around her so tight it hurts. His chin atop her head makes everything okay for a little bit.

By the middle of December, Sara can carry five-gallon buckets of ground up feed and ride Leo without pain – so long as she sinches her wrap tight. Between her opioid tolerance and Babe's medicine basket going unreplenished, she is forced to ween herself off. Fortunately, her physical pain is tapering off and missing Babe is less painful than watching him hurt.

Her withdrawals are blamed on the flu.

Once able to use a shovel, Sara buries the counterfeit cash in Lady's garden – minus a handful for Christmas presents. Mostly healed by the time she is wrapping Christmas presents, the last 10% of recovery proves elusive. Sara is very excited about her first Christmas.

With "the file", as Sara calls it, hidden in a place where only barn swallows and mud daubers might find it, the young woman goes about fulfilling her promises to Babe.

Saturday, December 20th, 2014

4:40 PM

Interstate 35 North, three miles north of Ankeny, IA.

The previous, dark green Ford Taurus long abandoned – and since found by authorities – Norman and his Natasha travel to her next assignment in the identical replacement dark green Ford Taurus.

A wintry scene all around, the two killers are over halfway to their destination: Minneapolis, MN.

Earlier, Twelve told Norman, "You can't pick out a new car worth a fuck."

Norman's response to her criticism was: "The day I talk cars with a woman is the day I put the barrel of a shotgun in my mouth."

"So, you want to talk about cars?" Twelve asked shortly thereafter.

Not much has been said since.

Without looking his passenger's way, Norman forecasts, "This one'll be easier than the last one."

"Who said the last one wasn't easy?" Twelve smarts, eyes also straight ahead.

Norman chuckles. "You must remember the last one differently than I do."

"Another Shannon?" Twelve regrets having said something that brought Norman joy.

"Not this time," he answers. His tone shifts to curious. "Hey, how'd you kill the Shannon anyway? News said she was shot."

Appearing preoccupied with the picturesque landscape, the Natasha pretends not to hear. She knows Norman hates being ignored. His displeasure brings her joy.

Too proud to admit curiosity strong enough to ask again, the squatty handler clears his throat and moves on. "The target's name is Gordon Hart. Owns a nightclub in Minneapolis. Your job is to get him back to his residence."

And kill him? Twelve guesses with an upbeat tone.

"No, you little psychopath. You don't have to kill him," Norman huffs. "Your job is to get him back to his house, sedate him, then let me in. Got it?"

"So, you *don't* want me to kill him?" Disappointment.

"No," Norman sighs. "What I *want* you to do, is dress up like a little whore. Walk to his nightclub full of *other* little whores. And lure him *out* of the club and *back* to his house – like I said the first time."

"And *then* I get to kill him," adds Twelve, expressly for the purpose of antagonizing Norman.

"I don't give a shit!" Norman erupts. "Kill him if you want to so damn bad, just wait until *after* we're done!" Knuckles turn white as rolling palms grip the wheel.

"Well, now I don't even want to kill him," says Twelve like a snarky teenager. *I'm gonna kill you with a heart attack, you fat, grouchy old fuck.*

"You can cut his fucking head off for all I care, but not before you get all gussied up, push your tits up, and use that big fanny of yours to lure him *out* of the club and *back* to his house!" Norman's blood pressure rises. "...and by the way, you're getting fatter."

"I've gotten fatter?" the now 138-pound Natasha alludes to Norman's recent weight gain. *I'm Megan Fox level hot, mother fucker!* knows the less-than-humble Natasha.

"Let's not talk for a while. You're giving me a headache," Norman says with a dismissive flick of his wrist.

Her eyes ever forward, *Push my tits up?! As if they need pushed up! Blind old bastard. Shouldn't be driving if he thinks I'm getting fat...dumbass.*

8:01 PM
Holiday Inn Express

Sitting slumped at the end of the bed, near the television, Norman waits for Twelve to try on the dress he picked out for her. The Natasha marches around the corner from the bathroom – "You've got to be *fucking* kidding me!"

Proud of himself on many levels, Norman looks at the less-than-pleased Natasha standing before him. The "dress" he selected – a black, skintight, strapless miniskirt – is so short she must pull at the bottom to reach mid-thigh. "What?" he asks wryly.

"What do you mean, 'what'?!" Twelve bites. "This is what you expect me to wear?!"

"Hey, it's not my fault you got fatter," Norman defends, grin deepening his crow's feet.

"I hate you so fucking much!" Twelve grinds, stomping back into the bathroom; slamming the door.

"Did you find the underwear I got you?!" The door muffles Norman's laughs.

Grabbing her .40 caliber off the tank of the toilet, the scowling Natasha aims at him through the wall.

10:48 PM
36 degrees
Parking Lot of Club Drink

Having taken a little white pill a short time ago, the operative with a perfect "smoky eye" and layered auburn wig loves the way she feels; raised to a higher level, every nerve standing on end, the sensation of electricity coursing throughout her exquisite body. With a t-shirt draped across her lap (the miniskirt creeps up while sitting), Twelve peers over the dash. Like a lioness looking through tall grass, the predator sees nothing but white-tailed does flittering about. And dumb bucks strutting to impress them.

The line to get in is long but moving.

Tandems and groups of twenty-somethings pass between vehicles; breath puffing into clouds as they rush to join those waiting to enter the trendy spot. Dressed to be seen, and shivering, many waiting to have their IDs checked by the bouncers (wearing shirts two sizes too small) prefer being cold to the inconvenience of checking a coat. A scan along the brick front brings Norman's words to mind – *"Walk into his nightclub full of other little whores..."* Twelve smiles. *They do look like whores*, the Natasha agrees.

Showered in neon, three woman making duck-faces scrunch together for a selfie. Twelve shakes her head, *I hate women so much*.

Around the parked cars and SUVs snake in search of parking spots long taken.

"You sure he's in there?" asks the assassin cinched tight beneath her painted-on miniskirt.

"Yeah, he's definitely in there," answers Norman, shifting to ease a spasm in his lower back.

"Be nice if you had a picture." *I'm glad your back hurts. I hope you die.*

"Be nice if you didn't bitch so much," Norman grumbles.

"Be nice if the CIA could've given you a picture," says Twelve, slowing turning his way.

Norman's face falls lax. Her eyes bore into his.

Yes, I know you're CIA. And no, I don't care. Feeling she has taken the upper hand, Twelve turns from Norman's troubled stare.

Preferring to avoid the subject altogether, Norman clears his throat and moves on. "He's 5'8" or 5'9", about 170 or so. And his teeth are too big. He's got veneers...and he's got a ponytail. Real douche bag. Can't miss him."

You're calling someone else a douche bag...that's rich.

"I'm sure you can find him if you ask around."

"I won't have to ask for him," the Natasha says haughtily. "He'll come to me."

"He'll probably be coming *on* you the way you're dressed," scoffs the guy not caring for Twelve's Queen-of-the-Universe attitude.

Goddamn, you're stupid. Twelve rolls her eyes.

"On a serious note," Norman settles, "he's probably gonna wanna fuck you *inside* the club. Remember not to let him do that or you'll fuck up the mission. You've got to get him *back* to his house...remember that."

"It's a good thing you said something," Twelve scoffs in Norman's face. *Gee, I keep forgetting how pitted and fucked up your skin is.*

"You have to let him *think* he'll get to fuck you *if* he takes you back to his house — not a fucking hotel, not someone else's house, not behind a dumpster — his house."

Talking to Twelve like she is stupid makes her want to murder Norman more.

Holding a *Visine* bottle between his thumb and forefinger, Norman instructs, "Once you get to his place, do whatever you gotta do—*whatever* you gotta do..." stressing the word 'whatever' with a stroking motion, "...to make sure he drinks this shit...then let me in the house. Got it?"

A noisy group passes by her window as Twelve slides the tiny plastic bottle down her cleavage. "How much?" she asks the one being as patronizing as possible.

"A squirt oughta do," Norman says, eyes following the bottle down Twelve's bust.

"Norman?"

"Yeah," he responds, eyes darting up.

Yes, I just saw you staring at my tits.

"You'll need money," Norman says, embarrassed ay the lapse.

"No, I won't," Twelve lifts her door handle.

Norman reaches into the console as the Natasha steps into the cold.

"Here's a phone," Norman extends. "If I text you, text me back. Don't call. I'll follow you to his place." Twelve reaches for the phone with one hand; tugging her skirt down with the other. "And don't take all fucking night."

THUMP! the Natasha is quick to shut the door – in case Norman had anything else to say.

The sharp chill raises a sheet of goosebumps. Though she hates the skirt, the Natasha does love the night air. The way the Northerly wind bites her skin. A cold burn. Twelve feels alive.

With bold strides, the Russian with auburn bangs pushed aside, heads for the entrance. One of the puffed-up doormen taps another. Twelve has their attention.

"Holy fuck," the bigger, bald one says low. More heads turn. Steam crawling off her hot skin, Twelve smolders as though having emerged from a volcano.

"You ever seen her before?" asks the 5'6" bouncer turned 5'10" by lifts and spiky hair.

"Nope," answers the bigger of the two with an ID between his fingers. A woman is waiting impatiently for it back so she can go inside. By the time the buxom beauty passes the last row of cars, more are looking than not. Once stepping onto the street, most are looking. Once across the street, all are looking.

Having abandoned her feline grace, the Natasha takes shorter steps, causing her hips to sway. The bouncers puff out their chests even more than usual.

"I'm here to see Gordon," Twelve notifies, walking past as though she owns the place. Warmth and a club lights greet her as the woman collecting cover charges yells, "Hey! You forgot to pay!" over the pounding Rihanna remix.

The shorter bouncer is quick to let the woman behind the register know – "It's cool! She's here to see Gordon!" Twelve enters the fray of club goers.

Called a "meat market" for good reason, the operative senses primal desire. The atmosphere – thick with bass, body lotion, cologne, laughter, lust, and insecurity – reminds Twelve of somewhere else. *It's like high school with flashing lights and booze.* Also, same as high school, she can feel eyes crawling all over. A path magically clears as she makes her way

The Natasha seeks vodka and a close-up from a security camera.

Dance floor to her right, tables along the wall to her left, she cuts through the mass toward the bar along the back wall. A bit sadistic, Twelve takes pleasure in the way women shrink away when she nears. She also enjoys watching men's brains turn to pudding. *I can actually see your IQ falling*, thinks the Natasha as a guy's eyes dart from her breasts to face, to breasts, then face. *Dumbasses...*

Twelve places her hands on the bar. Those nearby shuffle away; men for a better look, women to avoid a side-by-side comparison.

So, this is what it's like to be Tiffany, thinks the Natasha staring at a wall of gleaming liquor bottles. *Being Tiffany is fun.*

To the pulsing beat of Beyonce, the more audacious males angle for approach. Twelve doesn't like club music. She likes what is played in weightlifting class. Bush, Chevelle, Metallica, Marilyn Manson and Nine Inch Nails.

In the mirror (above a row of every flavor of Pucker imaginable) she watches men inch nearer; bartenders hustle to supply the shoulder-to-shoulder crowd. Twelve stares into one of the cameras angled down. *Gooooordon...*she beckons as though calling a kitten from under a couch. *Goooordon...come on down here and take me to your house so I can killll youuuu.* The taunt in Twelve's head causes her to smile. She looks into the mirror straight on. *Fuck! My pupils are huge! And pretty!*

Natasha 712 is her own biggest fan.

"Can I get you something to drink, miss?" asks a bartender in his early twenties.

"Who's going to pay for it?!" Twelve questions over the music.

Baffled, the bartender raises his finger a little at a time... eventually pointing at the entitled one.

Full lips rise into a smirk, Twelve shakes her head as if to say *"Yeah, paying for my own drink isn't going to happen."*

"Okay," nods the Ethan Hawke look-alike. *God, what a little bitch!*

As the bartender steps away, a GQ guy with Abercrombie smile and abs that can be seen through his skin-tight shirt, sidles up alongside.

"Hi!" begins the former lacrosse player over the music. "My name is Der—"

"Buy me vodka!" barks Twelve.

"Uh..." Deric is taken aback by her jarring show of force.

Wow! What a bitch?! "Okay..."

Twelve watches the befuddled man signal the bartender. His brain below the belt told him to go ahead and buy the drink.

"Mike!" shouts Deric over Demi Lovato song. "Two! Grey Goose!"

"I said *vodka!*" shouts the Natasha unfamiliar with the brands.

"Okay..." *What is this chick's deal?!* "Two *vodkas*, then!" Not knowing what to make of the demanding beauty, he plays it cool. Once re-centered, he leans in for conversation. "So...you from around here?"

"No!" Twelve answers louder than necessary. The Natasha stares at Deric, challenging him. Her aggressive, but calm, gaze is like a heat lamp to his snowman of confidence.

Deric hands the bartender a twenty after the shots are placed in front of them.

Twelve gulps hers down before he even reaches for his.

"So," stumbles Deric, reeling from Twelve's Viking-like manner. "Where you from?"

Focusing on the smooth warmth travelling down her center, the assassin compares this vodka to the vodka Babe had shared with her sister. *It's different,* thinks Twelve, rolling her tongue. Though it appears she has forgotten the guy with perfect teeth, she hasn't. The Natasha revels in his increasing discomfort.

On his face, an expectant hope of a response. On Twelve's face, an expression of *'Why are you still standing in front of me?' I am done with you. You may go now.'*

His snowman of confidence reduced to a slushy puddle; the dejected Deric decides to abort his mission. "So, uh...yeah, I'm gonna be around...you know, later—"

Indifference. Twelve offers no response.

Deric retreats.

Dating is fun! chirps the Natasha in her head.

11:03 PM
Security Office

Before a wall of Hi-Def monitors sits Matt Williams from South Bend, Indiana. The offensive tackle looking fellow wearing wire-rimmed glasses and Rizzo Cubs jersey has eyes on every square inch of the club, save for the restroom and his boss's office.

Downward angles on each cash register, the entrance, the exit, DJ's booth, waitresses' station, dance floor, booths, tables, and a dozen shots of the parking area. Matt, laid back no matter how many Red Bulls he drinks, sees all.

Of the thirty-two screens in front of him, his eyes are fixed on one. Matt zooms in on the responsible for the stir at the entrance. He presses the button on his radio for the second time, "Hey boss, you *really* might wanna come check this out..."

11:05 PM
The Bar

Mistaking her wry smile for an invitation, a dashing young man with a Wall Street look steps up to the plate.

"Haven't seen you around here before!" he archs his voice over Britney's 'Womanizer.'

"Vodka!" Twelve shouts. She likes making the monkeys dance. *Being nice is for ugly people.*

"Yeah! Okay!" he grins, assuming she is being playful.

Men's' job is to get me vodka, thinks Twelve. *I say "vodka" and they get it for me.*

"So, are you from around here?" he asks. "I haven't seen you before!"

"That's what the last guy said!"

What a bitch! "I was just wanting to welcome you to the neighborhood—you know, if you *were* new!" Not about to let a dreadful personality get in the way, the sharp-dressed man forges ahead.

Twelve throws back her shot. "That's very nice of you!" she sits her empty glass down. Then picks up his shot.

Uh...she just drank my drink, too...

11:08 PM
Security Office
Gordon hovers over Matt's shoulder, watching the auburn-haired vixen dismiss the second contestant on monitor nine. Having planned to leave early, the guy notified by both the doorman and his 'eye in the sky' has decided to stick around.

"I'm starting to think this one's a cold fish," comments Matt, who used to be a bouncer himself.

"No, she just knows these guys are chumps," Gordon huffs. Still smelling of bronzer from tanning at the gym, the owner of the establishment decides to personally welcome the heartbreaker to his club.

11:09 PM
The Bar
After watching others fail, Andre – a wide receiver from the Vikings practice squad – decides to "show these white boys how it's done." Confidently, the muscular guy with a freshly shaved head and a tailored suit strolls up the "white girl" whom he believes needs some "game spit at her".

"How you doing, g–"

"No!" Twelve cuts him off the way a guillotine falls.

Shocked at being shut down so rudely, the wanna-be suiter softens his manner. "No, girl, it ain't like tha—"

"Get the fuck out of here!" She roars. His bug-eyes wide, the spooked guy in a nice suit can't get away fast enough. *Shit, forgot to get vodka first,* Twelve chides.

While onlookers stand in awe at her harshness, Gordon heads Twelve's way. He emerges from the crowd as though summoned. His reddish-brown hair pulled back and mouth closed, Twelve doesn't recognize him right away. "Buy me vodka!" she orders. High off amphetamines, booze, and crushing men's feelings, the Natasha is getting a little carried away.

Gordon smiles. Big teeth.

Twelve leans around to check for a ponytail. *Oh shit, that's him! This is Gordon!* realizes the operative using herself as bait.

"Was someone bothering you, miss?" Gordon asks, the air filled with Lady Gaga's *Paparazzi.*

"No," answers the suddenly charming Twelve. "Well, not anymore." Gordon's gaze falls to breasts pushed even higher by a stretchy wrap pulled tight. Twelve tugs down at her ever-crawling skirt.

"I'm Gordon!" he proudly announces, "I own the place!"

"I'm..." *Shit, pick a name, quick!* Twelve says the first name that pops into her head. "Tiffany. My name is Tiffany."

"Nice to meet you, Tiffany!" Gordon leans on the bar.

Holy fuck! Your teeth are too big!

"Can I get you something to drink?" he asks, leaning closer.

"Hmm..." Twelve considers in a snap. *I've already had three vodkas on an empty stomach AND I am on a mission so I probably shouldn't have more. But then again, I do like vodka because it's awesome. And I'm basically taking meth, and that's the opposite of drunk so...* "Give me vodka!"

"You don't want the vodka down here!" Gordon says with a sour face. "You want the stuff in the VIP, the good stuff!" Without so much as a nod, the man with an orangish tan is towing Twelve through the crowd and to the stairs leading up to the VIP. Presumed a high-dollar escort by many of those looking on, it takes Twelve a moment to fully comprehend just how much she doesn't appreciate the way he laid claim to her.

Gordon stops at the bottom step, gesturing for Twelve to go ahead. "Ladies first," he says with a smile she finds slimy. After giving her mini dress another tug, the Natasha starts up the narrow stairway.

Having taken three steps before Gordon takes one, Twelve feels not only the muffled bass of house music, but Gordon's eyes looking up her skirt. *Enjoy the view cheeseball,* she thinks, having already decided how Gordon's night is going to end.

White panties! Gordon bites his fist. The auburn doll reaches the top step. Upon entering the exclusive area, Gordon's hand firmly finds the small of her back. Twelve does not like this.

The VIP has an Eastern theme. Deep reds, and gold. Burgundy couches running the perimeter. A slanted wall of tinted glass overlooks the action below. Much quieter, the more intimate setting has but a single bartender and two platinum blonde waitresses serving only top-shelf booze. Black lights cause bleached teeth and hair to glow.

Enjoying the circulating air, Twelve decides she likes the VIP section almost as much as she hates Gordon's hand is *still* on the small of her back. Making sure each of the twenty-five or so people in the VIP know the head-turner is with him, the grinning guy with lifts in his shoes stays leads Twelve to the only couch out in the middle of the room.

Having changed into a tight, black t-shirt before leaving his office, Gordon likes showing off the results of working out six days per week. 5'9" and 175 pounds, the man who gets testosterone shots twice a month from his doctor has an impressive physique for forty-seven years old.

Twelve sits on the far end of the swede couch. Her skirt rises. *Fucking skirt!* She raises, tugs, and sits so as to hold the stretchy material in place. Gordon sits unreasonably close. *Of course, you have to sit right fucking there!* His hand finds her knee. Skin crawls.

In addition to one hand on her knee, Gordon reaches his other arm along the back of the couch.

When Gordon sees something he wants, he goes for it. "Best vodka we've got!" he booms for all to hear. "When you own the place, you oughta get the best, right?!" he yells in Twelve's ear.

"Absolutely!" Twelve says with an air of enchantment. *I think I just threw up in my mouth a little.*

"So," Gordon says, inching closer. "What do you think of the place?"

"I think it is very nice." *You smell like a tanning bed.* "It's the first club I've ever been to."

"Really?" Gordon replies boisterously, his arm casually falling from the back of the couch to Twelve's shoulders. "So you're like a *virgin*, huh?! To clubs I mean!" Porcelain veneers on full display, he gives her knee a little squeeze.

"I guess you could say that." Twelves lays her hand atop his to keep it from going any higher.

"I'm sorry, what?" he leans even closer.

You are way too close to my face right now. "I said, I *guess* you could say that!" Twelve is extra loud so as to give no excuse for him to lean closer yet.

"Well, since it's your first time, I'll be gentle!" Gordon laughs at his inuendo. "But *only* because it's your first time!"

You should tan less. Your skin looks like leather. I hate you a lot... "Thanks." Sinking down, the couch seems to be swallowing her.

As though sent from above, a waitress offers a momentary reprieve when she places a drink on the low table in front of them.

Gordon leans for the drinks; Twelve raises her behind, pulls her skirt down and sits again. While doing so, her thigh tenses under his grasp.

"Wow! Your leg is as hard as mine!" Gordon robustly comments, giving follow up squeezes higher and higher. "You play sports?"

"No, I don't play sports," Twelve has never been groped before. She doesn't like it. She really, *really* does not like it. He mistakes her grimace for a smile.

"Here you go!" Unreasonably close once again, Gordon all but shoves Twelve's shot into her face.

"Thank you," Twelve shrinks away. *You disgust me.*

Gordon raises his drink, says, "Cheers!" and clicks glasses, spilling vodka on Twelve's dress. "To virgins! Virgins going *to clubs,* anyways!" He sips and sets his down.

As Twelve tastes chilled vodka – *Cold vodka, what the fuck?!* – Gordon swipes at the wet spot on her dress. His meaty palm grazing her left breast. The Natasha sucks a sharp breath.

"I am so sorry!" he gushes through a smile. Twelve shrinks away, burrowing into the couch. "We'll send it to the dry cleaners in the morning."

"Not a problem," says Twelve, resisting the urge to drive her thumb into his eye. *You must be on drugs. No way you're this much of a dickhole on your own!*

"So, what are you in town for, a photo shoot or a fitness thing or something?" Gordon asks, now touching the pretty woman's hair.

"I'm in town on business," Twelves smiles. Oddly, she finds his touching her hair – wig hair – more unsettling than his hand on her thigh.

"Yeah, like I said – model!" bursts Gordon, his breath reaching her neck. "I hope it's nude modeling! Ha, I'm just kidding!" His hand roaming North, the very tip of his thumb slides beneath her creeping skirt.

Having kept cool as long as she can, Twelve pushes Gordon's hand away.

"What, too far?" Gordon laughs off the rebuffing. "You know what they say! You never know there the line is until you cross it!"

Whoever says that is a fucking moron! Twelve smiles, tilting her head. "Is this your only club?" she changes the subject. While feigning interest in Gordon's answer, she takes note not only of his two-inch and, approximately thirty-pound weight advantage, but his minor case of cauliflower ear. This tells of a wrestling background. With no sign of physical impairment, body strong from regular weight training and experience grappling, the Natasha concludes it crucial to avoid physical conflict.

"Yeah," he answers with disingenuous modesty. "But I have other businesses. This is just a sideline."

"Oh yeah?" Twelve's eyes, dilated from her pills and slightly glassy from the booze shine with legitimate wonder.

"Ever heard of Hart's Diamonds?" Gordon asks as though it were a household name.

No. "Yes."

"Well, I'm Gordon Hart."

"That's very nice to know." *What does the CIA want with a jeweler?*

"Hey, you want me to have the heat turned up?" he offers.

"No, why?" asks Twelve.

Gordon points with his eyes. "'Cause you're nippin' big time!"

Twelve looks down and sighs. *Kill him if you want to!* She hears Norman's growly voice in her head. Gordon sees Twelve's brightest smile.

Thirty-four minutes pass. Over the course of what seems three hours, Gordon tells the woman he keeps calling 'Tina' all about the club. Square footage, every detail of the sound and lighting system, the average total collected at the door each night of the week, the hourly averages of the registers, his plans for upcoming renovations, and how he just got in from Europe last night.

Enduring increasing contact, the Natasha nods and smiles on cue. Gordon's breath-freshener having long worn off, the heat from his mouth now smells like warm mayonnaise. Twelve does not like the smell of mayonnaise.

Unable to take it any longer, Twelve interrupts the ever-gropier Gordon. "I want you to take me to your house and fuck me." *This should move things along.*

Stunned into silence, Gordon stares into the siren's flushed face.

"I'm sorry – what?" Gordon wants to hear it again.

"You heard me." Twelve repeats, brow seductively raised.

"Um – is, uh…" Knocked off center by the offer so boldly put forth, he wonders, "Is this a money thing? I mean, if it is I–"

"I'm not a prostitute, dumbass!" Twelve fires.

Gordon throws up his hands. "Sorry! No offense!" Both freaked out and turned on, the guy with a chiseled-on smile informs, "You know, uh…my office is right up–"

11:56 PM
The Entrance of Drink
Rather than exiting the rear of the club, near his vehicle, Gordon walks his prize past as many bouncers, bartenders, wait staff, and doormen as possible. With his coat on – and hand in the small of her back – he escorts the Natasha out the front and into the sharply chilly night. Past the patrons waiting in line. Along the East side of the building. Along the South side of the building. Then lengthwise through the employee parking lot.

Passing the dumpsters and the rear exit, Gordon escorts the frozen Twelve to his tricked-out Escalade.

Don't act like you're not impressed. Gordon unlocks his SUV with the key fob.

Saturday, December 21st, 2014

12:01 AM
Employee Parking Lot, Club Drink
Made louder by a modified exhaust, Gordon's SUV roars to life. Arctic air rushes from vents on full blast. Having not said much since lashing out, Twelve remains quiet as Gordon takes off his coat.

"Sure you want to go all the way to the house, huh?" Gordon double checks before putting the vehicle in gear. *It would be a lot less hassle to do this in my office.*

Biting her lip, Twelve nods.

Gordon eyes Twelve up and down, reminding himself why he's going through all the trouble. He puts the SUV in reverse.

Tired of fighting the skirt – and 99% sure she will be murdering Gordon a little later – Twelve doesn't bother pulling it down. Panties peek from underneath.

12:09 AM
I-35 South
Travelling at 76 mph, Gordon casually requests, "How about a blowjob for the Captain?"

"No."

12:27 AM
Gordon Hart's Neighborhood
Once past the guard shack, Twelve realizes wealth on a scale she has never seen before. Each estate along the roving path more grand than the one before, Gordon flips his blinker upon nearing the third residence from last.

Wow, Twelve is in awe, *I've never murdered anyone in a house this nice before!*

The house makes Twelve think of a governor's mansion. A beautifully scaped lawn. Marble fountain. Manicured hedges. Bulbs lining the crescent drive. His palatial home – white stone face, tall windows, columns hinting Greek influence – is lit up as if a ball or state dinner were underway.

"Welcome to my humble abode–" Gordon smarms. He veers off the circle drive, rounding to the garage on the side of the house.

"It's very nice," Twelve compliments. "Is anyone else here?"

"Nope," he grins. "Just me and you."

"Perfect."

12:28 AM
Gordon carefully pulls into the nearest spot in the seven-car garage.

Unarmed and alone, with a much stronger male, inside a sealed structure. Apprehension rises as the garage door lowers. Knowing Norman is nearby offers the Natasha no additional comfort. In the garage with a BMW, a Denali pickup, a Harley, two jet skis, a snowmobile, two four-wheelers, a speedboat and every tool imaginable, Twelve knows she's on her own.

"You have a lot of nice things," she says to Gordon, switching off the ignition.

"You know what they say," Gordon quips to the woman opening her door. "'He who dies with the most toys wins!'"

- 430 -

Only a total douche would say that, thinks Twelve, rounding the front fender of the SUV. His line of sight blocked for a moment; Gordon doesn't notice the smooth palming of the flat-head screwdriver laying on the bench.

"Ladies first," he says again, same as following her up to the VIP. Twelve passes by, screwdriver unseen… *beep, beep, beep, beep* sounds the alarm on the wall.

8-8-7-5, Twelve watches Gordon's finger switch the security status from AWAY to HOME.

Standing in the mud room, Twelve sees a state-of-the-art washer and dryer to her left, oak cabinets, marble counter tops, an area for hanging coats, a table for charging electronics and a bench running along the wall, should one wish to sit while removing their shoes. Bigger than Lady's kitchen, the Natasha never knew such rooms existed.

Soon barefoot, Twelve enters luxury rivaled only by something Sara saw on MTV. Taken aback by grandeur, she looks around with awe. *Hollly shiiit.*

To one side, a contemporary living area. Windows running floor to high ceilings, dark hardwoods, industrial colors, ornate rugs, marble end tables, beautiful couches, sculptures, a spiral staircase leading to the upstairs and an 80-inch television on the wall.

To her left, a kitchen of granite and stainless steel. An assortment of pots and pans hanging above the island, an elaborate range, gleaming appliances, and an elegant faucet craning into a sink un-like anything in Twelve's memory. Imported cabinets compliment the dining table with seating for eight. Beyond, the bay window overlooking a sprawling cedar deck.

Between the two spaces, an aquarium casting an electric hue. Exotic fish, both Asian and tropical.

"What do you think?" Gordon asks, hand suddenly caressing Twelve's rear.

The Natasha tenses.

"Oh my God! Your ass is made of *steel!*"

The Natasha twists away.

"Do you *live* in a gym?!" Gordon steps close. He is ready to get things going.

Screwdriver behind her back, Twelve buys time. "Can't a girl get a drink first?"

Gordon huffs, "Sure." He turns, grumbling something under his breath. "Bar's in the basement." Pouting and agitated, his once overly affable mood has steadily declined since being denied a blowjob on the ride over.

Keen to notice this, the Natasha follows down the stairs. *How am I going to get him to drink this shit?* wonders the woman going deeper into what feels like a lair.

After a few steps down the carpeted stairs, the operative with a galloping heart beholds a basement with more square footage than most people's homes.

A sportsman's dream, the walls are lined with memorabilia dating back to the 1920's.

Three pool tables. Fully stocked bar. Off to one side, a full gym; free weights, machines, dumbbells, and one of every kind of cardio machine. In the middle of the open expanse, a 'horseshoe' sofa facing the 72-inch screen lowered at the press of a button.

After a beeline to the bar, Gordon offers, "Vodka?" with a tone betraying his frustration.

"That's fine," Twelve answers as Gordon tosses ice cubes into a shaker, pours vodka, then runs it through the strainer into a scotch glass. Tired after a long day, he acts much like a child not getting his way.

Plopping the glass down on the bar, he slides it across so quickly some sloshes over the side. "There you go."

Shit, I need him to drink something. Twelve reaches for her glass. "You're not gonna make a girl drink alone, are ya?" she bites her lip.

"No," he says sharply, hands falling on the varnished top. "I gotta drive us back."

Twelve does a frowny, pouty face. "Not even *one* drink?"

"Fuck it. *Fine*. Not like I have to get back to work or anything," Gordon huffs.

Situation critical! Sounds the alarm in Twelve's head.

His mood rapidly deteriorating, Gordon slams his glass down on the bar.

Giving the angry male space, Twelve walks around to the sofa. While en route, she scans for more weapons... Pool sticks, pool balls, decorative plate above fireplace, the glass in my hand, hand towel on the bar.

Fingers down her cleavage Twelve retrieves the tiny plastic bottle.

Sitting in the middle, so as not to get pinned against an arm, Twelve tucks her borrowed screwdriver in between the cushions.

Gordon soon upon her, she notices, S*hit! He didn't bring his drink!* The Natasha looks back to see his glass sitting on the bar. Without warning, Gordon makes his move. Soon with his mouth on her neck and hand inside of her thigh, Twelve's groan mistaken for a moan. A hot, slimy tongue swirls its way along her jawline. Hand kneads its way near her private place. Revolution stirs within Twelve's core.

Holding perfectly still – denying her screaming urge to close her legs and twist away – the Natasha pushes emotion aside. Zeroes her focus. Crowded and at a disadvantage, she knows her immediate solution will not involve the screwdriver, because the guy now rubbing through her panties is sitting on it. *Eeeeww.* Twelve's stomach twists. Despite Gordon slobbering on her neck, she maintains her calm. Deliberate, even as her underwear are being pulled aside, the Russian forms a plan.

Visine bottle palmed in one hand – her drink in the other – the operative with few options and little time raises her arms above her head. "Pull my top down."

Removing his hand from between her legs, Gordon yanks down the polyester blend. He finds layers of stretchy, beige wrap covering her breasts. "What the fuck is this?"

"Something for you to take off," the Natasha answers, hands still high.

While Gordon unwraps Twelve's torso like a Christmas present, the contents of the tiny squirt bottle are emptied into the drink above. Squeezing too hard at first, Twelve is surprised the sound of jetting stream doesn't prick his ears. With her top down and rings of flesh-colored wrap loosely looped about her waist, the Natasha is exposed. Gordon places his mouth on her left nipple. *And now to get you to drink this shit!* Plots the repulsed Russian.

The assassin with the imprint of stretchy wrap pressed into her skin endures Gordon's hands and mouth on her body; same as riding out a joint lock or choke hold. She knows the keys is to stay calm. Skin crawling, Twelve regains her center before proceeding.

Gordon's hands between her legs once more, Twelve pretends sip of her drink – "What the hell?!" she bursts out.

"What?!" A perplexed Gordon looks up.

"What's wrong with my drink?!" A lousy actress, the Natasha does her best.

"What about your drink?!" Gordon shrugs.

"Something is wrong with my drink! What did you do to my drink?!"

"I didn't do *anything* to your drink!" He indignantly defends.

"Oh really?! Try it and tell me there isn't *something* wrong with it because something is *definitely* wrong with it!"

Anxious to disprove her claim and get back to business, Gordon snatches the drink and takes a quick sip. Not a drink, but a sip.

Curiously suspicious, Gordon rolls his tongue in search of whatever may be amiss. Tilting the glass, he notices a violet hue. An oily film riding the liquid surface... a slight, but unmistakable taste of chemical. Gordon sniffs the drink.

Fear surges upon the sight of Gordon firming his mouth. His jaw clenches. Breathing slows. *Barefoot. In a basement. House sealed. Tits out. Ribs unsecure. Looped in wrap. And he's sitting on my screwdriver. Fuck. This is bad.*

Pretending to be calm, Gordon turns to set the tainted drink on the end table. Her heart racing, Twelve begins pulling her top back up.

Wearing a look of disappointment, Gordon shakes his head at. "You know..." is all he says before—

POW!

Head rocked, blood streams from Twelve's broken nose.

"You wanna play games with me?!" shouts a Gordon now on his feet. "Huh, you little bitch?! You wanna play fuckin' games?!" Veins bulging in his neck, Gordon spits on Twelve now bleeding into her cupped hands.

Seeing stars, it takes a moment for the Natasha to gather her wits. Concussed. Vision blurred. Slumped forward. Head between her knees. Twelve slyly slides her hand between cushions for the screwdriver. *I'm going to kill you for that!* Unable to find the screwdriver, she hears a belt buckle coming undone. *Oh shit!*

Gordon's hand seizes Twelve's throat. Overwhelmed by his strength, the Natasha is pushed onto her back and straddled.

Choking. Sinking into the cushions. Blood running down her cheeks. Twelve feels she is drowning. Gordon grabs a handful of hair. The wig slides off.

Held in place by his left, the woman with blood in her eyes takes a bludgeoning punch to the side of her head. Bright flash. Ears roaring. A heavier blow than the first, Twelve's consciousness dims.

Bearings return to the words, "Are you still tricky bitch?! Huh? You still tricky?!" Gordon's belt buckle jangling, he steps out of slacks now hanging off one ankle. Twelve's world spins.

Blinking clears her vision enough to see furious eyes. Intentions clear, the guy pinning Twelve's body uses his free hand to pull his black t-shirt over his head. "You said you wanna get fucked, huh?! You come *all* the way out here to get fucked, huh?! You think this is a joke?! You think *I'm* a fucking joke?!"

Vessels rising in her cheeks and eyes bulging, the object of Gordon's ire wriggles and twists. Neck slippery with blood, Twelve fights for consciousness. Clawing at his arm, she coils to keep her knees from being pried apart. Resistance further enrages Gordon.

Shifting, crimping, writhing. *He's so strong!* Twelve cries out in her head. Black miniskirt bunched around her waist; she is tangled in circles of lax wrap.

Infuriated, he taunts, "You wanna be a fucking tease, bitch?! Huh?! You wanna be a fucking tease?!" Though impeded, Gordon manages his left knee between Twelve's thighs. His free hand reaches down for her panties...*POP!* is the sound of thin, lacy material swiftly ripped away.

Legs blocked apart by his knee sunk down into the cushion, the feral Natasha cannot defend against his upturned hand.

"Is *this* what you came to give me?" Gordon demands, two fingers sliding up inside. SQUEEZE! He seizes with curling fingers.

"Unnngh!" grunts Twelve upon his violating grasp. Dominating the one who vexed him sends a surge of pleasure through Gordon. Fingernails digging into both her throat and insides, she can but quiver under his authority.

"What'd you put in that drink, you scandalous little bitch?!" Gordon growls.

Her answer is a snarl. Shirking. Clawing. Struggling against arms hard as stone. Fighting so long as fight remains.

Gordon gives a clutching jerk by her pelvis — fingernails raking. "Answer me bitch!"

Twelve tries to bite his hand. Gordon clamps her throat even tighter. Though bloodied and swollen, the woman who made him feel small continues thrashing.

Her strength dedicated to keeping Gordon at bay, Twelve doesn't know if the sip of the chemical will have any effect at all. If Norman will come along at any point. If Gordon might kill her when he is done. But she does know he is leaning closer. And that his eyes are within reach.

"I said—" the Natasha gurgles, drawing him a little closer... JAM!

Twelve's palm shoots up Gordon's slippery wrist, driving French tips into his eyes as she bucks with all her might.

"Aaaargh!" Gordon screams, hands clasping his face. "YOU FUCKING BITCH!!"

In a rage, Gordon unleashes fury upon the choking and coughing Natasha *PUNCH! PUNCH! PUNCH! PUNCH!* A flurry of blows rain down upon Twelve, defending from her back. Using a triangle defense (forearms reenforced by overlapping palms facing outward), she blocks and deflects many of what seems a hundred punches. But some get through. *PUNCH! PUNCH! PUNCH!* Mostly blows to her brow and top of her head. The bloodied Natasha weathers the storm. Gordon begins to fatigue.

Finally gaining separation, Twelve kicks up from her back – heel splitting his lip. Gordon rages.

"You fucking bitch!!" *Huff, puff*. "You fucking bitch!" *Huff, puff*. "You fucking–"– Gordon slips, falling onto Twelve. Her legs wrap around his waist. She pulls him close. He is shocked at her strength.

Stretchy band entangling them both, Twelve tries to crush Gordon's ribs with her legs. *If I can't breathe, you can't breathe, motherfucker!* Wrenching his ponytail with one hand, she fishes for her screwdriver with the other. *Where the fuck are you?! You should be right there!*

Head pounding. Strength failing. Chocolate hair goopy with blood. Face swollen. Unable to breathe. The Natasha fights on.

Gordon is suddenly hampered by dizziness. Like being drunk. Heaviness fills his limbs.

Where the hell is that screwdriver?! wonder the Natasha, right hand fishing between the cushions. *WHAM* Gordon's knuckles drive into her side. *Shit!* "Uuggffth!" *I'm hurt!* Wind knocked out of her lungs, Twelve could swear her ribs are rebroken. Channeling all her rage, she scissors his guts even tighter.

Twelve sips air as a faltering Gordon struggle against her hold.

Given up on the screwdriver, the Natasha still yanking ponytail digs her nails into Gordon's face. She feels his strength lessening.

Disorientation and fatigue weight heavy on the man wearing silk boxers. Another punch to Twelve's side. This hit, thumping against her folded arm, has little effect. Another punch, even less. Falling deeper under the chemical's spell, Gordon braces his arms. His world is spinning. Growing woozy, Gordon is unaware of the elastic band wrapping his neck. *What the fuck?!* wonders the guy with his torso in a vice. He claws at the stretchy band now digging into his neck. The tide has turned.

Rolling her wrist to tighten the stretchy strip, Twelve's hand soon turns white, Gordon's face, purple. The whites of her eyes appear through her mask of smeared blood. Now the aggressor, she glares, drinking in Gordon's agony.

The scene is almost silent, save for gurgles and strain as bodies rustle on moaning leather. Twelve arches her back in search of breath. Sinuses flooded, the Russian with hair matted to her sucks air through gritted teeth.

"Who's the bitch, now?" Twelve taunts, with what little breath she has. Too weak to escape, Gordon remains posted, his hands along the edge of the cushion.

Consciousness slipping, the man bleeding from his eyes and lip collapses. Both Twelve and Gordon slide off the edge of the couch onto the floor.

"Get off of me!" Twelve kicks at the guy laying atop her leg. Gordon, choking and coughing, stares up from his back. A victim of the mystery chemical and strangulation, he is confused. Unsure where he is or how he got there. Twelve staggers to her feet.

"I guess that shit kicked in," she sneers, sounding as though she has a cold. Returning the favor from earlier, she spits in Gordon's face. The stretchy band harmlessly looped about his neck, and pants still hanging off his ankle, Gordon lays on the floor with his legs apart. *STOMPS!* Twelve's heel smashes testicles.

Curled in the fetal position and shuddering, Gordon vomits on the carpet.

Tilting her head to slow her bleeding, the Natasha situates the dress she can't wait to throw away. She is no longer exposed.

While a disoriented Gordon quivers and cries, Twelve walks to a mirrored sports display to assess the damage. She gasps at the sight of her face. Touching the sides of her nose with the flats of her fingers, the Natasha is too angry to comprehend just how angry she is. She lightly presses about the knots on her forehead and scalp.

Her hair line gooey is from sweat and blood. Forehead bumpy, bruised and streaked. The fact that Gordon touched her at all makes her angry. But her nose...her nose is a whole *other* thing. *You wanna be a fucking tease, bitch?! Huh?!* Gordon's words ring in Twelve's pounding head. *Are you still tricky bitch?! ...You came all the way out here to get fucked, huh?!*

Every pulse a jackhammer to her head. Every breath a struggle. And her ears are hot. The Natasha hates when her ears get hot.

Twelve peers at Gordon through eyes nearly swelled shut. His mouth foamy at the corners, the weeping man begins to crawl away. Pulse felt through her nose twice as wide as usual, she asks, "*Where in the fuck do you think you're going?!*"

To the side of the man on all fours, she lines up the kick. *THUMPH!!* Gordon is lifted by the Russian's bare foot. Ribs cracked by the hearty boot; he lay purple-faced, unable to scream.

And don't take all fucking night! Twelve remembers Norman's last words before shutting the car door. This makes her want to take longer. To the song of Gordon's visceral groan, Twelve walks over to the bar, splashes water on her face, drinks three handfuls from the faucet and pours half a scotch glass of vodka. Gordon begins to cry.

Drink in hand, Twelve rounds the couch, flipping cushions to find her screwdriver. *"There* you are!" She picks it up and turns to Gordon.

Twelve kneels over the pitiful sight and takes a sip... "Hey," she pokes him lightly. "Look at me." Shivering as though freezing, and mumbling something unintelligible, the wheezing Gordon fails to do as he is told. "Hey," blood drips from her nose onto his side. *"Look* at me!" Wincing, Gordon closes his eyes tighter.

"Hmm," sounds Twelve, feeling as though someone squeezed an entire bottle of Elmer's glue up her nose. She raises the screwdriver above his calf. "Gordon!" *STAB!*

"AAAGGHH!"

Twenty-one minutes later

Gordon, tied to a chair, is jarred awake by a pitcher of ice water dumped over his head. Foggy and nearly blind from the gouging, the wheezing man realizes; zip-ties digging into his wrist behind his back, ankles secured to the legs of the chair, Norman smiling and Twelve (wearing an over-sized Randy Moss jersey and a pair of white sweats she took from his closet) holding a bag of frozen peas to her face. Gordon begins sobbing.

Twelve, with most of the blood wiped off her puffy face, leers over the frozen bag. *You just wait until we're alone again... you just wait.*

Hockey memorabilia behind him, Gordon looks up through tendrils of wet hair. Panicked eyes dart between Norman and Twelve. He feels drunk. And sorry. And helpless. Boxers soaked with urine and ice water, he begins in a shaky voice, "I don't–"

"Shut up," says Norman, cold as the water pooled in Gordon's lap.

The massive basement is dead silent. Despite the openness of the area, the moment feels intimate, as though all three are in a place no larger than a bathroom or a closet.

An eternity passes, Gordon speaks again. "I just want–"

"I said *shut up.*" Norman repeats like a gavel falling.

Gordon realizes his captures beyond reason. Hopelessness sets in. Soon blubbering, he wails upon notice of the screwdriver sticking out of his calf.

"Shut up!" barks an annoyed Norman.

Like a child, Gordon does his best to stop crying.

"Why'd you hit the girl?" asks Norman, almost sounding unhappy about it.

Rather than answering, the sniffling man just lowers his head. Lip swollen, eyes raked, red marks around his neck, hair a mess; Gordon is a pitiful sight.

Cry bitch! Twelve finds melody in Gordon's misfortune.

"Look," Norman interrupts Gordon's dulcet whine, "I know why you hit her. I've wanted to hit her since I met her, but not in the nose. Why'd you hit her in the nose? I've gotta look at this bitch, you know?"

"I'm, I'm sorr—"

"I don't give a fuck about her." Norman's words chop the air. "What I *do* care about is the safe. Where is it?"

A safe?! Twelve looks to Norman. *What the fuck?!*

"Safe? What safe?" Gordon plays dumb.

Yeah, what safe? wonders Twelve. *Is this a fucking robbery?!*

Unamused, Norman calmly reaches into his pocket of his slacks and pulls out a collapsible knife. Without looking her way, he hands it to Twelve.

Saying nothing, she opens the 4 ½ inch blade and slashes across Gordon's bare chest.

"AAAAHHH!" Gordon screams, his chair rocking and jumping as blood streams from the long, shallow cut. "You fucking bitch! You fucking bitch!" Gordon shrieks, mouth twisting in agony.

Finding Gordon's words offensive, Twelve steps for another swipe, but Norman shouts, "No!" with an arm out. "Down girl! Down!" The Natasha's handler thinks this is funny.

Shrinking in fear, Gordon is grateful for Norman's intervention.

Face throbbing. Knots on her head throbbing. Throbbing between her legs. Twelve glowers at the man who hurt her.

Jesus Christ! Norman thinks to himself. "All right, gimme the knife back." His hand lay open for a time. "Give it here."

Twelve reluctantly gives back the knife, never taking her scowl off Gordon.

"A real charmer, I know," Norman jests just as Twelve sidearms the bag of peas squarely into Gordon's face.

SMACK! "AARRH!" Gordon howls, the bag smacking him square in the mouth.

"Goddammit!" Norman growls at Twelve. "Will you stop?! Please?!" He stares at the one feeling a little better. "You're worse than my third ex-wife!"

Crying again, Gordon looks at Norman, blood still running from the slash.

"Don't look at me pal, I gotta ride home with her," Norman shrugs, combing his white hair forward with his hand.

"I'm sor-re-rry," Chest heaving erratically, Gordon tries to make amends.

"Now let's try this again before I let this crazy bitch have her way," Norman groans low. "Where's the goddamn safe?"

"It's upstairs! It's upstairs!" Gordon can't answer fast enough.

"See how easy that was?" Norman says as though talking to a child. He waits a moment... "So, you gonna make me ask for the combination?"

"There is no combination," Gordon mumbles, any trace of bravado long gone. "...my fingerprint is the combination."

The corners of Norman's mouth rise. "Which finger?" he asks, black eyes gleaming.

"My thumb," Gordon croaks, his head hanging down.

Norman leans in. "Which thumb?" Twelve smiles. She sees where this is going.

"My ri-ight thumb."

"And this safe," Norman pries, "is it in your closet?"

Gordon swallows hard. "...noo. It's un-under my bed."

"Under the bed, huh?" Norman repeats, his short, wide teeth showing. "Right thumb?"

"Yeah, under the bed," Gordon shamefully affirms. His chin rises. "If you promise to l-leave, I wi-will go up with y-you and—"

"Shhhh." Norman shushes, stubby finger to his lips. "There's no need for you to get up..."

Terror floods Gordon's heart as Norman reaches back into his pocket. He sees the knife once again. "No. No. Noooo!!"

"Natasha," Norman hands Twelve the knife once again. "Bring me his thumb."

"No! Nooo!!"

Seven very loud minutes later

Laying on his side, still fastened to the chair with his hands behind his back, Gordon softly blubbers. Spent from howling, bucking, and blood loss, he is no longer capable of the ear-piercing shrieks that filled the basement a short time ago. Twelve doesn't know if the chemical she slipped him dulls pain. She hopes not.

Aside from Gordon's slobbery sniffles and choppy breathing, it's quiet as Norman goes about whatever he is doing upstairs. Twelve stares at wrists raw from digging zip-ties, the gory mound where Gordon's thumb was attached. His hands swollen and purple, she is surprised at how little the thumb bled. Regardless, the cream-colored carpet is ruined.

Fading in an out of consciousness, Gordon looks up at the woman who wrenched his hand open and sawed his thumb off. Twelve removes the bag of peas from her face as to say, *Remember what you did?* The despondent man lowers his eyes in shame.

"What?" asks the Natasha, face more swollen by the minute. "Nothing to say?"

Sodden with regret and fear, Gordon dares ask, "Are you g-gonna ki-kill me?"

"Maybe not," the Natasha allows a ray of hope. After a pause… "Maybe I will kill you…maybe Norman will kill you. But definitely," Twelve flippantly teases, "*one* of us is *going* to kill you."

Gordon weeps. Twelve smiles behind her frozen peas.

Two minutes pass.

Curious, Twelve decides to ask Gordon – who lost consciousness once again – about the contents of the safe. Kneeling down beside, she lightly pries the handle of the screwdriver still sticking out of his calf.

"AAAHH!" Gordon screams, recalled to the hell of his reality.

"Shut up!" Twelve hisses. "What's in the safe?"

"Diamonds!" Gordon cries, his right cheek on the carpet. "Dia–"

"I said shut up!" Twelve shushes. *Diamonds? What the fuck?!* the Natasha questions as Gordon whines. *Yeah, this is a robbery, plain and simple.* Half a minute later, a jovial Norman comes down the stairs. Twelve has never seen her handler look happy before.

"You ready?" he asks rhetorically.

"No," says the scorned woman. "Not yet."

With a curious look on his face, Norman watches Twelve drop the bag of peas. She extends her open hand.

"I need your pocketknife."

She's going to slit this guy's throat, assumes Norman, digging into his pocket. He hands the knife to his roughed-up colleague.

Realization sinking in, Gordon looks to Norman. Then at Twelve. Then back to Norman. Then Twelve. "No! No! Nooo!" he shouts, losing sight of her as she steps behind.

Craning his neck to look back, the frantic man wriggles and bucks in horror. Knelt down behind, the Natasha 712 seizes a handful of hair. She jerks his head back.

Flick! sounds the metallic scrape of a pocketknife opening. Hope gone; Gordon summons the last of his strength to spit– "You fucking bitch! You fucking bi–!" a rolling gurgle soon drowns his squalling act of defiance.

The slicing blade sends a wash of shiny red into the plush carpet. Gordon's eyes roll back.

Taking delight in her grizzly task, Twelve pries his head back farther as she saws. Norman – not usually squeamish – winces at the sound of stainless-steel scraping vertebrae. A gruesome sight, it reminds him of the terrorist beheadings streamed online.

"There we go," grunts Twelve, pulling Gordon's head loose. Chin down, wet hair draping her battered face, the Natasha stands.

Though deeply disconcerted, Norman pretends to be bored with the Natasha's antics. "You done?" he says to the savage with upturned eyes and a pool of blood at her feet. He makes it a point not to look at Gordon's vacant face. His swollen eyes barely open as if to be peeking down.

Without a word, Twelve drops the head where she stands, steps over Gordon's body and turns for the stairs. "Clean that up," orders the Natasha disappearing up the steps.

Norman takes a deep breath. *What. In. The. Fuck?*

Twelve enters Gordon's kitchen. *I hope he has Hawaiian Punch.*

1:44 AM
The Driveway of Gordon's Residence
After a shower and helping herself to Gordon's closet again (while Norman doused the scene with household cleaning agents) Twelve and her handler pull away from the 6000-square-foot residence.

Damp hair soaking her neckline, the Natasha with her pistol in her lap pulls down the visor lined with tiny bulbs. Every time she looks, it's worse. More swelling, more discoloration. She touches the sides of her nose twice as wide as normal. Regretting having not tortured Gordon more, she flips the visor back up.

Unsettled by the beheading, Norman has been quiet.

Having found an ice pack frozen solid as a rock, the crabby assassin uses another bag of peas until it softens. Angrier as time goes on, Twelve wants to go back and cut Gordon up, but she doubts that will make her feel better. Wishing she had an ice pack she could wrap around her entire head, the Natasha stews. *Fucking Gordon!*

Despite her fixation on the late Gordon Hart, Twelve keeps an eye on Norman and a hand on her pistol. On high alert, she believes that *if* her handler is planning to kill her, he will most likely try it on the way home. A lot of fields and wooded areas between Minneapolis and St. Charles.

Usually crotchety, Norman's uncharacteristically buoyant mood has Twelve all the more wary. Preferring a better mood herself, she takes a little white pill.

Norman slows for the guard shack.

Dragging her mussy hair across her face, the passenger clad in pink Victoria's Secret pajamas appears asleep. Norman rolls to a stop.

Not wishing to wake the young lady, the night watchman with a jelly doughnut and belly hanging over his belt waves the dark green car through.

"You can wake up now," says Norman as the car accelerates.

"I'm asleep. Don't wake me up," Twelve smarts, shifting in search of breath. Stiffness and ache spreading throughout her body, she is glad she brought Sara's pills this time.

Twelve washes down one Oxycontin with a sip of water...*Shit!* Realization strikes like a slap to the back of her head. *I should've taken Gordon's vodka!*

2:20 AM
Parking Lot of Convenience Store, I-35 South
Norman returns to the car with the items Twelve requested: two sports drinks – one red, one blue – a slice of pizza, a bottle of Ibuprofen, a bag of Starburst jellybeans, and a tube of Chapstick.

It's official. Twelve knows something is off when Norman doesn't complain about her laundry list of requests. Between the little white pill, Sara's Oxycontin, and the satisfaction of sawing Gordon's head off, Twelve is in much improved. So much so, that she doesn't really want to murder Norman that much right now.

Unable to breathe through her nose, the Natasha must inhale between bites of pizza and jellybeans.

Once back on the interstate, the two operatives are just another set of lights heading South through the night. Snow on both sides of the highway and a gray sky above, they travel behind a Ford F-150 with expired tags for the longest time. After finishing her first sports drink, and big bag of jellybeans, Twelve dips her chin... *BUUUURRP!* the Natasha's throat rumbles like that of a viking after a flagon of ale.

Equal parts awe and disgust, Norman turns to his uncouth passenger. At that moment, the vent blows a waft of pepperoni in his face.

Her throat still humming from her belch that would make a lumberjack proud, Twelve smiles.

4:17 AM
Altoona, IA
Truck Stop
Having peed on the side of the road twice already, Twelve decides to avoid another arctic chill on her backside and follows Norman inside to use the restroom.

She sweeps her hair behind her ears so everyone can see her face. When Norman's not looking, she makes a fist, indicating he's the one responsible for her bruises and swelling.

Norman receives unpleasant looks.

The Natasha finds this funny.

10:14 AM
Lady's Residence
Though warmer than Minnesota, home is cold. The Ford imprints in the frost as it climbs the winding Northern drive. Norman parks in front of the telephone pole near the fence.

Twelve is surprised to see Lady's car under the port. At the farm even more than Sara, the new widow spends little time in the house with so many memories.

Even more surprising is Norman having not made a single joke or smart remark about her face. *Must've made an impression with the head,* the Natasha muses.

Norman shifts the car into park. The engine still running, he turns in his gray leather seat. "You know," he says with a tinge of sympathy, "he shouldn't a hit you in the nose."

"He won't do it again."

Norman's pitted cheeks to rise. "No...no he won't." His black eyes scan knots and red streaks about Twelve's forehead. "Here, I'm gonna make this quick. I am going to be travelling for a while, so you're gonna get a little vacation–"

"To sell the diamonds?" Twelve interrupts. She wants him to know that she knows.

Norman's face falls flat. *Shit! What did Gordon tell her?!* After a short silence, he continues as though she'd said nothing at all. "You have some money coming."

I like money.

"I'm giving you this for now," Norman says, reaching inside the breast pocket of his jacket.

Not about to lower her guard, Twelve's trigger finger tenses as Norman removes an envelope bulging in shape of

- 448 -

cash. Sporting an expression of curious mistrust, she takes the envelope.

"I have something else for you, but if you shoot me, I'm not going to give it to you," sighs Norman, glancing down at the Glock in her lap.

"It better be nice then," Twelve smartly advises.

Norman digs his fat fingers into his breast pocket, grumbling as he fishes around. Finally — and very carefully so as not to drop it — he removes a beautifully cut, 1.5 karat diamond with the tips of his middle and forefinger.

He drops the stone into Twelve's palm, sparking as it tumbles.

"When are you coming back?" asks the Natasha with her left eye swelled shut.

"Couple of months, maybe three or four. Depends." Norman doesn't like answering questions. "You did good on this one."

Fuck your flattery. Ready to be out of the car and away from him, Twelve curtly asks, "Is that all?"

"Just keep your phone on you. Maybe see a doctor. You look like shit." With that, Twelve opens the door — diamond and envelope in one hand — pistol in the other. She gets her bag out of the backseat. Standing by the telephone pole, she waits for Norman to leave before turning her back.

Once at the bottom of the drive, Norman waits for three cars to pass and disappears to the East.

Stepping toward the gate, Twelve expects to fall away at any moment. Sliding her pistol into her bag so it doesn't get dropped and scratched again, she lifts the latch, cautiously walking through. Though the Natasha doesn't like getting bumped out of the driver's seat, she has come to terms — for now. Though not wanting to go back to sleep, Twelve does like the idea of leaving Sara with a broken nose. She thinks this is funny.

Walking along the patio, the sister with muddy blood in her sinuses and a bag slung over her shoulder expects that any second...aaaany second now...she will fall away.

Twelve walks up onto the porch. Aaaany moment now. Twelve opens the door. *This is fucking weird.* She enters the house. Stepping lightly, the Natasha passes Lady's rumbling dryer on her way into the kitchen.

Waiting for whatever is next, the bedraggled Natasha stands in the middle of the kitchen.

She hears a toilet flush... a faucet turn on... a faucet turn off and the bathroom door open...

This should be interesting, thinks Twelve, remembering her last encounter with Lady.

"AHHH!" Lady jumps at the sight of Twelve's face. Heart pounding, she is further jarred upon realizing she isn't looking at Sara.

Like holding her ground in front of a dangerous animal, Lady hides her fear. Silence hangs heavy for a time.

"I'm not going to hurt you." Twelve says plainly.

"I know." Lady responds in kind.

Both expecting something to happen, but nothing does. Silence resumes.

"What happened to your face?" Lady eventually asks.

"I got in a fight."

"Well, you look terrible," Lady comments, her mouth tight.

"I agree," Twelve returns Lady's coldness.

"So, who keeps beating you up?" Lady pries, long wishing to know. "I've been wondering."

"Different people."

"Where are these *different* people?"

"Underground mostly," Twelve smirks.

"So that's what you do when you leave here?" Lady asks disapprovingly. "You kill people?"

"Yeah, pretty much." The Natasha shrugs.

"He's not here. He passed away," the lass informs, in case the assassin is here to talk to Babe.

"I know."

"You know, do you?" Lady asks accusingly. "What else do you know?"

- 450 -

"Everything."

"Hmm…" Lady tenses her mouth. "Well, what does *she* know? What does Sara know?"

"I don't know what she knows," Twelve honestly responds.

"She says she doesn't remember much–"

"She's probably telling the truth. She isn't smart enough to lie." The timbre of Twelve's unkind words serve to reenforce Lady's belief that she truly is a different person. The Natasha sounds nothing like her girl.

"*One* of these times you're gonna get that sweet girl killed." Says Lady, her words coated in acid.

"Not for a few months at least," Twelve dismisses. "Norman is going to be gone for a while."

Hands on her hips, Lady inhospitably asks, "Will *you* be gone, too?"

"I don't know how I'm still here now."

Struggling with her emotions – and somewhat disarmed by Twelve's calmness – Lady can tell she is telling the truth. "Well, you look like shit."

"That's what Norman said."

"Nice to know me and him can agree on *something*," Lady sighs. She turns toward the bathroom for the first aid kit under the sink. "Did Norman buy you that outfit?" she inquires of the Victoria Secret pajamas.

"No."

"If not Norman, then who did?" asks Lady from the bathroom.

"I got it from a guy who didn't need it anymore," Lady hears as she grabs the dusty metal kit and a washcloth from under the bathroom sink… while still squatted down, she hears a low cry building around the corner.

Sara! Lady's alarm sounds.

Swift footsteps carry Lady into the kitchen. She finds her girl, puzzled and with puffy eyes welling. Lightly touching the sides of her nose, Sara sadly asks, "What happened to me?" Chin quivering and tears streaming, "Whut…whut happened to my nose?"

Her heart melting, Lady rushes to comfort. "Oh child – you're back." For a moment, she feared Twelve was here to stay.

"My face," Sara cries louder. "Wh-what ha-happened to my face?!" Sara heads for the bathroom, but Lady steers her to the kitchen table.

"You're gonna be-" Lady stops to pull Sara's hands down from her face. "You're gonna be okay. We're gonna get you fixed *right up!*" She says in her most upbeat tone. The woman rounding up pain pills, ice, and a wet washcloth, knows this is going to be a tough fix. *At least my girl is back.* Lady focuses on the positive. *At least my girl is back.*

"Clint? Has Clint seen my face?!" asks a balling Sara. "Has Clint looked at my face?! I wanna see my face!" Difficulty breathing worsens her anxiety.

We're gonna get some ice-"

"I wanna see!" Sara interrupts. Lady struggles to keep her in her seat. "Will Clint still think I'm pretty?!"

"Oh heavens yes, child!" Lady exclaims. "You're just a little puffy!" The woman who grew up with bare-knuckle boxers for brothers knows this will pass.

"But I can't breathe through my nose!" Sara arches a high whine. She can't stop touching her face. Crestfallen, the slumped girl down completely.

"Let me get you a pill, child." Though Lady doesn't want Sara to slip back into her pill habit, she doesn't want her to hurt either. And she needs to calm down.

11:18 AM
Kitchen Table
After a glance in the mirror – and a squall that could've been heard near the road – Dilaudids have simmered the scene. Whimpering with her head hung low, Sara just knows Clint isn't going to think she's pretty anymore. Lady assures won't be the case.

Exhausted, beat up and convinced life is over, Sara doesn't even hear what Lady is saying as she goes about applying makeup gently as possible.

Relieved upon finding nothing more than bumps, bruises, and what appears to be rug burns, Lady suspects Sara hasn't slept since abruptly leaving the house early yesterday. She doubts Clint has slept. She herself hasn't sleep a wink.

Lady called Clint and told him that Sara was home but asked that he not arrive until she called him back.

Though Clint promised not to arrive until Lady called him back, he *didn't* promise not to be right around the corner awaiting the call. This last disappearance has brought the young man near his breaking point.

Caking on foundation, Lady tells the girl in a stupor, "You just need to tell him."

"Tell him what?" Sara asks despondently. She just knows he isn't going to want to be with her anymore.

"Everything."

"No." Sara is ashamed of the truth.

"You're going to have to tell him something," informs Lady, remembering the day Babe told her the truth.

"*What* then?" says a frumpy Sara, folding her arms. "If I tell 'em it'll only make stuff worse!" For the first time in a while, Sara has regressed.

Lady knows Sara's age can rise and fall during peak stress. While giving her girl a chance to calm, a number of points come to mind; *You can't expect him to live in the dark. I don't know how much more that boy can take. If you love him as much as you say you do, you'll tell him...* but upon opening her mouth, a question enters the air, "Do you know what I said when Babe told me he was a spy?"

Sara's face rises. "No, what?"

"Okay."

"Okay, what?"

"'Okay' is what I said. I cared no more that he was a spy than I would if he were a baker or a shoe salesman."

"You didn't care?" Sara asks with hopefulness.

"Well, actually-" Lady blushes, "I actually thought it was a little...sexy." Sara smiles for the first time since returning home. Doing so reminds how painfully puffy her face is. The reminder wipes the smile away as fast as it came.

Clint's not gonna think I'm sexy ever again, Sara sullenly thinks to herself.

"Tell me this," Lady says with a chirp, "What did he say when he saw your scars?"

"He freaked out," Sara answers somberly.

"Okay, but *after* he freaked out, what did he do?" Lady tries opening Sara's eyes to the bigger picture.

"I don't know…" mutters Sara, feeling underneath rock bottom.

"He got over it and you two moved on. You gave him some truth, and even though it was tough, he was able to handle it."

Sara perks up a bit.

"I've been in his shoes, on the *other* side of the equation. And let me tell you, the truth is the *only* way to go. Lying is a sure way to lose someone."

"Did Babe ever lie to you?" asks Sara, warming to the idea.

If he did, I don't know about it, thinks Lady while saying a flat, "No."

"What if he asks details?" Sara begs guidance.

"That would be too much truth. Besides, you don't really know any details, do you?" asks Lady, applying yet another layer of liquid foundation under Sara's eyes.

Straining for recall on this most recent outing, Sara comes up with nothing. No flashes. No faces. Nothing. "Not really, no."

"Okay then," Lady nods, hoping she's not giving terrible advice. "You can't hide what you don't know," she shrugs. "Besides, the *truth* is good, details… sometimes *not* so good. While I don't know everything, I do know that boy loves you every bit as much as I love Babe." Like a balloon filling with helium, Sara's spirits lift.

"But did Babe ever kill anybody?" Sara asks balefully, her balloon sinking back down.

"Well, no...not to my knowledge," Lady thinks back. "But then again, neither have you," points out the woman who didn't believe in split personalities until recently.

Sara's spirits rise again.

"Let me ask you this," says Lady, hoping to build on progress, "How long do you want to be with Clint?"

"Forever." Sara answers without hesitation. She hopes Lady is doing a good job with her makeup.

"Forever is a long, long time. And *trust* me, *even* under the best of circumstances – which aren't the kind of circumstances you two have – it takes honesty and teamwork."

"But not too much detail," Sara circles back.

"Exactly!" Lady pokes the air with her finger. *Even busted and bruised she is still beautiful.* "Teamwork is the key. And speaking of teamwork, we need to come up with a plan."

Leaning forward, Sara is anxious to hear any plan her Scottish fairy godmother might have. "What are you gonna tell him?"

"What am *I* going to tell him?!" Lady laughs. "I'm pretty sure it's gonna take *both* of us to handle this or Clint'll whip every guy in the world, one after the other, *just* to make sure he got the guy who did this to you!" Seeing Russell Martin staggering back with blood pouring out of his nose, Sara has no doubt Clint could whip every guy in the world if he were mad enough.

Together, as Lady applies makeup and Sara holds still, a plan is worked out.

11:45 AM

Knowing she has done all she can – and reminding herself that the goal isn't to fool Clint, just blunt the initial shock – Lady closes the compact and sets the brush down.

"How does it look?" Sara asks, hopefully.

Howard's saying, *Looks like shit, but it's better than it was!* comes to Lady's mind. But she only says, "It looks better than it did." While caked-on foundation and concealer blanket the bruising (and a swoop of hair covers a bumpy forehead), she has found eyes swollen nearly shut and a broken nose rather difficult to hide.

"Can I see?!"

"Umm," Lady looks into a face wrecked from the nostrils up. *She looks like someone who had a really bad allergic reaction to something!*

Sara watches Lady hop up from her chair and disappear around the corner, soon to return with the big, dark pair of sunglasses Devon gave her. Verrrry carefully, she slides the arms through Sara's hair and sets them down across the bridge of a widened nose.

"There!" Lady leans back. "*Now* you can look!" ...with bated breath, she follows Sara into the bathroom. *Please be happy enough, please be happy enough, please be happy enough...* Wringing her hands, the gal who did her best watches Sara in front of the mirror above the sink. "Now let's keep the glasses on for now," Lady softly suggests.

Sara, fuzzy from the pills, is surprised for the better. Showing hardly any reaction at first, she raises and lowers her chin...turns her face side to side...rotates her head round and round. "You know..." Sara dares smile, "it might pass the forty mile and hour test."

"What's the forty mile an hour test?" Lady tilts her head.

"Well," Sara references a Howard-ism, "if someone drives by forty miles an hour, they *just* might not notice-" Thankful, she turns to Lady and smiles.

Relieved, Lady laughs. "You want me to call that boy?"

"Yeah," Sara nods her stiff neck. "Yeah, I do."

11:55 AM

"He's here!" Sara says at the sight of Clint's red Chevy hurrying its way up the South lane.

Little rocks would be kicking behind the tires, were the ground not frozen.